CW01467198

Gloves *Off*

Stephanie Archer writes spicy, laugh-out-loud romance. She believes in the power of best friends, stubborn women, a fresh haircut, and love. She lives in Vancouver with a man, a dog, and a baby.

For spicy bonus scenes, news about upcoming books, and book recs, sign up for her newsletter at:
https://www.stephaniearcherauthor.com/newsletter

Instagram: **@stephaniearcherauthor**
TikTok: **@stephaniearcherbooks**

To check content warnings for any of Stephanie's books, visit www.stephaniearcherauthor.com/content-warnings

Gloves Off

THE VANCOUVER STORM SERIES
STEPHANIE ARCHER

ORION

For Mr. Archer, my accident-prone sleepwalker.

An Orion Paperback

This edition first published in Great Britain in 2024 by Orion Fiction
an imprint of The Orion Publishing Group Ltd
Carmelite House, 50 Victoria Embankment
London EC4Y 0DZ

An Hachette UK company

The authorised representative in the EEA is Hachette Ireland, 8 Castle-
court Centre, Dublin 15, D15 XTP3, Ireland (email: info@hbgi.ie)

1 3 5 7 9 10 8 6 4 2

Copyright © Stephanie Archer 2025

The moral right of Stephanie Archer to be identified as
the author of this work has been asserted in accordance with
the Copyright, Designs and Patents Act of 1988.

All rights reserved. No part of this publication may be
reproduced, stored in a retrieval system, or transmitted
in any form or by any means, electronic, mechanical,
photocopying, recording, or otherwise, without the
prior permission of both the copyright owner and the
above publisher of this book.

All the characters in this book are fictitious, and any resemblance to
actual persons, living or dead, is purely coincidental.

A CIP catalogue record for this book is
available from the British Library.

ISBN (Mass Market Paperback) 978 1 3987 2434 1

Printed and bound in Great Britain by Clays Ltd, Elcograf S.p.A.

MIX
Paper | Supporting
responsible forestry
FSC® C104740

www.orionbooks.co.uk

CHAPTER 1
ALEXEI

THE MORNING of the Vancouver Storm's season opener, I wait for the elevator up to Coach Tate Ward's office at the arena when I hear it—heels clicking.

She steps into my periphery, and a familiar scent washes over me—vanilla, violets, and sandalwood. My shoulders tighten.

Here we fucking go. My blood starts to hum. On my wrist, my watch beeps in warning as my heart rate rises above resting rate, and I silence it.

She looks up from her phone, those warm whiskey eyes cooling. "Oh. You."

I reach for the elevator call button and press it again. I don't want to spend more time with this spoiled brat than I have to.

I cannot fucking stand Dr. Georgia Greene.

"Thanks, Volkov." She offers me a mock grateful smile. "I don't want to spend more time with you than I have to."

Like always, her auburn hair is down around her shoulders, loose, wavy, and thick like one of those laughing women on shampoo commercials. It's not red, it's not brunette, it's something in between, with gold strands that catch the light. A crop of new freckles span her nose and cheekbones, probably from sunbathing on a yacht all summer, lounging topless while being served drinks on a silver tray by some employee whose name she doesn't know. My teeth grit.

She stands next to me and faces the doors as we wait, still reading emails on her phone while I try not to inhale her.

"I'm surprised you're back at work this season." Apparently, I can't stop myself from provoking her. "I thought you would have bagged a rich husband by now."

I give her a sidelong look, taking in her flawless hair, her makeup, the outfit she has chosen to fit her every curve. Her skyscraper heels. The expensive handbag dangling from the crook of her arm. The Greene family is notorious for owning half of Vancouver. She's exactly like my ex—superficial, self-centered, and obsessed with wealth and image.

"I'm ignoring you," she says, eyes on her phone.

I'll never get married, I heard her say last year. Still, it pisses her off when I talk about her wanting to find a rich husband, and the only thing I love more than pissing off the doctor is hockey.

"Isn't that your deepest desire?" I ask. "Land some old guy on the brink of death and cash in when he crosses over to the afterlife so you can quit your job and live out the rest of your days doing what you love most, spending money on yourself?"

I don't know why I act like this around her. I don't talk to anyone the way I talk to this woman.

At the words *old guy,* her lips curve into a sick smile. "Maybe I'll marry you."

"When hell freezes over." I would never marry, let alone marry *her*. "And I'm not old."

I'm thirty-six. For an enforcer defenseman, I'm old, but I'm still in incredible shape. The Norris trophy is awarded to the NHL's best all-around defenseman. I haven't won it three times because I let myself go.

"Hellfire," I add.

She stiffens, and I fight the urge to smile. She hates that nickname.

"Don't call me that."

"That's where you're from, isn't it? Forged in the fires of hell?"

A feeling expands in my chest, like the moments before a game starts, and the air between us crackles.

"You want to know what my deepest desire is, Volkov?" She whirls on me, eyes flickering with fire, and my heart hammers harder. "My deepest desire, which I wish for every birthday, is that you'll fall down a very narrow, very deep hole. You won't have your phone on you. It'll be in the middle of nowhere, and I'll be the only person around." She puts on a high, sad voice. "*Help me,* you'll call up the hole. *Please, Georgia, help me.*"

"I'd never ask for your help. And I don't sound like that."

"You will, because you'll be starving, thirsty, and very scared. It's a hundred feet deep, and there are snakes at the bottom."

"That's what you wish for on your birthday? That's kind of pathetic, don't you think?"

"You know what else I wish for? That you'll finally retire." Her gaze trails over me, cataloging every injury, every pin and steel plate in my body from seventeen years in the NHL. "And I never have to see you again."

Her words hit me in the gut like an arrow. I can control my diet to a tee, can do everything to heal and play my best, but I can't stop time. My impending retirement is the shadow I can't shake.

Where the hell is this elevator? I watch the number above the doors. "Do what you do best, Doctor, and make shopping your full-time job so we can hire a real doctor."

She doesn't say a word, but I can feel her irritation. Bull's-eye.

"Asshole," she mutters.

She's not wrong. A beat of silence stretches between us before the elevator doors open and we step inside.

"It must be Friday," I say to the doors as the elevator ascends.

"Excuse me?"

"It's Friday. How do I know that?"

"Oh my god," she whispers in mock awe. "You *can* read. This whole time, we weren't sure."

My competitive instincts wake up. "Making fun of my immigrant heritage? That's a low blow, Doctor, even for you."

She gives me a flat look. "That's not what I meant."

My parents fled Russia when I was a kid, and worked around the clock to pay for hockey. "Not all of us could afford private school."

Our upbringings couldn't be any different. *We* couldn't be any different.

Her face turns a shade of pink that makes my watch go off again. I silence it, victory coursing through me. She's about to say something when I cut her off.

"Violets. Every Friday, you wear the perfume that smells like violets." It took me months to identify that note. I only figured it out because I was picking something up at my mom's flower shop and the scent stopped me in my tracks.

She blinks up at me in shock. I bet she hates that I know this about her. I bet she hates that I'm on to her.

"That's the one you wear when you go out, trying to catch a rich husband, isn't it?"

She straightens up an inch but she's still almost a foot shorter than me. Deep in my lizard brain, I like how much taller I am. In her heels, she's tall, but I'm taller. I'm twice her weight. It would be no problem to throw her over my shoulder.

"Don't be such a stalker, Volkov." She turns back to her phone.

My gaze dips to her shoes. Tall and spiky, designed to castrate her victims with one sharp kick to the balls. Way too high, with dumb little straps that look like they'll break at any minute. So fucking impractical. Real doctors don't wear shoes like those. The soles are red, I remember, from her wearing them to an event last year. The same color her eyes probably turn when she doesn't get what she wants.

In my nightmares, her shoes are as tall as buildings, taunting me with their clicking sounds as she walks up and down the hall. So unprofessional. Doctors are supposed to wear ugly Crocs, not sexy little fuck-me heels.

I hate them, and I hate how much I think about them.

"Are you going to get that?" She sends a pointed glance at my wrist.

Goddamnit. My watch is going off again. I silence it, taking a slow, deep breath. The program helps me keep my heart rate low when I'm supposed to be resting, to aid recovery and performance, but it's going haywire today.

"They're Christian Louboutin," she adds with a smirk, "in case you want to buy a pair to jerk off onto at night."

My lip curls. "I don't jerk off to your shoes," I grit out. "This may be hard for you to understand, Doctor, but some people aren't attracted to you."

I let my gaze rake down her body, lingering on the long line of her neck, the smooth skin above the collar of her silk shirt, the dip at her waist, and the swell of her hips.

I don't hate her because she's so similar to my ex, Emma—charismatic, friendly, confident, gorgeous—and I don't hate her because she knows exactly how hot she is. I don't even hate the doctor because she comes from wealth and privilege.

I hate her because she doesn't believe in me.

Two years ago, I had one meeting with her where she ran her hands all over my body, over all the injuries I'd accumulated, before I got a concussion during a game and landed myself in the hospital.

"You're transferring me to another doctor?" I asked her the day after I was discharged.

She didn't meet my eyes. *"I'm not the right physician for you."*

"Too much work? I'm going to cut into your shopping time, huh?"

Those whiskey eyes flashed with irritation. *"You're held together with pins and K-tape, Volkov. I've recommended you for retirement. I'm not going to invest time into a lost cause."*

One meeting. That's all it took for her to give up on me.

Fucking finally, the elevator reaches the floor at the top of the arena, where the offices are. It pings and the doors slide open.

"Have a great day, Volkov. Don't knock any more teeth out tonight."

She strides out and down the hall to her office, head held high, wearing those pants like they were designed for her.

"I have all my teeth," I snap after her.

I hate her, but the doctor has a great ass. My watch goes off again.

"Everything okay, Volkov?"

Coach Tate Ward stands at the reception desk, watching me watch the doctor, wearing a curious but amused expression.

"Everything's fine." I silence this stupid fucking watch. It's probably broken or something. "You wanted to talk to me?"

"You bet." He tips his chin at his office across the hall. "Come on."

I FOLLOW Ward into his office, taking a seat in one of the club chairs in front of his desk, across from him.

"What do you think about Luca Walker?" he asks.

The twenty-two-year-old rookie who cares more about having fun, partying, and chasing girls than playing in the NHL? He's a cocky little shit who needs a reality check. When my last defensive partner, Hayden Owens, moved to offense at the end of last season, Ward signed Walker as a free agent and paired us together.

"He's young."

No one makes me feel my age like Walker, baby-faced, bright-eyed, and full of optimism. The kid's a ray of sunshine, fresh as a fucking spring daisy.

Ward waits, watching.

"Inexperienced," I add.

More of that patient eye contact. The ex-player turned coach is only a few years older than me but has this unnerving calm and wise thing going that makes him seem decades older.

"He'll have to work hard this year if he wants to keep playing at this level." For every guy in the league, ten wait in the wings. One fuckup and he's gone, sent packing to the Storm's farm team.

"And I don't think he's cut out to play with me."

Ward's dark eyebrows lift. "Really."

"Rookies don't play in the first defensive pair. They start in the third-tier pair and work their way up."

Hockey teams have three defensive pairs. The first is for your top players, like me, not the guys who are still finding their feet with a new team, playing at a new level.

Ward knows this. We used to play against each other when he was in the NHL years ago, when I was with Montreal and he was with the Storm here in Vancouver. He rose from first round draft pick with a record yearly contract to the top scorer in the league. The guy won the Hart trophy for MVP of the year eight years in a row until a knee injury ended his career. He disappeared for a few years until he cropped up, coaching women's hockey at the local university, and was hired as head coach on the Vancouver Storm two years ago.

"My philosophy is that working with people better than you is the best way to improve." Ward leans back in his chair, folding his hands over his stomach. "What do you think of that?"

I rub the back of my neck. "You're the coach."

"I still want to know what you think."

I don't want to do this. Any moment not in a game, practice, or training is spent healing the multitude of injuries I've sustained over the years.

Besides, no one showed me the ropes. No one mentored me. I had to figure everything out myself.

"I don't have time to babysit."

Ward's mouth twists in a wry smile. "I would really like you to make time. I want you to mentor Luca Walker and turn him into the player the Storm needs."

What am I going to say, no? It doesn't work like that. Ward's a good guy, probably the best guy who's ever sat in this office in the history of the Storm organization, but I'm not interested in incurring his wrath if I ignore a direct order.

He could buy me out of the remaining seasons on my contract and force me to retire, if he wanted to. He could trade me at a discount to make room for a younger guy.

I give him a firm nod. "Okay. I'll do it."

From the changes he's made over the past few seasons, I suspect he has a grand plan for this team.

Jamie Streicher, one of the best goalies in the league, in net. Rory Miller, the league's top scorer, as center forward and now captain. Hayden Owens, moved from defense to offense and surprising everyone with the jump in points on the board.

And now he's set his sights on the rookie, Luca Walker. If there's anything I love, it's this team, and hell if I'll stand in the way of our run for the Cup.

I sigh with frustration. "Why can't you be an asshole like the last guy in here?" The last Storm coach was terrible. Red-faced, angry, always yelling at us. Berating us for every mistake, every loss.

Ward lets out a short laugh. "Thanks, Alexei." He gives me a nod of approval. "I appreciate it."

"Don't thank me yet." I head to the door.

"One last thing." He frowns at his computer, pulling something up. "There's a problem with your citizenship application."

"Again?" My gut drops. This nightmare won't end. Ward gives me a strange look as worry tightens in my chest. "This has been happening for years."

"I wondered why you didn't have citizenship yet."

My family immigrated to Canada from Russia when I was eight. "We had visas and permanent residencies, but when I joined the NHL and we applied for citizenship, it all went to shit."

Years of drawn-out issues over misspelled names, lost applications, rejections for no reason, and requests to resubmit. Headache after fucking headache.

If I could throw money at it, I would—god knows I have enough of it as one of the highest paid players in the league—but that's not how the Canadian government works.

"The team's legal staff is handling it now." Ward gives me a reassuring smile. "They know what they're doing."

"Did they say how long it'll take?"

"Usually a year for processing, interviews, and final acceptance. Could be up to three years, though."

I don't know if I have that much time. The reality I rarely admit is, one bad injury and I'm done. It happened to Ward. It could happen to me.

"And with the way your visa works," Ward adds, "you'll need to be with the team or have citizenship to stay in the country."

Alarm races through me. I'm not interested in going back to Russia. I haven't been back since we left. I definitely can't let my parents be sent back. They were outspoken against the government—that's why we left—and fled the country when their arrest warrants were issued. It's not safe for them to return.

When I was growing up, they worked so hard to keep me in hockey, an expensive sport. They did everything they could to give me a better life here in Canada.

I have to fix this. This is our home. Our lives are here.

Through the glass walls of Ward's office, dark red hair catches my attention, and I watch the doctor stride up the hall in those infuriating heels. My nostrils flare as she smirks at me.

No one gets on my nerves like her.

As she passes Ward's open doorway, she shifts her attention to Ward and her smile turns genuine. "Hey, Tate."

Ward gives her a friendly nod. "Dr. Greene."

An ache throbs in my chest, thinking about what I said to her two years ago, after finding out she transferred me. After finding out she didn't believe in me.

There's no way I'd let someone treat me who bought her way into medical school with Daddy's money. You're clearly incompetent.

The hurt in her eyes didn't feel as good as I wanted, though.

You said that to Ward? she asked.

Yes, I lied. *I told him you were incompetent.*

She disappears around the corner, and I realize Ward's watching me with a glint in his eye.

"Too bad you aren't married to a Canadian."

"Married?" After Emma, I would never, ever get married.

He looks out the window. "It would really speed the application process along."

A long beat of silence stretches between us. "Are you saying I should marry a Canadian for citizenship?"

My first thought is the doctor before I shove that thought away, fast. I hate that she pops into my head at random times.

He leans back, watching me in that steady, calm way. "I didn't say that. I would never tell you to do something illegal." He shrugs again. "It'll be fine. You've got three years left in your contract. They'll sort it out by then."

Nausea rolls through me. I don't know if I have three years left with the team, and with the way things have dragged out with my citizenship application, I can't afford to wait that long.

I say goodbye to Ward and head to my car, aware of every pin and plate in my body. Every injury that didn't heal right because I played through it. On the ice, I use my body like a weapon, playing brutal and physical hockey.

One injury could end everything and send me and my family back to Russia.

Ward's right. I need to get married, and it needs to be fast.

THAT AFTERNOON, I sit in my office at the hospital, eyes narrowed as I stare out the window at the giant banner hanging from the nearby arena—a hundred-foot image of Alexei Volkov in his Storm uniform.

My arena office looks out onto a Storm billboard with the same image. The universe is laughing at me.

I flip both middle fingers at the banner. What a waste of a sharp jawline, strong nose, and thick, dark hair, just long enough to curl at the back of his neck. Long enough to twist your fingers in and give a sharp tug.

How unfair that the universe gave that set of broad, sculpted shoulders to *him*, made *him* that towering height.

Even his voice is a waste, with that low, rumbly timbre, free of a Russian accent but with slightly clipped consonants.

Volkov's hot in a scary way, my friend Darcy said once. Dark, soulless eyes rimmed in thick lashes. Perpetual under-eye circles that are probably hereditary, but I like to dream that our arguments keep him up at night, frustrated and unable to sleep.

He's bad boy hot. The kind of hot you shouldn't want, but you do.

I mean, *I* don't. Some people do. Volkov's far too much of a dick for my liking.

Make shopping your full-time job so we can find a real doctor, he said. It's the first time I've seen him since the Hawaii trip our friends made us go on this summer. A full week of ignoring each other, not even looking at each other.

"Two minutes."

I jump out of my skin. Dr. Heather Joshi, the director of the athlete recovery program here at the hospital, leans on my doorframe with a knowing smile.

"That's how long you've been staring at him."

My face burns. "I was *glaring*. Because he's a dick."

She sits in the chair opposite me, nodding sagely. "Mmm. Yes. Right."

"I hate him." She knows this.

She taps her chin with a manicured fingernail. "Mhm. And that's why you let him think you're a spoiled little princess?"

Heather's known me since I broke my ankle as a teenager and she was the physician overseeing my recovery and rehabilitation. Her passion, enthusiasm, and dedication to her work showed me that athlete injury recovery is my passion and purpose, and her flawless style showed me that you could be great at your job and look incredible doing it.

The athlete injury recovery program we designed together is one of my favorite things in the world, along with sparkly dresses, my two pet bunnies, and heels that make me feel powerful and hot.

I glance at her heels. "New?"

"Don't try to distract me."

"So I let him believe his assumptions. So what? He doesn't get the privilege of knowing me."

Despite what Volkov thinks, I did not grow up wealthy. I

grew up with teenage parents scraping by. Yes, my last name is Greene, and yes, it's *those* Greenes, but my wealthy, powerful grandfather cut my dad off when my mom got pregnant at seventeen. I went to public school, I worked my ass off to get scholarships to university, playing for The University of British Columbia's Women's Soccer team, and then I worked even harder in medical school. Everything I've achieved, I've earned.

I get a sick sense of satisfaction from letting him believe the worst of me, though.

Not all of us could afford private school.

God, Volkov's such an asshole. So controlling and arrogant —like my ex, Liam. Like so many men in medicine. Like my grandfather, who left me an inheritance when he passed a few years ago, but with the caveat that I need to be married to inherit.

I'm not *touching* that money. I don't need it, and I love the idea that he's glowering up at me from hell, furious that he can't control me.

Besides, after how Liam manipulated me, I would never get married. It's too easy for men to use marriage as a tool to control women.

I refocus my attention on Heather. Under her lab coat, she's wearing a tailored dress in striking fuchsia, her favorite color. It matches her lipstick, a stunning contrast to her brown skin.

"That is your color," I say, like I always do when she wears it.

She smiles to herself. "I know." Her expression sobers. "I met with the hospital board this morning, and I have bad news."

Uh-oh. It's the warning shot. They teach us this in medical school when we learn how to tell the patient's family their loved one has passed.

"The program didn't obtain the next round of funding," she says.

I stop breathing. In research, funding is everything. It pays for our salaries, the lab and office space, equipment, everything.

A loss of funding is a death sentence. I feel sick. "So we're done."

She gives me a sad smile. "As of May, yes, the program is done."

"We have until May, though."

She shakes her head with an empathetic expression. *No, your loved one is not coming back.*

"If we don't have funding by January, the hospital will book the space out to someone who does." She sighs, and I can see she's trying to be strong for me, but she's pissed as hell. "It's all money," she says with a touch of bitterness.

I'm reeling, head spinning with questions and emotions. The program has grown to two hundred athletes. Our work is groundbreaking. We're finding methods for injury recovery that will become the norm in sports and help athletes around the world.

On top of that, healthcare is publicly funded in Canada. Many of our participants wouldn't be able to afford this level of care otherwise.

"But we—everything was going so well. Our last publication—"

"I know. We're doing incredible work." She takes a deep breath. "The good news is, we both have long careers. Many private clinics need specialists."

I don't want to work at a private clinic that only caters to rich people, though.

"And you have the Storm," she adds.

I'll admit, I took the job on the team's medical staff because it would lend credibility to the research program, and to my résumé as an athlete recovery specialist.

It didn't hurt that Liam, now an orthopedic surgeon in Toronto, was a massive hockey fan. A job with a hockey team would be his dream. It felt good, taking his dream job, when he never believed in me to begin with.

I ended up loving it, though. I love working with athletes, keeping them healthy and overseeing their recovery so they can do *their* dream job.

Except Volkov. He can go to hell for telling Tate Ward I was incompetent. Fuck that guy.

Motivation rockets through me. "I'm not ready to give up," I tell Heather. "So we raise the funds. We have the benefit coming up. We can get the media involved. I don't need a salary—"

"Georgia." She puts her hand on mine. "We need ten million dollars. The benefit brings in a couple hundred thousand at most." She gives me that sad smile of defeat. "It's okay. This is how research goes."

Like a lightbulb, my mind flicks to my inheritance—for ten million dollars.

No. No way. Marriage is designed to benefit men, not women. How many women have I seen in medicine get married and then fade away to run the home and raise the kids while their husbands ascend higher and higher in their careers?

Years ago, when I learned that Liam, my now ex, unenrolled me from medical school, he proposed. *If you stay here in Toronto,* he had said, *we can get married.* No romance, no declaration of love. From how sullen and irritable he became when I shared my academic wins and accomplishments, I suspect he was threatened, but I was so stupidly love-drunk and desperate for his approval that I said yes. For one week, I considered deferring my dreams so I could basically be his unpaid assistant, attending events on his arm, quiet and small in the background.

I thank the universe every day that I didn't marry that guy. Men like him don't want a woman who can hold her own. They want to feel like the king, the top dog.

I'm going to come up with the money for the program, but I'm sure as hell not getting married.

———

Early that evening, before I need to be back at the arena for the Storm's opening game, I stride across the soccer field in my leggings, windbreaker, and stylish sneakers—because you don't need to be wearing heels to look hot—carrying a big box I know will make the girls scream with joy.

My absolute favorite part of the athlete recovery program? The Vancouver Devils, a team of incredible, hilarious, gritty teenage girls.

"Is that what we think it is?" one of the girls asks from where they're waiting in a group, talking and laughing.

I give them a beaming smile. "You know it."

I'm Dr. Greene at work, but here at soccer practice, I'm Coach Georgia. I'm still technically their doctor, but the goal of the team is for recovering athletes to maintain a team environment appropriate to their ability.

Being on a team has incredible benefits—support, friendship, structure, staying active, competitive, and happy—but when players return to their regular team, they often reinjure themselves because they're competing with non-injured players. They push themselves too hard. Players who do nothing fall behind on their physio and often experience depression, because when their sport is everything to them, losing it can leave a gaping hole in their life.

Thus, I created sports teams with the program participants. I run the soccer team for teenaged girls and some of my fellow doctors run other teams.

I set the box down and give them a sly smile. "Are you ready to see your new uniforms?"

They cheer. I grin and pull out a red and black jersey.

"Power colors!" Tasha, a seventeen-year-old recovering from an ACL tear, pumps her fists in the air, making me laugh. "We're going to look so hot."

"Power colors," I confirm.

We don't play regular games, the girls just scrimmage against one another every week, but looking the part and feeling good is important. What we wear can boost our confidence when we need it.

"When you put this jersey on, I want you to remember what a bad bitch you are."

A few of them catcall and I laugh, read out the name on the back of the jersey and toss it to the smiling player. I don't think I'm supposed to say *bitch* around them, but whatever. They go to high school, they've heard much worse.

"I want you to remember that with hard work and passion, you can do anything."

Another cheer. I toss another jersey.

"You are gritty, you are relentless, you are smart and fierce, and no one can hold you back from doing what you love."

They cheer again, and once everyone has their jersey on, we warm up and do their prescribed physio exercises before they scrimmage. With their brand-new jerseys, the girls want to play hard, but I encourage them to slow down, take it easy, and focus on their technical skills.

This is why the program matters. A lot of these girls were on track to play for universities around the world on full scholarships. Some of them could go pro. They can still have those things, with proper recovery and attention.

If the program gets cut, the Vancouver Devils go with it. Motivation surges through me. Like hell I'm going to let that happen.

I'm going to find a way to save the program.

BEFORE THE GAME THAT NIGHT, I wait in the arena concourse with the other players, shifting back and forth on my skates to stay warmed up. Energy buzzes throughout the building, fans roaring as the lights go down and the music starts.

The other players talk in low voices, some staring at the floor, deep in concentration and head already in the game, and some staying warm like I am.

I should be focusing on the game and what we practiced this morning, but instead, I'm thinking about my citizenship problem.

"Vancouver Storm nation," the announcer calls, *"welcome back for the season opener!"*

The crowd roars again, raring to go. Fans have been waiting for this since the end of last season, when we were eliminated from the third round of playoffs, the furthest this team has gone in the Stanley Cup playoffs in almost a decade.

In front of me, Hayden Owens, my old defensive partner, gives me his typical beaming smile. "Admit it, Volkov. It's good to be back."

I make a low noise of acknowledgment. It's *everything* to be back. With eighty-two games in the regular season, our schedule is grueling and packed—but I spent all summer bored and itching to play with my team again.

Physically, I feel good tonight. My shoulder doesn't hurt. My ACL feels okay. I've been following a strict low-inflammation diet, training hard, resting hard, and doing everything I can to play my best this season.

Mentally, I'm back in Ward's office. In this game, everything can end in the blink of an eye. I need to figure something out, fast.

In the arena, the announcer lists team staff, the trainers, and the physios.

"Hazel Hartley," he announces, and Rory Miller, the Storm's captain, cups his hands to his mouth.

"That's my girl!" he yells down the hall toward the arena. His fiancée, Hazel, is a physiotherapist with the Storm, probably standing at the bench with the other staff. Off my flat look, Miller grins, ear to ear, patting his chest over his heart. "It doesn't matter that she can't hear me. "She can *feel* my support."

"Darcy Andersen," the announcer calls, now listing off the team analysts, and Owens claps his gloves together with enthusiasm.

"Yeah, Darce," he hollers. "Go get 'em, tiger!"

"Jesus Christ." These fucking guys and their relationships. "Control yourselves."

Miller elbows Owens. "You ready to pop the question?"

After practice this morning, Owens showed us the engagement ring he had made for Darcy. The two were best friends for years until last season, when she convinced Owens to be her wingman as she started dating again.

That didn't last long.

Owens grins. "Not yet. I'm enjoying messing with her too much. Soon, though."

Again, I think about what Ward said. *Too bad you aren't married to a Canadian.*

The announcer lists the team medical staff, and I glare at the floor, getting my head in the game.

"Dr. Georgia Greene."

My neck tenses.

"Aren't you going to cheer on your girlfriend?" Miller asks with an innocent smile, his eyes glittering with mischief.

They know we don't get along. They don't know why, though.

Finally, they announce the players. The crowd goes wild as Miller, Owens, and our starting goalie, Streicher, hit the ice.

"From Winnipeg, Manitoba, Luca Walker!" The crowd cheers again for our rookie, this time higher-pitched, and Walker flashes us that annoying cocky grin over his shoulder as he steps onto the ice, waving. Walker's already getting attention with the female crowd.

"From Vancouver, BC, Canada, our homegrown boy and three-time Norris trophy winner," the crowd starts roaring louder, and I skate onto the ice, *"Alexei Volkov."*

The arena noise is deafening as I do a lap, nodding at the fans, feeling that familiar wash of adrenaline race through me. Something I love about the Vancouver fans is that they don't care where you were born—if you played hockey here at some point, you're from here. Are they cheering because of that, though, or because they think this will be my last season?

It isn't. I'm too stubborn to quit. They can drag me into retirement in a coffin.

I skate a loop around the ice, the fans roar, the spotlight follows me, and the energy in the arena vibrates. There's nothing like this. Playing for the NHL has been my dream since we moved to Canada. I'm not giving it up for anything. I can't help but glance at the doctor at the bench as I skate past, our eyes meeting before I look away fast.

The players take our places for the anthem, Walker standing beside me, shifting his weight from leg to leg, gazing around the arena with wide eyes like a kid on Christmas. He joined the team mid-season last year, so this is his first season opener.

"Does it ever get old?" Walker asks me.

I look around the arena, taking in the roaring fans, the music playing, the blue lights traveling across the fans. The sea of Storm jerseys. The fans who want us to win almost more than we do.

Here, on the ice, I'm part of something. It means something.

"No," I tell him as the music ends. "It never gets old."

———

Halfway through the game, the other team's defenseman cross-checks Miller from behind, shoving him forward into the goalie. My spine straightens as sharp protectiveness races through me. It's a dirty hit and worthy of a penalty, and the fans immediately start booing, a low rumble of disapproval and outrage rippling around the arena. They pound on the glass, furious.

The whistle blows, but instead of the ref calling a penalty on the other team, Miller gets a penalty for goaltender interference.

The fans' booing gets louder as Miller skates to the penalty box.

"Are you fucking serious?" he yells at the ref in shock.

The Storm players on the ice look to me, but I'm staring at the player who cross-checked Miller. He glares back at me.

He knows how this works. I'm the Storm's enforcer. I'm the biggest guy on the ice and the strongest, most aggressive fighter.

And now it's my job to even the score and show the other team that they can't pull shit like that without consequences.

Two minutes later, there's a scramble in front of the net for the puck, the whistle blows, and I get my opportunity. I grab the jersey of the guy who cross-checked Miller, and he shoves me back.

Do I know what I'm doing on the ice? Yes. My record-high contract for a thirty-six-year-old player proves that.

Can I back up my team and protect my guys? Yes. My protective instincts are raring to even the score and show them they can't fuck with us.

Will I win this fight? Also yes. Adrenaline courses through me, sharpening my senses as my heart rate picks up.

And yet, I'm so fucking tired of this shit. This is the part I would say goodbye to in a heartbeat.

My gaze flicks up to the owner's box, open to friends, family, and team staff during home games. Is she still here? Is she still watching?

I yank my gaze back to the ice. I don't care about her, and I definitely don't care if she's watching.

Circling the other player, my heart beating out of my chest and adrenaline racing through my veins, the fans roar with approval as I throw my gloves on the ice.

CHAPTER 5
GEORGIA

A WEEK LATER, I walk into the Filthy Flamingo, a crappy dive bar tucked away in the Gastown neighborhood, and take a seat at the bar in front of Jordan—my friend, my roommate since university, and my bartender.

The narrow, wood-paneled bar has vintage band posters framed on the wall; soft, pretty string lights across the ceiling; and a hundred Polaroids tacked up behind the liquor bottles. There's one of me giving Jordan a big, smacking kiss on the cheek while she laughs. That one always makes me smile.

A few Storm players already sit at a table in the back. Jordan hates hockey and this quiet bar is the only place they can go where they won't be hounded by rabid fans. I usually avoid the bar on game nights, when the team is sure to be here after the game. It's not to avoid a conflict of interest, because I don't treat the players I'm friends with, like Hayden Owens, but I hate running into Volkov.

"I need to get married," I tell her, dropping onto a barstool.

She pours me a glass of wine without pause. She knows all about the inheritance and the program losing funding.

She opens her mouth to say something but I jump in. "Marry me."

"No." The corner of her mouth ticks up.

Despite her delicate, fairytale looks—long, shiny dark hair, emerald eyes, pale porcelain skin with dainty features straight from her late mother—she isn't fazed or rattled by anything. She doesn't take any shit, and nothing gets to her. She's tough as nails.

We've been together through thick and thin—through her mom passing away and her dad basically abandoning her from grief, through the whole Liam thing. Through medical school for me and her sports psychology masters. I tried to bring her on as a consultant to the research program, but she said no.

I give her a winning smile. "Please."

"I really don't want to."

"I'd do it for you." I actually would. She's the only person I'd marry. "It's perfect. We already live together. You'd just have to come to events with me and stuff, call me your true love, pretend to kiss me, etc."

She arches an eyebrow, amused. "I'm not really into the whole fake dating thing."

I give her a wry smile. I didn't actually think she'd say yes. It's a ridiculous ask. "Okay, fair."

More players arrive, saying hi to us as they pass. She mixes drinks for a few minutes before she sets the shaker down, takes a deep breath, and holds her expression neutral. Her dark nails tighten on the counter. "You could ask my dad for the money."

I'm ashamed to say, I've already considered this. I know what he'd say, and so does Jordan. The one person in Vancouver who has more money than my grandfather did, he'd want the one thing money can't buy him—time with his daughter, who wants nothing to do with him.

She'd do it for me, too, but I can't do that to Jordan.

"Nah." I wave a hand like I'm turning down seconds at a meal. "I'd rather get married."

She gives me a tiny, relieved smile. "I can think of a dozen guys who'd marry you. Go find one of them. Who's that guy at the hospital, Dr. Handsome?"

"Dr. Handley." He would totally marry me, but then he'd get attached and I'd feel bad breaking his heart. "I don't want that kind of marriage. I want a business arrangement."

Jordan's nodding. "No feelings."

If anyone would understand, it's her. She doesn't do relationships, either. "Ideally, we don't even like each other."

The door opens and Volkov walks in. Jordan raises her brows at me with a teasing question in her eyes.

I give her a dry look. "As if."

I head to the washroom, but when I return, Volkov is sitting two barstools away. He and Jordan have their heads together, talking in low voices. They see me and he stops talking. She sends a pointed look at me.

"What?" Jordan knows how I feel about him, but they're friends, and she refuses to take sides.

"Volkov has something he wants to ask you."

"No, I don't." He glares at her. "Be quiet, Jordan."

I whirl on him. "Don't tell her to be quiet. This is her bar." Back to Jordan. "What is it?"

"Volkov asked me to marry him."

I probably look like I've been slapped, jaw hitting the floor and blinking with wide eyes. "Why?" Does he have a thing for her? I never caught that before. Sharp unease twists in my stomach.

Jordan smiles to herself, mischief sparking in her eyes. "I'll leave you two to talk."

I lift a hand to stop her. "No—"

Too late. She's already walking away, and I'm left with Volkov. We sit in silence, both looking straight ahead at the

Polaroids. There's one of him somewhere. My eyes scan—there. With the Hayden and Rory, from last season.

I can't take this anymore. I turn to face him. "Why did you ask Jordan to marry you?"

His cold gaze flicks to me, then away. "You first."

So she told him that. "It's really not your business."

"Fine."

"Good."

I turn back to the Polaroids. Does he have an inheritance, too? He doesn't need the money. The guy's loaded. All these hockey players are, especially stars like him. He makes millions per year.

"I have an inheritance," I say for some reason. "I need to be married to receive it." He doesn't need to know the rest.

He's quiet for a long moment. "I need citizenship."

My eyebrows go up. "But you've been here for years."

"I know." His nostrils flare. "I don't want to get into it. I'm on a work visa while I'm still with the team."

"Lucky for you, you're the most stubborn bastard I know." I give him a sparkling smile. "You'll be playing well into your nineties."

The unspoken truth hangs in the air: Volkov has three years left in his contract, and it probably won't be renewed after that. He's still one of the best defensemen in the league, but one bad injury could take him out. Physical defensemen like him hardly play as long as he has.

Our eyes meet. Oh. Oh no.

"No," I tell him, shaking my head. "No. No, no, no. No fucking way."

He scowls.

"You can't be serious," I choke out.

"I am." He says it like it's causing him physical pain.

"Volkov." I steeple my hands together. "Did you hit your

head again?" Two years ago, he was in the hospital with a bad concussion from a head shot. "Knock a few more teeth out?"

He rubs the bridge of his nose, closing his eyes. "Like I fucking said ten thousand fucking times, I have all my teeth."

I look around, ensuring we won't be overheard, before I lower my voice. "I'm not going to marry you. It would be a disaster."

A long beat of silence stretches before he answers. "I have no other options."

"I hate to admit this, but there are women who would marry you. Women who have no idea what you're actually like."

His expression darkens. "I don't want a real marriage."

I don't want a real marriage, either. Something snags in my head, and for the first time, I actually consider this.

Incompetent, he called me. He said that to Ward. Top of my class in medical school, but because I wear lipstick and heels and get my nails done, apparently I don't know what I'm doing.

No. I'll find another option. Anyone but him.

"No." I gather my things, pulling out my wallet and tossing a twenty on the bar. "It would never work. We hate each other. Everyone knows this."

"That's why it *would* work." He watches me shrug my jacket on, gaze trailing over me while his lip starts to curl in distaste. "I would never develop feelings for you."

I laugh to myself, dropping my head. "Wow. Just when I was getting my hopes up."

"It won't get complicated. We'll both get what we want."

Again, the logical, problem-solving part of my brain pauses and turns this over. He's not wrong. I hate this man with every fiber of my being. He's exactly like Liam. Powerful. Controlling. His career comes first, above everything.

Maybe that's why it would *work,* my brain whispers. It wouldn't be a real marriage. It would never be love. And what other choice do I have?

After Liam, the idea of marriage makes me feel claustrophobic. Like I can't get enough air. Like the walls are closing in on me.

"No," I say again. I can't marry a guy like Volkov, even if it is fake. "Final answer. Go find some shy little wife to bully, because it won't be me."

His jaw flexes but he doesn't say a word as I stride out of the bar, waving goodbye to Jordan.

I'll figure something out. I have to.

DAYS LATER, Volkov darkens my doorway at the arena.

I keep my eyes on the patient file on my screen. What's he doing here? He's never been in my office before. This is so weird.

"What's the matter, Volkov? Get lost on the way to the underworld?"

"No." He closes the door behind him. "I found it just fine."

I fight the urge to laugh. I hate him, and that wasn't funny. He leans on the glass, crossing his arms over his broad chest, watching me with that unnerving, cold expression.

"Despite you thinking I'm not a real doctor, I actually have work to do with my tiny lady brain." I make a *shoo* gesture. "Go away."

"Have you thought about what we discussed?"

I close my eyes, exhaling slowly. This again?

"No," I lie. "I haven't."

It's *all* I've thought about this week. I had another lawyer look through the will to see if there's any wiggle room—there isn't.

I have no other options. A sick feeling rolls through me. I

hate feeling trapped like this. I hate feeling like I have no choice, like my hand is forced.

"Fine." He starts to leave.

"How would it work?"

He pauses, turns around, and closes the door again, watching me.

"Like, how long are we talking?"

"My immigration lawyer says it could be up to a year."

A year. Okay. "My inheritance will be distributed after three months of marriage." Mid-December, if we did this quickly. Just in time for the funding cut off at the hospital.

We're silent, darting glances at each other. I can't believe I'm actually considering this.

I keep thinking about the girls at soccer, though. It's important. It helps them. It matters.

Am I really going to fuck that all up because I can't put up with Volkov for a year? I would never fall for him. He's always traveling for the team, anyway. He'd be like a terrible roommate who I'd never see.

Maybe I can do this. For the girls, I think I can do this.

Holy hell. I can't believe I'm actually doing this.

"Fine."

He arches an eyebrow. "Fine, what?"

"Fine, I'll—" Through the glass walls of my office, Ward walks by, and I give him a weak smile and nod hello. He waves back, glancing between me and Volkov with curiosity. "I accept. I'm in."

Volkov watches me, and I fight the urge to shift under his gaze. It's that old feeling from medical school, from childhood, from my residency years, when a man is trying to intimidate me. He does it so effortlessly, without even knowing he's doing it, because society has told him he holds all the power.

I cross my legs, kicking a foot out, and his gaze drops. I'm wearing the tall, spiky heels today. His jaw tenses like it always does when I wear this pair.

"Meet me at the Italian place across the street tonight and we'll figure out the details." He clears his throat.

What? I don't want to get dinner with him. Ew. "Let's go to the bar."

"We need to be seen. Photographed."

Right. Volkov attracts attention wherever he goes. All these hockey players do. In Vancouver, hockey is a religion, and these men are gods.

"Eight," he says.

"Nine." I like working late because there are less interruptions.

He nods once. "Don't be late." As he's about to leave, he pauses. "Why do you need the money?"

I can't tell him the truth. Even if he doesn't care, I don't want him to know. It's personal, and it's mine, and I can't trust a guy like Volkov with something so special. Besides, his hate fuels me. Every time Volkov shows his true colors and acts like an asshole, I get a little ping of the *I was right* feeling.

I shoot him a pleased, smug smile, straightening my leg and letting my heel dangle. "For my shoe collection, of course."

A beat passes. He doesn't actually believe I'd get married for *shoes,* does he?

He shakes his head with a disgusted expression. "Incredible, Doctor. I underestimated how superficial you are."

His words pinch, but before I can respond, he's gone.

"Dickhead," I mutter, flipping him the bird behind his back as he walks away.

There's no way I'd ever fall for that asshole.

"DON'T FALL in love with me," the doctor says by way of greeting when she arrives at the restaurant that night. "Write it on a sticky note and put it on your dentures case, Volkov, because I will never, ever love you back."

Thank fuck I reserved a table in a more private area of the restaurant, where we can be seen but not overheard. People glance over at the woman across from me, because a woman who looks like Georgia Greene draws attention, but no one is within ear shot.

"That's not going to be a problem, Doctor." I know better than to fall for someone who values image and wealth above all else. I'd never make the same mistake twice.

She gives me a knowing smirk, those warm whiskey eyes sparkling. "I know I'm your type."

My eyes trail over her, lingering on her neckline, where freckles peek over, scattered across her pale skin. Her skin looks soft, probably from drinking virgins' blood.

"You aren't."

Does she think I would actually make a move on her? That I'm attracted to her?

My gaze trails over her form. Curvy. Tall. Thick hair I can

wrap around my fist. Sharp, assessing gaze and even sharper tongue. And those shoes. I hate those shoes.

The server comes by and she orders a glass of wine, I order a nonalcoholic beer.

Her eyebrow lifts. "You don't drink?"

"Not during the season." After even one beer, I can feel the inflammation in my body the next day. Old injuries ache more. It's not worth it.

Her gaze lingers on me, interest and focus in her eyes, and she looks like she wants to say something.

"I'm sorry to interrupt your date," the server says, glancing between us with a nervous smile, and I fight the urge to correct her. From the way the doctor stiffens, I'm certain she's stifling the same urge. "Would we be able to get a photo with you?"

She gestures at the bartender on the other side of the restaurant.

"We're huge fans," the server admits.

"Of course." I clear my throat and stand. "Let's go to the bar."

I spend a few minutes signing autographs and taking photos with the staff before I return to the table.

"Wow," the doctor drawls. "You *can* be nice."

I'm about to tell her I don't mind spending time with fans, that when I was a kid and my dad would take me to minors games—the only ones we could afford—I'd be thrilled to meet the players. Hockey isn't just a game, it's part of our culture. It brings people together. It gives people something to get excited about, something to hope for.

"It's part of the job," I say instead.

Her gaze lingers on me with a little frown, like she knows there's more I'm not saying, but she lets it go. "So, one year."

"One year. Or until my citizenship and your inheritance

come through." I take a deep breath. "We need to live together."

Her gaze narrows on me.

"I'm not moving," we say at the same time.

Her jaw drops. "Why should I move? I live close to the arena. It's convenient for you."

"Don't you live with Jordan? I'm not going to fight over the shower in the mornings like I'm living in a frat house. You'll move into my place."

"Is your place even livable?"

I shake my head, in awe of how fucking spoiled she is. "I may not have a fountain and circular drive like you grew up with, but I assure you, my place is good enough for the average hockey wife."

Her nostrils flare. Was it the comment about her being used to wealth, or reducing her education and career to her impending marital status? Looks like I just found another nerve to hit.

"Careful, Doctor." I raise my brows. People have been subtly glancing at us this whole time. "Don't look so demonic. People are watching."

As I say it, some guy passes by the table, gaze snagging on the back of her hair. My hand tightens around my glass.

She puts on a smile, but her gaze cools, pretty amber eyes turning frosty.

Not pretty. Just interesting. Sparkly, with tiny threads of gold. Rich like a glass of bourbon. A little is perfect but too much would kill you.

"Maybe I want to stay in my place. Maybe I don't want to move," she adds, glancing at her nails, inspecting them. They're a deep maroon purple, neat and trim.

"I'm sure you'd love to stuff me in some broom closet and

call it my bedroom, but my place has plenty of room for both of us to stay out of each other's way."

A few years ago, I bought and renovated a home in North Vancouver. It wasn't the largest home I looked at, but it had good bones: tucked away in the forest, overlooking the trees, arched and slanted ceilings, loads of natural light, and a massive stone fireplace. Mid-century modern, my real estate agent called it. It's private, quiet, and the neighbors don't bug me.

"I'm not moving. Besides, during the season, I'm either away for hockey, at a game, or training. I won't be home to see you carting in your shopping bags."

She sighs like talking to me is exhausting. "It would probably be too much hassle to move all your medical equipment anyway. I'm sure your place is set up like a care home." She rests her chin on her hand, narrowing her eyes. "I'll need a big closet."

"Yes, Hellfire, I'm aware you're a consumer." My eyes drop to her shoes and her eyes flash at the nickname she hates so much.

"You'll have to cut out comments like that or no one will believe us."

"You have your own comments to cut out."

"I'll save those just for you, Volkov."

Our gazes hold, and my shoulders tense. This year is going to be fucking terrible.

"We need to get our stories straight," I tell her. "People will ask questions about how we got together and why we didn't tell anyone."

"Easy. I was humiliated." She gestures at me. "You're twice my age."

"In that case, you look terrible for eighteen."

The corner of her mouth tightens like she's trying not to

laugh, and I get a weird hit of something warm in my chest. Annoying.

"We'll tell people we hooked up after the double date."

Last year, Owens clearly had a thing for Darcy but wouldn't make a move, so I asked her out in front of him to spur him into action. It worked like a charm—except Owens insisted on bringing Georgia.

"We didn't want a relationship. We just wanted to," she arches an eyebrow, "blow off steam."

Fuck, she means. We just wanted to fuck.

I bet the doctor is incredible in bed. I picture her beneath me, naked and desperate while I thrust into her, those plush lips parted and eyes on me, letting me do what I want to her. Arousal pounds through me.

My thoughts slam to a halt. Even if we put our weapons down, messing around with the doctor would be a fucking disaster. She's marrying a guy she hates *for money*. Her morals are paper-thin.

She'd tear my heart out and sell it for this season's newest heels, and she wouldn't feel an ounce of remorse while doing it.

My watch is beeping—that fucking heart rate alarm again—and I silence it, ignoring her raised eyebrows and tilting, catlike smile.

"Are you picturing it, Volkov?"

"The thought of fucking you makes me feel sick."

"Right." She smirks like she doesn't believe me. "Sick in the excited way? Like your pants feel tight?" She sends a pointed glance to my crotch.

I close my eyes, rubbing the bridge of my nose. This woman is infuriating.

"So we didn't think it was going anywhere, we were just hooking up, and then we decided to get married." I make a face. "Who's going to believe that?"

"You're an intense guy. You fell madly in love with me and insisted I marry you."

"Maybe you fell madly in love with *me* and begged me to marry you."

She snorts, unamused. "I would never beg, Volkov."

My groin tightens, and my watch starts beeping again. I turn off the program that monitors my heart rate outside of training and games. When I'm not exercising, I need to be resting and recovering, but being around the doctor torches all of that.

"Besides, you're controlling enough that demanding I marry you is actually believable."

I ignore the dig. "We didn't tell anyone because I'm private. I don't like people knowing my business."

Against protests by the Storm publicity department, I don't have my own social media. I'm rarely photographed except with the team, and I never do postgame press because they're always asking about my fucking retirement.

The amusement falls from her expression, and her delicate fingers toy with the stem of her wineglass. "We're really doing this, huh?"

My gaze snags on the pinch between her eyebrows. "No one can suspect a thing. If people find out this isn't real and the government thinks people are lying for us, they could get in trouble. My parents could be deported. If you're not in, tell me now."

"I'm in." The long line of her pale throat works as she swallows, and our eyes meet. "We'll fake it and fool everyone. No one will know but us," she adds. "And Jordan."

We both know she won't say anything, though.

There's a steel edge to her voice I haven't heard before. She never takes anything seriously, but this, she cares about.

For shoes, though? This doesn't add up.

I gesture to the server for the bill. "We'll get married tomorrow." I got the license this afternoon, as soon as we talked in her office. "Courthouse. Two pm."

The doctor's eyes flare with surprise. "Tomorrow?"

"I want this process started as soon as possible."

Her gaze flicks to my bad shoulder. If anyone should know I'm on a ticking clock, it's her. My gut knots. I hate that she knows all my weaknesses. I hate that I wasn't worth her time as a patient.

I don't know if I expected her to fight me on this, to insist on a big, flashy, expensive wedding, but she just nods, frowning to herself.

"Tomorrow." She stands, and puts her coat on. "See you there, Volkov."

She walks off without a second look. I watch her leave, my gaze catching on the flutter of her light jacket, the flash of her heels, before she's gone, and the realization sinks in.

The doctor and I are getting married.

CHAPTER 8
GEORGIA

THE NEXT DAY, I stand outside Vancouver City Hall under the cool September sunlight, questioning my life choices.

It's a beautiful day to get married. My hair and the wedding dress I found last minute flutter in the light breeze and I take a deep breath. September is the best month in Vancouver, still warm from the summer but before the rainy winter season starts. I always tell people to visit in September.

If I wanted to get married, I'd get married in September.

"Congratulations," an older man says as he walks down the steps.

"Thank you." I clutch my small bouquet, hold my smile until he passes, before I let out a long breath and glance around.

If this were a real wedding, I'd get married under that big tree over there, the one that looks about fifty years old, solid and steady, branches reaching up to the sky. On the grass beneath it, sunlight dapples through the leaves. I'd stand under that tree and hold the hand of my dream man, gazing up into his eyes in adoration.

In another lifetime, maybe.

Inside city hall, more people give me encouraging, friendly

smiles. Everyone loves to see couples getting married. When I reach the floor where they do the wedding ceremonies, I spot him immediately. Hard not to, with a guy his size.

He's wearing a suit, arms folded, shoulders tense, impatient energy radiating off from him. Clean, tailored lines and rich, dark gray fabric. The way the suit fits him is a strange contrast to the brutal lines of his face.

If I didn't hate Alexei Volkov so much, I might think he was handsome. I might be attracted to his broad shoulders, the way his dark hair is thick with a slight wave, or the sharp, intelligent focus in his eyes. I might have the urge to run my fingers over the scar in his eyebrow, or press my palm into his abdomen to test if his torso is truly as firm as it looks.

If I were attracted to him. Which I'm not.

His gaze flicks to me, pausing, lingering, sweeping up and down. "That's what you're wearing?"

Irritation throttles through me. How dare he? I look hot. "Wait until the wedding's over before you spit on my new dress, okay, Volkov?"

The gown is floor-length silk with a deep V and flowing sleeves. Seventies bridal goddess is the look I'm going for. I found it on the rack this morning at the wedding dress store I pass every day on the way to work. The fabric is smooth and drapey, skimming over my curves with a slight pearlescent sheen. My hair is down around my shoulders in smooth waves, and my makeup is light and simple except for a swipe of blood red lipstick, which I wear when I need confidence. Or to establish dominance.

More than ever, I need the confidence boost of looking incredible.

His eyes linger on my neckline, my waist, and a rush of adrenaline hits my bloodstream. "Last chance to change your mind."

Am I sure about this? No. I'm petrified. Even though it's just on paper and it would be a frigid day in hell before this marriage between me and Volkov includes real feelings, every cell in my body screams at me to run.

This marriage will never be real, though.

"I'm sure. Let's get this over with."

He nods once, scowling over his shoulder where an older woman with a sweet smile waits. She steps forward and he tilts his head at the door. "We're doing it outside."

As we walk, he tucks his fingers beneath his shirt collar, pulling it away like he can't breathe.

"Don't worry, Volkov," I tell him in a low voice so we aren't overheard. "The nightmare of being married to me will be over before you know it."

As we pass a window, I catch our reflection. We look spectacular together, I'll admit. He's all towering height and broad shoulders, brutal features, and a sharp, expensive suit, and I'm feminine elegance, red lips, and long wavy hair.

What a shame. What a waste.

We make our way out of city hall in silence, people sending glances our way.

"Is that Alexei Volkov?" someone whispers.

As we descend the front steps, I lift my hem so I don't trip. Like always, his eyes go to my shoes. A victorious feeling bubbles up my throat.

"Like them?" I'm all innocence. "They're my something new. You know how much I love to shop."

His eyes cut to mine, flashing with fury, and my grin broadens.

Like most of my shoes, they're outrageous and impractical. A deep, bloodred to match my lipstick. A red that says, *I am here to fucking play, and I will win.*

"This necklace is from my mom, handed down from

my grandmother. Something borrowed." I push my hair back to show him the amber stone hanging from the thin chain, and his eyes dip to my collarbone. My mom lent it to me when I was a teenager and insisted I keep it, but good enough for a fake wedding that's probably already cursed.

He sighs, exasperated with me, and deep in my chest, I feel joy. The more I talk, the more annoyed Volkov gets.

"My 'something blue,' well..." I press my lips together like I've said too much, my smile turning coy. "That's hidden beneath my clothes."

His jaw flexes. Ooooh, I'm really getting under his skin now. He shakes his head and mutters something to himself.

I lower my voice so the officiant, walking a few feet away, can't hear. "Don't you want to know what my 'something old' is?" A smile stretches across my face. To an outsider, I'm the picture-perfect bride, beaming at my groom, excited to hitch my wagon to his and sign my life away.

"I wish you would stop talking," he mutters under his breath.

"It's you." I'm still beaming at him like he's the love of my life. "You're the *something old,* Volkov."

He glares at me like he's regretting all of this.

"Tell me," I whisper, because around him, I just can't help myself, "what happens to our prenup if you kick the bucket early?"

"Here," he tells the commissioner, ignoring me. "Let's do it here."

With a start, I realize he's led us to beneath the big maple tree I admired earlier.

"Why here?" I ask.

I'd rather get married inside city hall, under ugly fluorescent lighting, listening to the hum of the air-conditioning and people coughing or arguing parking tickets. Not out here, where the sun is shining.

I don't want any of this to feel real. I don't want it to be nice or romantic or memorable.

"It's public," he says in a low voice.

When I glance around, I spot the people already looking at us. A couple marrying outside city hall already attracts attention, but there's an aura of power around Volkov that draws notice. I think about the restaurant last night, how my eyes went to him like a moth to a flame.

He has a point—the Storm social media accounts will be buzzing within minutes.

The officiant smiles again, her innocent, pleasant nature so out of place next to me and Volkov. A lamb in a snake pit. "Are your witnesses joining us?"

My stomach drops and I look to Volkov. I didn't even think of witnesses. Of course we'd need them.

"They're here." Volkov tilts his chin at an older couple approaching. She's wearing a dress and he's wearing a suit. They look to be in their sixties, and they're speaking in Russian, beaming at Volkov.

Oh god. His parents are here? He invited his parents?

They say something to him in Russian, the woman giving him a hug and the man shaking his hand. The woman's eyes sparkle like she's holding back tears.

She turns to me with a big, cheerful smile, and pulls me into a tight hug. "Congratulations," she says with a Russian accent. I give a startled look to Volkov before the woman steps back and the man shakes my hand.

"So happy for you," he says.

I force a smile. "Thank you." I keep that smile pasted on my face as I lean in to the man I'm about to marry. "You invited your parents?" I ask through my teeth.

He looks at me like I'm insane. "Svetta is my housekeeper, and Dmitri is her husband."

"Thank god." My exhale is pure relief. I don't want to meet his parents. This isn't real, and the less ties to our personal lives, the better. Knowing him and his personality, his parents are probably assholes, just like him.

"Everyone ready?" the officiant asks us.

"Ready." Volkov's gaze slides to me, challenging and assessing. *Last chance,* his expression says.

Uncertainty flickers behind my ribs. What choice do I have, though? I can't let the program lose funding. Those girls need it. They need one another and they need me.

I draw myself taller, inhale a steadying breath, and nod at the officiant.

"Ready."

CHAPTER 9
GEORGIA

FOR MOST OF MY WEDDING, I'm barely listening. The officiant talks about love, commitment, and devotion to each other—all things I couldn't care less about.

A respectful distance away, people gather and take photos. He's so private, I bet he hates this. That gives me a tiny boost.

"Did you prepare vows?" she asks us.

Volkov and I stare at each other. Another thing I didn't think of. Neither did he, by his stricken expression.

I cover up the fumble with a warm smile. "We did, but we'd love to say them in private, if that's okay." I nod to Volkov. "He's shy about these things."

The officiant melts. "Of course." She steps away ten feet and turns her back on us. Our witnesses shuffle away, giving us space.

Volkov holds my gaze with that cold, pissed-off look, leaning in until his mouth is inches from my ear. Alarm shoots through me as his scent washes over me, clean and sharp, deeply masculine, and the back of my neck prickles.

For a startling moment, I think he's going to kiss me.

"I don't love you and I never will," he murmurs.

I huff a silent laugh. "This isn't a real marriage, and when it's over, I won't miss you."

He stares down at me, nostrils flaring, and god, I fucking hate him.

"Glad we're on the same page."

He calls the officiant back, and we continue the ceremony. She makes us repeat things. I'm only half listening, focused on saying the right words, not on what they mean. It doesn't matter. It isn't real.

"Do we have the rings?" the officiant asks, and my heart stops.

Was I supposed to get a ring for him? Before I can panic, he reaches into his suit jacket and pulls out two rings, one small and one large. They're cold, plain, and ugly, two bands of metal.

I make a horrified face. "Oh god," I blurt out before I can stop myself.

The officiant looks between us, concerned, and I school my expression into a smile.

"These are heirlooms." I'm scrambling. "I thought they were lost."

"How romantic," she says softly, clutching her chest.

This is probably a good thing. I'd get attached to a pretty ring. I'd miss it when this was over. I won't miss this ugly thing.

She says more words, and he takes my hand and slides the ring on my finger. My nerves jump from the surprising warmth of his hands. My focus narrows to where his fingers brush mine.

The ring is at least two sizes too big. He stares down at me, daring me to challenge him.

More words I barely listen to as I repeat, and I slide the ring onto his finger, holding his strong hand in mine.

It's weird, touching him like this. My stomach dips.

"Very well." She sends us a serene smile, and when I look

to Volkov, my heart does a weird, confusing clunk. "I now pronounce you husband and wife."

Our witnesses clap happily, the officiant beams between us, and the onlookers start applauding.

"Yeah, Volkov!" someone hollers.

The officiant pauses with meaning. "You may now kiss the bride."

I stiffen. My cool mask of composure slips, and panic races up my spine. He's not going to actually—is he? A question rises in my eyes.

He stares back at me with a cold glare.

"Mr. Voklov?" the officiant asks.

I'm not breathing. I clutch my stupid bouquet—why did I buy this? I feel like a child playing wedding with her friends.

"Would you like to kiss the bride?" the officiant asks gently, like she suspects he's so overcome with love and devotion that he hasn't heard her.

I see the barely perceptible curl to his lip, though. He's disgusted at the idea. I don't care about him or what he thinks, but still, the rejection stings. My face burns, and I pray he doesn't notice. The only thing more embarrassing than him rejecting me at our wedding would be him realizing it hurts me.

He takes a deep breath. Oh. We're doing this. Okay. My pulse picks up. We're actually going to kiss. Of course we are. We can't pretend to get married without a kiss. My heart hammers, my spine goes ramrod, and I'm frozen as he lowers his mouth to mine.

My eyes close, my palm comes to his chest, and under his dress shirt, I feel his granite muscles tense. People are applauding and cheering. I guess they can't see how uncomfortable he is, kissing me. He probably hates my perfume, too, because he's not even breathing. His lips don't move. It's like kissing a statue.

We pull apart. He blinks, stunned, like I just stabbed him in the gut.

"That was the worst kiss of my life," I whisper so only he can hear, smiling serenely like the besotted bride I'm supposed to be. "That was like kissing the dead body at a funeral."

A terrible kiss and absolutely no spark. Exactly what our marriage will be.

His eyes dart all over my face. There's something weird in his expression—confusion. Or maybe surprise. Bemusement?

"That's not how I kiss." He frowns.

Relief covers up the fading sting of rejection. Imagine if the kiss with Volkov was actually *good*? Then I'd have real problems.

Deep down, though, I'm a little surprised. I hate the guy, but I have this annoying feeling he's incredible in bed. I don't know why I think this—these hockey players are rich, gorgeous, and famous. They don't need to be good at sex.

Not that I'm thinking about it. And not that I think Volkov is gorgeous, either.

We thank the officiant, thank the witnesses, and walk back toward city hall to file the certificate.

"Put your arm in mine," he demands under his breath as we walk, as the onlookers call their congratulations.

My pride crackles with defiance at him telling me what to do, but I force myself to slip my hand over the crook of his arm. His arm is like a steel bar, and the fabric of his suit is smooth and high-quality. Wherever he goes for suits, they know what they're doing.

Inside city hall, it's much quieter.

"I'll file the marriage certificate." He sends me a dismissive look, like when the officiant asked if he wanted to kiss me. "We're done here."

So arrogant. Before I can say something sharp and devastating, the elevator doors near us open and he steps inside. They close and he's gone without another word.

"What, no wedding night?" I mutter to myself as I head to my car. "I thought we had something special." I glance around to make sure no one can see before I free-throw my bouquet into the nearest garbage can.

And like that, I'm married.

"VOLKOV IS A MACHINE," my dad says at dinner that night, shaking his head with admiration. The food in my mouth turns to dry sand. The Storm game is on mute in the other room so my dad can keep an eye on the score.

He's a huge Storm fan.

Across the table, Jordan and I look at each other. After getting to know them while we were roommates in university, she's close with my parents. She always comes to these dinners, and tonight especially I need her here for support.

"Can we turn the game off during dinner, please?" I ask with a forced smile.

My dad looks at me like I'm ridiculous. "This is an important game." His eyes go back to the screen. It's the only time he's distracted from his family, when hockey's on. "It sounds like his work ethic is beyond any of the other players. That's probably how he's had such a long career." He looks to me. "You should study him in your program. The guy recovers from injury like no one else."

I'm well aware. I clench my molars together. Jordan makes a muffled noise behind her hand, and I point my fork at her. "You better be choking and not laughing."

My dad gives me a teasing look in between glances at the game. "Georgia, you always get so twitchy about the guy. Do you have a crush on him or something?" His eyes glint and my mom laughs.

Jordan's eyes bore into me. *Do it now,* her expression says.

"He's going to win the Norris trophy again," my dad says.

I take a deep breath. Photos of the wedding are already surfacing online. I don't want them to find out from someone else.

Ugh. That terrible kiss. My stomach rolls at the memory. "I have something to tell you guys."

"Again?" my mom asks my dad. "He's won it more than once?"

"Three times." He nods with enthusiasm. "That's what's so impressive—"

"I got married," I blurt out, and both my parents slowly turn to me. Jordan puts her head in her hands.

My dad blinks, fork hovering in midair. "Excuse me?"

"Did you say you got *married*?" my mom repeats.

My heart hammers up into my throat. If anyone's going to see right past me, it's them. "Yep." I can't get a full breath. I feel sick. "To Volkov."

My dad turns the game off, and silence stretches between all of us. I can hear my pulse in my ears. I stare at the table, but I can feel their gazes searing me.

My mom is the first to break the silence. "You called him a stubborn, conceited, sexist pig who thinks he knows better than everyone."

Well, he is. My chin dips in a nod. "Yes. I said that."

"You hate him." My dad rears back. "I can't say a word about him without you going red in the face."

I just keep staring at the table. Also true. Why did I think this would work? I'm a day in and the plan is crumbling into dust.

My parents look at each other before they break out in beaming grins.

"Knew it." My mom shakes her head, eyes sparkling. "What did I say, Shane?"

Uh, what? I'm flooded with relief. Guilt follows, because I'm lying to them.

"You knew it," he confirms with a proud nod before he gives me a teasing look. "Honey, you can't fool us. We know you too well."

"You didn't know it." My voice holds a touch of defensiveness.

"We did," Mom insists. "He's the only player you have such a strong response to."

"Because he's such an *asshole*." She gives me a strange look. "Because he *was* such an asshole," I amend. "When we first met. And now he's great. I—" I force the words out. "I love him."

Jordan closes her eyes, her mouth tightening like she's trying not to laugh.

"How long have you two been together?" my mom asks. "Why didn't you say anything?"

I think about what Volkov and I agreed upon. "We just, uh... didn't think it was going anywhere."

My discomfort must be written all over my face, because my mom reaches out and gives my arm a squeeze. "It's okay. We know being vulnerable is hard for you after the whole Liam thing."

My blood pressure skyrockets. I hate when she brings it up so casually like that. "I don't want to talk about it."

I thank the universe every single day that my mom called and asked three times if I was very, very sure this was what I wanted, and on the last time, when I didn't answer, she booked me a flight home to Vancouver before calling the UBC admissions people to reverse the change.

"I'm just saying, we're thrilled you're in love." She gives me a soft smile. "I'm not surprised he fell in love with you. You're extremely lovable." She winks at Jordan. "You, too, baby. You two are catches. Anyone would be lucky to be with either of you."

"Thanks, Mom."

"Thanks, Cece." Jordan gives her a tiny, amused smile.

"So when do we get to meet him?" my dad asks.

"He's really busy with games and training."

Maybe I can put them off until the spring, when his season is over. By that time, we could already be separated, and there would be no point.

"Next weekend? Let's set a date." My mom pulls out her phone, bringing up her calendar. "Or we can come to your place." Her eyes light up with realization. "Are you already living together?"

"We're in the middle of moving my things." Sort of. I spent most of this afternoon packing while my two pet bunnies, Stefan and Damon, became increasingly nervous.

I doubt Volkov would let me bring them when I move in, so I'm going to have to sneak them into his house.

My mom makes a sad face between me and Jordan. "Aw. End of an era."

I sink a little, because I'll miss living with Jordan. She knows every version of me and still loves me, and I still love her.

It's only temporary, though. One year maximum. Maybe we can live together after.

"Thanksgiving?" My mom's still scrolling through her calendar. Canadian Thanksgiving is in a few weeks.

Ugh. The idea of Volkov meeting my parents is bad enough, but at an intimate family gathering? God, no.

"He's away for a road trip." I think I remember seeing that on the calendar.

"Don't tell us you're embarrassed of us." My dad pretends to look offended. "We're the cool parents. I won't even ask him for an autograph."

I start to smile. Growing up, my parents were at least a decade younger than all the other parents. All my friends had crushes on at least one of them, sometimes both.

They aren't going to let this go. An idea hits me.

"I'll bring him to the Halloween party."

My parents' Halloween party is a yearly event. My mom is a costume designer on film sets, so she goes all out on costumes. As a kid, my costumes blew everyone's out of the water. I still remember her staying up until the early hours of the morning, sewing sequins onto my princess dresses. With help from her set design colleagues, my dad wires up elaborate, spooky lighting in the front yard, making the house look haunted. All my mom's film friends show up, and everyone's costumes are intense.

My mom sinks in disappointment. "That's ages away."

And there will be a ton of people packed into this house. They'll be busy hosting, with no time to focus on how much I definitely am *not* in love with Volkov.

I glance around at my parents' modest home that they bought a few years ago, once my dad's electrician business took off. Am I ready for Volkov to learn I didn't have the upbringing he thought I did?

It doesn't matter. He's going to find out eventually.

"He's really busy," I repeat. "And with my work at the hospital, schedules can be tricky."

"Okay." My mom shrugs. "We'll wait until Halloween. I can help you source a costume if you'd like."

I try not to look too gleeful at the prospect of forcing Volkov into a costume. I already have ideas. "I'd love that."

When I glance at my dad, though, he's giving me a scrutinizing look. "Are you sure about this, Georgia? It seems fast."

We're close enough that I could probably tell them everything, and they'd probably understand why I'm doing this. They could be interviewed about Volkov and his parents' citizenship, though, and I'd never want to get them in trouble.

"I know it's fast." I need to think of something convincing. "He's unlike anyone I've ever met."

Not a lie. I look to Jordan. *Help me,* I say with my eyes.

"They're perfect for each other," she tells my parents. Her mouth curves into a wry smile. "You'll see."

I give her a strange look, but my dad steeples his hands together with a deep breath. "Okay. Georgia, you're a grown woman, you can make your own decisions. We just want you to be happy and healthy." He lets out a short laugh. "I guess you get that inheritance now."

A weight clunks in my stomach. I'm not stupid enough to hope they forgot. They were furious when they found out about the clause in the will. And I'm definitely not stupid enough to pretend *I* forgot.

"Mhm." I sip my water. My blood pressure rises.

"It's okay if you feel weird about accepting the money." My mom leans her chin on her palm, giving me a sympathetic look. "It's not from a good place, but it doesn't matter. It's yours."

"I, um, I'm going to accept it. I'm giving it to the hospital." I look up, meeting their eyes. "For the athlete injury recovery program."

They stare at me for a long time. Terror spikes up my

throat. I haven't said a word about the program getting axed, but they know what it means to me.

They've figured it out.

"God, we're proud of you." My dad hangs his head, smiling. "How did we get such a good kid?" he asks my mom.

"We raised her right." She glances down at the floor. "Hugo Greene is probably rolling in his grave at you using the money to help people."

I laugh. "I didn't think of that."

"And you know what we always say," my dad adds.

"The higher the heels," I raise my glass, "the closer to heaven."

My mom laughs. "That's my girl."

"Not quite." He grins between us, amused.

"More sequins, more sparkles."

He chuckles. "Also no. Money doesn't buy happiness."

"Hear, hear." My mom toasts with Jordan, who knows that lesson better than anyone.

My dad looks to Jordan. "We're proud of you, too, kid. Running that bar by yourself. Self-made, working hard."

"Your mom would be proud," my mom says.

"Thanks, guys." Jordan's eyes flicker with emotion before she blinks and it's gone.

That's what I love about my parents—they treat Jordan like another daughter.

My stress level descends to normal as the conversation moves on. On the ride home, Jordan looks over at me from the driver's seat.

"They bought it."

I nod, staring out the window as we pass the houses in my parents' neighborhood. "Let's hope everyone else does, too."

CHAPTER 11

GEORGIA

"WELL, NOW," I say to Darcy a few days later at the Filthy
Flamingo for her engagement party, wrapping her in a tight
hug. "Let me see it."

Earlier today, Hayden gave everyone a heads-up that he
would be proposing to the woman who had been his best friend
for eight years. The bar is filled with Vancouver Storm players,
partners, and team staff.

She obediently holds out her hand, blushing, her lavender
hair around her shoulders in soft waves. I inspect her ring, a
sparkling cluster of white lab-grown diamonds around a pink
diamond, like the cherry tree blossoms that bloom around
Vancouver in the spring.

So soft and romantic. So Darcy.

"It turned out beautifully. Just beautifully."

Seeing someone head over heels like Hayden is for Darcy
makes my heart ache with sweetness. They're so meant to be. I
can already picture them living out their lives together, hand in
hand, teasing each other, smiling at each other, laughing at their
private jokes.

The back of my neck prickles, and my eyes cut to Volkov,

glaring at me while in conversation with Rory and Hayden. He's kept to the other side of the bar all night with rigidity, like the distance between us is court mandated.

I picture us in fifty years. I'm at his funeral, watching his casket being lowered into the ground, flipping him double middle fingers.

"Isn't that his ex-wife?" someone would whisper.

"Great choice on the dress," I tell Darcy. She's wearing a floral sixties-style A-line I found on a consignment site the other week and sent the link to her. "I told you you'd have somewhere to wear it."

When we met last year, Darcy was fresh out of a long-term relationship, stuck in a boring, soul-sucking job, dressing in a way she hated, living a *life* she hated. It took a bit of peer pressure from me but I've converted Darcy to wearing clothes she loves, that make her feel beautiful.

"Wait." Her gaze snags on my left hand before she grabs it, ogling the plain, thin band. Nothing sparkly like what she has, but on this finger, the meaning is crystal clear. "What's this?"

"Oh, that?" God, I really didn't want her to find out *now,* during *her* engagement party. The timing is terrible.

"Yes, *this.*" She wears a funny, curious smile.

I'm surprised she hasn't seen the photos yet. "I got married."

"Married?"

She looks like I slapped her. Of course she does. *I will never get married,* I've told her. I've told everyone that.

And I still won't. Not for real.

"To who? When? *Why?* I didn't even know you were seeing someone."

I didn't realize how hard this part would be—lying to my friend. I like Darcy. I respect Darcy. She's smart and funny and wonderful.

"Volkov."

Her sea-green eyes go wide as saucers. "I have a million questions."

Just like with my parents, I want to tell her the truth, but I don't want her complicit in anything. "It's your engagement party. We don't want to steal your thunder."

She makes a face, waving me off. "You know I don't care about that. We should celebrate."

"No," I say too quickly, with a desperate edge, and she gives me a strange look. "I mean," I clear my throat, laughing a little, "I'm still wrapping my head around it."

Not a lie, technically.

She studies me before she nods, smiling softly. "Okay. I understand."

The guilt doesn't go away, though. "I'm sorry I didn't tell you."

Darcy is the kindest, loveliest person on the planet, and I am a bag of trash for lying to her. I'm worse than fashion designers who destroy unsold items instead of putting them on sale.

"I did always wonder if you guys were going to," she lowers her voice to a whisper, *"hate fuck."*

My face burns hot. "Darcy."

She starts laughing. "What? You two have all that sexual tension."

This again? My parents announcing that they "knew it" plays in my head, and my hackles rise.

"I can't believe you got married," Darcy says to herself just as Hazel Hartley walks by.

"Wait." Hazel stops in her tracks and grabs my arm before lifting it to look at my hand. "Married?"

"Married?" Her sister, Pippa, a singer-songwriter, married to Storm goalie Jamie Streicher, pops up out of nowhere.

"Married?" I hear Hayden say on the other side of the bar.

"You got married," Rory Miller repeats loudly like he can't believe it, while Volkov stands there, looking irritated.

Even calm and serious Jamie Streicher looks baffled. One by one, the guys look over to me. My stomach dips with nerves. The bar falls silent as the news spreads like wildfire. I can hear my heart pounding in my ears. Everyone is staring between me and Volkov.

I force an embarrassed smile, my face burning hotter than the sun. "Surprise."

"There she is," Hayden singsongs as he approaches. "Dr. Georgia Volkov."

"Nope." I shake my head. "Still Georgia Greene. Not changing my name."

Hayden wraps me in a tight hug, squeezing the air out of my lungs. "I *knew* there was something between you guys. Didn't I know it?" he asks Darcy. "I said it, right?"

"Mhm." She smiles. "You said it."

I make a low noise of frustration that thankfully no one hears over the music and conversation.

"Georgia, congratulations." Rory wraps me in a hug. "Maybe we can finally get some peace and quiet now that you two have an outlet for all that tension."

Hayden, Hazel, and Pippa start laughing, Darcy presses her lips into a firm line like she's trying not to smile, and Jamie just raises his eyebrows, but his eyes are sparkling.

Volkov and I meet gazes, and it's on the tip of my tongue to say something like *in his dreams,* but we're supposed to be happily married and having loads of loud, passionate sex.

I picture Volkov in bed. I've seen him without a shirt—he's ripped, like most hockey players, and the guy is six foot five. I bet that in bed he'd be like he is the rest of the time—pushy, controlling, overbearing. Selfish. High-handed.

Heat twinges between my legs.

"Yep." I swallow half my drink. "Doing lots of . . . that stuff."

Volkov gives me a strange look and I busy myself with finishing the rest of my drink.

"So, you liked him all along?" Hayden presses, still wearing that teasing smile.

Volkov arches an eyebrow, knowing and arrogant. My spine stiffens, and it takes every ounce of my control not to set Hayden straight.

"Yes." It's like eating dirt. This is so humiliating. "I liked him all along."

The athlete recovery program, I chant in my head as I catch a glimpse of his cruel smirk.

Rory gives us a *go on* gesture. "When did it start?"

Behind the bar, I meet eyes with Jordan. *You're on your own,* her expression says.

"We hooked up after the double date."

"Cool." Hayden grins at Darcy. "So did we."

She blushes. They're all probably thinking that once Hayden and Darcy left, the tension between me and Volkov simmered to a boil before I dragged him by the collar into the bathroom and had passionate, furious sex with him.

In reality, we watched Hayden jealously haul Darcy out of the restaurant before Volkov got up without a word, paid the bill, and left without looking back at me. Just another secret we'll have to keep.

Volkov clears his throat. "We didn't think it was going anywhere. That's why we didn't tell anyone."

Everyone glances between the two of us, and my blood pressure peaks again. Hazel's eyes narrow.

They don't believe us. We can't just spout off practiced answers. We need to actually look like a couple.

My pulse picks up as I move to Volkov's side, and with everyone's eyes on me, I awkwardly rest my hand on his chest.

It's like touching a brick wall. The guy's body is made of armor, and he's giving me nothing. His T-shirt is strangely soft, though, like it's been washed a hundred times. A hand on the chest, though? That doesn't exactly scream *true love*. No, I need more. What would Darcy do with Hayden?

I tilt my head so it rests on his shoulder. This feels so awkward, but a moment later, his hand comes to my waist. Warmth seeps through the fabric of my dress. Except for putting the ring on my finger a few days ago, he's never touched me. I touched *him* during our initial meet and greet, when I examined his injuries to see how they'd healed, and he looked like he was about to throw up.

My heart beats out of my chest. My nervous system is warning me of danger. Is his heart beating faster under my hand? It seems like it. Maybe his nervous system is warning him of danger, too.

"Sometimes you fall for the last person you expect." I give him my prettiest smile, and his nostrils flare. "Right, handsome?" *Fucking say something,* my expression says.

"The doctor's right," he tells everyone. "She's the last person I'd expect to fall for."

Incompetent. I hear the word he said two years ago like it was this morning.

He yanks his hand away from my waist, and tucks it in his pocket. Embarrassment twinges behind my ribcage as I lift my head off his shoulder. Of course he doesn't want to touch me. He hates me.

Good. Him finding me repulsive means nothing will get complicated between us. He'll never hit on me, and even if he did, I'd laugh in his face.

I wonder what that would be like, Volkov hitting on someone. Probably him clubbing her on the back of the head and dragging her back to his cave. I haven't heard of him dating anyone. Maybe he's celibate. Maybe he's one of those types who thinks sex or even jerking off is bad for his testosterone.

My gaze roams over his broad shoulders, the way his dark hair curls slightly at his nape. The brush of stubble over his sharp jaw. So he's hot. So what. There are tons of good-looking hockey players here tonight. It doesn't give him an excuse to act like an asshole and remind me how disgusted he is by me.

Competition fires through me, and I have the urge to get him back.

"You know what I've always loved about Volkov?" I ask Darcy. "He's a beast in bed. The second we step in the door, he's all over me. We don't even have time to take my heels off."

My gaze cuts to him, catching the flex of his jaw. Delight spreads through me. Pissing off Volkov is going to be my lifeline during this year.

He glowers. I smile wider.

"He has a lot more stamina than you'd think," I continue. "Don't be fooled by his age. He can go *all night*."

I wonder how big his dick is—an unwelcome thought that I swat away fast.

A big, warm hand comes to the back of my neck, gripping firm but not tight, and a rush of heat moves through my body. The biting quip I'm about to say disintegrates. With his hand on my neck like this, I can't think.

He brings his mouth to my ear. "Behave, Hellfire."

A shiver runs down my back.

"All I need to do is flash a couple bills from my wallet and the doctor's all over me," he tells Darcy, still gripping the back of my neck. "She's surprisingly good at begging."

Low in my abdomen, fury clenches. I would never beg, and especially not with him.

I take a deep breath to clear my head, but instead get a deep inhale of his scent, clean and masculine.

"You're so funny," I manage, scrambling for control. With a sweet smile, I give his bad shoulder a playful slap, the one with a metal plate and a handful of pins. His jaw flexes again like he's biting back a groan of pain. "You know what's also *so* funny? How much you love being tied up and spanked." I give Darcy a knowing look. "It's always the big tough guys who like to be told what to do, *if you know what I mean*."

His hand squeezes my neck and I get another rush of warmth low in my abdomen. I always choose guys who are laid back, affable, and easy to push around, especially in the bedroom. The last thing I want is someone telling me what to do with my own body.

Darcy looks concerned. "This is a lot of personal information."

I get the feeling Volkov isn't interested in being told what to do during sex, though. I don't know why I'm thinking about this. It doesn't matter.

Thankfully, his hand drops, and my brain works again.

"But you know what he's best at?" I stare Volkov down, my mouth curling into a smug grin, thinking about that stiff, awful kiss at our wedding. "Kissing. He's an *incredible* kisser."

I barely hold back the laugh as his eyes flare with irritation.

"Sorry, Darcy." He turns to her. "My little *gniloy kluben* loses her filter when she gets horny."

My smile hardens. "Your what?"

His cold eyes flickers with challenge, fire, and something I've never seen before. "It's Russian for *sweetheart*." The corner of his mouth tightens. "It's an endearment, saved for the ones you love the most."

"Aw." Darcy melts. "Alexei. Who knew you were such a teddy bear?"

"Yes." My eyes narrow. "Who knew?"

His eyes glint with dark amusement. He's not smiling, his mouth is still a cruel slash across his face, but he looks pleased with himself.

Too pleased.

I don't believe him, but I've already forgotten the words he used so I can't look them up later.

Darcy gasps, like she just thought of something. "Hawaii."

The trip to Hawaii this summer with her, Hayden, Hazel, Rory, Pippa, Jamie, and Volkov. The one Darcy pleaded with me to join.

"Oh yeah." Hayden gives us a cheeky grin, shaking his head. "You guys were hooking up the whole time?"

More like, Volkov glared at me in my swimsuit while I attempted to read fashion magazines at the pool.

I wait, giving Volkov a look like, *your turn*. He can take a turn being humiliated.

He stares me down. "Yes. Georgia kept sneaking into my bed at night."

My face burns hot. He wishes.

Darcy gets pulled into a conversation with Rory and Hayden, leaving me alone with Volkov.

"Nice work," he mutters. "This is going to be more believable if you don't ramble incoherently."

My temper flares, hot and angry. "Shut up, Volkov. At least I'm trying. You're just standing there and letting me do all the work. It's probably what you're like in bed."

"You sure seem interested in what I do in bed. You keep bringing it up."

Heat washes through me again, and I take a deep, calming breath so my head doesn't explode. Why does he get under my skin so easily?

Later, when I can't stand beside my new silent, brooding

husband any longer, I pay my tab with Jordan and pull my jacket on.

"You weren't going to leave without saying goodbye, were you?" he says at my side, eyes cruel and mocking.

That's exactly what I was going to do.

"I'll walk you out." He grabs his jacket. "I'm leaving, too. Darcy. Owens." He nods at them. "Congratulations."

"You too, buddy." Hayden claps him on the back.

I give them both a hug, whisper my congratulations in Darcy's ear, before I walk outside, Volkov's looming presence right behind me.

In the cool autumn air, I can breathe again.

"Hold on," he says as I start to walk away without a word. He reaches into his pocket and hands me something. "Here."

It's a key. Right. We agreed I'd move in on Saturday. I'm already dreading it.

"Did you decide to stow me in the dungeon or the rotting garden shed?" I ask, studying the key.

When my gaze shifts to him, he yanks his gaze up from my mouth. "I could give you the master bedroom and you'd still turn your nose up at it."

I roll my eyes, tuck the key in my coat pocket, and start to walk away but he catches my sleeve, frowning.

"Where are you going?"

"Home." I give my sleeve a tug but he doesn't let go.

His eyes flick down the dark alley. "Take a car."

Ugh. So controlling. "Jordan and I live three blocks from here."

He hesitates, something odd in his eyes. Concern, if I didn't know him better. For a horrifying moment, I think he's actually going to offer to walk me home.

"Don't walk through the alleys." His throat works, eyes moving over my heels. "It's dark."

"Don't tell me what to do, Volkov. Learn that rule and this agreement is going to be a breeze."

This time, when I pull my sleeve from his grip and walk away, he doesn't stop me, but I feel his gaze on me until I turn the corner.

CHAPTER 12
ALEXEI

THE NEXT DAY, I'm at the rink with the rookie, practicing defensive drills.

"Again." I gesture at the fourth-line forwards I've wrangled into a scrimmage. "This time, use your body weight. Get physical, Walker. Shove the other guy out of the way, get him against the boards, do what you need to do to disrupt the play."

We run the play, but the forwards sail past Walker with the puck.

"Walker," I yell across the ice. I don't know why this isn't getting through to him. "What did I say?"

"Get physical." I can hear the frustration in his voice, and his usual smirk is gone.

"Okay. Again."

We try again and again, but it's not working. My mood sinks, and the rookie can feel it. At the bench, Ward watches me fail.

"Let's take a break," I tell Walker before skating over to Ward.

"How's it going?" he asks.

Terrible. I don't even know where to start with the rookie. "He has a long way to go."

"That's why I paired you together. Be patient with him. You guys will figure it out." His gaze flicks to my shoulder. "How's that shoulder doing?"

"Great. Feels brand-new."

Even now, the dull ache throbs. Exercise releases pain-relieving endorphins, but the pain always returns.

Ward watches me like he doesn't believe me. "You'll talk to me if anything changes?"

"Yes." Never. I'll just get better at ignoring the pain.

"Good." His eyes warm. "I saw the photos online. Congrat-ulations."

I pull my glove off and we shake hands. "Thank you."

I glance up to her office overseeing the rink. The light's on, so she must have gotten home okay last night. Yes, I can't stand her, but her walking down that dark alley replayed in my head all night.

If Ward suspects anything about the reasons for our marriage in relation to my citizenship, he doesn't bring it up. Instead, his brow wrinkles. "My admin didn't see your response to the team dinner tomorrow night."

The welcome back dinner for players and staff. I wasn't planning on going. "I can't make it."

"Dr. Greene is going but you can't?"

"Family stuff." There. Nice and vague.

"If there's any way you can reschedule, I'd like you to be there. It's important to show the new players and staff that we're all committed, especially experienced players like yourself."

The thing about Ward is he knows exactly how to get you. He knows I feel a responsibility to this team. Maybe it's that I admire his hands-on coaching style, that he's incredible at uniting a group of strangers to work toward a common goal, or maybe that he genuinely seems to want the best for us, but I want to make him proud.

I clear my throat and nod. "I'll be there."

"Good man. Thank you."

The dinner will take an hour or two, and I can slip out early. There will be so many people there, I won't even have to talk to the doctor.

I think about our wedding, how beautiful she looked as she spat insults at me. How the hairs on my arm rose when I put the ring on her finger. The way my heart beat out of my chest as I kissed her. The second our mouths met, an electric shock ran through me.

I froze up. I never freeze up. I don't know what happened.

As Ward's about to leave, he pauses. "You didn't get a honeymoon."

Honeymoon? The idea of being stuck alone in a hotel room with the doctor for a week is a nightmare.

A real couple would go on a honeymoon, though.

Worst kiss of my life, she'd said. I remember the way her soft lips felt, and my jaw tightens.

"We'll do it at Christmas," I lie. "Before Miller and Hazel's wedding."

Fuck. Why'd I say that? I don't go to weddings. Miller and Hazel are getting married on New Year's Eve in Silver Falls, a tiny ski town in the interior of British Columbia where her and Pippa's parents live. I've already RSVP'd no.

Three months is a long time from now. A lot could happen. I'll find an excuse to get out of it.

My mind flicks to the doctor's extensive shoe collection, and I wonder which pair she'll wear to the wedding.

Ward nods with a pleased expression. "That's great. There's more to life than hockey."

No, there isn't. "Okay."

"This career doesn't last forever and once it's gone . . ." He shakes his head, a wry smile pulling up on his mouth. "Some guys have a tough time after retirement, when they don't have anything other than hockey." He gives me a quick wave, a nod, and he's gone.

Don't I fucking know it. My retirement looms closer with each day.

THE NEXT MORNING, I pace in the kitchen, waiting for the doctor to get here.

I'm not used to living with someone, especially someone I can't stand, but we'll never see each other. I spend half the season on the road. When I'm in town, I'm at games, training, or working with health professionals, trying to undo years of damage on my body.

My gut drops when I hear the doctor's car pull up outside. At the front windows, I watch an old sedan park in the driveway.

I frown. Is that rust on the wheel well? The car is old in the barely-running way, not in the vintage, collector car way. My new wife is way too superficial to drive something like that, but I'm not expecting anyone else—

The doctor gets out of the car. Is this a joke? That car is probably older than I am.

A moment later, there's a knock at the door.

I open it and lean on the doorframe. She's in leggings, a windbreaker, and sneakers, and I've never seen her dressed so casually. Even dressed for the gym, she looks hot. Annoying. She's breathing heavily, a little flushed, with strands of auburn hair escaping her ponytail, and my mind goes to dirty, depraved places. I bet this is what the doctor looks like in bed, rumpled and breathless.

Right before her jaw unhinges and she bites her partner's dick off.

"Yes?" I act like I don't recognize her.

She gives me a flat look. "Is this how you act when company comes over? No wonder you're still single."

My gaze drops to her feet. "Didn't know you owned a pair of sensible shoes."

"Go jerk off to my shoes in private, Volkov."

The back of my neck heats, and I let my gaze trail over her again. As much I can't stand this woman, those leggings on her are something else.

My gaze lands on the giant thing on the step behind her.

"Uh." My lip curls as she hoists it up. "No. That's not coming inside."

The crystal is at least four feet tall. A soft pink with jagged edges, tiny particles on its surface sparkling in the morning sunlight.

It looks like a giant dick.

I stare at it in horror, stepping back as she carries it into the foyer.

"I'm not leaving my crystal outside."

She can't be serious. "Why do you have it?"

"Because I love it." She lowers it to the floor beside the entranceway table where I keep my keys and wallet. Jesus Christ, those leggings fit her ass like a dream. "And it's pretty. Isn't that enough?"

"It's heavier than you are. How are you going to get it up the stairs?"

She dusts her hands off, and admires it. "I'm not. It's going right here."

"No, it's fucking not. This is a man's home. Men don't have crystals."

I can't have a crystal in my foyer that looks like an erect cock.

"What's the matter, Volkov?" She rests a hand on the tip. The *top,* I mean. "Does it . . . intimidate you?"

She trails a hand over it suggestively and I look away in alarm. I don't like this game.

"Don't tell me you're one of those quacks who think crystals gives you powers, Doctor? Maybe it can help you fly." I give her a condescending, indulgent look that makes her eyes flash with anger. "Or maybe it'll attract some poor sucker who wants to give you all his money."

Her gaze sparks with fury, and a thrill runs through me.

"I don't need any help with that," she says with a tight smile before walking past me into the front room, gaze moving over the high windows, vaulted ceilings with warm wood beams, and stone fireplace.

Is that admiration in her gaze? If it is, I don't care. Light filters in through the windows, catching on gold strands in her auburn hair, and my frown deepens. Her scent wafts over to me —violets, again.

My teeth grit. Dr. Georgia Greene has the personality of a fire demon but smells like pretty flowers, and I don't like it. My florist mother has a book with flower meanings. *Purple violets— my thoughts are occupied with love.*

Unfuckinglikely.

She looks at the mid-century modern furnishings a decorator chose. "It'll do."

"So fucking spoiled," I mutter under my breath. This home is nicer than any place I ever lived growing up, but the doctor and I had very, very different upbringings. She probably has a trust fund, had everything she ever wanted, and never heard the word *no,* whereas my family had to work their way up from nothing.

The corner of her mouth curves up at my disdain and her eyes linger on the built-in bookshelves around the fireplace.

"No family photos," she says like she's not surprised.

I removed them in anticipation of her moving in. I have nothing to hide and I'm proud of my parents, but I don't want her snooty, nose-in-the-air attitude anywhere near them. If she insults my parents, their heritage, or their jobs, I don't know what I'd do.

"I don't see them much," I lie.

My mind burns with the memory of Emma's parents meeting mine. How they barely spoke to them. I was in my fourth year in the NHL, already making millions, but it didn't matter. What we came from was shameful to Emma's old-money family.

For the next year, I'll keep my family far, far away. I told them I'm doing renovations. I can drag that out for a couple months at least.

"You can park on the left side of the garage." I hand her the garage door opener, careful not to touch her hand again like when I put the ring on. Like last night at the bar when she smoothed her palm over my chest and I almost passed out. "What time is the truck getting here?"

She gives me a questioning look. "What truck?"

"The moving truck."

"I didn't hire a moving truck."

"Then how are you moving your stuff in?" I ask slowly, and my condescending tone makes her nostrils flare. A thrill of satisfaction runs down my spine.

"My car."

My gaze swings to the window, and I crane my neck to see her car in the driveway. It's packed to the roof with boxes.

"That's all your stuff?" I thought she'd show up with a semitruck.

"Almost. I'll have to do another trip or two."

I almost offered to help her outside the bar after Darcy and Owens' engagement party. If she were anyone else, I would have. I'd have roped in Owens, Miller, Streicher, and Walker, too. It's the way I was raised. My parents would be horrified to learn I'm letting her fend for herself.

Acting like a decent person would give the doctor the wrong impression, though.

Something occurs to me and I frown. "You need furniture, then."

Her cool mask slips, and she blinks with uncertainty. "I got rid of everything. You said I'd stay in the guest room."

I cleared out the room I'm putting her in, moving all the furniture to the room beside mine. I gave her the room farthest from mine, at the end of the hall. It's the smallest. Let her be miserable in there with not enough room for her precious shoes and tiaras, I figured.

Now I have to move it all back? I'm meeting my physio in twenty minutes.

"Fine," I grit out.

Fuck. Now she'll be in the room beside mine, sharing a bedroom wall with me. Sleeping a few feet away from me.

I lead her up the stairs, fighting my urge to take the box from her. When we reach the open door beside my room, I gesture inside.

"Here."

I have to admit, everything looks better in this room than where it was before. There's more daylight in here. The windows are bigger, and the bathroom is nicer, with a deep soaker tub. Just like the rest of my home, everything was chosen by a design team—the low, king-sized bed with a thick white duvet, the mid-century modern style bedside tables and the reading chair by the window, and the stupid little decor things my housekeeper, Svetta, must have put out.

It's too nice for my new wife.

The woman beside me lifts her eyebrows once with a flat expression, like she's unimpressed. "Great."

My teeth clench. What a spoiled brat.

"Do you sleep in a bed?" I ask. "Or do you hang upside down from the rafters?"

"A coffin, underground if possible." She yawns behind a delicate, manicured hand.

"Tired from a wild night?" I can't hide the irritation in my voice.

"Absolutely raucous." She holds my gaze, challenging me. "I've been busy every night this week."

Tension snaps in the air. My attention snags on her mouth, how it tilts like she has a secret. She was probably out in something short and tight, laughing at some guy's dumb jokes and tossing back free drinks. She probably left her wedding ring at home, too. My gaze drops to her other hand, to the plain silver ring I put on her finger a few days ago.

Before I can respond, she shoots me a wink, flounces down the stairs, and it's hard to look away from the curve of her hips in those leggings.

———

Late that afternoon, I return, listening for sounds of my new wife moving like a tornado through my home. She has probably rearranged half the furniture by now. Or sold it.

Silence.

Upstairs, half a dozen moving boxes sit outside her closed door. A few are labeled *Fragile—shoes!*

"It's not forever, Damon," she's saying quietly on the other side. "It'll be over before you know it and then it'll just be us again."

The sweet softness in her tone has me standing straighter, listening harder. Damon? I've never heard the doctor speaking to *anyone* like that. Who the fuck is Damon? Hot, sharp alarm races through me.

My fake wife failed to mention she has a *boyfriend*.

My teeth clench so hard my jaw hurts as I glare at her door, burning a hole in it. I picture some faceless guy all over her, hands in her hair. Does he take her out and spend money on her? Is he a nice guy, someone the doctor can push around, or is he an asshole like me?

It pisses me off because she didn't tell me, and her having a boyfriend could blow up this entire deal. That's why I'm mad.

Before I can stop myself, I lift a fist and pound on the door.

MY TWO BUNNIES stare up at me forlornly.

Damon and Stefan are twenty-pound lionhead rabbits, so fluffy I can barely see their eyes, but I sense their distress at the new environment. Poor guys. I offer a piece of lettuce to each of them but they just gaze up at me with sadness.

To my utter shock, Voklov's home is *beautiful*. I expected his aesthetic to be *dirty man cave cluttered with empty beer cans* but his home is like a spread out of *Architectural Digest*. Open, spacious, masculine, and stylish. I'm sure he had someone choose everything for him. Powerful men like Volkov don't do anything home-related. They make the money, have the big career, and expect a pretty little wife to do the rest.

The guest room is almost bigger than the apartment Jordan and I shared, and nicer than any place I've ever lived. His home gym is better equipped than the one the players train in at the arena, complete with a sauna and an ice machine and tub for cold plunges. He has a fully-stocked wine cellar, a library with a stained-glass window too pretty for a guy like him to own, and a sprawling kitchen overlooking the emerald forest out back. I hope there are paths through that forest so I have somewhere to scream after Volkov and I argue.

Living in his home will be an unexpected perk of this arrangement, as long as Volkov isn't here.

And as long as I don't sleepwalk.

When I'm going through periods of extreme stress, I sleepwalk. Like clockwork, it would happen during exams in university and med school. The whole summer with Liam, when I knew something was wrong and wasn't ready to admit it. During my medical residency. I usually end up in Jordan's bed, clinging to her like a cuddly koala while she squirms to the edge of the mattress to get away from me.

I take a deep, calming breath. That's not going to happen here. Even unconscious, my body wants nothing to do with Volkov. I would sleepwalk to Jordan's bed because it's *safe*.

Volkov's bed is probably made of nails.

A pounding sound on the door has me nearly jumping out of my skin.

"Just a second, I'm naked," I call, hoisting the bunnies up and hiding them in the bathroom.

He can't know about them. He'd probably step on them "accidentally" or put them outside where they'd get scooped up by an eagle or eaten by a coyote.

"Talking to more of your crystals in there?" he calls through the door. "Does the Canadian Medical Association know about this?"

I bet he'd love to have my license taken away. He already thinks I'm terrible at my job. I open the door and adopt an inconvenienced expression, like it's *my* house and *he's* the guest.

On the other side of the doorway, his nostrils flare. He looks livid. Good.

"Who were you talking to?" He glances past me but I step into the hall and pull the door closed behind me.

"I was on the phone," I lie.

His Adam's apple bobs and his nostrils flare again before he jerks a hand at the boxes in the hallway. "What are all these boxes doing here? They can't all be full of shoes."

"You can't be surprised. You should be thrilled, actually, that you have such a stylish and hot wife."

His eyes cut to me, his eyes raking over me like I'm wearing a dirty, grease-stained paper bag instead of yoga leggings and the cute windbreaker I wear to soccer practice.

Fuck him, I look great.

"The kind of woman I usually go for doesn't need expensive shoes to feel confident." His cold gaze is steady on me. "It comes off as insecure."

My lips part. *Insecure?* My vision goes red with rage. I just —he's so fucking—I can't. He's a fucking asshole. Heat rises to the surface of my skin and an angry knot tightens in my throat, but I send him a cool smile, like his words bounced right off me.

"The men I'm with usually don't mind. In fact," I lower my voice, lean closer, and hold his cold gaze, "they love my heels. *Fuck-me* heels, they call them."

Men? What men? I haven't slept with someone in forever. Volkov doesn't know that, though, and I'm hoping what he doesn't know *will* hurt him.

He glowers down at me, a muscle tight in his jaw. "Those guys are going to have to wait until this arrangement is over."

Again, what guys? But something in the controlling, commanding way Volkov says this turns a knife in my stomach.

"That wasn't part of the deal. And besides," my voice is light and casual, and I'm winning this argument so hard, "why should my beautiful shoes go to waste?" Our gazes are locked, and a weird, tense energy snaps between us. My skin feels hot and prickly. "No, Volkov, I'm going to be wearing my fuck-me heels all year long."

"No fucking other guys," he bites out, eyes raging.

Are we standing closer than before? Blood pounds in my ears. "Oh, I'm going to."

I don't know what I'm saying. Of course I'm not going to sleep with other guys and screw everything up, but Volkov telling me what to do in *that* tone makes me want to scream. My emotions are at the wheel, joyriding.

"I'm going to fuck every guy I want. Every guy I *meet*."

What? I'm acting ridiculous, but I can't stop. I'm possessed with the need to piss him off. Volkov's jaw looks so hard it could crack.

"I'm going to be out every night in a short dress and my sparkly little fuck-me heels, getting *railed* by some nameless guy while he gives me mind-blowing orgasms."

Like that would ever happen. The only guy who's ever been able to make me come is rechargeable and safely tucked in my nightstand, but wounding Volkov's overinflated ego makes my heart pound so hard I swear he can hear it.

I feel sick. Or excited. Or like I could fly or fight a lion. Fighting with Volkov is like a drug.

"No." He swallows, towering over me, and his lethal expression sends a shiver down my spine. "You will not."

The air between us feels flammable.

"Yes," I whisper, "I will."

"You're going to jeopardize everything."

"I'll be discreet."

We're inches apart. His eyes flick down to my mouth. Something cutting and hot surges through me, spiraling and sparking. His scent is in my nose—sharp, masculine, and dominant—and the back of my neck tingles.

This year is going to be hell, but I won't back down. I won't let him win.

"I'm going out." I give him my most charming smile, like

I'm not replaying the word *insecure* in my mind like a broken record.

"Now?"

He raises an eyebrow. God, I hate when he does that. It's his sign that he thinks I'm making the wrong choice. That I'm just a dumb little woman with a dumb little woman brain.

"Yes. Now."

"The dinner is in—"

"I *know* when the team dinner is." My smile is razor-sharp. "I can tell time, Volkov." He's getting the best of me again. "Don't you worry your bruised skull. I'll be home with plenty of time to slip on a pair of those heels you love so much." My expression is innocent. Maybe even a little sweet. I am the devil reincarnate. "Maybe I'll even find someone tonight who likes them."

His dark eyes flare but I'm out the door before he can respond.

———

An hour later, after blasting one of Jordan's angry lady rock playlists, I return to Volkov's home. Not *my* home. This place will never be my home. Not with him living there.

The front door's unlocked, to my surprise. I wouldn't put it past him to lock the house up tight so I'm forced to ring the doorbell and beg to be let in.

No sign of my horrible husband, thank god. Outside my room, though, my gaze snags on something.

The packing tape is torn off the boxes. They've been opened. My heart jumps into my throat as I flip the cardboard box open.

Empty. Alarm bells ring in my head.

I yank my bedroom door open and head to my new walk-in

closet, praying for Volkov's sake that he had a complete personality transformation, felt remorse for our argument, and neatly unpacked my beautiful shoes in the closet like a good husband would.

The closet is empty, though, and my new husband is still a fucking asshole. My lungs feel tight, my heart beats harder, and my stomach clenches into a hard knot. If I were an egotistical jerk, where would I hide my shoes?

A thought occurs to me, and my lips part with shock and horror.

He wouldn't.

He would, that voice in my head says. *He hates you and he totally would.*

I fly through the house, out the door, and around the side where the compost, recycling, and garbage bins sit. When I flip the garbage lid open, my vision blurs with white-hot rage.

CHAPTER 15
ALEXEI

THE ENTIRE STREET probably hears the doctor's shriek. My fingers still while I work on my tie, a rush of adrenaline hitting my bloodstream.

Over my dead body will she be fucking other guys this year.

Why didn't I think to ask if she had a boyfriend before we made the deal? Of course she does. I've never seen eyes like hers. The doctor is a rare kind of beautiful. If you're into women like her, that is.

Which I'm not.

I'm not jealous. I don't care if she has a boyfriend. I'm only mad because it'll jeopardize my and my parents' citizenship. That's all.

The front door bangs closed, and my pulse trips. I can hear her opening and closing doors downstairs, looking for me. Anticipation sways and peaks inside me. I haven't felt this wired since my first season in professional hockey. Her footsteps move up the stairs, slow and steady like a predator.

I take a seat in the lounge chair by the window, spreading out and folding my arms over my chest, wearing a smug look that'll make her blood boil.

My bedroom door bursts open, fire in her eyes, color on her cheekbones, and hair rumpled. Her chest rises and falls fast as she glares daggers at me, holding up the clear trash bag.

"What," she growls, and my groin tightens, "is this?"

"I don't know, Doctor. Trash?"

"Not trash." Her eyes turn wild, and she slowly walks toward me. Anticipation rises in my gut. "You threw out my shoes."

"Svetta must have thrown them out when she was cleaning. Were they on the floor?"

"No, they were not *on the floor*."

She stares at me with hate in her eyes. Good. Let her hate me. It fuels me, makes my heart race, makes me feel alive.

"So this is how it's going to be," she says.

I think about the guy she was talking to earlier, and frustration courses through me all over again. "I guess so, Hellfire."

———

Forty-five minutes later, I'm hit with her next move.

I sit in the front room, reading through team emails on my phone, when she descends the stairs. My eyes land on her shoes, first. Sparkly, strappy, and sky-high.

Fuck-me heels.

MY HORRIBLE HUSBAND does a double-take at my outfit, gaze snagging on my legs, my waist, my neckline, my hair before his jaw tightens.

His lip curls in disgust. "That's what you're wearing?"

I dug all the way to the back of my closet for this dress. Long sleeves, a low square neckline, a mid-thigh hem, every inch covered in copper sequins. Bold and loud and showy. A showstopper, my mom called it when she gifted it from one of her film sets.

His disapproval makes me see red. *Fucking asshole!* every cell in my body chants. Liam never liked me wearing flashy stuff, either. *That sure is bright,* he once commented about a dress I wanted to wear to a mixer for the new medical students and their partners. He didn't like attention being drawn to me when it could be on him.

"Yes, Volkov." I summon all the feminine power I can, straightening my shoulders. His eyes flick back to my cleavage, and I get a hit of satisfaction. "I want everyone to know how *insecure* I am."

Clothes say something about us. They're a way to communicate with the world. People see what we wear and interpret a message, whether we mean it or not. Sometimes it doesn't matter. Sometimes I wear sweatpants, my hair in a messy bun, and a T-shirt with a hole near the armpit I've had since university, and I don't care what message people infer.

Tonight, though, after the blowup we had this afternoon, I'm wearing a dress that says *I'm not backing down. I'm ready for a fight.* This dress says *I know I look good* and *eat your heart out* and *I don't need you.*

Something flashes in his eyes. On a normal person, I'd call it regret, but I'm sure the only thing Volkov regrets is that he didn't twist the knife in deeper.

"Besides," I tuck my phone and cards into my clutch, "I'm sure your teammates won't mind."

I love my body. I'm hot. I have nice boobs and a great butt. I'm toned and strong from soccer. My body is awesome. Do I look like my mom or Darcy, petite and thin? No. But different doesn't mean worse, or less.

It's what I always say to the girls at soccer: you don't need to look like the Photoshopped people in magazines to be gorgeous.

It's clear what body type Volkov prefers, though, as his gaze finds the hem of my short dress, and he looks like he's going to be sick.

He stares at me, unamused, before his gaze flicks to my heels. "Never miss a chance to show off, do you?"

The silver lining of this whole situation is that Volkov was forced to marry a woman he doesn't find hot. These hockey players are used to getting everything they want. They're so competitive, and they love to win. He won't be able to change this ass or these boobs, though. He'll have to live with them for an entire year.

My mouth curves into a smug smile. I'm about to make an

aloof comment and breeze out of here, when something on the foyer table catches my eye.

A small bouquet of bright blue flowers sits in a short vase. Each bloom is the size of a large coin. They're not ugly, they just don't look like a typical floral arrangement.

"For you." He watches me with a weird look in his dark eyes. Interest mixed with . . . not amusement. Entertainment.

He's laughing at me, but I don't get the joke.

"For me." I arch an eyebrow. Why would Volkov buy me flowers? "Are they poison or something?"

The corner of his mouth twitches. "Now, why would I poison my wife, Doctor?"

He probably got them as a gift and is just messing with me. "I can think of a few reasons, but you'll have to wait a bit longer."

———

The car ride is silent and tense.

How the hell am I going to do this for an entire year? Maybe I can move out but leave enough of my things at his place to make it *look* like I live there.

"What, are you nervous or something?" he asks, breaking the silence.

We're almost at the restaurant, driving through Stanley Park on our way to the Teahouse. His eyes drop to where I'm fiddling with my necklace.

"You've been to this dinner before," he says. "It's for the new players. No one will be looking at us."

Concern flickers in his eyes.

"I gave you my word," I tell him as he parks in the crowded parking lot. "I'm not going to screw this up."

"I know," he says, and it feels like he means it, but I don't wait for him to go on before getting out of the car and striding into the restaurant. I hear the chirp of his car before his footsteps follow.

"As long as we don't have to kiss again," I toss over my shoulder with a smirk, "no one will know the truth."

He's about to argue but the host greets us with a bright smile and leads us into the restaurant.

At the front of the dining area, I stop short at the giant image displayed. Alexei's hard chest bumps me from behind.

"You've got to be fucking kidding me," he mutters.

It's the picture from our wedding day, of our terrible kiss. Beside the photo, a *Congratulations!* sign. All the Storm players and staff in the restaurant fall silent, smiling at us.

I turn to Volkov with wide eyes, heart pounding up into my throat. "No one will be looking at us, huh?"

This isn't a dinner to welcome the new players.

It's a wedding reception—for us.

ALARM BARRELS THROUGH MY BLOODSTREAM, lighting up my nervous system.

Tonight, all eyes will be on us.

Oh god. What if there are games? What if we have to dance? What if we have to kiss again?

"Did you know about this?" I hiss to him through a smile, pretending everything is fine as all our friends and colleagues watch us.

"Of course I didn't know," he mutters back, running a hand over his hair. "You think I wouldn't warn you so you can put your knives away?"

"Fuck you," I whisper, still smiling.

"Fuck you, too, sweetheart."

Tate Ward steps forward with a cautious look. "I see we've taken you by surprise."

I force out a light, tinkly laugh. "You sure have." I sound a bit manic.

"I hope this is okay." He searches our expressions. "The team really wanted to do this for you."

"It's great," Volkov says. "We really appreciate it. Thank you."

"Yes." I take deep breaths. I can do this. "Thank you so much."

Tate reaches into his jacket and pulls out an envelope, handing it to us. My arms apparently aren't working, but Volkov accepts it. "A little something from the team to say congrats."

Volkov opens the envelope and arches an eyebrow at me, expression unreadable.

"A week in the honeymoon suite at the Silver Falls resort," Tate explains. "Alexei said you were planning to take your honeymoon there before Miller's wedding on New Year's."

"Did he, now." I turn to Volkov with a hard stare. "That was our secret, *darling*."

"That's very generous," he tells Tate, ignoring me. "Thank you."

"Yes, very thoughtful." I'm still smiling. Smiling so hard it hurts. "Can't wait."

There's no way I'm spending a week in a hotel room with him. Especially not the *honeymoon suite*. Volkov doesn't even go to weddings; to the surprise of his entire team last season, he skipped Jamie and Pippa's. I'll go myself and have the perfect week: drinking champagne and watching *The Vampire Diaries* in the bathtub—alone.

"We're happy to." Tate gives us a proud look. "Another two of our own getting married? It's a big deal."

A pang of regret twists in my gut. Tate Ward's one of the few male bosses I've had who treats women like equals. He hires women, and even more, he pays us what we're worth. When Darcy didn't believe in her ability to work as an analyst for the team last season, he encouraged her. Team doctors are usually hired based on who the coach golfs with during the offseason, but Ward reached out to Heather and asked if any experts in athlete recovery would be interested in something with the team. When I preferred a part-time role so I could stay with the hospital, he made it happen.

And now he's looking at me and Volkov like he's proud of us. I want to puke.

"Have fun tonight," he says before stepping away, and we're surrounded by our friends.

"Surprise!" Darcy clobbers me in a tight hug. "Are you surprised?"

I let out a weak laugh. "I sure am."

She admires my outfit. "Dressed to kill, as always. I'm sure Alexei's having a hard time keeping his hands off you in this dress."

From wringing my neck, maybe. I make a high noise of amusement, glancing at Volkov, who's deep in conversation with Rory, Hayden, and Jamie. "Something like that."

It seems everyone arrived earlier than us to surprise us, and now we've arrived, people are taking their seats for dinner.

"You two are up front," Rory tells me and Volkov with a cheeky grin, "at the head table, so everyone can see you."

Of course we are.

CHAPTER 18
ALEXEI

DINNER GOES QUICKLY, thank fuck. My new wife and I are distracted by the constant stream of teammates and colleagues coming up to congratulate us.

"Dude." Walker swings by, drink in hand and eyes all over my mouthy wife as she's in conversation with another team doctor and Hazel. "Georgia's your *wife*?"

I cross my arms over my chest. Another victim straying too close to the doctor's web. Walker's young and stupid. He doesn't know the damage a woman like the doctor can inflict.

"Holy fuck," Walker drawls, still staring at her, and something sharp twists in my gut. "I want a wife."

My shoulders stiffen from the way he's looking at her.

"No, you don't," I snap. "Close your mouth. And you can call her Dr. Greene."

She does look hot tonight, though. That dress. I fucking hate that dress. I *love* that dress. I'm trying to ignore her but I'm obsessed with it, sneaking glances when she's not looking.

Her legs are long and bare, and the short, sparkly dress barely covers her ass. Something that fucking annoys me about the doctor is her ability to make clothes look like they were created just for her, fitting every curve and swell of her body in a way that's hard to ignore. Her auburn hair is down, wild and curly, and she's wearing more makeup than before, drawing my attention to those captivating whiskey eyes and that fascinating mouth.

Beneath the boiling frustration in my gut, a minuscule grain of respect lingers. She's winning again and I'm scrambling to get ahold of myself.

Well played, Doctor.

And then I remember that she has a boyfriend, and my teeth grit.

Walker turns back to me with a grin, his eyebrows bobbing up and down. "My wiener feels funny."

I make a disgusted face. "Walker."

"Yeah, yeah." He rolls his eyes with a teasing grin. "Focus," he says in a low, sharp voice, putting on a frown. "Determination. Discipline. Ice baths."

"Is that supposed to be me?"

"Yes, sir." He salutes.

I shouldn't like this stupid kid, but I do. "Walker?"

"Yeah, boss?"

"Fuck off. And don't call me that. I'm not your boss."

The doctor twists around and smiles at Walker, her eyes warm. "Hi, Luca."

His smile stretches ear to ear and he leans down to rest his hands on the back of her chair. "Hi, Georgia."

"Dr. Greene," I correct him.

He ignores me, the little shit, smiling harder at my wife. "Congratulations. Volkov's a lucky guy. You're really pretty."

I curse under my breath. He's like a fucking puppy stumbling over himself to climb in her lap.

His eyes dip to her cleavage. "Can I get you another drink?"

Irritation throttles through me. "She has a drink. Go sit down, Walker."

If anyone's going to get her drinks, it'll be me.

The doctor presses her lips together as Walker returns to his seat, smiling at her over his shoulder. "He's sweet."

"He's a child. He has no fucking clue what it takes to play in the NHL."

"Good thing he has you."

I stare at her mouth as she sips her drink. "What does that mean?"

I brace myself for a sharp, cutting crack about how I'm due to retire or how my body only has so much time left in the league.

"If anyone knows what it takes to play a long career, it's you." She glances around the restaurant. Anywhere but me.

"Doctor, that almost sounded like a compliment."

Her cheeks turn pink, and her lips part like she's about to say something.

"Okay, lovebirds," Miller's voice projects throughout the room. He's at the front, holding a microphone with a cocky, knowing grin. "We're going to get to the dancing and cake in a bit, but first, a little entertainment. We were torn on whether to include this portion of the evening, but in the end, we were just too damn curious about the two of you and your relationship. What can I say?" He winks at us. "We're nosy."

My expression hardens. I know where this is going.

"We're playing *Newlywed Trivia*!" he says with a beaming smile. "How well do the two of you *actually* know each other?"

The doctor and I exchange a tight glance. I know she likes shopping, shoes, and getting her nails done. She knows every injury I've ever had, but we've never had a real conversation that didn't end in one of us wishing the other was six feet under.

We're fucked. We don't know each other at all.

"Come on up, you two," Miller says as Owens places two chairs at the front, back-to-back, and Darcy sets a whiteboard and erasable marker on each.

"When's your birthday?" I mutter as we head over to the chairs.

Her eyes are panicked. "What?"

"When's your birthday? Do you have any siblings?"

She stares like I'm the dumbest man on the planet. "Haven't you been to a wedding before?" She catches herself. "Right. You don't go to weddings. They're not going to test us on boring stuff. They're going to ask funny, cute questions. So fucking act like you like me," she hisses through a smile.

We take our seats at the front, a hundred pairs of eyes on us. Miller explains the game—he'll ask questions that the team and our friends have submitted, and we'll write down our separate answers. If we were in a real relationship like our friends are, we'd know everything about each other.

"Question one," Miller reads off a note card. "This one's from Pippa Hartley. Who made the first move? Write it nice and big so everyone can see."

Our markers fly, and when we hold up our boards to the audience, everyone laughs. I wrench around to see her answer.

We've both written each other's name.

"I would never make the first move with you," she says under her breath, pretending to laugh along with everyone.

"Like I would?"

"I see the way you look at my shoes, Volkov."

"Because they're ridiculous." I sound defensive. "Not because I'm—"

"Off to a rocky start," Miller says into the microphone, and we wipe our answers away. "This one's from Hayden Owens. Who's the better kisser?"

The crowd laughs again when we hold up our answers. This time, we've both written our own names.

She lowers her voice so only I can hear. "Your teeth probably fall out every time you kiss someone."

"Like I've told you a hundred times, *I have all my teeth.*"

"We knew they were stubborn, folks." Miller's eyes sparkle. "In case you've lost count, you're oh for two. Let's try again. This one's a two-parter from our very attractive and slightly terrifying physiotherapist, Hazel Hartley." He winks at his fiancée and she rolls her eyes, smiling. "Part one: What is Georgia's favorite gift from Alexei?"

I wrack my brain—what gift would I give the doctor? She's materialistic and shallow. *Jewelry,* I write.

She holds her board up and the audience chuckles. *A pair of fuck-me heels.*

Our argument from earlier replays in my head. "We're at a work event. You should be more professional."

"God, you're such a prude."

"I'm not a prude."

"Part two," Miller says. "What is Alexei's favorite gift from Georgia?"

She holds her board up again with the same answer as last time. The audience laughs again. Walker gives me an enthusiastic nod and a thumbs-up. *Nice,* he mouths.

The implication that the doctor gives me sexy gifts makes the back of my neck feel hot.

"Volkov, hold your board up," Miller says, and I display my answer. "A cheap wedding," he reads.

A weird tension ripples through the room, and some people laugh awkwardly. I glance at Owens. He's pulled Darcy's hand into his lap. He'd never write something like that for his answer.

I bet the doctor's boyfriend wouldn't say something like that, either. My jaw clenches.

"Nice," my wife mutters. "World's number one husband, right here."

I let out a heavy exhale. I'm fucking this up. She's getting under my skin, but everyone's watching. *Head in the game,* I tell myself.

CHAPTER 19
ALEXEI

"THE LEAGUE'S best goaltender and Vezina Trophy winner three seasons in a row Jamie Streicher wants to know, who's messier?" Miller asks.

We hold up our boards and Miller lights up with surprise. The audience applauds.

We glance at each other's boards—we've both written her name.

"Wow." I turn back around. "You admitted a fault. A first for you."

A quiet scoff. "Because I'm so insecure?"

A weird feeling stabs beneath my ribcage. I didn't mean to say that earlier. I don't know why she gets this reaction out of me. I lose control around her, say things I don't mean.

"Our favorite bartender couldn't make it tonight but Jordan wants to know, where was your first date?"

I write down my answer, praying the doctor writes the same one. We hold our boards up and Miller reads the name of the restaurant where Owens, Darcy, the doctor and I went last year on the double date.

Our gazes meet, the hostility in her eyes dimming. She gives me a subtle nod, and I nod back. See? We can do this.

"They're finding their rhythm," Miller says. "Coach Tate Ward wants to know, what was Alexei surprised to learn about Georgia?"

I scrawl my answer, and the corner of my mouth twitches. I hold my sign up and the crowd laughs. *Her morning breath can wake the dead.*

"Volkov, I swear to god," she mutters as everyone chuckles.

"It would look weird if I suddenly started acting too much like Owens or Miller."

"This one is from a new member to the team, Luca Walker. What's Alexei's dark secret?"

Big fan of dog shows and cries when the dogs win, the doctor writes.

Everyone *awww*s. On the mic, Miller shakes his head, smiling. "Volkov, under all the pins and plates holding you together, we knew you had a heart."

Beside me, the doctor stiffens before she flips her hair over her shoulder.

"This next question is inappropriate." Miller's grin turns mischievous. "I want to know, who looks better naked?"

For a split second, I picture it—the doctor spread out on my bed, beneath me, all that pale, soft-looking skin on display, wearing only that wicked smile.

My groin tightens.

We both write the doctor's name. It would look weird if I wrote my own name for this. Anyone can see she's a knockout. This whole thing would crumble into dust if I can't even admit she's attractive.

Her boyfriend sees her naked, an ugly, irritating voice whispers in my head, and I grip the marker. Whoever Damon is, I hate him.

"Who's more likely to burn the house down while cooking?"

We both write the doctor's name.

"Who has the better hair?"

Again, obviously the doctor, but she surprises me by writing my name. I lift my brows at her. "You like my hair?"

Her gaze skates over my hair, lingering. "It's not your worst trait."

Huh. Another almost-compliment.

"Who snores the loudest?"

We both write my name, and when the crowd laughs, we glance at each other. There's something in her expression, a flicker of what my teammates and I feel when we score a goal. She's competitive, and she likes winning. One of the very few things we have in common.

"All right." Miller tilts that smile at us. "I'm beginning to see why these two work so well together. This question is from Darcy Andersen of the analytics team. Which pair of Georgia's shoes is Alexei's favorite?"

I pause with my marker hovering over the board. She has this black pair with little bows on the ankles. Sharp and pointy. Bright red soles that flash like the flick of a tongue as she walks away, swaying her hips. They're terrifying and aggressive and look like they'd hurt if they connected with your shin.

Something about those heels piss me off. Something about those heels make her ass look incredible. Something about those heels sticks in my head, and I can't stand it.

I bet her boyfriend bought her those. I wish I could get that asshole out of my head.

Black with bows on the ankle, red soles, I write, and hold my board up. She's written the same ones.

"Lucky guess," I mutter, turning my back to her. "I had to pick one."

"Mhm. Probably has nothing to do with the fact that your eyes fall out of your head every time I wear them."

I make a face. "They do not."

"You remember them in staggering detail, Volkov."

"This one's from Ross Sheridan." The team owner and ex–Storm coach sits quietly near the back of the room, watching with a calm smile. "Alexei, what is Georgia's favorite moment from your hockey career?"

Probably the head shot and resulting concussion that landed me in the hospital two years ago, right before she transferred me to another doctor. Instead, I scribble out an easy one —*defense assist record*. I still hold that record to this day.

She hesitates before her marker flies. I've lobbed her a softball, she better get this one right.

"Calder trophy," Miller reads.

My eyes meet hers in surprise. The Calder trophy is given to the rookie of the year. I won it my first season, and even though it was almost eighteen years ago, I still remember how my parents looked on with pride at the award ceremony.

All their hard work. Every double shift and coupon clipped to pay for skates and sticks, every five a.m. ice time. That award wasn't for me, it was for them.

When I think about retiring, that's what my mind wanders to.

I don't know what it means that she wrote the Calder trophy down. I haven't told a soul what that moment means to me. Before I can say anything, though, the game continues.

"Last one. Another two-parter. What does Georgia love about Alexei?"

My money, I write, before I erase it. I'm supposed to be playing nice. *My perseverance,* I write as a painful joke to myself and my ex-fiancée. If I had given up on that relationship like I should have, she never would have humiliated me and my family the way she did.

We hold our boards up, and the crowd lets out another collective *awww*.

His determination, she wrote.

Our eyes meet. I'm frowning, and she looks away. A weird tension simmers in my gut.

"I had to write something." A hint of pink washes over her cheeks. Is she embarrassed?

I look down at my board, feeling like an asshole for what I wrote originally before erasing it.

"And the second part to the question, what does Alexei love about Georgia?"

What would Owens, Miller, or Streicher say about their partners? They'd pick something that has nothing to do with looks. Nothing material.

Her intelligence, I write.

My hilarious sense of humor, she wrote.

Our eyes meet again.

"I had to write something," I echo.

"On that adorable note, folks," Miller sets his notecard aside, and I try not to let my relief be too obvious. "The game is over. Clearly, these two are meant for each other." He looks to the audience. "Are we ready for the first dance?"

"YOU'RE TOO FAR AWAY," I say quietly as we take our spot on the dance floor while Pippa plays a slow, romantic song on her guitar.

Everyone's watching, their eyes on us like a weight.

"Not like this." I press my hand into her lower back, bringing her closer. Flush against me. "Like *this*."

Her scent floods my nose again. Warm, sweet, but spicy. I let myself take one deep inhale for immunity—the more I'm exposed to it, the less it'll affect me—before my gaze slides to her shoulder, where her bra strap would sit beneath the fabric of the dress. Maybe she's wearing one of those strapless ones. Maybe it has lace on it. Maybe her panties match.

With a spike of arousal, I picture her in lingerie, but the image is soured by the addition of this faceless *Damon* she's with.

"Where would a guy like you learn to dance?" she asks, interrupting my thoughts.

Dance lessons in preparation for my first wedding. A real wedding that never happened. The memories make me feel sick.

"My mother made me learn when I was a teenager." A lie.

"She wants you to get married."

"More than anything in the world." The truth.

"Won't she be thrilled. Tell me, Volkov, is she going to use her mother-in-law powers for good or evil?"

My mom's the kindest person on the planet. "Doctor, you don't need to worry about that because I won't let you get your claws anywhere near her."

Besides, I don't want my mom getting attached to someone who will be out of the picture in a year.

The corner of her mouth tugs up in a wry smile. "I wouldn't have it any other way."

We've danced alone for enough time that other couples join us on the dance floor, and even though her cool, confident expression doesn't change, she relaxes under my touch. I study her features.

"What?" Her gaze flicks to mine, her whiskey eyes losing some of the spark from earlier.

"Tired?"

"Nope."

She's too proud to admit it, and for some reason, I don't like that idea. I don't know why she's tired—she works part time as a doctor for the team. She doesn't even work weekends.

Maybe *Damon* kept her up late, and I don't like that idea, either.

———

When they bring the cake out, the little figurine groom on top has a black eye.

"Like it?" Owens laughs. "We had it specially made for you, Volkov."

"It's accurate," I admit.

At my side, my fake wife's smile is tight and forced.

"What's the matter?" I tilt my chin at the cake. "He's not missing enough teeth?"

She lets out a dry, humorless laugh.

People surround us, smiling and taking photos. I take the knife, about to slice into the cake, but Darcy makes a strangled noise of protest, eyes wide.

I freeze. "What?"

The doctor covers her mouth with her hand. I think she's hiding a laugh.

Owens shakes his head, grinning between us. He lowers his voice. "Volkov, I know you're not a wedding guy, but you need to cut the cake *together*." He gives me an emphasizing look. "It's symbolic. I think." He looks to Darcy. "Right?"

She gives him a sweet smile and nods.

My new wife steps in front of me, taking the knife, and I hesitate before covering her hand with mine. Her hand is warm and soft, like at our wedding when our fingers touched. It's the size of her hand, though, that snags my senses. Deep in my caveman brain, my instincts like that she's so much smaller than me.

Which is fucking dumb. I'm six foot five. Most women are smaller than me.

Most women aren't my new spoiled, selfish wife, though, who smells like that and wear those shoes and has that thick hair I want to sink my fingers into.

And who is messing around with another guy. She's probably in love with him, from the tone of voice she used. I wish I could stop thinking about that.

My other hand comes to her waist, the sequins warm from her body heat. Under my gentle grip, she presses the knife down into the cake. Together, we cut a slice, and the guests cheer. More photos. Lots of smiles and applause.

"Great." I let her go, and she sets the knife aside. "Is that all?"

The doctor gives me a sick, serpent-like smile before she picks up a piece of the cake. Alarm rockets through me and I open my mouth to say *No fucking way* but she's too fast.

Everyone laughs as she smears it across my face. Some of it gets in my nose.

"I just love you *so* much."

People howl. Her eyes dance as she licks icing off her finger, pretty plump lips closing around the tip as her cheeks hollow out.

Deep in my chest, something wakes up. It's not the blood rushing to my cock that has me frowning, though; it's the rising pressure behind my sternum, like a balloon expanding. I have icing up my fucking nose and yet I have the urge to laugh.

I lift the plate with the remaining cake before my gaze locks on hers. "My turn."

"No." She shakes her head, stepping away. "No, thank you." She gestures at her exquisite face. "I don't want to ruin my makeup."

The spark's back in her eyes, and a weird feeling loops through me, light and buzzing. My competitive instincts rise. I could go after her. I could chase her and shove cake in her face. Her makeup would be ruined and there would be cake on her dress and she'd be furious.

Or maybe she'd shriek with laughter. My eyebrow inches higher and I take a step toward her. Her eyes flare.

"Alexei, don't," Darcy calls, laughing.

With a dry look, I set the plate down, and people laugh, thinking it was a joke. Someone hands me a towel and I wipe the cake off my face before cutting a finger-sized sliver of cake.

"Hold on, Hellfire," I say as she steps away. I lift the piece I cut off. "We're not done here."

Defiance snaps onto her features, eyes burning me, and I feel my mouth tilting into a cruel smile. I love that stubborn scowl on her pretty face when I tell her what to do.

"Eat up," I murmur.

"I will get you back for this," she whispers, holding my eyes.

There's something new pounding through my body, though, as her lips part and I slip the cake between them. She's so stubborn, but when she bends for me, Jesus... it's like a drug.

Her tongue flicks out to catch a dot of icing on her bottom lip. Fuck—I'm getting hard.

"What, no kiss?" someone calls.

My stomach drops. The doctor's expression falters.

"Kiss, kiss!" another person echoes. That goddamned rookie again. "You didn't kiss for the photo."

The doctor and I exchange a wary glance.

"He doesn't like PDA," she tells them with an apologetic expression.

"Nice, blame me," I mutter.

Through a tense smile, she shoots me a look. "I'm not going to kiss you again."

I bet her boyfriend would hate it. He probably hates that she's living in my house, one bedroom away, telling everyone she's married to me. I bet he's jealous as fuck.

Something proud, possessive, and territorial beats through me. I think about our terrible kiss at the wedding, how I froze up, and how she said it was like kissing the dead body at a funeral. The desire to prove her wrong, to *compete* with her again, roars through me.

"What's the matter?" I keep my voice low. "Scared you might enjoy it?"

She laughs under her breath. "As if."

Something primal inside me likes her light, feminine scent. The way she looks up at me as I tower over her. How her long lashes fan out. The plump curve of her mouth, begging for my attention.

It's cruel, how hot the doctor is. The universe designed her just to torture me.

Every cell in my body wants a do-over, to show her how it could be. I lower my voice to her ear, hand on her waist again. "Maybe *you're* the bad kisser."

"It's not me."

"Prove it." My blood beats in my ears, adrenaline in my veins.

The long line of her pale throat bobs. "Fine. Let's get this over with."

She sets a hand on my chest. That intoxicating scent of hers washes over me again, hooking around my neck like a collar, and I lower my mouth to hers.

This time, I don't freeze up.

MY INFURIATING husband grips my hair, tilts my head back, and kisses me hard. I forget where I am, who I'm with, and why we're here.

With a low, pleased groan, he coaxes my lips apart and strokes against my tongue. Some instinct deep within me has me stroking his right back, hands fisting the front of his shirt, leaning into his firm chest, arching against him like a cat in heat.

It's a *good kiss*. No, it's a *great* kiss.

I don't even like kissing. It's the thing I do to get to sex, which is usually disappointing, anyway, but with my husband's stubble lightly scraping my skin, his clean scent in my nose, and the hot, searching slide of his tongue against mine, my blood turns molten.

I'm on fire. His mouth on mine is too good, too mind-bending and demanding and confident, like he knows exactly what he wants. Like I'm just strung along for the ride.

Did he always smell this incredible?

Where did he learn to kiss like this?

Why is his hair so soft and thick?

Why is him gripping my hair like that so hot?

I didn't know this kind of kissing was a thing, like I can't stop and I never want to. Like my entire existence depends on this kiss going forever. Shivers run up and down my spine, and when he sucks my tongue, my brain short-circuits. He groans, my head spins, and I don't know what the fuck is happening.

Every time I tug the thick strands of his hair, he lets out another low, hungry noise. The third time I do it, he pulls me to him, hard body flush against mine.

Someone nearby moans. It isn't me. It can't be me, because I'm busy thinking about how I hate him. I nip his bottom lip and a shudder runs through him.

I like kissing. I like it a lot. I could do this for hours. I hate that it's with Volkov, though, and I really hate that he's so good at it.

He makes a low noise in his throat like he's just as annoyed as I am before the kiss deepens. Electricity spirals through me. Low in my abdomen, pressure builds as he pulls me closer to him, one big arm wrapping around my shoulders and the other still firmly rooted in my hair.

If this is how he kisses when he doesn't like someone, what's it like when he *does*?

Hoots and hollers rise up around us, hauling me back to earth. In a sharp rush of realization, I pull back. Right. He's doing this to prove a point, to get back at me, one-up me.

He glowers down at me, eyes glazed and pupils expanding wide, chest rising and falling fast. My horrible husband still hates me. I clear my throat and look away, gathering my thoughts and fighting the urge to fan my overheated face.

The team watches with big, proud grins. Luca gives us a big smile and a thumbs-up. A twinge of embarrassment hits me, because I'm supposed to be professional in front of them.

I don't know why I lost my head like that.

I want to say something cool and witty, because I'm unaffected and unrattled.

"What the hell was that?" I ask, instead.

He holds my gaze before his drops to my mouth. His hands flex like he's holding himself back.

"You're supposed to be a bad kisser." I press my swollen lips together, and his eyes flash, watching the motion.

He leans in, an inch from my ear, and I can smell him again —body wash or detergent, something clean and crisp. "Maybe you don't know everything about me."

A shiver runs down my spine. Maybe I don't.

VOLKOV and I head home in tense, awkward silence, pretending each other doesn't exist.

I replay the dinner: the dinner, the game, the dance where Pippa sang about finding someone who means everything, trusting them, and giving them every part of yourself.

Been there, done that, and I won't be doing it again.

I keep thinking about that kiss, though, and I have a sinking feeling I'll be thinking about it for a while.

At his house, I'm about to head upstairs without saying goodnight when his voice stops me.

"Hellfire."

Halfway up the stairs, my spine straightens. God, I hate that nickname. I hate the way he says it all low and arrogant, and I hate the way his mouth quirks when he says it, like he *knows* I hate it.

"Get rid of him."

I turn to look down at him. "Excuse me?"

His eyes flicker with possession. "Damon."

I freeze. He knows? How does he know? I snuck them into my room without him seeing, and they haven't made a peep.

Fuck, he's mad. He's doing that jaw-clenching thing again.

My stomach flips at the intensity in his eyes. Slowly, I descend until I'm at his level.

"How did you find out?"

"I heard you talking to him in your room. We had a deal. Cut him loose."

I stand as tall as I can, staring him down. He will not intimidate me. "No. They're a bonded pair."

"They? Who's *they*?" He folds his arms over his chest, his expression a dark cloud.

"He and Stefan."

"Stefan?" Outrage flashes in his eyes. "There are *two* of them?"

"They're a bonded pair."

"What does that even *mean*? No. Don't tell me. I don't want to know." He glowers down at my feet. "I bet you wear the shoes for them, don't you?"

I pause. That's a weird thing for him to care about. "I mean . . . I guess I try them on in front of them? But they don't seem interested."

He makes a noise of anguish, raking his hands through his hair, and I laugh. He's so uptight and serious.

"Look, I'm sorry I didn't tell you about them, but they're so quiet, you won't even notice they're here. And the only place they'll be is my room."

His eyes widen with shock. "They're not coming over to my house, and they're sure as shit not going in your bedroom."

"Where are they *supposed* to live?"

"They're living with us?!" His voice goes weirdly high. "What did I say, Georgia? I said no fucking other guys."

Silence stretches as I stare up at him in confusion. "What are you talking about?"

"No fucking other guys." He leans in, inches from my face,

glaring deep into my eyes. A shiver of anticipation runs through me. "I don't share. This year, you're *my* wife. Mine."

I like the way those words sound, and I like the brutal, furious, possessive way he says them. I shouldn't, because I hate him, but I do.

There I go—thinking about our kiss again.

Wait. "Who do you think Stefan and Damon are?"

"Your boyfriends."

A delighted choking noise scrapes out of my throat. I press my lips together so I don't laugh. Oh, this is good. This is *so* good.

"Or fuck buddies," he adds. "Whatever. It sounded pretty fucking *intimate,* though, telling them *it's only temporary* and *soon it'll just be us again.*"

The laugh bursts out of me and I clap my hand over my mouth as his expression turns outraged again.

"It's not funny, Georgia."

I laugh again. I can't help it. "You're right, it's not. It's *hilarious.*"

"Stop smiling."

"Volkov, Volkov, Volkov." I shake my head as victory fills my chest, warming me throughout. This must be what Olympians experience when they win the gold.

"What?" he bites out. Ooooh, he's mad. He keeps glancing at my smile like it pisses him off more.

"After what you did to my shoes, I have half a mind to walk away from this conversation and let you keep believing this." My smile turns wicked, and his eyes drop to my mouth again before he frowns harder. "But I pity you, because not only do you have such a bad personality," my gaze roams the brutally handsome planes of his face, "you're ugly, too. So ugly."

He arches an unimpressed eyebrow. "Are you done?"

"For now." I wink at him, heading to the stairs. "Come on, Volkov. It's time you meet my *boyfriends*."

THE DOCTOR SMILES the whole way up the stairs.

This is pissing me off. I don't like it when she smiles. I can't look away and my stomach feels weird.

And that kiss earlier. That fucking life-changing kiss. I keep hearing the little moan she made as our tongues met.

Unease threads through me as she enters her room and I linger in the doorway. There's no one here.

"Oh, darlings," she calls, opening the bathroom door. "I'm home. There they are," she says proudly, with that big grin on her annoying, gorgeous face. "My boyfriends."

On the floor, a giant ball of dryer lint makes a squeaking noise.

"Eugh." I make a face. "What the fuck is that?"

"Don't say *eugh*. This is Damon." She crouches down to pet the dryer lint. "He's the friendly, flirtatious one. Very outgoing," she says, matter-of-fact. "And that one," she points to the one hiding beside the toilet, "is Stefan. Very serious, brooding, and emo. I named them after the brothers on my favorite TV show."

Realization dawns. A bonded pair, she said.

They're so furry, I can't see their eyes. Maybe they don't have any. "But what are they?"

"They're rabbits."

"*This* is Stefan and Damon," I say, mostly to myself.

Her smile is smug, but I don't even care. Relief crashes through me, easing my shoulders down, loosening the knot in my gut. The doctor doesn't have two boyfriends, or even one. She wasn't talking to some other guy. She has *rabbits* and she was talking to *them*. My shoulder hurts a little less.

I slide a glance at her. "Those aren't rabbits."

"They're double-maned lionheads."

"Is that why they look all fucked-up?"

"They don't look *fucked-up*. God. You're so rude. They're just fluffy. They're cute."

"They look like stuffed toys that went through the blender and got sewn up the wrong way." I lean down to get a better look at the two massive piles of fur. "Are they even alive?"

She looks at me like I'm stupid.

"They're not moving."

"They're tired," she sputters.

"Tired from *what*?"

Her expression turns incredulous. "From the journey into your hellhole home. They don't want to be here any more than I do."

"Do they bite?"

Something about the wicked way she smiles makes my blood pump harder. "Yes, so stay far away from them."

"They look like the before picture on a pair of your shoes."

Her jaw drops in outrage. "I would *never* make them into a pair of shoes. That's horrible."

A smell hits my nose and I wrinkle it, sniffing. "They stink."

"That's the smell of their hay. It smells fresh."

"Smells like a barnyard. You're not keeping them in the house." I'm just trying to get a rise out of her now.

"Yes, I am." There's a fire in her eyes that I like. "They need space to run around."

I scoff, getting to my feet. "They don't look like they can run. Roll, maybe. Keep them in the backyard."

"No." Her eyes go wide and she stands, eyes flashing. "They'll get eaten by a coyote."

I make a face like, *well?*

"If they go, I go." She folds her arms over her chest, and my gaze snags on the way it pushes her breasts up in that dress.

"Fine." I drag my eyes up to her face. "They can stay."

As if I'd make these weird little things live outside. I don't care if they stay in here. I'm so relieved she's not involved with some other guy, I'd say yes to just about anything right now.

She opens her mouth to protest before she catches herself. "They can stay?"

"They don't leave your room."

The fight leaves her eyes, and she looks at me warily. "Fine."

"Fine." I make a noise of acknowledgment, crossing my arms. A beat of silence passes.

That fucking kiss sneaks into my head. My gaze drops to her mouth, pretty and full, and I think about how soft it was. How her hand sunk into my hair and how it felt when she tugged.

I don't like this woman. She's shallow and selfish. She recommended me for retirement.

She tried to take away my dream. I can't be thinking about kissing her.

ONE HEAVENLY WEEK LATER, during which I don't see Volkov once because he's away for games, I find my seat behind the net, where Darcy, Hazel, and Pippa always sit to cheer on their guys.

"We know the marriage is fake," Darcy says the second I sit down.

Fuck.

And here I was, worried she would feel like I had hidden my relationship from her.

"What?" I do my best shocked face. "What are you talking about?" I gesture at the jumbotron hanging from the arena roof, where a photo of Volkov in his uniform flashes on-screen. *Congratulations, Alexei Volkov and Dr. Georgia Greene!* it says. "That's my husband."

My mind flips to the kiss at the team dinner. Thank god I could get some space this week and clear my head. It wasn't *that* good, I've decided. It just took me by surprise. I've had better.

Darcy smiles. "I know he is. But I still think it's fake."

"I love him," I force out. Even saying those words makes me feel ill.

"Oh, do you?" Her smile turns secretive.

My face is going hot. "Yes. So much. More than anything. He's my everything."

Wow. Even I know that sounds fake as hell. Darcy gives me a knowing smile, eyes lit up with amusement, and I blow out a heavy breath. She's too smart, too analytical.

"Fine," I whisper, keeping my voice low so we aren't overheard. "I only get my inheritance if I'm married because my grandfather was a sexist, controlling asshole, and Volkov doesn't want to be deported the second his career ends. Also, who's 'we'?"

"Hayden and me. Don't worry. He won't say anything. He's rooting for you two."

"Stop rooting for us. There is literally nothing to root for."

"One of us, one of us," Hazel chants as she and her sister, Pippa, approach with their arms full of food.

"Hi, Georgia." Pippa hands Darcy and me a tray of nachos.

"Hey, little Hartley. How's the new album coming along?"

"It's hard, but I love it." She grins before her eyes go to Jamie, skating to his place in the net in front of us. He gives her one of those serious, intense gazes, and she blushes.

Pippa used to be his assistant. They got married last year in Whistler, a mountain-town ceremony made even more beautiful by Volkov's absence. Pippa and Jamie are the picture of newlywed bliss. They have a dog together and everything. That song Volkov and I danced to at the team dinner? Pippa wrote that about Jamie.

While we wait for the game to start, Hazel updates me on the body-positive fitness studio she started last year, Pippa talks about the new album, and Darcy fills me in on the upcoming Women in STEM events in Vancouver.

I'm the only one of us not wearing a jersey, I notice with a touch of self-consciousness. None of them says anything and I doubt they care, but I'd definitely look the part if I were in costume.

The lights go down, and the fans start to cheer. Around the arena, it's a sea of Storm jerseys.

I bet Volkov would just *love* to see me wearing his jersey. He'd get that smug, knowing look.

"Vancouver Storm fans, are you ready?" the announcer calls, and the fans roar.

The pump-up music starts and the players enter the arena, skating laps for their last warm-up. When I cover the game as a medical professional, I stay in the back, sewing up cuts, taping sprains, and assessing for concussions in the medical room. Sometimes, if I'm still in my office while the game is on, I'll glance down at the ice. I never, ever sit out here with the fans.

I can see the draw, though. There's an infectious energy in the air.

"Have you seen this?" Darcy asks, showing me her phone. It's a social media fan account for the Storm, and the latest post is a picture from the team dinner, of Volkov feeding me the piece of cake with a dark glower. The photo has almost a hundred thousand likes.

"Yes, I saw it." My private account has been bombarded with new followers. I stared at that photo for half an hour last night as I lay in bed.

Don't get between that guy and his wife, one comment said, mistaking the sick victory in his eyes as possession.

Those two are going to make good-looking babies, another person wrote. Gag. As if we would ever.

Is it horny in here or is it just me?

Those weren't Volkov's horny eyes. He was just playing another sick game. That's what we do.

Volkov hits the ice, and my heart rate jumps. He's easy to pick out; he's bigger than every other player.

"You should post a picture," Darcy says quietly, glancing pointedly at Volkov. "As his loving wife."

She's right. A loving wife would be proud of her big hockey player. I pull my phone out and snap a picture of him skating past before adding a filter.

Cheering on my man, I type into the caption box, trying not to laugh. Thank god Volkov doesn't have social media—I'd die if he saw this. The second I post it, my phone starts buzzing and dinging with notifications.

"So how's it supposed to work when it's over?" Darcy asks as I put my phone away.

"We divorce." I shrug. "Easy."

"What happens if you start to like each other?"

I nearly choke on my nachos. "You're kidding, right?"

A tiny frown appears between her eyebrows. "He's not as bad as you think."

"Ugh." I roll my eyes. "You sound like Jordan."

"It's true. And if you ever get to know him—"

"Which I won't."

"Or if he ever gets to know you—"

"Which he won't."

It's easier this way, I said to her last year, when she realized I'm not the spoiled little princess Volkov thinks I am. When she realized I encourage his inaccurate image of me.

I find him on the ice, stretching. I wonder if his shoulder hurts tonight. I wonder how his ACL feels. I think about him calling me incompetent and anger surges inside me.

"He doesn't get the *privilege* of knowing me, Darce. Guys like Volkov are a dime a dozen. They're controlling, and they only care about themselves. I don't care if he likes me. You know what's a major red flag? When a guy doesn't want a platonic relationship with a woman. It means he sees them as objects."

"He's friends with me."

"I guess it's just me, then."

She studies me for a minute. "Sometimes I think you purposefully keep him at arm's length because him knowing and rejecting the real you would hurt more."

Heat rises on my face and I give her a bewildered look.

"No." I shake my head, at a loss for words. "That's not it."

She shrugs.

"It's not," I insist.

"Okay."

The game starts with a face-off at center ice, and I watch Volkov use his body as a weapon, knocking guys out of the way like bowling pins. The puck comes to our end of the rink and Volkov and a player from the other team collide. It's loud, the glass and boards rattling with the impact, and my breath catches in my throat. That was his bad side, with the collarbone that didn't heal right.

The player from the other team bounces off Volkov's towering frame, and Volkov skates off like it never even happened.

He's fine. See? He's totally fine. He probably didn't even feel that.

The game continues, and even though it's been a while since I've watched one, I'm hooked. Hockey's fast-paced, loud, and intense. Time flies, and I can't look away. Volkov is so focused on the ice, so determined, and watching him skate hard, exert himself, and give it everything is weirdly fascinating.

It's the fighting I don't like. It's the players getting hurt that makes me feel sick. I'm a doctor. Of course I don't like that stuff.

"Go, go, go," Darcy murmurs later as Volkov passes to

Hayden. An opening appears in front of the net, and Hayden shoots the puck.

He scores, and the arena erupts in noise. Darcy jumps to her feet, smiling and cheering. The guys celebrate before Hayden loops past us, blowing a kiss to Darcy, looking goofy with his gloves and helmet still on. Volkov's right behind him, eyes on me.

He sends me an arrogant look. *Well?*

I give him an exaggerated thumbs-up and he scowls before skating off.

"You're going to need to work on that," Darcy says to me, grinning.

He does look good in his Storm uniform. Powerful and handsome. Not that I'd admit it out loud.

During the second period, the whistle blows for a penalty and the game stops.

"Hey, ladies." Some guy from the row behind us leans forward, breath smelling like beer. Ew. "We're from out of town and we're going to a bar after. You two want to join us?"

There's a knocking sound and we all turn to the glass, where Volkov stands, glaring at me, before his cold gaze slides to the drunk guy. He locks eyes with him and slowly shakes his head.

"Jesus," the guy's friend mutters. "That's Volkov."

The guy tenses. "Do you know him?" he asks me.

Darcy hides a smile as I give Volkov a flat look through the glass.

"That's my husband."

CHAPTER 25
ALEXEI

IN THE MIDDLE of the night, my bedroom door opens.

I sit up, frowning in the dark as her figure moves through my room to my bed. She's wearing a T-shirt and no pants.

My first thought is that she's trying to mess with me in my sleep—draw a fake mustache on me with a Sharpie or shave my eyebrows off—but instead, she pulls back the duvet and slides into bed beside me.

Uh.

I'm wide-awake now, stiff like a board with her firm ass tucked against my cock. Her familiar violet scent surrounds me, her soft hair spilling over my skin. She lets out a content sigh, relaxing against my body. Her bare legs brush mine as she tucks her cold feet under mine.

"Warm," she sighs.

I lie there, frozen, reeling. Is she drunk? She must be. I don't smell booze, though, and she didn't seem to be drinking at the game earlier.

"Doctor, what the actual fuck are you doing?" My voice rasps with sleep.

No answer.

"Doctor."

My full attention narrows to where we touch, where her soft body presses into mine. I'm not a cuddling kind of guy, I remind myself, and I hate this.

In the back of my mind, I'm surprised at her sleep attire. She belongs in something expensive and lacy.

I catch myself. Because she's spoiled and loves to spend money. Not because her body would look incredible.

"Go back to your bed," I demand.

Nothing. Still fast asleep.

"Georgia."

"Mmm." She smiles into her pillow. *My* pillow. Not hers.

I shake her shoulder. "*Georgia*. Wake up. I'm going to put your shoes in the garbage again." I give her cheek a few pats and her eyes flutter open.

She squints in the dark, bleary-eyed, before she looks over her shoulder at me, her eyes go wide, and she's out of the bed, fast like lightning.

"What the fuck?" she screeches. "Were you cuddling me, you fucking pervert?"

I gape at her. "Are you serious? You were in my bed. You came here!"

I can't tell if she's furious, embarrassed, or both. I don't know what I am, either.

"Don't do it again," she sputters, before she hightails it out of my room and slams the door behind her.

Her fast footsteps move down the hall until her bedroom door closes with another slam, and the house goes silent.

What the fuck just happened?

CHAPTER 26
GEORGIA

A FEW EVENINGS LATER, I pull my car into the garage. His car is here, all sleek black lines, which means he's home.

My face burns hot with mortification at the memory of his shocked and weirded-out expression after I *climbed into his bed*. My god. It's like the universe hates me or something. There's nothing like the jarring realization that I'm not in my own bed. Waking up in Volkov's, though—

I'm ashamed to admit how comfortable I was. Warm and sleepy against him, so at home I could have stayed there forever.

I shudder.

Liam thought the sleepwalking thing was bizarre. *Creepy*, he called it. That summer in Toronto, I'd wake up on the couch, at my desk, at the kitchen table. One time, on the floor of his closet. Anywhere but his bed.

Since I woke up in Volkov's bed, I've been avoiding this house—and him. Svetta, his housekeeper, was thrilled at the sight of the bunnies, and although she speaks very little English, she communicated she would be happy to help take care of them.

I think about her over-the-moon enthusiasm for our

marriage. *A good man,* she kept saying about him. Right. I'm sure. *My husband snores, too,* she said about our separate bedrooms situation.

When I tried to repeat the Russian phrase he called me, the one that apparently means *sweetheart,* she made a face and started waving her hand in front of her nose, like something smelled bad. I don't think I got the phrase right.

Inside the house, he's leaning against the kitchen counter, almost like he's waiting for me.

"Hello." My tone is polite and unaffected, like I'm talking to a stranger on the street. Like the sleepwalking thing never happened.

His gaze trails over my clothes and his expression turns unimpressed. "Where were you?"

I was at soccer practice, but he doesn't need to know that. "Don't worry your pretty little head about where I've been."

Please don't bring up the sleepwalking, I pray.

"Ross Sheridan sent us a gift," he says, nudging his chin toward a box on the counter.

It's a framed picture from the team dinner—the shot of me shoving cake in Volkov's face with a wicked smile while he glares at me.

"Wow," I drawl. "Look how hot I look. Maybe I'll use this as my dating profile pic after we're done."

His jaw tenses, and his eyes drop to the protein bar wrapper in my hand. "Was that your dinner?" Disapproval drips from his tone.

"Let's not do this, Volkov. I don't need a lecture."

I've grown to hate the texture of the protein bars I buy in bulk—way too sticky and chewy, like glue—but they're a decent source of nutrition when I don't have time or energy to cook for myself. I keep a box in both my offices and another handful in the glove box of my car. If I don't eat enough, I get cranky.

"Someone your size needs more calories per meal."

I close my eyes, laughing at the situation I've found myself in. "Someone my size. Okay, thanks. Goodnight. Don't die in your sleep."

His head tilts back in exasperation. "I meant—"

"I know what you meant." I walk out of the kitchen, but he steps forward and wraps a big hand around my arm, stopping me.

He's about to say something else before he goes silent, tilting his head like he's listening. I open my mouth but he cuts me off. "Be quiet."

I'm about to tear him a new one for ordering me around when he strides out to the foyer. Curiosity has me hot on his heels.

He stares out the window at a car pulling into his driveway. "My parents are here."

I jolt. "What?"

He sighs.

"Now?" I ask, stupidly.

He runs a hand over his hair, like he's in distress. "Yes. Now."

"Should I . . ." I'm already backing toward the door to the garage. "I should leave."

I don't want to meet them.

He shakes his head. "Don't bother. She'll find you."

A cold knot gathers in my stomach.

For someone to turn out like Alexei Volkov, his parents have to be truly awful. Cold and brutal, like him. They raised him in an ice cave, making him do thousands of push-ups before his daily breakfast of gruel and old, dried bones. Emotions disgust them. They probably both have short, practical military haircuts, and take freezing cold showers every morning.

I'm already using all of my energy to deal with him, but three Volkovs? I'm going to crumble.

Beneath my hesitation, though, I *am* curious about them. He married me for their citizenship, too. He must care about them.

The doorbell rings. My stomach turns over with nausea. His eyes meet mine, hard and callous.

"If you're rude to my parents in any way, if you say anything to offend them, we're done. The deal is off."

Stunned and hurt, I blink at him. "Okay," I say, feeling two inches tall.

Just when I thought his opinion of me couldn't get any lower, it does. I swallow and brace myself.

HE OPENS THE DOOR, and I'm ready for Ms. Trunchbull from *Matilda,* mean and bitter. Towering over me at seven feet tall.

The woman on the front step is tiny, though, barely reaching my shoulder, holding a potted plant, her warm smile reaching ear to ear. Behind her, a tall man gives my husband a friendly nod.

She starts talking to Volkov in fast Russian, eyes shining as she launches into the house. She gives him a playful tap on the ribs, saying something in a scolding tone. I catch the word *Svetta* in there.

When she sees me, she falls silent and her smile broadens, the apples of her cheeks popping.

She's adorable. I could put her in my pocket. This can't be his mother.

"You must be Georgia," she says in a light Russian accent, handing the plant to Volkov, who's staring at it with a dark expression.

She beams harder, coming at me with outstretched arms. Is she going to try to strangle me? Is her warm, welcoming smile a distraction while she elbows me in the solar plexus?

"Maria Volkov. So happy to meet you. My Alexei didn't say a word about you. That's how I knew you were pretty." She looks me over like she's pleased with what she sees. "But you're more than pretty, aren't you? You're beautiful."

I blink at her. My words don't work.

Maria wraps her arms around me, squeezing me tight. I'm frozen. She's hugging me. Alexei's mother is hugging me. She smells nice, like lilacs.

She tilts her head at my giant pink crystal. "That has a very good energy."

"That's what I said." I smile in surprise. "Alexei thinks it looks like a—" I clamp my mouth shut, and Maria's lips press together. The man behind her coughs like he's covering a laugh.

"That shape and size can be very intimidating for men." Maria nods with a serious expression, but her eyes glitter. She gestures at the man behind her. "This is Alexei's father, Nikita."

The large man looks like an older version of Volkov, has the same dark, almost black hair but with silver at the temples. Same brutal lines of his face. His eyes are kind, though.

"Nikita Volkov," he says in a low voice, with a strong Russian accent, holding his hand out.

We shake hands. "Georgia Greene."

"Good to meet you."

He says it like he means it. There's an air of calm about Alexei's father that I don't see in men often. Ward has it, too. Jamie Streicher, sometimes, when he's with Pippa and his dog, Daisy.

"You too," I say absently.

Maria gestures to the plant Alexei's still holding. "This is for you. Myrtle. It represents good luck and love in a marriage."

"Oh." I guess I'll need all the luck I can get. "Thank you."

I can barely take care of myself, though. That thing's going to be dead within the week.

"Alexei will take care of it," she adds, like she can hear my thoughts. He says something in Russian to her, glowering; she responds in a firm tone. His jaw tenses, but he doesn't respond. "Alexei knows all about plants and flowers from—" Her gaze falls to the blue flowers from the other week and her eyes narrow as she slowly turns to her son. "—my florist shop."

His throat works, and he almost looks guilty.

"Your florist shop?"

"Yes." She loops an arm through mine, leading me to the kitchen. "He worked there growing up."

Back in the foyer, Nikita says something to his son in Russian, who answers in Russian, sounding irritated before he sighs and grabs my car keys from the bowl.

Over my shoulder, I shake my head at him, but his dad is already out the door with my keys.

Volkov calls something after him, probably directing him to the nearest source of water for his father to drive my car into.

"Where's he going?" I ask Maria.

She just smiles that warm smile that reminds me of the way the sun looks when it streams in through the library stained-glass window first thing in the morning. Over her shoulder, she glances at her son before looking pointedly at the bags she brought. Without a word, he picks them up and follows us to the kitchen.

I can feel him glaring at my back the entire time.

"Svetta said you're a doctor?" She gestures at the bar counter. "Sit, I'll make us tea."

"Oh, no, it's okay." My expression is apologetic. "I should be getting upstairs to bed—"

"No." She gestures at a chair at the bar. "Sit."

My husband's large, warm hand lands on my shoulder. "Sit, Doctor."

He raises his eyebrows. I raise mine. He knows I hate being told what to do.

His expression tightens like he's in physical pain. "Please," he murmurs, and when he presses into my shoulder again, I sink into the bar seat.

His mom moves around the kitchen like a hummingbird, opening cupboards and drawers with confidence like she's been here a million times while he hovers behind me, leaning against the counter.

"Have you had dinner?" she asks.

"Yes."

"No," Volkov says at the same time.

Maria digs into the bags she brought, pulling containers out and transferring food to plates and bowls.

"Maria, can I help?" I ask.

"No," she says firmly. "You probably worked all day. You're tired."

I start to stand. "I'm not tired."

Volkov's hand lands on my shoulder again, pushing me back into the chair. "She's tired," he says, and I shoot him a frown over my shoulder.

Maria gives him an arch look. "Would you sit down? You're making your wife nervous."

Your wife. A funny emotion perches in my throat, ready to escape. A laugh, maybe. Or a scoff. I'm this guy's wife and I didn't know a thing about his parents. Worse, I'm shocked at how nice they are.

She places a big bowl of soup in front of me with a spoon. "Eat." She puts another bowl beside mine before giving her son an expectant look.

"Thank you, Maria. This looks amazing."

"Thank you, Mama," Volkov murmurs, taking the seat beside me. He catches my eyes, and his expression is clear: *Eat the fucking food and don't you dare insult my mom.*

Maria's back is turned while she makes tea so I roll my eyes at him, slip a spoonful of soup into my mouth and—

"Oh my god," I moan, and a muscle in Alexei's jaw twitches. The soup is full of chicken, potatoes, cabbage, carrots, and what tastes like horseradish, among other herbs. "This is amazing."

"Excellent, Mama," Volkov echoes.

Maria waves us off, but she's pleased. "Food and flowers are my 'love languages.' I heard that phrase on a podcast."

She's so sweet. How could she possibly be this guy's mom? "Do you cook a lot?"

"Oh yes." She nods resolutely, with pride. Alexei's eyes are sharp on me, watchful, like he's waiting for something. "When I have time. My flowers keeps me busy." She sighs dramatically, the corner of her mouth twitching, the same way Volkov's does sometimes. "So many weddings."

Oh god. She probably wished she could have been at our wedding. Guilt pinches in my stomach.

I need to change the subject, fast. "Where's the shop?"

"Fourth and Lonsdale."

"Oh." I straighten up. "That's close to here."

"You should come visit me."

"The doctor doesn't have time," Alexei cuts in.

Her eyes close briefly. "Of course. You're busy with your job, I'm sure."

The embarrassment on her face makes me feel like the lowest scum.

"No, I have time." I don't know why I'm agreeing to this. I shouldn't be spending time with her. "And I'd love to come by and see it."

He glares at me, but I ignore him.

"Wonderful." She beams that smile again. Her eyes snag on my left hand and she grabs it, frowning at the ring. She gives Volkov a dark look.

"Alexei." Her tone is firm as she holds my hand up. "What is this?"

VOLKOV'S EYES cut to me in warning.

That feeling rises—I want to fuck with him. This woman is too nice, though, and I can't upset her. To my utter shock, I actually like her.

Besides, I'm not going to tattle on him to his mommy. That's not how I play this game.

Oh, and we're supposed to be happy newlyweds, totally in love.

"This is the one I wanted." I give her a bright, reassuring smile. "I take my rings off for work so often that I didn't want to lose it, and a big ring would tear up the latex gloves."

Her eyes narrow before they drop to my feet, where I'm still wearing my heels from when I got home. I can see her thoughts like they're written in the air. *No woman who wears shoes like* those *would be happy with a ring like* this.

I look to my silent husband. *Play the fuck along.* "Right, handsome?"

A muscle in his jaw twitches. "This is the one she wanted."

"Where'd your dad go?" I ask, changing the subject again.

Maria sips her tea, still looking at my ugly ring. "He's probably looking at your car."

"What?" My spine straightens in alarm. "Why?"

"He's a mechanic." Volkov gives me a sharp, searching look. "Is that a problem?"

"No, but nothing's wrong with my car."

"He just wants to check it," Maria says, waving me off.

I frown at Volkov, but he shrugs. "Don't look at me. This is what he does."

Heavy footsteps sound through the house and Nikita walks into the kitchen. He lights up at the sight of the food but Maria shakes her head.

"You've already had dinner," she says kindly with laughter in her eyes as he stares longingly at the food.

He heads to the sink to wash his hands. "Your spark plugs will foul soon," he says over his shoulder before looking to his son. "Bring Georgia's car in when you can and I'll replace them."

"I can bring it in," I cut in. Volkov wouldn't be caught dead in my car. He'd probably place a brick on the gas pedal and run it off a cliff. "Thank you so much."

"Nonsense." Nikita shakes his head. "Alexei will bring it. We can put your winter tires on at the same time."

"I'll do it next week." Volkov shifts, not looking at me.

"It's fine—"

"I said *I'll do it*." His eyes meet mine, full of challenge.

"Let him, *solnyshko*. He's your husband now." Maria gives me a teasing smile. "Alexei takes care of the people he loves."

I snort but catch myself, covering it with a cough while my pretend husband glares at me. She must know a different guy named Alexei.

"Okay." I smile pretty at him. "Thanks, *husband*."

"No problem, *wife*."

"You can make it up to him in other ways," Maria says with a cheeky wink, and I choke.

"Yeah, Hellfire. Why don't you think of some ways you can make it up to me?" He puts his arm over the back of my chair. Even though he isn't touching me, I can feel the heat from his skin. The challenging spark in his eyes makes my face burn.

"Don't be embarrassed," Maria laughs. "We were young once, too."

I make a humming noise of acknowledgment, forcing a smile. Our marriage isn't anything like theirs, I can guarantee that.

Later, Volkov and I stand at the front windows as his parents pull out of the driveway. We watch as the taillights fade down the street.

"I expected evil troll people, but your parents are actually nice." Something Maria said pops into my head. "What did she call me? Sol . . . something."

"*Solnyshko.*"

"Right. That. What does that mean?"

"*Sunshine.*"

"Oh." Warmth washes through me. That's something my mom would call me or Jordan.

"You can't get close to them," Volkov says quietly.

A ping of disappointment hits me right in the heart. "I know."

"I don't want them to be disappointed when it ends."

"I get it." So why do I feel bummed out? I just met these people, it doesn't matter.

Another beat of silence. "I'll take your car tomorrow."

"Tomorrow's not good for me."

He makes a derisive noise. "Save the shopping spree for the weekend so I can get it over with."

And like that, my temper snaps. "I'm not going shopping, you *dick*. I'm working at the hospital."

His stunned expression is the most satisfaction I've experienced in *years*. "The hospital? You have a job with the team."

My instinct is to keep details of my life secret and safe from him, but he should probably know for the citizenship interview we might have to do.

"I'm an attending in the orthopedics department, doing research on athlete injury recovery."

His dark eyes search mine, a frown creasing between his eyebrows.

"That's why Ward hired me," I add. "I'm a specialist."

And I'm not fucking incompetent, I think with a clench of anger.

"How many hours a week are you there?"

"I don't count. If I'm not at the arena, I'm at the hospital, and if I'm not there, I'm at soc—" I cut myself off. I've already said too much. He doesn't need to know about the soccer team. He'd probably make a crack about how I'm indoctrinating them to the Church of Shoes and Shopping.

He's studying me, and I don't like it. "So, not shopping."

"Sometimes I'm shopping."

He's still studying me with that unhappy expression. "I'll pick the car up and return it before your shift is over."

"No, Volkov, it's fine." I let out a light laugh and his gaze slides to my mouth before he looks away, fast. "I'll do it. You don't have to do my errands."

"I'm taking your car in, Doctor. Don't argue."

"Okay." What? "My shift is seven to seven tomorrow."

He nods once, folding his arms. A beat passes. "What was that the other night?"

Oh god. Nerves fire through me.

If I lie, he'll think I'm shamelessly trying to get into bed with him. *I liked him the whole time,* I was forced to tell people about us. What if he thinks I really did? I'd die of mortification.

He'll think the truth is weird, but he already hates me.

"I sleepwalk."

A stretch of silence before his eyebrow slides up. "You sleepwalk."

"Mhm."

He blinks, eyes cold and hard. "That's weird."

Predictable. Just like Liam. I start walking to the library, where I left a few of my things last night, when his voice stops me.

"This isn't going to be a recurring problem, is it, Doctor?"

God, I fucking hope not. "Don't flatter yourself, Volkov."

———

I'm grabbing my things from the library when a book slides out from between my laptop and my file folder.

Flowers and Their Meanings. The book is old, weathered, and dog-eared, with a broken spine. The pages are yellow with age.

I frown at it. I didn't put this here.

Earlier tonight, Maria excused herself for a moment before she returned minutes later, wearing a private smile. She must have slipped this into my stuff.

I flip through the old book. Water stains blur some of the illustrations, and I find the copyright page—it's almost forty years old.

Alexei used to work in my shop after school and on the weekends, she had said. I think about the way she narrowed her eyes at the blue flowers and the guilty look on his face.

He knows about flowers? His dark, glittering eyes and half smirk replay in my head. If the plant she gave me means *good luck in a marriage,* what do those flowers mean?

I don't know what they're called, but I find an illustration of the blue flowers, blooms the size of coins.

Blue Tansy—hostile thoughts, declaration of war.

My jaw drops and I laugh out loud. "Unbelievable."

I didn't think he had it in him. A tiny spark of respect glows in my chest.

I'm still going to get him back, though. I can't let him win.

Volkov wants to declare war? Game on.

THE NEXT WEEK, I'm about to take a seat beside Owens on the plane to Los Angeles when he gives me an odd look.

"I thought you'd want to sit with your new wife."

I lift my bag to the overhead bin. Rarely does she travel with the team to away games, a couple times a season at most.

He gestures over his shoulder and I catch sight of that familiar auburn hair. She's sitting five rows behind us, in the window seat, earbuds in and staring out the window.

She wasn't home when I left for the airport. Was she at the hospital again? When I picked her car up the other day, I used the spare keys she left in the kitchen, found the car in the spot she texted me directions to—with her name on it—and returned it without even going inside the hospital.

I wanted to, though. How did I not know she worked there?

What else don't I know about her?

"It's fine," Owens says. "Go sit with her."

My gaze lingers on her. She's wearing a little frown, like she's concentrating. It would look weird if I didn't want to sit next to her. We're supposed to be happily married.

When I put my bag into the bin above her, she pops an

earbud out and gives me a flat look. "What are you doing?" she asks quietly as I take the seat beside her.

I can smell that light, sweet smell of hers again. "Sitting beside my wife."

"I'm working." She's reading some medical journal, one long leg crossed over the other.

"I wasn't planning on having a conversation."

"Great." Her heels are a copper color with gold buckles. I haven't seen these before. "You don't normally travel with the team."

"What happened to pretending I don't exist? Let's do that again."

"I'm just wondering why you're here." And why I didn't know. This feels like something I should know. We live together, and yet we don't know anything about each other.

It never bothered me before, but now it does.

She puts her reading down. "Mei's kid is sick and she couldn't get her parents to watch him." Mei is one of the other team doctors. "I said I'd help her out."

Athlete injury recovery. My thoughts keep going back to that. No wonder Ward hired her.

Maybe she can help me. The thought surfaces before I stamp it down. She's a specialist in athlete injury recovery and she told me I was a lost cause. The message is loud and clear.

She goes back to her reading and my eyes snag on her shoes again.

"New shoes?"

"Volkov."

I have the weirdest urge to smile. "You weren't home this morning."

"I came straight from the hospital."

So she worked all day. "Tired?"

"Nope." She lifts her chin. "Not even a little."

Liar. I bet she's exhausted. "Have you eaten?"

"Not this again."

A bad feeling rises in my stomach. She needs to take better care of herself. "Have you *eaten*?" I give her a hard look and she narrows her eyes at me, starting to smile like she's realizing something. "You need to be lucid when you're treating the players." Even I can hear the defensiveness in my voice. "I don't care about you."

She snorts, turning back to her work. "I don't care about you, either."

We sit in silence while the team and staff finish boarding and the plane takes off, and shortly after, a flight attendant makes her way to our row.

"Dinner?" she asks.

"Yes," I answer in a firm tone, "for both of us."

"Controlling," Georgia sings under her breath, making my shoulders hitch. She thanks the flight attendant before her smile drops and she gives me an arch look. "I'm not eating because you told me to. I'm eating because I want to."

"I don't care."

"Good. Me neither."

"Great."

Her phone pings, and when she pulls it out, a video plays on the screen of Svetta and the bunnies. One of them is on the sofa in the living room.

"What are those rodents doing out of your room?" And why the hell is Svetta playing with them?

"Don't call them rodents. They don't like being cooped up. They need to roam."

My thoughts go to the other night, when she slipped into my bed. How warm and soft she was. The low, pleased hum she made as she nestled her ass against my cock. "You're not going to be doing a little roaming yourself tonight, looking for bed partners, are you?"

"Volkov, get real." She sounds uncertain, though.

I picture her stuck in the hall in a T-shirt and panties, forced to knock on my door and ask for help. An expanding, smug feeling fills my chest. She'd fucking *hate* having to ask for my help.

Maybe she'd run into someone else in the hall, though. They might take advantage of her.

My protective instincts lurch. I don't like that thought. Not one bit.

She opens the camera app on her phone and holds it out, leaning toward me. "Pretend you like me."

"What are you doing?"

"Taking a photo." She gives me an emphasizing look, lowering her voice even more. "For my social media. It helps with—" She gestures between us.

It helps with making this look real, she means. That makes sense. I don't have social media so I forget about this stuff.

"Okay." I lean on the armrest divider, toward her, but she frowns.

"Mmm." She shakes her head. "No." A tap of her fingers on my elbow has me moving my arm before she lifts the divider and slides close to me, against my side.

My lungs tighten as her scent washes up my nose. She's warm, like she was in my bed. Blood rushes to my cock.

In an instant, she's sliding back to her seat, doing something on her phone. I didn't even notice her taking the picture. I watch as she posts the photo. Her phone starts buzzing immediately.

"Is that your account?" I ask.

She nods.

"Show me."

She arches an eyebrow, skeptical.

"I'm not going to mess with anything, Hellfire. I just want to see what you've been posting online."

She must see that I'm telling the truth, because she hands her phone over.

The higher the heels, the closer to heaven, the caption on her profile says. I've seen her profile image before—it's a Polaroid tacked up behind the bar at the Filthy Flamingo. Big, sparkling smile, the kind that lights up a room.

In the photo she just posted, I'm looking at her with a tight, tortured expression, like I want to devour her.

Wife guy, someone already commented.

Another photo on her profile catches my eye. It's me on the ice, during the game she attended last week.

Cheering for my man, the caption reads. I give her a look, and a hint of pink washes over her face. Pretty.

She snatches the phone away. "Darcy told me to post that."

"Did she write that caption for you?"

She won't meet my eye, and I have the weirdest urge to smile again. "You should be thanking me. That photo got a lot of views. I look like the perfect little hockey wife, drooling over her husband."

I'm torn between asking to see the rest of her profile photos and teasing her harder about being *her man*—a phrase that's setting off an unfamiliar pressure in my chest—when Ward appears beside us.

"Hi, newlyweds."

On instinct, I reach for the doctor's hand, enveloping it in mine.

Like at the team dinner when we cut the cake together, I get a weird twist of pleasant warmth at the feel of her hand beneath mine. Delicate, with neat, glossy nails.

She doesn't pull her hand away as she smiles up at Ward. "Hi, Tate."

I nod a hello and he hands me my game packet, which contains information about the other team, diagrams of the plays we've practiced, and my hotel room number and key card.

"Dr. Greene," Ward adds, "your key is in Alexei's packet."

Beneath my hand, she stiffens. "Excuse me?"

"Don't worry." He gives her a smile. "I put you two in the same room."

My watch starts going off. Her eyes narrow as I silence it.

That's one way to keep an eye on her tonight.

Ward must read her weird energy because his gaze swings between us, eyebrows high. "Is that a problem? I thought since you're married now—"

"It's not an issue." I clear my throat, my hand settling on her bouncing knee. She stills. "We wanted to be professional. That's why we didn't ask to share."

"Oh." Ward lets out a short laugh. "I'm not worried about that with you two. You would barely kiss her at your own wedding dinner, Volkov."

Ward moves on, handing out more packets, and the doctor yanks her hand out from under mine, staring after him, chewing her lip, a worried expression all over her features.

"Is this going to be a problem?" I ask in a low voice.

"Not for me."

"Most of the rooms have two beds." Her shoulders are tight and she's worrying her bottom lip like she's silently freaking out. "I'm not going to bother you, Doctor. You're not my type."

As much as I don't like her, I don't want her to worry for her safety.

She lets out a light laugh, shaking her head. "Thanks, Volkov."

Nothing's going to happen tonight with the doctor, but that doesn't stop me from picturing us in a million positions.

I scrub a hand down my face. That's enough of that. Maybe I don't know her like I thought I did, but I'm not dumb enough to think blurring the lines of our agreement is a good idea. If I'm kerosene, my wife is the match.

We'd kill each other within the week.

HOURS LATER, after the game, I open the door to the hotel room, Volkov following behind me, and my stomach sinks.

We've been given the room with one bed.

Fuck.

I didn't bring pajamas.

Double fuck.

On team trips, I always get my own room. All I have are my work clothes, a tiny sleep T-shirt, my toiletries, a couple pairs of shoes, and my undergarments.

Lingerie. They're pretty and sexy, because I love to feel good about myself.

And now I'm stuck sharing a bed with Volkov.

Fuuuuuuuuuuuuck.

My eyes close. Why didn't I think of this?

"We can't ask for another room with two beds," he says with a warning look. "We have to share."

"I know, Volkov."

He heads into the washroom, the shower starts, and I run through my options.

Sleeping without pajama pants isn't a big deal. He won't even notice.

When I open my bag to pull out my sleep shirt, though, it's not there. My stomach flips. I have nothing to wear to bed.

Oh god. Okay.

We went straight from the airport to the arena. I was working at the game so I couldn't step away, and now it's late. Everything is closed.

I could sleep in my work clothes, but I know myself. I'll get too warm and in the middle of the night, fast asleep, I'll unzip my dress and yank it off. Volkov will wake to me laying on top of the covers with my ass and tits spilling out of my navy blue Agent Provocateur set.

I could ask Volkov if I can borrow a T-shirt but . . . no. It would smell like him, and I'd look adorable in it. No way. We're not going there.

When the bathroom door opens, I'm still standing over my bag, wracking my brain for any other solution. He leaves the room and by the time he returns with an ice pack, I've brushed my teeth and washed my face, but I still haven't come up with a solution. I'm back to standing over my bag, feeling the weight of his attention as he heads to the bed and settles on top of the covers, placing the ice pack across his shoulder.

It doesn't help that he looks painfully hot. He's shirtless, which I saw in Hawaii, but there's something about a man lounging against the headboard, all rippling muscles and broad shoulders. I'm rendered helpless by the smattering of dark chest hair snaking down his carved abs into the waistband of his boxers.

He's wearing glasses, too. Hockey players shouldn't wear glasses. It makes them look too hot.

He rolls his shoulder, wincing, and I frown down at my suitcase. "Shoulder hurting?"

He took a hard hit during tonight's game, the kind that made me feel sick.

"No."

"You should take an anti-inflammatory."

"Doctor." He sighs, reaching for his e-reader. "I'm not your patient anymore. You made sure of that."

In my mind, I see him and the player collide again before I shove the replay out of my head. Our gazes meet, and his eyes flick over me, standing tense and frozen over my bag.

"What's wrong with you?"

My face goes hot. After the sleepwalking thing, which he clearly didn't believe, he's probably going to think I planned this. "I didn't bring pajamas."

"What do you mean, you didn't bring pajamas?"

"I mean," I inhale a sharp breath, "I thought I'd be in my own room like *always,* and I didn't bring anything to sleep in."

"Nothing?"

My face is probably bright red. "Nothing appropriate."

His gaze sharpens. "What does that mean?"

"You know I love beautiful things, Volkov."

I study my nails without seeing them, acting aloof. My heart's beating out of my chest. A long moment passes in silence.

"I don't care what you wear," he finally says with disinterest like I'm one of his teammates. "You're about as attractive to me as a sack of potatoes."

My mouth parts in shock, and I let out a dry laugh. "A sack of potatoes."

Ouch. Really?

His gaze skims over my body, and his expression remains hard as he turns back to his e-reader. "Sorry to break it to you."

My instincts say he's lying. Is he embarrassed about finding me attractive, or is he telling the truth?

My skin prickles with that competitive feeling again, like I want to fuck with him. I was going to put my pride aside and ask to borrow a T-shirt, but now I'm going to shove his words in his face, make him choke on them.

"Well, if I'm just a sack of potatoes," I say lightly, "then I guess there's no issue."

"That's what I said."

With my back to him, I pull out the blue Agent Provocateur set. It's see-through. Am I actually doing this? I'm playing with fire, but he *did* call me a sack of potatoes and I *am* wildly competitive. Petty, too.

I'm about to head to the washroom to change when I stop. *Declaration of war,* the blue flowers meant, and I'm ready to retaliate.

My expression turns innocent. "You don't mind if I change in the room, right?"

God, I'm evil.

His gaze stays glued to his e-reader but his jaw flexes. "Doesn't matter to me."

"It's just that the humidity in the bathroom is going to mess with my hair." I unzip my dress.

"I said it *doesn't matter to me.*"

"Good." I slide my dress off, now standing in front of him in just my bra and panties. My heart thuds. He still isn't looking at me. "I'm so relieved."

I've never done something like this, taunt a man like this, but around Alexei Volkov, I'm not myself.

I turn to give him my back and unhook my bra. My skin prickles. Is he watching? I don't dare turn around. Slowly, I slide my panties down, bare-ass naked, heart hammering, adrenaline howling through me.

My instincts scream to sprint into the washroom and cover myself in a towel, but I put the set on as slowly as I can, dragging this out.

I take one steadying breath before turning around, and I'm

about to freak out that Volkov can see my nipples through the sheer fabric, but his eyes flick to my body and stay there. He doesn't look like he's breathing.

"Something wrong?" My voice is light and casual, but I'm sure my eyes glow with feminine rage and revenge.

He's still staring. "No."

"Good." I wander to my side of the bed and settle on top of the duvet, his eyes on me the entire time.

Sack of potatoes, my *ass*. Take that, you fucking asshole.

"Do you want to...uh." His gaze snags on my chest. My nipples pinch and his eyes darken. "...put a line of pillows down the bed or something?"

He actually looks nervous, and delight sparkles through me. His e-reader screen's turned off due to inactivity, but he hasn't noticed.

"I don't think we need that, do we?"

Silently, he shakes his head. His Adam's apple bobs as he swallows, gaze sliding down my stomach, my hips, my legs. I adjust the pillows behind my head, take a deep breath that makes my tits rise and fall, and close my eyes.

"Get under the covers." His voice sounds hoarse.

I can't look at him. If I see his expression, I'll burst into laughter. "I get too warm. This is fine."

I reach for the lamp and click it off before laying back down, purposefully pushing my boobs together, and my darling husband clears his throat.

"Sweet dreams, Volkov."

CHAPTER 31
ALEXEI

I'M LISTENING to my wife's slow, steady breathing, trying to ignore my hard-on and fall asleep when she rolls over and lays across my chest.

I open one eye, body going taut and alert. "Doctor?"

"Warm," she murmurs with a sigh, eyes closed and breath skating across my bare chest.

Just like last time.

A shudder of pleasure rolls through me. She's right, she does run warm. I try not to think about what she would feel like under me, looking up at me as I sink into her.

My groin aches with need again. I wish, under her clothes, she was covered in oozing sores and boils, or scales like a lizard, instead of soft, smooth skin. There are freckles all over her chest from the summer. A few on her thighs. I remember those from Hawaii.

You're about as attractive to me as a sack of potatoes. I can't believe I said that. No wonder she thinks I'm an asshole.

I should wake her up. Like last time, she'd be humiliated. That's not as appealing as it should be, though. Concerning.

I can't lie here all night with her on top of me or I'll never get any sleep. Careful not to wake her, I shift her off my chest and back to her side of the bed.

Two minutes later, she's on top of me again, clinging to my chest, one leg sliding between mine.

I groan. This isn't working, and I like this too much. I push her back to her side, haul myself out of bed, and lie down on the sofa. My feet hang off the edge, but I'll still get a better sleep here than with the doctor's hair in my face.

Soft hair, I should add. Soft like silk.

Tomorrow, I'll tell Ward her snoring keeps me up and we need separate rooms.

I'm just starting to fall asleep when I hear the rustle of sheets. The doctor lays down beside me on the sofa, arm looping around my waist, head against my chest, light violet scent washing over me.

I sigh, frustrated. We're going to be playing this game until dawn.

Resigned to my fate of being up all night with an erection so hard it hurts, I lead her to the bed, climb back in beside her, and wrap an arm around her waist, pulling her to me.

We're not cuddling, I tell myself, ignoring how her body feels tucked against me, her perfect ass nestled against my cock. I move my hips back. I'm not enjoying this. I don't even like her.

So she works more than I realized. She still transferred me to another doctor because she assumed my career would be over soon. She still recommended the team cut me loose.

We're complete opposites and any attraction I feel to her is misplaced.

I force myself to relax and fall asleep, praying she doesn't wake up.

———

The next morning, I wake with her tucked against me, breathing softly, warm and smelling like violets and vanilla, her hair brushing my arm. I'm on my bad shoulder, and it hurts from the game last night. My erection aches with need, pressed into that perfect ass of hers.

Still, I'm more comfortable than ever. That was the best sleep I've had in ages.

A warning feeling grows inside me. I ease away from her and head to the shower to get rid of this erection before she sees it. Under the spray of the water, I come picturing her on her knees, mouth tilted in an irritating smirk as she takes me between her lips.

When I get out of the shower, she's up and dressed—thank fuck.

Her gaze darts to me. "Any problems last night?"

I hate that I came thinking about her. If she knew, she'd laugh and laugh, her ego doubling. With the urge to even the score, I almost tell her about her sleep-cuddling me.

It feels like a low blow, though.

"Nope."

She lets out a soft breath of relief. "Good."

CHAPTER 32

ALEXEI

THREE NIGHTS IN A ROW, the doctor makes my life a living hell.

"You look like shit," Owens says at the warm-up skate on the last morning of our away-game stretch.

"Shut up." It can't be healthy for a man to have an erection for extended lengths of time like this.

He just grins. "Bad night?"

Three terrible nights. The worst of my life.

I didn't tell Ward we needed separate rooms, because what if she did sleepwalk into the hall? I'm not worried about her, but I didn't like that idea.

Three nights in a row, she slept half on top of me, her leg tucked between mine, her head on my chest, her scent in my nose.

Three mornings in a row, I woke up hard but well rested. The deepest sleeps of my life, once I let go and relaxed.

My wife apparently sleeps like the dead, waking up after me each morning. She has no idea about any of this, a thought that gives me a twist of discomfort.

"What's the matter, Volkov?" Miller asks as he skates past. "The doctor keeping you up late?"

"Yes." My mind goes to the freckles across her chest, and my mouth waters.

I can't wait to get home tonight so I can sleep in my own bed—alone.

"Only Volkov would take a good night's sleep over hooking up with his hot wife," Walker says, and I glare at him. "What? It's a good problem to have."

It's a problem, all right. It's a *problem* that the doctor is the hottest woman I've ever seen. It's a *problem* that she makes me feel like I'm losing my mind. It's a *problem* that I want to bend my wife over the bed and fuck those teasing words and smirks right out of her.

It's just because she gets under my skin. My body's confused.

———

That evening, we exit the plane in Vancouver, and I've never been so relieved to get home.

"Get some rest, Volkov." Miller claps me on the shoulder. "Never seen you so grouchy."

Beside me, the doctor's lips turn up.

"Something funny?"

Her eyes go wide with innocence. "Nope. Nothing funny at all."

She thinks she's keeping me up because of the lingerie.

When we get to the arrivals area for the team's private plane, she starts walking toward a car waiting at the curb.

"I already booked a car," I tell her.

"Good job." She keeps walking past me. "So did I."

"Doctor." I wait, but she's still walking away. "Georgia," I call again. She stops, turns, and waits with an expectant look, like I'm inconveniencing her. For fuck's sake. I lower my voice. "We're not taking separate cars home."

"I'm not going home."

My eyebrows pull down. "You're going to work *now*?"

"Don't worry about it." She gives me a pretty smile and a wink. "Don't wait up."

I don't know whether it's the unsettling realization that I sleep better when she's tucked against me, or the way she's looking at me like she can't stand me, or maybe it's that I can't stop thinking about fucking her in the position I woke up in this morning.

Or maybe I'm angry at myself for saying she didn't turn me on when she did.

There are players and staff everywhere, waiting for their own rides. For whatever reason, challenge and determination fire through me.

"Give your husband a kiss goodbye," I call in front of everyone. "Hellfire."

Her nostrils flare.

I'm thinking about those little scraps of lace barely covering her, and how fucking delectable her body is. How my body responds to hers with sharp, powerful arousal.

My heart's in my throat, beating hard, as she stares at me.

"I'll see you in a couple hours, *darling*." A brittle smile forms on her mouth but her eyes are pure rage. "Surely you can wait that long."

"I can't." I set my bag down, straightening up to my full height. "I'm going to miss my wife way too much."

This is for teasing me with that lingerie, my eyes say. *Two can play at this game.*

I fucking hate you, her eyes say right back.

Fire burns in her eyes and I feel like smiling. She starts

walking toward me with slow, steady steps, and my watch goes off before I silence it.

"Come on, Hellfire. Show me how much you love me."

She starts to smile, that furious glint still in her gaze, and my pulse stutters.

"You sure about this?" she asks quietly. "You sure you want to start this?"

"*You* started this." From the outside, it looks like we're having an intimate conversation. "You said I was a terrible kisser."

"You are."

"Worried you're going to enjoy it like you did at the team dinner?"

She laughs, delicate and amused. "With you? Never."

"I think you're worried you'll like it too much." With my mouth an inch from her ear, I lower my voice. "I remember how you kissed me back. I think you're worried you'll get turned on."

"I'm worried all your fake teeth will fall out." She winces. "That would be so humiliating for you."

What a little chicken. "I'm willing to take that risk."

"Volkov, this is sad." Her eyes lift to mine with mock sympathy. "This isn't going to work, and then you're going to feel bad about yourself."

"Keep stalling, Doctor."

I don't know why it's so important that we kiss. I don't know why I need to win this round so badly. I'm competitive, but not like this.

Never like this. She brings out the worst in me.

"All right." She flattens a hand to my chest, running her thumb back and forth over the fabric of my T-shirt. My pulse skips. "Don't freeze up on me again, though."

Something about her low, teasing voice combined with the

look in her eyes makes the hairs on the back of my neck rise. Competition courses through me and I step close enough so our bodies are touching—her breasts against my chest—and my blood hums with energy.

My pulse pounds as I wrap a hand around the back of her head, sinking my fingers into her soft hair, and her eyes widen as I lower my mouth to hers.

The second our lips touch, I know I've lost this round.

VOLKOV'S KISS IS HARD, urgent, and desperate, like he has a point to prove. His tongue slides against mine, his stubble scrapes my skin, and a low, hungry groan rumbles in his chest. His fingers flexing on my scalp, sending sparks of pleasure down my neck. My thoughts whirl, pinwheeling and spinning out.

For someone who didn't bat an eye at me laying in lingerie next to him three nights in a row, Volkov kisses me like he wants me. Heat spills through my limbs, rising on my skin, settling between my legs.

He said he wasn't attracted to me, but he kisses me like he's powerless. He kisses me like this is going to go so much further, like we're seconds from tearing our clothes off.

My backside hits the car. I didn't even notice him walking me backward.

Another noise slips out of him—kind of a *huh,* like he's surprised but not upset about it. Like he knew it.

The memory of the team dinner kiss rushes back at me, full force. I was wrong about that kiss. It was *that good.* Just like this kiss is *that good.*

I hate that I'm clawing right back at him, tugging his hair, feeling his hard chest, his soft T-shirt, inhaling him, letting him coax my lips apart and taste me.

Letting him take control. He kisses me like he's in charge, and deep down, a tiny speck of me likes that.

The kiss changes, turning deeper, like he's trying to consume me. My thoughts blur, my skin goes hot, and every nerve in my body feels charged. My brain is full of Pop Rocks, sparking and cracking as Volkov kisses the hell out of me.

How am I going to coach soccer tonight? After this, I won't be able to see straight.

His big arm loops around my waist, hauling me to him, our hips flush against each other. Something hard notches between my legs, and my eyes go wide and unseeing.

He's hard. I want to say something cool and witty, like *how's that for a sack of potatoes.*

I don't, though, because more than anything, I want to keep kissing him. Helpless, I melt into him.

Who kisses like this? Where'd he learn these moves? I scrabble at his chest, fisting his T-shirt in my hands.

A startling realization hits me—his arm around me feels familiar. Too familiar. My eyes go wide, gazing up into his with shock. I stiffen; he drops his arm and steps back, breathing hard.

Any problems last night? I'd asked the first morning. *Nope,* he'd said, but he didn't meet my eyes.

I did sleepwalk. He lied. Oh god. My face burns hotter. Who knows what I was doing all night? Oh god oh god oh god.

I hate being out of control like this in front of him. I hate him seeing my weakness. He was probably saving it for the right moment so he could wield my humiliation like a knife.

He's still breathing hard, watching me with a slant to his mouth. His throat works. "Have a great night, Hellfire."

Without another word, he gets into a waiting car and I watch it drive away, arousal, surprise, and confusion swirling through me.

A FEW EVENINGS LATER, it's the second period in a home game against Atlanta—and we're losing one to three.

"Remember what we practiced," I tell Walker as we line up for a face-off. "Be physical. Disrupt the play. Get in there."

He nods, and when the whistle blows, the other team snags the puck before he and I are off, skating hard to intercept the puck. The other team brings it toward our net, and Streicher's on high alert as they pass it back and forth, trying to find their moment while Walker and I get in the way.

Walker blocks their forward from receiving the puck—*good*—but then he skates to their other forward, the one I'm covering.

I shake my head. What's he doing? This isn't the play. This isn't what we practiced.

Walker tries to snag the puck but their defense checks him out of the way with ease. Their forward snaps the puck at the net and they score.

A collective groan of disappointment ripples through the arena, and I let out a heavy exhale, frustrated.

———

"Aren't you going to remind me to play more physical?" Walker asks after the game as we head upstairs to the owner's box reserved for staff, friends, and family. His usual cocky grin is gone.

I think about the way he got slammed into the boards by the other team tonight. He wasn't hurt, but he could have been. Walker's not big like me, he's lean like Miller. Guys' careers end due to injuries all the time. Look at Ward, who had been on track to be the next Gretzky when he blew out his knee.

The rookie's only twenty-two. I don't want his career to be over before it even starts. I'd never forgive myself.

"I don't know, Walker." I could tell him to play more physical, but what's the point?

Nothing we're doing is working.

"I'm sorry," he says as we step into the box, and I feel like fucking garbage. I don't know why I care. I have my own game to focus on, and the last thing I need is mentoring this arrogant rookie.

"Luca!" A taller guy in his fifties with a deep umber skin tone waves at him, smiling. Beside him, a blond guy about the same age wears his own proud grin.

Walker lights up and gestures at me to follow. "Come on. My dads are here."

I begrudgingly follow the kid to his parents. When he's within arm's reach, they pull him into a tight hug, squeezing the life out of him, telling him what a great game he just played.

My gut sinks. I didn't know they were here, and I wish they'd seen a game where Walker had played better, where some of what we've been practicing had actually worked, instead of a loss.

"This is Michael," Walker gestures to the taller man, who gives me a broad grin, "and Terrence." Walker's other father wears a quiet smile.

I shake both their hands with a firm nod. "Alexei Volkov. Nice to meet you both."

"We've heard so much about you." Michael sends a pointed glance to my left hand, where I slipped my ring back on in the dressing room. "I hear congratulations are in order. Is your wife here?"

"No." I glance around, rubbing my thumb against the band on my ring finger, thinking about that fucking airport kiss again. About how it felt when she wrapped herself around me every night. "She's working."

Probably. I don't know her hospital schedule. All I know is that she's in her office at the arena in the mornings, and she doesn't get home until late.

My cracks about her shopping and spending money replay in my head. During the three-day road trip, I don't think I saw her stop working once, except to sleep or get ready in the mornings. She was always on her laptop, talking with players, stitching guys up, or helping them retape their injuries.

A bad feeling, like I've been very wrong, moves through me.

"Georgia's one of the team doctors," Walker explains to his dads.

"Georgia," Terrence repeats, smiling. "What a beautiful name."

"It is." My mom said the same thing after they met. *Beautiful name for a beautiful woman,* she said to me.

Again, my mind goes to that fucking airport kiss. I thought challenging her and proving her wrong would feel like victory, but it was me who enjoyed it too much.

"We want to thank you so much for everything you've done for our Luca," Michael adds. "We really appreciate it. It's hard when we're all the way out in Winnipeg."

My mood sinks even further. "I haven't done anything except bark his ear off."

"No shit," Walker says with a snort, and Terrence gives him a scolding look before smiling up at me.

"That's not true. He's told us all about you. You have a very impressive career and we're so grateful that he has someone like you to show him the ropes."

There's a weird feeling in my chest, watching his parents look proudly at their son. Maybe it's that they remind me of my parents. Maybe it's that I know Ward signed him for a reason.

Maybe I'm the problem.

On the way home, I realize that I don't know the rookie's story. I hardly know anything about the kid. Maybe his background is like mine, where his parents worked their asses off to pay for hockey. Regardless of where he comes from, playing in the NHL is his dream. It's all our dreams. His parents want to see him succeed more than anything, just like mine.

Maybe figuring it out for himself is the better option.

Tomorrow, I'll talk to Ward, and tell him it isn't working.

———

The next morning, my trainer and I are leaving the gym in the arena when Ward finds me.

"Got a second?" he asks.

"Sure. I want to talk to you about something, too."

I nod goodbye to my trainer and follow Ward up to his office. We make easy small talk on the way, but I'm distracted by my resolution from last night—to tell him it isn't working out with the rookie.

"I have some good news," Ward says as we enter his office and I take a seat.

My first thought is that he's found someone else to mentor Walker.

"You're getting a lifetime achievement award."

My face falls. "What?"

Ward laughs. "I know. While you're still playing? Incredible, Alexei. Very proud of you."

Only a couple guys are given the award every season.

It feels like I just got boarded hard enough to knock the wind out of me. "I don't want it."

Ward seems taken aback. His eyebrows lift. "You don't want it."

"No." I scowl. "I don't want it."

"Can I ask why?"

"They give that to retired guys."

"Ah." He nods. "Okay. I get it." Ward glances out the window. "Volkov, I'm not going to tell you what to do or how to feel, but I didn't go to mine, and sometimes I wish I had."

After his career ended abruptly, Ward disappeared. I was still playing and we weren't friends, but I heard rumors that he didn't do well with retirement. Most guys who experience a career-ending injury don't.

Another wave of worry moves through me.

"You don't need to give me an answer yet," he adds, eyes meeting mine. "Just think about it, okay?"

Saying no after his admission would be a slap in the face, so I give him a tight nod.

"Thank you. What did you want to talk to me about?"

This is probably where I should tell him I can't mentor the rookie anymore, but I hold back. It doesn't feel like the right moment.

"Nothing." I stand. "Everything's good."

"Good."

I'm almost at the door when he stops me.

"Hey, Alexei? If you decide to accept the award, and I hope you do, it would help having someone by your side. Someone you trust. For support."

He's not referring to my new wife, is he? She'd probably howl with laughter at the idea of me getting a lifetime achievement award. I can just imagine the old and injured jokes.

"You bet," I say before leaving.

There's no way in hell I'm bringing her to that award ceremony.

"WHAT ARE YOU DOING?" Alexei asks a few nights later as I stand in the foyer of his home, applying lipstick in front of the hallway mirror. His gaze catches on my mouth, flickering with distaste before it drags down my sparkly floor-length gold gown.

Right—those are his horny eyes. Poor guy is attracted to the last woman he'd ever want to be with.

"Waiting for my ride." Why is he home so early? He wasn't supposed to get home until late tonight.

A bouquet of flowers arrived at my office today. Yellow carnations. The second I got home, I looked them up in the book Maria had slipped into my work stuff. *Yellow carnations— disdain, rejection.*

He won't ruin my good mood. I splurged on getting my hair done after work, big and wavy and shiny, and my makeup is practiced and precise. This dress has been hanging in my closet, waiting for the perfect moment. Between work and the soccer team this week, I'm exhausted, but there's something about dressing up and looking hot that supercharges my ego.

"Where are you going?"

"Wouldn't you love to know?"

His gaze drops to my mouth and heat flashes through me.

It's the same look he wore before he kissed me at the airport, pissed off and wound up.

Tension thickens in the air. He steps closer and my pulse jumps. Goddamnit.

"I'm going to a hospital benefit." I twist the lipstick tube closed and tuck it in my clutch.

"Isn't that the kind of thing you should invite your husband to?"

Honestly, I didn't even think to. I'm so used to being single. "You weren't supposed to be home in time."

He studies me with a frown. "You're wearing that perfume again. The Friday one."

I hate that he notices things like this, and now that I know he grew up helping Maria in her flower shop, I realize that's how he identified the violet note in my perfume.

"I don't just wear it on Fridays," I rush out. "I wear it when I want to feel—" I don't know why I'm talking about this with him.

"What?" His stare turns to a glower.

The perfume makes me feel pretty and optimistic and happy. "It doesn't matter. Breathe through your mouth if you don't like it. Or better, stand farther away from me."

He studies me, and I have the urge to squirm.

"The other night," he says, voice low, and my skin prickles. "At the airport."

The kiss, he means. I squint, pretending to think. "What happened at the airport?"

It's like I haven't even thought about it once. Haven't obsessed about what we did each of those nights.

His nostrils flare. "When we kissed."

"Oh. When *you* kissed *me*."

His eyes flash. "We shouldn't be doing stuff like that anymore. No more kissing, even if it's for show."

I'm both disappointed and relieved. "I agree. I'm supposed to be professional in front of the team." I'm actually impressed at how cool and disinterested I seem. The devil inside me lifts her head, though, and the words slip out before I can stop myself. "Besides, it wasn't very good."

A muscle jumps in his neck. "You kissed me back."

"I was thinking about someone else," I lie.

He stills. "What?" he asks in a low, deadly voice.

My blood starts sparkling the way it always does when we spar. "I was picturing someone else." I wince up at him. "To get through it."

My grandfather can expect me in about seventy years, because I'm going to hell.

"Who were you picturing?" He's still using that low, scary voice that makes my stomach dip.

"It's not important."

"Georgia." He steps into my space and I step back, hitting the wall. His scent surrounds me, making me dizzy. "Who. Were. You. Picturing."

"Just a colleague."

Volkov clenches his jaw so hard it looks like it hurts, and his gaze locks to mine before it drops to my lips. Is he going to kiss me again? My pulse pounds in my ears. I don't know why I love fucking with him so much.

"He's going to be there tonight?"

It takes every ounce of me to hold his gaze, lifting my chin. "Yes. Dr. Handley is picking me up any moment. Dr. Handsome, the nurses call him."

His gaze hardens, and my stomach flips at the furious, possessive look in his eyes.

This game feels dangerous, but I can't stop. Adrenaline whizzes through me. Dr. Eric Handley is gorgeous in that big blue-eyed, corn-fed country boy way. A true nice guy, like

Hayden Owens. Safe and kind. We're 100 percent platonic, though.

Volkov's eyes drop to where I hold my clutch. "Where's your wedding ring?"

"It doesn't go with my outfit."

His glare turns to a raging glower. More adrenaline floods my body.

"Oh, come on," I laugh. "You bought me an ugly ring on purpose."

He holds up a hand, where his glints. "I'm wearing mine. What do you think it looks like, when you don't wear yours?"

Why is the sight of that ring on his big hand so hot?

He sucks in a deep breath, closing his eyes, and when they open again, they flash with something possessive. "Tell Dr. Handjob you don't need a ride." He starts walking up the stairs. "I'll be down in ten minutes."

My heart stops. "What? No."

He ignores me.

"You don't have a ticket," I call after him, panic spilling through my stomach. My colleagues know I got married—they saw the photos online—but I don't want Alexei Volkov anywhere near the work I love.

"Figure it out," he yells from upstairs, before his door closes.

Ten minutes later, he returns with damp hair and dark eyes, wearing a sharp, navy blue tux. It's clearly bespoke, with the way it fits his broad, towering form. For a man who spends all his time working out or playing hockey, I'm surprised to admit Volkov has style.

Hockey players shouldn't wear tuxes. It makes them look too hot.

My nerves whir as our eyes meet, and the clawing, desperate, hungry airport kiss replays in my head. Best kiss of my life. Not good, I tell myself. Very concerning.

And tonight, with him looking so deadly handsome? This is a bad idea.

Before I can say anything, though, he tosses something through the air, and I catch it. My wedding ring. His hard, determined expression burns me.

"Put your fucking wedding ring on. *Now*."

"SO, is he Dr. Handjob because he gives himself hand jobs," my irritating, stunning wife asks when we arrive at the grand old home in Shaughnessy, "or is it because you think *I'm* going to give him one tonight?"

Jealousy pounds through me like a drum. She's trying to get a rise out of me. I can tell from the teasing tone of her voice, the spark in her warm whiskey eyes.

Jesus fucking Christ, she looks good tonight. Took my goddamned breath away when I saw her standing there in the foyer, looking like a million bucks. My fingers itch to run through her soft, wavy hair like I did during that kiss at the airport.

And those shoes. Black velvet, red soles, with a bow on each ankle. I'm going to be thinking about those bows all week.

My teeth grit. "You are not giving him a hand job."

Her lips curve. I can't stop looking at her. I can't stop thinking about the kiss. I can't stop thinking about *her*.

I hate this.

A staff member for the event ushers us through the mansion and into the ballroom. This house is so big, it has a fucking *ballroom*. She probably grew up in a home just like it. My eyes flick to her dress again.

"Why are you always wearing this sparkly shit?"

"Because I love *this sparkly shit*. It makes me happy. Do you know what 'happy' is, Volkov?"

She kissed me back. You can't fake that kind of kiss—but apparently she was picturing someone else.

"Yes, Hellfire, I remember what happy feels like. When we divorce, I'm sure I'll feel it again."

Her eyes flash with competition, her pretty lips part, and she's about to say something when we're interrupted by some guy with his eyes all over her.

"Georgia."

Her face lights up with a radiant smile. "Eric."

So this is Dr. Handjob. This is who she actually wanted to kiss.

"You look beautiful, as always." He leans in to kiss her cheek.

My eyebrows go up. Is this guy for real? Calling her beautiful, right in front of me?

She is, but still. That's for me to say, not him.

My hand comes to her waist, pulling her against me. She gives me an amused, sidelong look that I ignore. He's still gazing at her with wonder, admiration, and longing. Fucking *longing*?

He likes her. This guy wants my wife.

"Thanks. Sorry about the last-minute change." She flicks an unimpressed look at me. "Volkov got home early."

The event was sold out, but with a sizable donation to the hospital and a few photos and autographs, the organizers hurried to find a seat for me. Being a professional hockey player opens doors like that, thankfully, because there was no way I was letting this guy hang on to the doctor all evening.

Dr. Handjob's eyes move to me. "This must be your husband." He sticks his hand out. "Eric Handley."

"Alexei Volkov." We shake hands. Mine is bigger.

He looks to the doctor with a teasing smile. "You call your husband Volkov, Georgia?"

I don't like how friendly they are. She doesn't joke with me like that and she sure as shit doesn't smile at me like that.

She blinks, caught off guard, and on her waist, my hand flexes.

"She's called me that for years," I cut in. "It's a hard habit to break."

Dr. Handjob smiles. "Right. She complained about you more than a few times."

"Did she now?" I don't know why that makes me so happy.

"Okay," she interrupts. "I didn't complain that much."

This fucker grins wider. "Remember that meniscus reconstruction the other week? I had to hear—"

With my hand still on her waist, I pull her away without saying goodbye. Something ugly and tight gathers in my gut at the thought of these two teasing each other at work.

"I'll catch up with you later," she tells him over her shoulder as I drag her away before she turns to me with a sharp look. "That was rude. He's my friend."

I laugh, cold and cruel. "He's not your friend, Hellfire. Don't even try to tell me this wasn't going to be a date."

She blanches. "It wasn't."

"Has he ever asked you out?"

She hesitates.

"He has." I fucking knew it. "What's the matter, he's not rich enough for you?"

"I don't date colleagues." Her gaze cools. "But maybe I'll marry him after we divorce. Dr. Handsome and Dr. Hellfire. Has a nice ring to it."

I know she's joking, but I don't like it. My gaze trails over her in that fucking phenomenal dress, the way it dips into her cleavage. For the millionth time, I think about our kiss. I think about what would have happened if we'd kissed like that somewhere private.

The kiss would go a lot further.

———

"You've got a good one here," a senior nurse tells me during dinner, pointing at my wife. "She has a good head on her shoulders, she works harder than everyone else, and she loves to learn—"

"Thank you so much, Margaret," the doctor cuts her off before she changes the subject.

I lean in, bringing my mouth close to her ear. "You didn't tell me the theme for tonight was people raving about you."

She's extremely well-liked among her peers—just another thing I didn't know about her.

"They're just excited to meet you."

They are, but not because of hockey, for once. It's because I'm married to *her*. I don't know how to feel about that. "Why do you work at the hospital? You don't need the job."

The team probably pays her more than enough. She sips her drink, not looking at me.

"They might ask this during the interview," I add.

More so, I need to know. I have a sinking feeling the reason has nothing to do with money.

"I love what I do." Her expression has never softened like this while talking to me. "I help athletes recover and regain mobility so they can do what they love. I get to make their lives better. There's nothing like it. It's like flying."

I'm stunned speechless at the conviction in her eyes. She's telling the truth. That's how I feel about hockey—it's like flying.

A weird, pleased pulse goes off in my chest. She has no reason to trust me, but she did. I don't know what this means. I don't like how I feel, confused and intrigued.

"Thank you for coming tonight, everyone," a woman says into a microphone at the front of the room. "I'm Dr. Heather Joshi, the director of Lionsgate Hospital's Athlete Injury Recovery Program."

Applause rises around the room.

"I can't talk about the program without highlighting the efforts of one person." A photo of the woman beside me appears behind Dr. Joshi on the screen, wearing a lab coat, working with a teenager on crutches. It looks like she's saying something encouraging to him.

"Georgia volunteered to make this speech, but I knew she'd leave out all the nice things about herself." A few people laugh, and at my side, the doctor rolls her eyes, but she's smiling.

"I had the pleasure of meeting Dr. Georgia Greene when she fractured her lateral malleolus—also known as a broken ankle—at sixteen. She was sent to the sports medicine clinic where I was a new physician. We worked together for six months so she could return to playing soccer with her high school team."

She played soccer?

The photo behind her changes. It's a younger Dr. Joshi and the teenage version of Georgia. Same whiskey eyes, same auburn hair. Big grin, with braces.

A few *aw*s rise around the room. People smile at her.

Dr. Joshi wears a fond expression. "That's us. Even back then, Georgia was a joy to work with. Smart, curious, and enthusiastic. Incredibly dedicated. Very interested in my shoe collection."

The room laughs and she flicks to the next photo. It's Georgia on a soccer field, mid kick. Ponytail flying, a look of concentration on her face. Legs strong and toned.

"Georgia went on to get a full scholarship to the University of British Columbia Women's Soccer team."

I turn to her, shock written all over my face. To play on a university team, you have to be good. I didn't know she was an athlete. She ignores me.

The photo changes, and it's my wife and Dr. Handjob. My shoulders tense. I hate that she seems to genuinely like him.

She'd never smile at me like that.

"Fast forward fifteen years, and she's Dr. Greene, applying for government grants and convincing me to start our own athlete injury recovery program at the hospital. She has lured orthopedic surgeons, internal medicine physicians, physiotherapists, and other specialists from all over the world, and I am proud to say we run one of the most advanced programs in the country."

The room breaks into loud applause.

"Is that all true?" I ask, even though I know the answer. I want to hear her say it, though.

She doesn't meet my eyes. "Mhm."

"We can't talk about the program, though, without mentioning Dr. Greene's favorite part."

The photo changes to the doctor with a group of teenage girls on a soccer pitch.

"One goal of our research is to speed up recovery, and Dr. Greene's hypothesis is that being part of a team environment is a critical part of rehabilitation. Participants have the option to play on a team of other injured athletes within the program. They have weekly practices tailored to their current ability, where they can reap the community and motivational benefits of a team environment under medical supervision. The teams are organized based on age, gender, and skill level." She smiles at the photo of Georgia and the teenage girls, the one I can't stop staring at. "This is Dr. Greene's team, the Vancouver Devils."

I turn to my wife, who's still ignoring me. She coaches soccer?

That's where she goes at night, I realize. She's either at this hospital program she clearly puts everything into, or she's coaching soccer.

Dr. Joshi talks more about the program, the other doctors, and some success stories, before she beams at the audience.

"And now, the part we've all been waiting for—the doctor auction."

A ripple of interest moves around the room. My gaze cuts to Georgia. "What is she talking about?"

"We'll start with the lovely Dr. Greene," Dr. Joshi says.

"Hellfire," my tone is sharp, low enough so only she can hear. "What is she talking about?"

"Fucking relax." She smiles as everyone looks over at her. "They're auctioning off dates with the doctors."

Dr. Joshi sends a cheeky grin our way. "We roped Dr. Greene in for this portion of the evening before she was married, but hopefully her new husband doesn't mind."

"Someone gets to go on a date with you?" I don't like that idea. Not one bit.

"We'll start the bidding at a thousand dollars." Dr. Joshi points to Dr. Handjob, who has his hand in the air. "We've got Dr. Handley for one thousand."

The fuck? My gaze whips to that fucker, alarm blaring inside me. He sends Georgia a friendly wink.

"Do we have two thousand?"

A few hands go up, including mine.

"Two thousand, from Dr. Greene's handsome new husband."

"Volkov." My wife's fingers dig into my thigh. My cock jumps. "Do not."

Dr. Handjob glances from me to Georgia..

"Do we have three thousand?" Dr. Joshi asks.

His hand goes up. My nostrils flare.

"Five thousand?"

Mine goes up. The room starts to buzz.

"Volkov," she hisses through a smile. "Stop bidding."

"Ten thousand?" Dr. Joshi lights up. "Ten thousand to Dr. Handley."

"His family is wealthy and they were going to donate anyway," she whispers. "I asked him to bid on me. We're friends. I didn't want to be humiliated if no one bid on me, and I didn't want to be stuck with some creep."

"A friend who calls you beautiful?"

My wife. Not his.

"Do we have twenty thousand?"

"Twenty thousand," I call, and the tension in the room thickens.

Dr. Joshi looks like she's about to detonate. "I guess Dr. Greene's new husband wants to stake his claim. Do we have thirty?"

"Thirty," Dr. Nutjob calls.

Wait. I frown at Georgia. "You thought no one would bid on you? In *that* dress? Are you delusional?"

The doctor has a smile that could stop traffic and perfect tits. Her body is a fucking dream.

She looks like she wants to say something, but Dr. Joshi interrupts.

"Do we have forty? Forty to Dr. Handley. We just broke a record, folks. Do we have fifty? Fifty thousand dollars?"

My hand goes up. "Fifty."

Someone whistles.

A strangled noise slips out of her. *"Alexei."* It's the first time she's said my first name. I like the way the *l* and *x* sound on her lips. "Stop. Bidding. Now."

The determined look in her eyes makes me feel reckless. Or maybe it's the way that guy is looking at her like he wants her.

That asshole wants my wife.

"One hundred thousand," I call, blood beating in my ears, and the room lights up with gasps.

"Dr. Handley?" Dr. Joshi asks, but he gives the room a rueful smile, shaking his head.

Victory pounds through me as the audience roars with applause. At my side, my wife smiles through clenched teeth.

"Congratulations to Alexei Volkov of the Vancouver Storm for winning a date with his new wife, Dr. Georgia Greene, and a massive *thank you* for your generous contribution to our program."

Did I just spend a hundred grand because I was jealous? Yes, and I'd do it again.

While everyone watches, I lean in to kiss her cheek, inhaling her, brushing my lips over the shell of her ear. Smug male pride beats through me.

"Don't tell me what to do, Hellfire."

WHILE HEATHER AUCTIONS off another doctor, I drag Volkov out of the ballroom, pushing him through the nearest door.

It's a library, with floor-to-ceiling bookshelves, dark wood paneling, and soft, dim lighting. Through the walls, we can hear Heather in the ballroom as the bidding continues.

"What was that?" I demand.

His eyes burn me. "A tax write-off."

In the low lighting, the planes of my husband's face look especially sharp, his under-eye circles even darker, and that pissed off, jaw-clenched expression only makes him hotter.

Anger pools in my abdomen. Or arousal. I'm not sure.

"That was you getting territorial. Control yourself, you animal."

He glares down at me, stepping into my space. "That asshole was making a move on my wife. I had to do something."

My stomach flips. "I'm not your wife."

"Yes, you are." He takes another step forward. My back hits the wall.

He looks to my mouth. Is he thinking about that kiss again? My pulse races with fury. He's *such* an asshole.

An asshole who just spent a lot of money on me because he was jealous. I want to be mad—I *am* mad—but a tiny, miniscule part of me preens.

"I can't stand you," I whisper.

His fist comes to the wall, beside my head. "I hate you, too, Hellfire."

He brings his mouth down to mine, hovering. It's a new game for us—who will break first?

It won't be me. I press my hand to his hard chest. Under my touch, his heart pounds. His scent makes it hard to focus.

"No more kissing," I remind him, and his eyes flash.

His fingers trail along the neckline of my gown, sending sparks over my skin. I think my lashes flutter, like some swooning leading lady in an old Western. Holding my eyes, his fingers drag lower, beneath my neckline, challenging me. *Daring* me. Under his rough fingertips, my heart races, but I give him a cool, disinterested smirk.

I will not back down. I will not let him win.

"Tell me to stop."

No. God, no. "I don't care."

I can play this game of chicken all day.

My gaze drops to the front of his pants, stretched out with an impressive erection. I swallow hard, heat moving through me. Volkov's huge.

His fingers reach the valley between my breasts. Blood whistles in my ears, but I lift a hand and fake a yawn.

His lips come to my shoulder, stubble brushing my skin as I burn hotter. "A bow on each ankle like you're pretending to be a good girl or something." I shiver, and he makes a low noise of amusement. "Like that, do you, Hellfire? You like being called a good girl?"

The words *good girl* make my stomach dip. "No. I hate it."

"Don't lie."

"I'm bored." My full focus narrows to his lips following my neckline, moving down my chest. Between my legs, heat swirls, and—oh god—I'm actually wet.

This horrible game is actually turning me on. It's not possible. There's no way.

His fingers hook into my neckline and he pulls it down an inch, lips latching onto the sensitive skin between my breasts before he sucks. My eyes close, but I don't dare make a sound. I'd never give him that satisfaction.

"Last chance," he says, voice low and rasping, his eyes are dark like sin. Dark like midnight. Pupils blown wide, eyes glazed with desire.

"It's okay if you've never gotten past this part." My voice comes out breathier than I meant. This level of adrenaline in my bloodstream can't be healthy. "I'll point out where the clit is."

He gives a short, unamused laugh before he drags my neckline down more, taking my bra cup with it, and pulls the stiff peak of my nipple between his lips.

My teeth clench at the intense sweep of pleasure through me as he sucks. Every roll and slide of his tongue on my breast tugs at my clit, like there's a cord between the two. My panties are wet. My heart races harder than ever. Alexei Volkov, supreme asshole and controlling dickhead, has my nipple in his mouth, but I'm finding it difficult to care. This feels too good to string thoughts together.

His hand comes to my thigh, skimming over me, sending goosebumps across my skin. I vaguely remember wondering if the slit in this dress was appropriate for a work event.

"What are you doing?" I ask. "You hate me."

"I do hate you." He doesn't look away. Why is that so hot? "But I still want to fuck you."

"Maybe I should go get Dr. Handsome," I say for some reason. I like playing with fire, I guess.

His gaze sharpens. "Don't you fucking dare."

His hand slips higher, pressing between my legs, over my damp panties, and hot, delicious sensation shoots through me.

Holy hell. Volkov and I are actually messing around right now. My body responds, insides turning molten, blood thickening, and intimate muscles clenching around nothing.

A low, stifled noise of pleased surprise rumbles in his chest. God, he's tall. So broad, towering, and powerful. His fingers slip beneath the fabric of my panties. Immediately, he finds my clit, working it with the perfect friction. My knees wobble at the growing ache, and I bite back a moan.

It's not because of him. I've never done this kind of thing with all my colleagues in the next room. It's a thrill. Perhaps I'm an exhibitionist.

Clarity slices through my blurred thoughts. "Anyone could see."

His strong throat works, eyes clouded with lust as his fingers work tight circles that make me feel like I might explode.

"After what just happened, do you think anyone would be surprised to find me in here, fucking my wife?"

Another shocking clench of heat. With his free hand, Volkov reaches for the door we just came through, flips the lock, before he waits, not moving, just watching me, breathing hard, searching my eyes.

"Tell me to stop, Hellfire."

Inside me, something snaps. I want to fuck him, too, and it's not just this messed-up game we're playing. I want to make him lose control. Every time he looks at me, I want him to remember that the woman he finds so repulsive made him lose it.

"This is just sex," I whisper.

We need to relieve the tension so we can spend the rest of this fake marriage ignoring each other. There's no way I'm going to come from this, with *him*, but the urge is still there, shoving me forward.

"What else would it be?"

"Just so we're clear."

I reach for his belt, fumbling. He pushes my hands out of the way, pulls himself out of his boxers, and I gape at the size of his thick cock, jutting out with moisture beading at the tip.

Every quip I made about his age, about his difficulty in the bedroom, skips around my brain, taunting me. Volkov having a cock like that has got to be a joke from the universe.

"Intimidated?" He arches an eyebrow.

"Hardly."

A low, quiet laugh. A condom appears, he rolls it on, before he hoists my thigh up, slides my panties aside, gaze lingering on my heels for a moment before he nudges inside.

My head falls back, eyes closed, jaw slack as I accommodate the intense thickness. My god, he's big.

"Okay?" he grits out, and deep in my chest, something twists. He's not supposed to be checking in on me during a hate fuck.

"Barely feel it," I gasp, palms flat against the wall. "So tiny. Like a baby carrot."

I can barely string words together, it feels so good, and he's not even fully in. He lets out a low, silent laugh like he knows I'm a dirty little liar, his hips thrusting and his cock stretching me until he's fully seated.

Pleasure spirals around the base of my spine at the deep, intense fullness. Oh god. My pulse pounds in my ears. He pulls out and sinks back in with a hard thrust, and my spine bends at the urgent, delicious heat spreading through me.

He thrusts again, and then again, finding a punishing pace

and dissolving my thoughts. The weight of his gaze winds me higher. The pressure inside me grows, doubling, tripling, electric currents running up and down my spine, a desperate ache gathering between my legs.

I stare at his mouth, slanting and taunting me, and desire pounds through me. His eyes burn, pupils blowing wide.

"We said no kissing," he reminds me in a low voice.

"I know." I swallow.

His head falls forward, resting his forehead on the wall as he tilts his face into my hair, inhaling deeply. "I'll make an exception if you ask very nicely."

"No, thanks." I try not to moan the words.

"You want to."

"I don't." I do.

"Beg me, Hellfire. Beg me to kiss you and I will."

I'm so, so tempted, but I'd die before I gave him the satisfaction. "Never. You're bad at it anyway."

"Keep telling yourself that, *good girl*."

My muscles clench around him. Volkov fucks me harder, like he hates me. Like he's putting all his frustration into this. His bowtie has come loose, dangling around his neck.

I hate that I'm going to be thinking about this for the rest of my life.

A spark ignites low in my abdomen. Oh god. This is actually working. No—absolutely not. I don't come during sex. Like he can tell I'm having an existential crisis, my husband fucks me harder, faster, with more urgency.

"You look like you're enjoying yourself, Doctor."

There's something about his sarcastic, knowing, high-handed tone that makes tension coil tighter between my legs. I shouldn't like being spoken to like that, by *him*, but I do.

"Go fuck yourself," I whisper. Not my wittiest insult but I'm struggling to remember my name. I'd rather burst every blood vessel in my brain than give him the satisfaction of a moan, though.

His mouth hooks in a cruel smile like he knows I'm holding back. "It's okay, you can admit it."

Hot. So fucking hot. Who knew he had this in him?

I stare at a spot on the other side of the room, unseeing, thinking about the grossest things I've seen in my job, scrabbling for control. Anything to distract myself.

Orgasms are mental. I hate him and I won't come. He's not even touching my clit. He's using me like a sex toy, hardly even touching me.

Another swirl of heat. Oh god. Do I actually like that? What's wrong with me? Sensations swirl together, tightening and clenching. My skin burns hotter. I can't think. I suck in a sharp breath. Oh my god. *Not going to come not going to come not going to come.* Not here. I can't. I hate him. My eyes close as the heat inside me gathers, that intense unfurling feeling starting. I can hear myself panting.

Is this what sex is like for other people? Because it's never been like this for me.

"Oh, no you fucking don't," he growls in my ear, and a jolt of lust spikes through me at the low, hungry tenor. "Don't you dare come." He fucks me harder. Harder. Oh god. I can't hold back. "This is for me," he rasps.

His thrusts turn jerky and urgent before he tenses. With a stifled groan, he buries his face in my neck. Inside me, I feel him pulsing.

For a long moment, we're frozen. He's still inside me, we're both breathing hard, and in the ballroom next door, I hear Heather wrapping things up. I have the sensation of stopping short at a cliff's edge, pulse racing with adrenaline, left completely unsatisfied.

I look up, and my heart stops at the surprise in his eyes. So that wasn't normal for him, either. I don't even want to think about that.

Alarm bells go off in my head. What am I doing? I can't be having sex with Volkov. He didn't even let me come, the asshole.

With a sharp, sobering breath, I press a hand to his chest. He steps away immediately. Arousal still twists low in my abdomen as I put myself back to rights, adjusting my dress and neckline, feeling the weight of his gaze before I walk back through the door without another word.

"GEORGIA, ARE YOU FEELING OKAY?" Dr. Joshi asks in a low voice after my wife stumbles back to the table. "You're flushed."

The doctor clears her throat. A pretty pink color washes over her cheeks, and I force myself to look away.

We shouldn't have done that, but my blood is humming with interest and satisfaction. The way she looked up at me with that defiant look on her face, fire flashing in her eyes, it just—

"I'm fine," Georgia answers.

Her eyes flick to mine and away again, and all I can think about is the way she looked up at me in the library, like she couldn't look away. How her hot, tight cunt felt around my cock. The fury in her eyes and the powerful surge through my blood when I wouldn't let her come.

Best fuck of my life, I realize with alarm. That's not good.

Never in my *life* have I done something like that. I don't know what came over me. I have the frustrating urge to haul her back there and finish what I started. Watching her disintegrate would be the sweetest thing I ever saw.

Hearing about her work woke up something in me. With

every detail I learn about her, the feeling that I've been wrong grows.

Jesus. I run a hand through my hair. *Get ahold of yourself.*

That Dr. Handjob is looking at her again, and jealousy tightens in my gut. It doesn't matter that she's only my wife in name. He doesn't know that. As far as he's concerned, she's mine.

"You've barely touched your dessert," Dr. Joshi adds with concern.

Georgia's gaze cuts to mine and her shoulders straighten. What happened back there won't happen again, and this arousal lingering low in my gut? It's a natural physical response. I still don't like her.

She's just so fucking *mouthy* all the time, and taking control over her and seeing the way she responded to it gave me a sense of victory I rarely feel these days.

"The smell of my husband's aftershave turns my stomach," she tells Dr. Joshi.

My mouth twitches. There we go. There's the woman I know and love to fight with.

I lean back and settle my arm over the top of her chair. "Maybe you're pregnant."

She chokes on her water. At the next table, Dr. Handjob drops his fork with a loud clatter.

"Oh?" Dr. Joshi looks stunned but pleased.

"I'm not," the doctor says quickly. "Definitely not pregnant."

"You don't know that." I find the ends of her hair. "We're not always careful."

It's a wonder I don't burst into flames right here, with the way the doctor's glowering at me. My chest expands with pressure and I bring my mouth closer to her ear.

"What's the matter, Hellfire?" I murmur. Her hair's soft, just like I thought it would be. "You seem tense."

The doctor's hand settles on my thigh and my cock jumps, but a moment later, something sharp pokes me. My knee jumps and hits the bottom of the table, making the plates and glasses clink.

I look down to see the doctor's retreating hand wrapped around her fork.

"Muscle spasm," I explain to the table before lowering my voice again. "Did you just stab me with your fork?"

She smiles, fire raging in her eyes. "Sorry, *baby*. My hand slipped."

"Brat."

She rolls her eyes, and I have the weirdest urge to laugh.

Our gazes hold, and an ache throbs low in my abdomen. Such pretty eyes, such a mesmerizing, unique caramel color. Long lashes that fluttered as I fucked her.

I shouldn't have done it, and it won't happen again. We can't be doing stuff like that.

———

"We're never doing that again," she says as we drive home.

A sickening thought slams into me: Did I go too far?

A curl of shame unfolds in my gut—I don't act like that during sex. I've wanted to, but I never act on it.

"Did I hurt you?" I ask in alarm. Our eyes meet, hers confused. "Earlier?"

Maybe I went too hard or fast. Maybe she's sore. The idea of causing the doctor actual pain and discomfort splashes cold water over my arousal.

"No." She snorts.

"I'm serious."

"Volkov, I'm fine. Relax. I'm not going to go to the media and ruin your career."

"That's not what I was worried about." The thought never crossed my mind.

"You didn't hurt me."

Relief settles in my body and I loosen my hold on the steering wheel.

"This is an agreement." She studies her nails. "Let's do ourselves a favor and keep it uncomplicated."

I think about what I learned about her tonight. She created a world-renowned research program studying athletes. It's clearly her passion. Her colleagues rave about her, she's got this guy at work bidding thousands of dollars to take her out as a *friend,* and she had a university scholarship to play soccer.

I think about earlier, and the desperate frustration in her eyes when I wouldn't let her come. I picture myself carrying her up the stairs to bed and burying my head between her legs to reward her. The urge to take care of her pounds through me.

And *that* is why we can't do this again. I'm not going to do something stupid and start caring about this woman.

"Fine by me."

What else don't I know about her? For the first time, I wonder why she needs her inheritance so desperately.

I don't care. I don't want to know.

"We need to go to these kinds of things together," I add. "I don't want to catch you going on another *date*."

She huffs a laugh. "Lucky you, then. My parents are having a party next weekend. They've been begging to meet you."

The Greenes want to meet me?

A bad taste fills my mouth. The Greenes run in the same social circles as Emma's family. Georgia might even know Emma. Their party will be catered with staff in uniforms, serving the finest champagne. The out-of-touch guests will complain about the government using their tax dollars on the poor, or how many immigrants are being let into the country.

I was wrong about her being spoiled and selfish. I was wrong about her wanting to marry rich and live a life of leisure.

Maybe I was wrong about her family. Maybe they're nothing like Emma's.

I thought I had her all figured out, but now I'm realizing I don't know *anything* about my wife.

I'M SITTING in the kitchen, waiting for the doctor to get home so we can go to this party with her family, trying not to think about what we did after at the benefit last week, when curiosity gets the best of me, and I open that social media app she was using a few weeks ago.

I'm forced to make an account to view her profile. She's easy to find, with a surprising number of followers, and I hit the 'follow' button before spending a few minutes browsing through her photos. Lots of her with Jordan and Darcy, a few at work, a selfie in Hawaii from the summer. I remember exactly how she looked in a swimsuit—lush curves on display. I'm clicking different parts of her profile when I find the tagged pictures. Another collection of images pops up with her in them.

One of them, though, looks different. @doc.georgia.-greene.queen is an account dedicated to her outfits. Some images are pulled from her own account, some are from people spotting her out in the wild, usually walking in or out of the arena.

She has a fan account? I hit Follow.

I'm looking at the picture of us on the plane the other week

—hottest couple in the NHL, one comment says—when I get a waft of that familiar violet scent.

"Stalking me?" she says over my shoulder and my watch goes off again.

"Jesus." I tuck my phone away. "Don't sneak up on me."

She lifts her brows and sends a pointed look at my phone. "I saw that. My favorite comment is the one that says, *Volkov looks at his wife the way I look at a double quarter pounder with cheese.*"

No, I don't. Do I? The back of my neck feels hot.

She smirks, cool and indifferent, like the library never even happened. Like she hasn't thought about it once.

And then there's me—who can't stop replaying it. Can't stop jerking off thinking about being buried in her tight, hot pussy. Can't stop hearing the little panting noises she made as she got closer to the edge, as she started to clasp me harder inside her.

She wants to pretend it didn't happen? Fine. I will, too.

"Are you ready to go?" I ask, glancing at the time.

"Not even close." She gives me a strange look before gesturing to the garment bag she draped over the stool beside me. I was so absorbed in looking at photos of her that I didn't even notice. "We need to go in costume."

I unzip the bag and recognize the superhero costume in an instant. "Batman? Do you have a mask kink or something?"

"What's the kink called where I don't want to look at your face?"

My mouth twitches and the urge to laugh tightens in my abdomen. After what happened at her work benefit, though, the last thing we need is to be laughing together. I'm already having a hard time not thinking about it.

Night and day, all I think about is fucking her. The flare of lust in her eyes when I didn't let her come.

She liked being told what to do, and even worse, I liked it, too.

Her hair's down around her shoulders, glossy and wavy, begging to be touched. Makeup done in a way that makes her eyes sparkle harder, her lips more distracting. She's wearing a T-shirt and those leggings again. "What are you going as?"

She smirks. "You'll see." She makes a shooing gesture. "Go get changed. I'll meet you down here in twenty."

Twenty minutes later, I sit in the living room wearing the surprisingly high quality Batman costume, holding the mask in my hand, inspecting it.

Where'd she get this? It fits me like it was made for me.

The sound of her footsteps has me looking up to the top of the stairs, and my jaw goes slack. My wife makes her way down in a tight black catsuit, every curve and dip of her body hugged by leather. Heels sky-high, pointy, and sharp.

In an instant, I'm half hard.

My watch goes off and I silence it. Why did we agree not to have sex again?

"You're wearing that to your parents' house?" I scratch the back of my neck. "Won't they, uh."

Holy fuck, she looks hot. This isn't good.

"Won't they what?"

"Hmm?" I jerk my gaze up, and her smile turns deadly. "You're dressing like *that* to a family event?"

She snorts. "My mom was the one who lent me these costumes."

What? I picture a stiff-lipped older woman dripping in jewelry, with a permanent sour look on her face, like Emma's mother.

This doesn't make sense.

"Whatever." I rub the bridge of my nose, praying for this evening to end quickly. "Let's get this over with."

———

The doctor directs me to a modest, two-story home in a quiet, middle-class suburb of Vancouver.

The feeling that I've been wrong gathers energy inside me.

My parents live three blocks away. They wouldn't let me buy them anything expensive when I started getting the big paychecks, because my mom didn't want to clean a big house. I said I'd hire a cleaner, and she just laughed.

Those Greenes wouldn't live in this neighborhood. They'd live in Shaughnessy, in something like the mansion where the benefit took place.

We park the car, my wife gets out, and as she walks in front of me, my gaze falls to her ass in that catsuit. Her body looks incredible. Georgia Greene was born to wear a black leather catsuit.

She leads me to a house where the front lawn has been made to look like a graveyard, realistic-looking gravestones spaced out across the grass, fog spilling out among them. Ghost-like figures hang from the trees, swaying in the wind and illuminated by creepy lights. In front of the gravestones, mounds of dirt and—

"Fuck!" I yell as a hand shoots out of the mound nearest me. My watch goes off again.

Georgia snorts. "It's wired to a motion sensor."

The hand retreats back into the dirt, and I give her a baffled look, my pulse returning to normal. *This* is her parents' house? It's average. Middle class. We can hear people inside, talking and laughing. Music playing.

She reaches to open the front door but my hand comes to her arm. "You'll need to call me Alexei." It never bothered me before, but it bothers me now. "We're married. Married people don't call each other by their last names."

"You call me Doctor."

"That's different. Everyone thinks it's a cute nickname." The corner of my mouth threatens to tug up. "I could call you *gniloy kluben* if you prefer."

If she knew what it meant, though, she wouldn't prefer it.

"Right." Her eyes narrow, the cogs in her head turning. "What does that mean again?"

"Sweetheart."

"Hmm." Her eyelids are tiny slits now. "I don't believe you."

"I don't care." I shrug. "But you're my wife. You should call me Alexei."

"Alexei," she repeats slowly, and I'm distracted by the way her lips look.

"There you go. Not so hard, is it?"

"Shut up, Alexei," she says to herself. "Don't choke on your dinner, Alexei. Your tooth fell into your drink, Alexei. Hmm. You're right. It's not so bad."

I clear my throat, shaking my head to myself. There she is. "Done?"

"For now."

"All right. Let's go."

"BELLA, WHERE HAVE YOU BEEN, LOCA?" A man in his late forties approaches with a big smile—and vampire teeth. He wears a gray wool coat, button-up shirt, and jeans, but has pale makeup and silver glitter all over his skin.

"Dad. No." My wife closes her eyes briefly, trying not to smile. "Your character doesn't even say that."

This is her *dad*? He's so young.

"There's my little troublemaker." Her dad wraps her in a big hug.

I glance around the home, at all the Halloween decorations, the partygoers who look like average people.

"Shane." A woman wearing a long brown wig with red contact lenses approaches. Also late forties. Also wearing the vampire teeth. "The line is, '*This is the skin of a killer, Bella.*'"

They both turn to me, smiling with their weird vampire teeth. My gaze snags on the woman's smile, and I'm hit with the resemblance to her daughter.

"This must be our new son-in-law," the guy says, beaming at me.

"Alexei Volkov." My heart thumps.

"Oh, we know. I'm a huge fan. Shane Greene." We shake hands, and I try to conceal my confusion. "And this is my wife, Georgia's mom, Cece."

"It's so nice to finally meet you." Cece beams. I reach to shake her hand but she bats it away. "No way. I'm a hugger."

She wraps her arms around me and squeezes. Emma's parents never hugged me once. I don't think they even shook my hand when they first met me.

"Georgia's told us such nice things about you," she says when she pulls back.

"Has she?" I give my wife an arch look. "That doesn't sound like her at all."

Cece cackles and Shane starts laughing.

"Well, Jordan told us you're a good fit for our Georgia," she says. "Congratulations. We're very happy for you two." Her mom steps back to look at me in approval. "The costume fits!"

"It does. Thank you?" I give her an odd look. Is it hers? Georgia didn't say where it came from.

"I'm in film," she explains. "Wardrobe department."

She works. Of course she does, because these are clearly not those Greenes.

Fucking hell. Just another thing I've been so wrong about.

Shane says something to Cece, who laughs. I'm not listening. I'm just confused, turning over the pieces of information I have about Georgia and her family, inspecting them for where I went so wrong. My eyes slide to my wife, whose mouth tilts in a smug expression, eyes sparkling.

A weird rush of adrenaline hits my bloodstream.

Cece lights up. "I almost forgot." She reaches for my wife's hand. "Let me see the—oh." She stares at the plain ugly ring on Georgia's finger. "Well. That's very subtle." She's surprised, but not upset. Maybe a little confused, though.

Georgia gives her mom a tight smile. "I didn't want anything too flashy. It would cut up the gloves at work."

"That makes perfect sense," Cece says.

I have to give Cece credit—she's a lot more polite than my mom was. *You want to keep her?* my mom said. *Spoil her.*

That won't be happening. Before, I would have said the doctor spoils herself enough, but now I don't know.

I look around at this house. I don't know anything anymore.

"Alexei, do your parents live local?" Shane asks.

I nod, trying to focus. "My dad's a mechanic and my mom is a florist."

Cece frowns. "Wait. What's your mom's name?"

"Maria."

Her jaw drops. "Shut up." She starts to grin, and again, I see resemblance to Georgia in her smile. "Shut *up*." They even sound the same. "I know Maria. I go to her shop all the time." She nudges Shane. "Maria's Flowers."

Georgia and I glance at each other with concerned expressions. "You know my mom?"

"She said her son was a hockey player and I didn't put two and two together." She gives me a good-natured shrug. "Shane's the hockey fan. I don't really follow it."

Shane shakes his head. "What a small world."

Georgia and I look at each other in shock. Our parents are already *friends*?

I don't like this.

"We'll have to all go to a game together," her dad says, and her mom lights up.

The doorbell rings and her parents excuse themselves to answer it, leaving my wife and me alone. She leads me to the living room, where people are gathered. A few say hello and introduce themselves. Photos sit on shelves, hanging from the wall, and I have the urge to study each one, gathering more clues about the woman who I clearly don't know anything about.

This doesn't add up. I stare at her, as if her thick lashes and the freckles across her nose and cheekbones hold clues.

My hand comes around her waist. The leather is warm from her skin, and there's a dip above her hip where my hand fits perfectly. Our eyes meet and we both look away fast.

"Did your parents have you when they were twelve?" I ask.

"Close. Seventeen."

They had her at *seventeen*? My expression must show my disbelief because she tilts her chin at a nearby photo of a very young version of her father holding her. He looks like a teenager.

"You don't have to keep a hand on me at all times, you know."

"We need to look married," I mutter. And I . . . just want to. I look around at their house again. "I thought you came from money."

She snorts. "With two teenage parents trying to raise a baby and finish school?"

"So you're not from those Greenes. Who's the inheritance from?"

"My grandfather, one of *those* Greenes." She presses her lips together, gaze darting to mine. "He cut my dad off when my mom got pregnant with me and my dad stayed with her," she admits.

What an asshole. Between that and the clause in his will, no wonder she's always calling me controlling.

The bad feeling intensifies. The spoiled, self-centered, superficial picture I've built of Dr. Georgia Greene begins to disintegrate.

"But your shoes."

I'm scrambling for something, *anything*, that means I haven't been treating her like shit for two years for no reason.

Yesterday, I caught a glance of her at the arena, wearing high, black velvet heels with little ankle straps. Her ankles looked so delicate, like I could wrap my hands around them, and the buckles were so tiny, I doubt I could even undo them.

I don't know why I'm thinking about taking her shoes off.

"Yes, I love beautiful things. I love that clothes make me feel amazing, and I love quality fabrics and pretty, pretty shoes, but I don't spend nearly as much money as you think I do." Her eyes sear me, defiant and annoyed. "Besides, what's wrong with spending money on myself? I work hard. I paid for school myself. So what if I want to buy myself things once in a while."

"You didn't pay for school yourself." She couldn't have.

Full scholarship, Dr. Joshi said at the benefit, about Georgia playing soccer in university. I've been so distracted, thinking about fucking her hard in the library, that I forgot.

"Why do you think I drive such a crappy car? I just finished paying off loans. I'm not about to jump back into debt." At whatever my expression is, she smirks. "What's the matter, *Alexei?*" She puts extra emphasis on my name, even though we're speaking so quietly, we won't be overheard. Her pink tongue flashes as she says the *l.* "Doesn't match up with the spoiled rich-girl princess image you had in your mind?"

"You didn't correct me."

"Maybe you don't know everything about me," she adds, looking away, and there's an ache in my chest.

In an instant, I hate myself.

I thought she was spoiled, selfish, and privileged, but she's dedicated to her career, hard-working, and well-liked by her colleagues.

I thought she had everything growing up, but she may have had even less than I did.

I thought her parents would be conceited, insufferable snobs, but they're warm, down to earth, and welcoming.

I thought I hated Dr. Georgia Greene, but I think I may have been very, very wrong.

"TELL us how you two got together," Cece urges later.

Georgia and I exchange a look.

After Cece insisted on leading us through the haunted house in the backyard that she and Shane created, we're inside again, in the living room with Cece, Shane, and a small group of their family friends. Every so often, the doorbell rings with a trick-or-treater and Shane gets up to answer it.

"I didn't ask her out for a long time because I thought she had a boyfriend," I say, holding her gaze.

Her eyes narrow.

"Actually," I tell Cece, "I thought she had two boyfriends."

Georgia looks away but her mouth slides to the side in a half smile.

"Two boyfriends?" Cece asks, laughing. "Georgia?"

Georgia gives her a wry look. "He heard me talking about Stefan and Damon. My rabbits," she explains for everyone else, and they laugh. "He was so jealous."

"I was a little jealous," I admit.

Georgia gives me a look of amused disbelief, and I know she's also thinking about me saying *no fucking other guys*. "*Very* jealous."

"Okay. Yes." I rub the back of my neck. "Very jealous."

Everyone's chuckling and smiling. We're selling this like pros.

"I always thought you two didn't get along." Cece exchanges a smile with Shane. "She spoke about you like she hated you."

"She did. We argued every time we saw each other." I look down at my wife, gaze snagging on the mesmerizing color of her eyes. "I wanted her, but I couldn't have her."

The words slip out so easily, and from the way the women around the table melt and exchange smiles, they must sound believable.

I put my arm over the back of Georgia's chair and let my fingers toy with the soft ends of her hair.

"One day," I add, "I got tired of waiting."

Georgia turns her head, bringing her mouth close to my ear, lowering her voice. "And *I'm* the spoiled one, huh?"

I give her hair a light tug and surprise mixed with something else flares in her eyes. Amusement, maybe. Arousal?

Probably not. I doubt it.

Shane shakes his head. "I knew Georgia liked him."

Under my arm, she stiffens. "No, you didn't."

"I did," he insists, laughing, and the pink growing on my wife's cheeks distracts me. "I knew she had a crush on you because of how she always got so twitchy when your name came up."

I don't know why this makes me feel like laughing. Maybe because I can picture the pissed-off expression she'd wear. I tug on her hair again, and the deadly look she sends me makes my pulse skip a beat.

"Has Georgia made you watch *The Vampire Diaries* yet?" her mom asks.

At my dumb expression, Georgia's eyes widen in an

emphasizing look. "It's the show I love, remember?" Her eyebrows lift. "The one about teen vampires, that I named my bunnies after?"

If our marriage was real, I'd know this about her.

"Right." I nod. "That one. We've watched a few episodes."

She pushes her hair back over her shoulder, and my gaze catches on her ring. I bought the cheap piece of metal online. One day shipping. The thought of her having to wear something so cheap and ugly nearly made me smile.

Now, buying her a cheap ring just feels like a low blow. Possessive feelings race through me. She's getting a bigger ring. Something flashy and expensive that tells everyone within eyesight that she's taken.

"You named your rabbits after two teen vampires?" I mutter back.

"They're not teenagers, they're hundreds of years old. They just go to high school and date teenagers."

She says this like it's normal. I grimace. "That's weird."

"It is weird, but in a hot way, so we don't think too hard about it." Her eyebrows bob up and down. "Careful, Volkov, or I'll get you hooked on the show and make you eat your words."

Her mouth curves into that half smile she does, the one where her eyes glint with mischief, and my pulse trips, but she turns to address the table.

"I wasn't fooled." She gives them a smug smile. "Alexei was always drooling over my shoes. It was only a matter of time before he was begging me to marry him."

"You're the one who would be begging," I mutter, but energy hums through me.

"Never." She's speaking so low only we can hear, giving me a gentle, pretty smile as if we're talking like lovers. "There's nothing you could do that would make me beg."

My thoughts still. My blood pumps harder as I replay her

words over and over again in my head. Through my body, electricity crackles.

I like the idea of the doctor begging.

"How'd you propose?" someone asks.

"Which time?" The doctor's mouth quirks and when she flicks that knowing, smug look at me, my cock twitches. "He had to ask a couple times."

"I wore her down eventually." I let my arm fall so it's resting on her shoulders. "My little Hellfire."

Georgia turns her head to me slowly, her eyes flashing with warning and fury.

"Hellfire?" Shane asks, grinning. "Is that your romantic nickname for my daughter, Alexei?"

"No," Georgia says, shoulders tense.

"Yes," I say at the same time. "She used to get on my nerves so much that I swore she was forged in Hellfire." My gaze flicks to her hair, strands of auburn glowing gold under the dining room lighting. "And the hair."

"The nickname suits you, honey," her mom says, smiling.

"It doesn't suit me." Georgia rolls her eyes. "He's just teasing."

As the conversation moves on, a realization strikes me.

Hugo Greene died years ago. It was in the news. She's had the option to get the inheritance for years.

"What do you need the money for?" I ask her quietly.

Our eyes meet, hers going guarded and wary.

"You obviously need it for something if you were willing to marry me," I add. "And don't even try to tell me it's for shoes."

I can't believe I fell for that.

"I saw these bunny palaces online." Her eyes spark. "Stefan and Damon will get a whole house and staff. There's a waterslide, too."

"Very funny."

She rolls her eyes. "Don't worry what I need the money for."

I'm going to find out why she needs that money.

CHAPTER 42

GEORGIA

A FEW EVENINGS LATER, I'm sitting in the front room of Volkov's house, waiting for my rideshare to soccer, when Darcy texts me.

Have you seen this? It's a link.

The social media profile has no picture, no photos, and no bio, but a *lot* of followers. A new account, it seems.

@alexeivolkov.

I make a face—why'd he make an account? He doesn't care about this stuff. When I click to see who the two accounts he's following are, though, my heart stops.

One is mine. With my new hockey wife status, I get more new followers now than I can keep up with. I didn't notice him adding me.

The other account is @doc.georgia.greene.queen, a fashion account dedicated to my outfits. A funny feeling loops through me.

Interesting. He must have clued in that social media is a way for us to fake it without having to interact. I find the picture I took with Volkov at my parents' Halloween party and post it. My phone starts buzzing immediately with comments and likes.

Volkov can park his Batmobile in my cave anytime, someone comments, and I laugh, studying the image.

God, he looked hot in that costume.

I can't stop thinking about what we did in the library. He didn't let me come—*asshole!*—and I should hate that. He showed his true colors. Controlling, dominant asshole.

I shouldn't be thinking about it so much. The day after the Halloween party, a bouquet of flowers arrived at my hospital office.

Candytuft—indifference.

The message is crystal clear. I can't be thinking about him, and I definitely can't be thinking about how hot he is.

He clears his throat and I drop my phone. I didn't even hear him get home.

"Staring at a picture of me?" he asks, mouth crooking.

"I was staring at myself," I volley back, face going hot. "Because I'm so self-absorbed."

His eyes trail over my outfit—leggings, raincoat, and sneakers. He's wearing a casual navy blue jacket, the same luxurious navy as the tux he wore to the benefit last week.

He folds his arms over his chest, gaze flicking over me. "I guess asking where you're going will get me nothing but a middle finger."

"I'm going to soccer." I don't know why I told him that.

"Why aren't you taking your car?"

"Something's wrong with it," I say absently, glancing up and down the street.

"I thought my dad fixed your spark plugs."

"He did. I think it's something else."

A tense pause. "Why didn't you tell me?"

I give him an alarmed look. "Why would I?"

His throat works before he pulls out his phone. A moment

later, he's speaking Russian. The conversation ends in a few sentences and he slips the phone back in his pocket.

"Let's go." He gestures to the hall leading to the garage. "I'm driving you."

"I've already called a ride."

"Cancel it."

My shoulders hitch at being told what to do, and again, for the tenth time this hour, I think about us in the library. A shiver runs across my skin, and I take a deep, sobering breath.

I really need to stop thinking about what we did. I open my mouth to protest but he gives me a hard look.

"I'm not letting my wife take a Lyft late at night."

A light laugh slips out of me. "It's six pm."

"It's dark out."

We narrow our eyes at each other and my pulse does another one of those excited jumps.

"Georgia." He sighs, rubbing the bridge of his nose like I'm the most exasperating woman on the planet. "Get in the fucking car before I make you."

A thrill runs up my spine. In my hand, my phone buzzes with a message. My car is delayed.

He takes a step toward me, glowering. "If I need to—"

"Okay, *fine*." I stand. "Wow. Bossy." I cancel the ride on my app and head to the garage as my husband's heavy footsteps sound behind me. "You don't need to follow me like a body-guard, Volkov. I'm not going to make a run for it."

He gives me a dark look, and when I return it with a pretty, patient smile, his jaw flexes.

"Where am I going?" he asks when we climb in the car.

"Fir and Twelfth."

We drive in silence for a few minutes before he flicks an irritated glance at me. "You're buying a new car."

"Volkov, I didn't ask you to drive me. Besides, I don't need a new car. Don't tell me what to do."

"Your car is a piece of shit. It isn't safe."

We're approaching the school where we practice. "Here's fine."

"This intersection? Tell me where you're going and I'll drive you there."

Why won't he drop this? "Volkov, stop being so stubborn."

Outrage flashes in his expression. "*You're* the stubborn one. I'm not letting you traipse around dark alleys in the middle of the night."

"Again, it's *six thirty*. If you let me out here, it's easier for you."

"Since when have you cared about making things easier for me?"

He doesn't say it unkindly, and there's a tiny, minuscule spark in his eyes when he glances at me sidelong that *almost* looks like he's laughing.

"If I didn't know you better, I'd say you were making a joke."

He stares at me and makes a low, growly noise in his throat that I find annoyingly hot. "I want to make sure you're safe," he says quietly, still wearing that serious, hard expression, and for some reason, I actually believe him.

This is weird. We don't act like this with each other. Volkov's an asshole—he doesn't get protective and caring.

The light turns green. "Up another half block and then turn right onto Helmcken."

A minute later, he parks in front of the school. I can already see the girls gathering at the field. I open the door and slide out.

"Thanks for the ride." I close the door behind me, but his door opens, and he gets out of the car. "No. No, no." I'm shaking my head. "What are you doing?"

He gives me a look I can't decipher. "You're just going to end up calling me for a ride home, anyways."

As if. I'd never ask for his help. And now he's going to spend the night watching me coach, judging me and telling me how bad I am at it?

"Fine." I shrug like I'm unaffected. "Make yourself useful."

CHAPTER 43
ALEXEI

"LAST FIFTEEN MINUTES," my wife calls to the girls forty-five minutes later. "You know what that means."

"Scrimmage?" one of the girls asks with a hopeful smile.

Georgia grins and nods. "Scrimmage."

Excitement ripples through the team, each player wearing a sharp-looking red and black soccer kit. The Vancouver Devils. Everything tonight has been about rehabilitation and healing. They've done an easy warm-up, physio exercises, and low-impact skill work, but I can tell they're itching for more.

"Easy mode, though," she tells them with a *this means business* expression. "Slow it down. This is not the time to push too hard."

They divvy up the teams and start the game.

"How's the knee, Isabel?" she asks a player who's wearing a knee brace.

"Fine," the girl calls back.

"You sure?"

The girl gives her the thumbs-up.

"Sometimes she forgets she's injured and goes too hard," Georgia says quietly, still watching Isabel.

Within a few minutes, one girl steals the ball and kicks it at the net. It sails past the goaltender.

"Yes!" Georgia shouts, clapping hard, smiling like she never smiles at me. "There we go. That was beautiful. It's okay, Beth," she calls to the goaltender. "That was a tricky shot. You'll get it next time. Thank you for not diving."

The goaltender blows a raspberry, and Georgia laughs.

Speechless, I watch her. I don't know what I expected, but it wasn't this. The game continues, the girls scramble for the ball, taking shots at either net. They're laughing. They're having fun. They love her.

She's a great coach. I've never seen her so at ease, so determined and enthusiastic. She never shows me this side.

This is the version of her from the photo at the benefit. This is the person Darcy, Owens, and Jordan are friends with.

It hits me. The inheritance the doctor needs so badly? It has something to do with this.

———

Half an hour later, after the soccer equipment has been locked away in the storage room and the girls have all been picked up, Georgia and I walk to the car.

"What?" She gives me a strange look, and I realize I'm staring.

I clear my throat and look away. "Nothing."

Frustration tightens in my shoulders. So I was wrong about her. We're complete opposites. She said I was a lost cause.

When we get to the car, I have the urge to open her door for her, but that would be weird. She'd think it was weird.

I do it anyway, and she raises an eyebrow at me.

See? Weird.

I start the car and glance over at her just as she's reaching for her seatbelt. "Put your seatbelt on," I say, because I feel like playing with her.

"Don't tell me what to do."

The corner of my mouth twitches. Such a fucking brat. "Don't tell me you'd go without a seatbelt just to piss me off, Doctor." I rev the engine once in warning.

"I don't know. I really love getting on your nerves."

"You're good at it, too."

That pretty mouth curves before she clicks her seatbelt into place.

We pull onto the road. Something about the way she was with the soccer team keeps snagging my thoughts. Across the front seat, she's staring out the window, playing with her necklace.

She wrenches around and reaches into her bag in the backseat, pulling out one of those protein bars she's always eating.

"Do you ever eat real food?"

She arches an eyebrow at me before her eyes narrow. "Yes."

"Because all I ever see you eat are those protein bars." I'm picking a fight, but I can't seem to stop myself. "You need to eat a balanced diet."

"You know I went to medical school, right? I don't need you to lecture me on how to eat."

Our gazes hold, tension snapping in the air, and I'm back in the library with my tongue on her nipple, listening to her shallow breathing. Frustration rages inside me. She's just so—I can't even—god-fucking-damnit, the doctor gets under my skin. She's doing this just to piss me off.

And it's working, which pisses me off more.

We never should have done what we did.

I yank my gaze back to the road. "You need your inheritance for this, don't you?" I tilt my head in the direction we came from.

Our eyes meet, hers flaring with something guarded.

"I'm right, aren't I?" I press.

She tucks her hand beneath her thigh, and I think about how that thigh felt, hitched up as I buried myself inside her.

Jesus. I need to stop thinking about that.

"The program's funding was cut." She doesn't meet my eyes.

There we go. So that's why she didn't marry some guy when her grandfather died a few years ago. "What about the proceeds from the benefit?"

"It's not nearly enough. The program costs at least a million a year."

"And your inheritance is . . . ?"

"Ten million," she says simply.

Something clunks in my chest. "You're giving ten million dollars away?"

"I don't know why I told you that," she says quietly, and I don't like the way I feel. I don't like that she can't trust me with these things.

I deserve it, after how I treated her, but I don't like it.

"It matters to you." I glance over at her.

Her eyes meet mine, and her chin lifts half an inch, eyes determined. "It matters to me."

Another heavy, uncomfortable clunk in my chest, and I yank my gaze back to the road.

"I met Walker's parents," I blurt out, running a hand over my hair. "They came to the game a couple weeks ago."

A beat passes where she stares at me and I feel like a fool. I don't know why I said that. I guess I just—I found out something about her, and I didn't like how uneven we were. We always even the score.

She regards me with curiosity. "What are they like?"

"Nice. They're proud of him." I hesitate. "They thanked me for working with him." A lick of shame hits me in the gut.

Her eyebrows lift. "What's wrong with that?"

"I haven't done anything. I'm going to tell Ward it's not working out." I've been flipping back and forth on it in my head since that meeting with Ward, since he told me I was getting a lifetime achievement award from the NHL.

For some reason, I want to know what the doctor thinks about it, though.

"What? Why?" Her eyes go wide with alarm.

"Because nothing I'm doing is helping. The kid's playing worse than he did last season when he joined the team." My gut twists. "If things stay the same, he's going to get hurt."

It'll be my fault. I'm failing him.

She's quiet for a moment, studying me. I wish I knew what she was thinking. "He needs you."

I rear back. "No, he doesn't. He's better off without me. I thought you'd be the first to agree."

"He needs you," she says again. Her gaze is pensive and searching. Determined, too. My heart beats harder. "These rookies are scared shitless their first year in the NHL. The guys are bigger and faster and meaner and want to win more. The pressure's more intense. They were one of the best guys on the team in the minors or in college but now they're back on the bottom rung of the ladder. And they're alone. Ward's the best coach I've ever worked with, but his attention is split between an entire team and staff."

My throat feels tight as I think back to my first few years in the league, when everything was so uncertain. Walker's an annoying, overconfident little shit—but I hate the idea of him being scared.

"Luca's a good kid," she says.

"I know." I sound defensive.

"He needs you." The piercing way she looks at me makes me uncomfortable. "He's talented."

And yet I can't figure out how to help him.

She frowns out the window, chewing her bottom lip. It's addictive, seeing the doctor like this, without her tough armor. Soft and thoughtful.

"He could be really great, you know?" Her wistful tone tugs at something behind my ribcage. "And you could be a part of that, if you wanted to be."

"Halfway out the door to retirement? Glued together with pins and K-tape?" I'm baiting her, trying to get her to insult me. It's easier when we play that game.

She shakes her head, still watching me in that way that makes me feel exposed. "He'd be lucky to get that far, Alexei. If he could have the career you've had, I bet that would make Walker and his parents very, very happy."

Silence stretches between us. I don't know what to say. I'm trying to think of some rude quip or comment but I'm coming up blank.

She called me Alexei again. She complimented my career.

We spend the rest of the drive home in silence, saying a stilted *goodnight* to each other before heading to our separate rooms.

When I get into bed, instead of passing out immediately like normal, I lie there for a long time, thinking about the way she looked at me when she told me Walker needed me, the emotion in her eyes, and how she called me *Alexei*.

CHAPTER 44
ALEXEI

FIRST THING THE NEXT MORNING, I find the rookie in the gym, lifting weights. "Question for you, Walker."

He checks his form in the mirror before starting another set. "Shoot."

"Are you scared shitless?"

He freezes and his eyes meet mine. "What?"

"Are you scared shitless? Because this is your first year in the NHL?"

He blinks like this is the last thing he expected me to say.

All night, I thought about what she'd said. He doesn't have a contract. He's a free agent, so at the end of this season, Ward needs to decide what to do with him.

"Yeah. Of course I am." His eyes dart to mine again. "This is my shot, you know? I screwed it up once and was sent back to the college team."

Right. Darcy mentioned that when she was looking through his old game tape.

His throat works. "I don't want that to happen again. I want to stay on the team more than anything."

He meets my eyes, and Georgia was right—the rookie's scared shitless.

A renewed sense of purpose courses through me. I can't give up on this kid. More than ever, I need to help him succeed this season. I need to figure out how to get through to the rookie.

"You'll get there," I say for some reason. "You're talented and smart, and if you've come this far, you know how to work hard. We'll figure it out together."

Walker gives me an odd smile, and I clear my throat, embarrassed.

"Did you actually just pay me a compliment?"

"Don't let it go to your head," I tell him with an eye roll. "Like I said, you have a lot of work to do." I turn and walk away. "Don't be late to our practice tomorrow."

In the mirror, I see Walker salute me. "Yes, sir," he says with that annoying cocky grin.

Determination races through me as I head to meet my trainer. How could I even consider cutting the rookie loose? I'm going to help him have an incredible season, but now I need to figure out how.

This matters to me, she said last night in the car about her program at work, about her soccer team.

Looks like I just found something that matters to *me*.

VOLKOV HAS BEEN AWAY for two days when the doorbell rings. Alexei's tiny, lovely mother stands on the doorstep.

"Hi." I blink down at her and she beams up at me.

"I didn't know Cece was your mom!" she says by way of greeting, giving my arm a squeeze and breezing past me into the house, carrying two big bags. "I brought food. You need to eat."

Why is your mother here? I text him as she heads to the kitchen.

"Alexei isn't home," I call after her. "And I was just about to leave."

I wasn't, but I need to get rid of her without hurting her feelings, because if I hurt Maria's feelings, I'd never forgive myself. My phone buzzes in my hand.

I mentioned you were alone for a couple days.

I give my phone an emphasizing look, eyes wide, as if he can see it. What happened to *you can't get close to them*? He was right. This whole thing is going nowhere.

Te hate fuck was distracting, but I have a new memory taking up space in my head these days: Alexei driving in the car after soccer, admitting that he doesn't know how to help Luca.

Another bouquet arrived at my office today. *Sainfoin—agitation.* Honestly, it's a relief. The last thing I need is him losing his head over me. No feelings, no attachments, no complications. That's what we agreed to, and that's what's easiest.

Maria's making noises in the kitchen, opening drawers and turning on the oven. "It won't take that long," she calls to me. "Alexei said something about you surviving on protein bars."

———

After I've eaten so much I might die, Maria insists on sitting in the front room with the bunnies, who freely roam the house when my horrible husband isn't home.

"Who's the sweetest baby in the world?" Maria strokes Stefan's head and he lays there with his eyes closed. "You are." She looks to Damon, sitting on my lap. "And you are, too." She meets my eyes and smiles. "Alexei was worried about you, alone in this big house all week."

I stifle the urge to snort. No, he wasn't. "Worried I'd set the place on fire, maybe."

She gives me an odd look. That's not the kind of thing a loving wife would say.

"From my cooking," I add. "I'm a terrible cook." Something jumps into my memory, the perfect distraction. "There's something I was hoping you could help me translate. I don't know how to spell it. *Gniloy kluben?*"

Her brow furrows in confusion. "Say it again?"

I repeat it. I've googled variations of it a hundred times but I can't find it.

She squints for a long moment before recognition dawns. "Oh. Rotten tuber."

I couldn't have heard right. "I'm sorry, Maria, can you repeat that? It sounds like you said *rotten tuber*."

"Yes. Rotten tuber."

I'm going to murder him.

"*Dirty* rotten tuber," she adds. "My parents were farmers, and they'd feed scraps and anything that's gone bad to the pigs, but sometimes a vicious mold would infect the turnips. The mold is dangerous. Very deadly. You have to watch out for these decaying turnips because if the pigs eat them, they get very sick. They're also quite stinky." Her nose wrinkles. "The entire town would stink from it."

Dirty, stinky rotten turnip? My mouth parts in shock, and I don't know whether to laugh or scream.

"It's expensive when the animals get sick," she adds.

"Of course." Don't laugh, Georgia. "You'd have to call a vet in."

Volkov has been calling me his dirty, decaying, rotten turnip that you wouldn't even feed to the pigs. I have to hand it to him—I'm impressed, and very, very entertained.

But I'm still going to get back at him.

She tilts her head at me. "Why do you ask?"

"Uh. Something I heard in the news." I'm going to get him back, but I'm not going to tattle on him. My gaze swings to the bag she brought. "What's in the bag?" I ask, changing the subject.

She reaches over and pulls out a photo album. "I brought photos of Alexei growing up."

My heart lifts. God, I hope he was an ugly child so I can mock him mercilessly.

Maria flips the book open, and on the first page is the cutest, chubbiest baby with leg and arm rolls and huge eyes. He's wearing a little blue shirt and pants and gazes at the camera with a grumpy little frown.

"Oh my god." I lean in, taking a closer look, melting. "I'd recognize that scowl anywhere. He's so cute. How old is he here, like a year?"

"Four months," she says gravely.

"My god." My eyes bug out. "He's huge."

"I know." She stares at the photo before shaking herself. "All he did was eat. Always eating. I couldn't get a moment to myself." She laughs before she gazes at the photo with affection, and a little plink of emotion lands in the center of my chest. "Having a new baby is hard, but I miss those days."

The next page has a photo of naked baby Alexei laying on his front on a bed, giving the camera a gummy smile.

"Hah." I pull out my phone. "I need to save this one so I can tease him about it later."

Maria laughs while I snap a photo and send it to him. The phone starts buzzing with his replies but I silence it and turn back to the album. I flip through it for a bit, laughing at Maria's commentary, and when I'm almost done, she stands.

"I'll just text Nikita to come pick me up."

She leaves the room, and I keep turning pages.

On the last page of the book, something catches my eye. It's a photo of Alexei in a Montreal jersey, the team he got drafted to when he first started in the NHL. There's a photo behind this one, though. I can see the corner peeking out.

I pull the plastic protective covering up, but when I slide the photo out, I almost drop the book.

It's a picture of a younger Alexei, maybe early twenties, and a very tiny blond woman, about the same age. It's one of those stiff studio portraits where she's sitting with a smile that doesn't reach her eyes and he's standing behind her, serious and surly.

Alexei and Emma invite you to celebrate their marriage.

I stare at the invitation, reading and rereading. He was married?

He wouldn't go to Jamie Streicher and Pippa Hartley's wedding. At the double date with Hayden and Darcy, he said he didn't go to weddings.

Is this why?

I study the woman in the photo. Emma. Blond, tiny, thin. So this is his type. My throat feels tight.

"Oh."

I flinch to see Maria standing right beside me with a surprised expression.

"I forgot that was in there," she says quietly.

"He was married?"

"Just engaged." She watches me with concern. "You didn't know."

The sharp ache of rejection moves up my throat. I don't know why I care. I know this isn't real.

"It wasn't serious," Maria says, and I give her a look of disbelief, gesturing at the wedding invitation with a wry smile. She sighs. "It wasn't like it is with you."

A complete farce? A business agreement? I'll bet it wasn't.

"I kept it because I wasn't sure if they would patch things up, and then I forgot about it." She looks sad for a moment before she smiles at me gently. "Georgia, he's so different with you. This was years ago."

"What happened with them?" I don't know why I'm even asking. I don't care. I don't want to know.

She hums, pressing her lips together. "That's for Alexei to tell you."

I'd rather die than ask him about it. Instead, I give her a tight smile, close the photo album, and change the subject, asking Maria about her florist shop, what her favorite flowers are, keeping her talking until Nikita arrives to pick her up. He comes to the door to say hello, asks me how my car's doing, and when they leave, I thank her for coming over and give them both a hug goodbye.

The entire time, my mind flits back and forth to that wedding invitation, and my reaction. Our marriage is a business agreement. That kiss at the airport was for show, and it was a way for him to get on my nerves and get back at me for the stuff in the hotel room. Us messing around at the benefit was a power thing for him, because I made him jealous.

None of it's real, and yet I'm concerned at the sharp, ugly sting in my chest at the idea of him marrying someone else.

THERE WILL BE *a grocery delivery tomorrow morning,* Alexei texts while I sit in my car after soccer, waiting for the tow truck and watching highlights from his game on my phone. *Svetta will take care of it.*

I respond with a thumbs-up.

He had been engaged. Was he heartbroken? Does he still think about her?

I left the window open in my gym. Can you close it? A moment later, *Please.*

I'll check when I get home.

Home? You're still at soccer practice?

Outside, sitting in my car.

The typing dots appear, disappear, and reappear. *And why are you sitting in your car, Doctor?*

I can hear the disapproval in his voice across the continent. I shouldn't say anything, it's just going to rile him up.

I kind of like riling him up, though.

Doctor.

I press my lips together. I can hear the tone, imagine the deep, exasperated breath he's taking and the way he's rubbing the bridge of his nose.

Do not tell me that fucking car broke down again.

Okay. I won't.

Lock your doors, and share your location with me. Right now.

Controlling, I text back.

I swear to fucking god, Georgia, if you don't share your location, I'll call my parents and they'll be over in a heartbeat.

Ugh. He's no fun. My good humor pops like a balloon. They would show up, too, because they're kind like that. *Don't do that. Of course my doors are locked.*

Share. Your. Location.

I roll my eyes, but I do as he says.

Good. Thank you.

I hate being told what to do, but a tiny part of me arches at him saying *thank you.* I bet he had to force it out.

How long until your ride gets there? Alexei texts.

Not sure. They said the tow truck could be a couple hours.

In my hand, my phone starts buzzing.

"It's fine—" I start.

"A couple *hours*? I'm calling you a ride."

"It's fine. I can't leave my car here overnight, anyways. There'll be nothing to come back to."

"We can only hope," he mutters, and I snort. "There's a car on the way for you."

"Alexei." My tone is sharp. I hate when people make decisions over my head like this, without involving me.

"The car will be there in ten minutes. I'm arranging for a tow truck. A faster one."

"You're so controlling," I tell him, but my words have no heat.

"Georgia, I'm not letting my wife sit alone in the dark in her car."

The words *my wife* arc through me like electricity. I have

the urge to keep playing with him like this, but then I think about his wedding invitation and the fun gets sucked out of the whole thing.

"What does the car look like?"

He rattles off a make and model.

"Okay. Thank you. I'll look for it. Bye."

"Hold on. Stay on the phone until he gets there."

"You can see his location and my location, can't you?"

"Just . . ." He lets out a heavy exhale. "Stay on the phone with me, and don't argue."

There's something in his voice, a tiny shard of softness, that makes me pause.

"Okay."

Another pause. "Thank you."

"Wow." My mouth curves again. "Two *thank you*s in one night. You hit your head or something, Volkov?"

I say it without thinking. In my mind, I see the hard hit he took tonight during his game, and a ball of worry knots in my stomach.

He makes a low, amused noise. "I can say *thank you*."

There's a beat of silence that almost feels comfortable.

"Good game tonight," I say, for some reason.

"You saw it?"

"I checked the score." And watched a few highlights, even though I normally avoid them.

"The rookie did well."

"So did you." He got an assist.

"An actual compliment? Maybe you hit your head, too."

I laugh before I catch myself. This conversation has veered into something new for us.

I don't want to stop, though.

"You're okay this week?" he asks. "Alone in the house?"

"Of course."

"I can ask my parents to come stay."

"Don't do that. You'll be home tomorrow. And even if you weren't, I would be fine."

"For next time, I mean."

"I don't want to put them out."

"You wouldn't. They like you."

My heart glows. What happened to not getting attached? I guess there's no point, when our parents already know one another.

"I like them, too." I smile, thinking about the way Maria teases Nikita. "They're funny, and kind. Somehow that skipped right past you."

He does a low laugh. "Yeah, yeah."

"Anyways, where would they sleep?"

"You'd have to sleep in my room, I guess."

Arousal fires through me at the thought of sleeping in his bed, inhaling his scent.

"Have you been sleepwalking?"

Blood rushes to my face as I remember waking up in the middle of the night in his bed, and then his smug, condescending expression at the airport after we shared a hotel room for three days in a row. "No. Of course not." I swallow. "Alexei?"

"Mmm?"

"When we shared a hotel room on the road."

He waits. My heart thumps erratically.

"What did I do?"

Another beat. "You cuddled me."

Horror floods my nervous system, followed by humiliation.

"What are you stressed about?" he asks.

"Excuse me?"

"I read that people sleepwalk when they're stressed."

"You did *reading*?"

He hesitates. "We agreed not to mess around anymore. I don't want you sneaking into my bed in the middle of the night."

The humiliation in my chest burns hotter. "I wasn't *sneaking into your bed*—" I shake my head. "You know what? Lock your door. That'll solve everything."

A car matching his description earlier pulls up beside mine.

"My ride's here."

"Stay on the phone with me."

My instinct is to say *no* the way it always is when he or any other man demands something, but I suspect he'll call back—or worse, call the driver.

And very, very deep down, in a place I'd never admit out loud, I want to keep talking with him. I get out of my car, lock it, and open the passenger door of the other car.

"For Alexei?" the driver confirms.

"It's under my account," he says in my ear.

"Yes, for Alexei," I tell the driver. I close the door and he drives away, leaving my car alone in the dark parking lot.

A memory from this afternoon hits me. "I forgot to say thank you for the flowers."

They were delivered to my office, a bright pink bouquet in a vase, sitting on my desk for everyone to see. *Gladiolas,* my book said when I hurried home between work and soccer. *Readily armed.* I keep smiling when I think about them.

"It'll make this look more real, me sending you flowers."

"Right. Yes." That's why I thought he sent them. For show. Nothing's changed between us. "Good idea."

We sit in silence, and I think about his engagement again, but there's no subtle way to bring it up. Finally, the driver pulls up to the house.

"I'm home now."

"Inside?"

"Mhm."

"Door locked?"

"Yes."

"Good."

Silence stretches between us. "Goodnight." I clear my throat. "And thank you."

"Don't mention it."

We hang up, and I play with the bunnies before getting ready for bed, thinking about that hit he took tonight on the ice.

This is why I don't watch replays—I can't stand watching people get hurt.

Not people, my brain whispers as I lie there in the dark. *Just him.*

———

The next morning, before my eyes are even open, I inhale a clean, masculine scent. Cool, soft sheets brush my bare legs. Complete silence—no squeaks or rustling of the bunnies around the room. Eyes still closed, I skim my hand over the bed. Sometimes they jump and cuddle against me during the night.

My palm slides over the duvet—but it isn't my duvet.

My eyes snap open. I'm not in my room. I'm in *Alexei's* room.

I don't want you sneaking into my bed in the middle of the night. Oh god. My pulse picks up. Again?

What are you stressed about? he asked, and I think about the replays of him getting hurt. I think about all the times I've seen him get injured, like the big one two years ago, and nausea rolls through me. During the away-game road trip, I watched the games. I saw him get hurt, and in the evenings apparently I clung to him like a magnet.

A sinking feeling gathers inside me.

I know why I'm sleepwalking.

A FEW EVENINGS LATER, I lie in bed, trying to scroll on my phone while my other hand throbs with pain. I intercepted a puck during the game tonight—and broke a finger.

That fan account has posted a photo of Georgia wearing the heels with big black bows on the ankles.

Dr. Georgia, please step on me, one comment says, and a strange mix of possession and amusement twists in my gut.

I don't know why I keep scrolling through this account, studying the photos like there's going to be a test. I set the phone down and reach for the bottle of ibuprofen on my bedside table, but when I try to open it, my hand hurts like hell, and I let out a low groan.

The door bursts open, and the doctor glares at me.

"How am I supposed to sleep when you're acting like a fucking baby in here?"

She folds her arms over her chest before she puts her hands on her hips, then folds them again. Her eyes are wild, frantic, and a cute pink color rises on her cheeks. Energy crackles between us.

"I can't sleep." She throws her hands in the air. "You're making way too much noise."

My eyes drop to her mouth. "I made one little sound."

Her gaze lands on my hand. "You broke a finger." Her voice sounds weird. Unhappy. I don't like it. "Did you take something for it? You're supposed to be taking an anti-inflammatory every four hours at least. Where's your ice pack?" She frowns at my hand. "Why is your splint all messed up like that? Who did this?" She strides over, sits beside me on the bed, and takes my hand.

"I took it off after Mei splinted it. It was too tight."

She gives me an irritated look, removing the splint with care. "It's supposed to be tight so it can heal properly." Her gaze lingers on me, on my glasses.

"Miss me, Hellfire?"

"Not even a little bit." She shifts her gaze to my hand. "You look like hell."

"Isn't that a compliment, where you're from?"

A tiny twitch at the corner of her mouth and she glances up at my glasses again. "You should really get LASIK."

"LASIK freaks me out," I admit. "I don't want a laser near my eye."

"Oh my god." She rolls her eyes. "You *are* a baby."

I can smell her violet perfume again. "Were you working tonight?"

She nods, eyes on my splint. I stare at her mouth, trying not to think about at the airport.

No more kissing. It's a good rule to have, especially when I'm thinking about her all the time like this.

"Question for you, Hellfire."

She makes a *mmm?* noise, still working on my splint, frowning in concentration. Prickles run up my arms from her fingers brushing me, and I can feel her body heat from where she sits beside me on the bed.

"Why didn't you want to get married?"

Her eyes flick up to mine, surprised and wary.

The question bothered me the entire road trip. I know why *I* didn't want to get married—because I don't need anyone. I have hockey, I have my teammates, I have my family, and I like my life as is. The last thing I'm going to do is introduce someone into my life only for them to leave. Only for it to be one-sided the whole time.

Georgia could find someone who's crazy about her, though. As much as I hate it, that Dr. Handjob guy stared at her with stars in his eyes. Half the guys on the team get tongue-tied and nervous around her. There's no shortage of men who would be happy to marry her.

"I don't want to give up my career," she says simply.

I make a face. "Why would you have to give up your career?"

"It's just the way it goes with men and women."

"No, it isn't."

She gives me a look like I don't know what I'm talking about.

"You know what I saw when I started working? Two doctors would get married, and she'd go on maternity leave and never come back. Or she'd work for a bit, but it's hard when she's been out for a year. Every gain in his career widens the gap between them and makes it harder for her to catch up, and eventually she throws in the towel. I've seen it too many times to count, Alexei. The primary caregiver for kids is the one whose career suffers, and it's always the woman."

"So don't marry another doctor." There's an ugly stab in my gut, thinking about her getting married for real one day. Having kids with someone.

"It's not just doctors. It's most men. Look at you. Your schedule is ridiculous. You're traveling half the year. Would you retire to take care of your family if your wife wanted to work?"

I can't even imagine being ready to retire. If I'm not a hockey player, who am I? Hockey is everything to me.

"You could have married someone you didn't hate for your inheritance," I say instead. "Your Dr. Handjob would say yes in a heartbeat."

I hate that idea.

"It would end up meaning something to him." She frowns to herself. "I could never lead someone on like that."

I stare at the splint. That warning feeling's back in my gut. This is why I can't be thinking about her. She isn't thinking about me back.

"There." She sets my hand down and stands, my side going cold from the loss of her body heat. "Don't move."

She leaves, and returns holding an ice pack.

"Fifteen minutes on, fifteen off," she tells me in a firm voice that makes me feel weird. Taken care of or something. Her eyes glint. "Doctor's orders."

"You were right," I say when she heads to the door again. I have the frustrating desire to keep her here, keep her talking. "About Walker being scared shitless."

She leans on the doorframe, unsurprised.

I've been thinking about it since I met his parents but coming up with nothing. The kid and I are complete opposites. I don't know why Ward paired us together. The rookie would be better off with someone like Miller or Owens.

"How'd you know?"

Her mouth twists in a wry smile. "Medical school. Everyone's the smart kid. Everyone loves it and works hard. Everyone wants it just as badly as you do. It was a whole new level of competition."

That sounds like the NHL. "How did you deal with it? Maybe I can learn something that'll help the rookie."

But mostly, I'm becoming addicted to every new piece of information I learn about her. Those pretty lips turn up at the corners like she has a secret, and that twist of interest spirals.

"I wore ridiculous heels so they'd underestimate me, then go home and study until I fell asleep at my desk."

"So that's how you weed out the assholes, huh?" I clear my throat. "The shoes?"

I don't realize what I've said until it's too late.

She stares at me dead-on. "Yes. That's how I weed out the assholes. Especially the ones who call me dumb, or incompetent."

Deep in my chest, regret yanks hard. I hate that I'm in that group.

"I never thought you were dumb." I hate myself for how wrong I was. How quickly I believed the worst in her. "I know how hard it is to get into medical school in Canada."

The hurt is still in her eyes, though. "Just incompetent?"

This is where I should tell her the truth—that I was attracted to her, but she reminded me of my ex. That she thought I was a lost cause and I hate when people can see my weak points.

"I'm sorry," I say instead, hauling in a tight breath, holding her eyes. "I shouldn't have been such a dick."

She looks down, studying her nails. I wish I knew what she was thinking.

"It's okay, Volkov. It keeps things interesting. Besides, I graduated top of my class." Her mouth curves. "Probably out of spite, honestly."

I huff an amused sound. "Good girl."

Something flares in her eyes, and I remember when I said that in the library at the benefit.

Our eyes hold, and my heart rate picks up. "Thinking about the benefit, Hellfire?"

She lifts her chin, a defiant move that only gets my blood racing harder. "Nope. Not even once."

The air around us thickens. Sharp, crackling desire courses through me. Trying not to be attracted to her isn't working.

"My bed smells like you," I say, because I can't help but provoke her.

I thought I was delusional at first, but no, it's not just that I can't get that intoxicating violet scent out of my nose. My sheets actually smell like her.

Her throat works, confidence faltering. "Weird. I don't know why."

I'm a sick bastard, because I find her discomfort amusing. "You don't know why?"

"Maybe Svetta used different soap."

"You're a known sleepwalker, and you're blaming my housekeeper?"

"I'm not a *known* sleepwalker. Only you know. And Jordan."

I shouldn't like that I know something so personal about her, but I do. "Why do you sleepwalk, Hellfire?"

"I don't know," she says tightly, before she's gone, walking back to her own room.

"Liar," I mutter to myself.

She knows, but she won't tell me. My determination snags like a jagged edge. I'm going to find out.

Learning more about my wife is a dangerous game that I can't seem to stop playing.

———

In the middle of the night, I wake to my bedroom door opening.

"Hellfire?" I murmur, squinting in the dark.

The bed dips and I get another wash of that pretty violet scent. She snuggles in beside me, her warm curves tucked against my front, her hair on my arm.

I should lead her to her bed, but she'll probably come right back, like in the hotel room. Instead, I lie there, listening to her soft breathing.

It's nice, with her pressed to me like this. Maybe I don't mind cuddling as much as I thought I did.

I think about what she told me tonight. Her working hard in medical school. Encouraging me with the rookie. I bet she helps the girls at soccer with this kind of thing, too. I saw the way they looked at her, like they wanted to grow up to be her.

Admiration grows in the center of my chest. I wish I'd never saw this captivating, fascinating side of her.

These feelings I'm starting to have for my wife? They aren't going away.

CHAPTER 48
GEORGIA

THE NEXT MORNING, I wake up tucked into Alexei's warm, hard chest, his soft sheets against my skin, his scent in my nose, and the thick head of his erection pressing against my ass.

Need gathers between my legs, but I ignore it.

"I did it again, didn't I?"

He got hurt. I always sleepwalk after he gets hurt, but I don't want to think about why.

He rolls away, stretching and letting out a groan that sounds a lot like in the library, when he came. My lady parts flutter. He looks disgustingly hot first thing in the morning, hair a mess and eyes all sleepy. That broad, carved chest. The trail of hair into his boxers.

"You begged me to kiss you."

Alarm fires through me, and I sit up, searching his expression with shock. "No, I didn't."

God, I fucking pray I didn't.

"You did. You said I was the make-out king and you'd do anything for just one more."

My laugh is soft and relieved. He's fucking with me. I slide out of his bed. "Get real, Volkov."

I'm almost at the door, my legs and ass prickling with his gaze, when he says something that stops me in my tracks.

"You should just start sleeping in my bed."

Every brain cell in my head explodes. "You have to be joking." He's fucking with me again. He has to be.

He shrugs. "You just end up here, anyways."

I choke out a laugh. "In your dreams."

"Not *my* dreams." His mouth slants in a cruel smirk, like he can read my mind and count how many times I've thought about him lately.

"I'd rather sleep in a locked coffin."

A low, surprised huff slips out of him. "Fine. If you do it again, though, I'm getting rid of your bed."

———

That afternoon at the hospital, a purple orchid arrives for me. *From the make-out king,* the card reads. The second I have a spare minute, I hurry to my office and flip through the book, which I've started bringing in my laptop bag.

Purple orchids—Respect and admiration.

So he apologized for calling me incompetent, and he actually looked sincere and contrite when he did it. So he took my advice about the rookie. So our hate fuck was the hottest thing I've ever experienced in my life and I'll be thinking about it until I'm a deceased speck of dust floating in space.

So what?

My gaze swings out the window to the banner of him hanging from the arena, mid-skate with a determined expression on his handsome face. I'm not going to soften for this guy just because he did something decent and apologized. Alexei Volkov is still the kind of guy to put himself first. What we're doing isn't real. Even these flowers are for show, and the meanings are some sick little game he plays. It's a power thing.

Neither of us actually wants to be married, and I'm not going to forget it.

"DON'T BITE ME," Alexei warns to the kitchen floor as I walk in after work a few days later. There's a game on TV in the other room so he hasn't noticed me. "Don't believe anything she's said about me."

I peer around the island. The bunnies are on the floor, going to town on two plates of neatly chopped-up veggies. Alexei crouches between them, stroking a strong hand across Damon's fur. His wedding ring glints, and my stupid, stupid little heart gives an erratic thump.

"Hi."

He goes very still before he stands and folds his arm across his chest like he wasn't just talking to my bunnies. "Hi."

"What are you doing?"

"Checking for tumors."

I press my lips together. I need to get ready for soccer, but there's no way I can drag myself away without teasing him. "It looked like you were petting Damon."

"Demon, more like. You've been gone for hours." He shrugs. "They need attention."

"Svetta gives them tons of attention during the day." A

sparkling, fizzy feeling goes off in my chest. Teasing him is like a drug. "I think you like them."

"I don't. I hate them. They stink."

"Mhm. Did you julienne those carrots? How do you even know how to do that?"

The corner of his mouth twitches. "I don't just play hockey. I can cook."

For the first time, I notice the chef's block of knives on the counter. The professional-grade pots and pans hanging from the ceiling rack.

The other night, when I came home late, it smelled incredible in here, like tomatoes and basil. Like someone had been cooking.

Him. Not Svetta. Alexei cooks. Why is that hot? That shouldn't be hot.

"Prove it," I say with an arched brow, even though I believe him.

His gaze sharpens with challenge. "Next time you leave work at a reasonable hour, I will."

My stomach dips. A meal together? Unforced, and not for show? We would never.

I'm holding his gaze, trying to think of something sharp and witty, when my phone buzzes.

At the reminder on-screen, though, my heart stops.

"Shit," I whisper.

He straightens, frowning. "What?"

"I have a work dinner." My mind starts to race. "There's a neurologist we're trying to woo to the program." We've been trying to arrange a visit with Dr. Emilio Reyes for months. "I don't know how I missed this in my calendar."

"What's the problem?"

"I have soccer." I glance at the time on the microwave. "I double-booked myself. Heather's out of town at a conference.

She and I have been the main contacts for Dr. Reyes. It would look rude and dismissive if I had another doctor take him out, like we didn't care. And I can't cancel soccer. That's my rule; I don't cancel on the girls."

I could, but even the idea makes my stomach sink. Soccer isn't just a chance to exercise under medical supervision. It's a social thing. They're all friends. And whether I want the responsibility or not, I'm a role model to them.

I need to be consistent and reliable for them.

I blow out a heavy breath, thinking. I don't know what to do.

"I'll do it," he says.

I stare at Alexei for ten long seconds. "Do what?"

He leans against the counter, arms still folded across his chest. "Coach soccer."

A slow blink. "You're going to coach soccer for me?"

"Sure." He says it like he's giving me a ride somewhere and not offering to take care of the thing that's most important to me. He pulls out his phone and taps out a text.

"You don't have training or something?"

He slips his phone back into his pocket. "I just cancelled it."

I blink at him. "Are you okay?"

He's not smiling, but his features soften into something amused. "I can take one night off."

"Do you even know how to play soccer?"

"Kind of."

"*Kind of*? What was your second sport?"

He gives me a confused look.

"Ninety-eight percent of professional hockey players competed in a second sport when they were teenagers."

"Oh. Baseball."

I'm really not sure about this. "So not soccer."

"Hockey is winter and baseball is spring. I couldn't play two winter sports. Besides, soccer's boring."

"Soccer isn't *boring*." My jaw drops at the blatant insult to my sport, and he looks away, mouth twitching like he's trying not to smile.

"No contact. No fighting."

A laugh slips out of me. "I'm not letting you tell my girls their sport is boring."

"I won't. We'll work on technical skills. I'll run different drills with them than they're used to. Cross-training is good for player development."

He actually looks sincere, and if I know one thing about Alexei, it's that when he does something, he gives it everything. All these hockey players do.

"Or I'll just do whatever you want," he adds.

"You'll be mean to them," I toss out.

"I won't."

"Promise?" I bite my bottom lip and his eyes drop to it before he pulls his gaze away, fast.

"I promise." He gives me a flat look. "What other option do you have?"

He's got a point. Is Alexei going in my place better than canceling? Two months ago, I would have said, hell no.

Now I'm not so sure.

Besides, he cancelled training. I doubt he does that often.

"Fine. Deal." My mouth slides into a smile and he looks at my lips again. "Good luck, Coach Volkov."

"STOP," I yell while the girls run the drills Georgia briefed me on earlier that night. "Bring it in."

The girls wander over to where I wait on the sidelines. It's cold out tonight, and our breath puffs in the air.

"Cara, you're on a low-impact plan. Why are you jumping?"

She shrugs. "I feel okay tonight. I can do it."

I've noticed a few of them ignoring their limitations, pushing themselves hard during the exercises tonight.

"Just because you feel okay doesn't mean you're at your ability before you got injured. Coach Georgia knows what she's doing. She's a world expert. Do you think the NHL hires just anyone?"

They shake their heads.

"Do you think she'd limit you if she thought you were fully healed?"

More head shakes. The girls look guilty, some wear frowns like they're pissed off or disappointed, and I feel a wrench of emotion in my chest.

"Look." I swallow. "I know how it feels to be injured. All you want to do is get back to where you were before."

"We want to play hard because we've always played hard," one girl says.

"That's how we got so good," another says.

"I know. Two years ago, I was in the hospital from a concussion and wasn't allowed to play for three months." Even the memory makes me feel sick. Watching from the bench while my teammates did all the heavy lifting. "Being forced to do nothing was torture. I know how hard it is to sit out from your sport when it's what you love. Rest isn't nothing, though. Just because you aren't pushing your body to the limit doesn't mean it isn't productive." I wiggle my bad shoulder. "My shoulder didn't heal properly and now it hurts most of the time." I give them a sidelong glance. "Don't tell Georgia that."

A few of them smile.

"Rest is part of training, so commit to it. If you're going to get better, do it right. Think of it like another hard thing. Another challenge. The better you heal, the better you'll play when you return. Coach Georgia wants you to regain full ability, even if it takes longer. She's rooting for you." I make a *let's go* gesture. "Let's run the drill again."

This time, they're careful. They check their form, slow it down, frown with focus. Cara isn't jumping. In the center of my chest, something squeezes.

"Good," I yell. "Nice work."

At the end of practice, the girls are tired. I can see it in their faces, in the way they move slower than before, and the way they laugh and smile less. I think back to Georgia and how much the girls like her. I think about how she was during practice, encouraging and fun, and the urge to impress her rises in me.

I don't want the girls to tell her I did a bad job at this. This is practice, but they should enjoy it.

I glance at my watch—fifteen minutes left.

Georgia would do something to lift their spirits. Something to make them feel good about their skills and progress.

"Bring it in," I call to them. "Drink some water and then line up in the middle of the field, single file, facing the goal.

"What are we doing?" one of them asks.

"Shoot-out."

A buzz of interest rolls through them. They're glancing at one another and smiling.

"*Fuck yeah,*" I hear one of them whisper.

"Which one of us do you want in goal?" one of the goalies asks.

"Neither." I point at where the rest of the team is lining up down the field. "You two get in line and take a shot."

———

I'm a terrible goalie. Really fucking bad. About half of the balls sail right past me. I'm not built for speed or agility the way guys like Walker and Miller are. For ten minutes, though, I forget about my impending retirement, I forget about trying to help the rookie, I forget about my citizenship, and I just have fun.

It's the strangest feeling.

"Is that all you've got?" I goad them. "Don't go easy on me."

"You suck at this!" they shout, wicked and gleeful like Georgia probably taught them. "You're the worst goalie we've ever played against!"

"Excuses," I yell back. "What's the matter, are you tired or something? Trying to buy yourself time? Quit stalling."

They're laughing, kicking balls at me one by one. I can see why the doctor likes coaching. Watching the girls practice skills with determined expressions, watching them smile and high-five when they figure something out, it's nice.

Rewarding, actually. I haven't felt this way in a long time

about anything. Being one of the better defensemen in the league was rewarding at first, until I got used to it.

"Wow," one of them says when we bring it in and stretch. Talia, I think. "That was really sad."

I lead them through a quad stretch. "Georgia didn't tell me how mean you all were." I don't know why I'm playing around with them like this. This isn't like me. "I hope you get back to playing on your regular teams, though. You girls are good."

They smile at one another. "We know," one of them says. Tasha? I think? "This was fun, though. You're a good coach."

"I'm not a coach." A weird, pleasant pressure notches in my chest. "I'm just filling in for my wife."

———

When I get home that night, the house is quiet. She's probably still out at the work dinner. It smells like her, though. Sweet and spicy. Violets. That stupid pink penis crystal sparkles in the foyer, scattering light on the walls and ceiling. Her car keys sit in the bowl.

If her car is here, that means there's something wrong with it again. Worry threads through me. It could break down while she's driving. She could get stranded late at night.

It's not safe. That's why I care. Because it's not safe. I don't want her to get hurt.

And maybe I still feel the need to even the score between us. For two years, I was a complete fucking asshole to her over assumptions I had made. No wonder she can't stand me. My gaze snags on her car keys again.

I know how to make it up to her.

CHAPTER 51

GEORGIA

A FEW MORNINGS LATER, I'm on my way out the door when I find Alexei in the kitchen.

"Thanks for helping out at soccer the other night." Between games and work, our schedules haven't lined up since. "You were a big hit."

He looks up, gaze lingering on me. "No problem."

The girls had flooded our team chat, asking when he'd be back. Later, at home, the light was on in his room and I considered knocking and asking him how it went, but the prospect of seeing him lying in bed, shirtless, reading, wearing glasses again seemed too risky.

I wish I could get that image out of my head. I've made extra effort not to consume any game content or watch replays where I could see him getting hurt. With him actually acting like a decent person now, the last thing I need is to wake up in his bed again.

We're not supposed to be messing around, I'm not going to tempt myself.

"Do you want an omelet?" he asks abruptly.

He wants to make me food? My heart thunks. "I have a meeting, I should get going."

He makes a noise of acknowledgment, and glances behind me at the door to the garage. "Sure. Next time."

"Next time."

For some reason, I'm walking over to him. My heels click across the floor and the way he glances down at them, the way heat flares in his eyes, boosts my confidence.

"Thank you, though," I say quietly, leaning up on my toes and pressing a kiss to his warm cheek. Under my touch, he doesn't move. "And thank you for the other night. You really did save me there."

His scent, the way his stubble scrapes against my lips, they blank out the giant question blaring in my head: *What the actual fuck am I doing right now?*

"You're welcome, Hellfire." There's a low, pleased tone to his voice that makes me flutter again.

He glances at my lips. The urge to kiss him for real pulses through me.

We can't, we shouldn't, we said we wouldn't, but god, I want to.

Oh god. I think I might be developing a crush on my fake husband.

"You're going to be late," he says, the corner of his mouth tugging up. Not a smile, but almost.

"Right." My face is flushing. "Bye."

At the door to the garage, though, I stop short.

My car's gone, and a dark green luxury SUV is parked in its place. Shiny and new. I frown. I parked my car there last night. I know I did.

Did Alexei's dad pick the car up this morning to fix something? I feel like one of them would have said something.

A bad feeling simmers in my stomach.

When I walk back into the house, he's waiting in the foyer, pacing with a weird, nervous energy.

"Whose car is that in the garage?"

He clears his throat, eyes on my face. "Yours."

The bad feeling in my stomach lands with a crash. "You can't be serious."

You're buying a new car, he said once. My throat feels hot and tight.

He crosses his arms, a spark of pride in his eyes. "It's yours. I bought it for you."

A knot forms in my chest and I can't get a full breath. I feel sick. "Where's my car?"

"Gone. I took care of it."

"Took care of it," I repeat. "You got rid of my car without asking me?" I blink in total fucking disbelief.

In an instant, I'm in the kitchen of Liam's apartment back in Toronto, asking him why I'm getting emails about my med school unenrollment.

"Are you serious? How could you think that was okay?"

His pleased expression falls like a ton of bricks. "It was a piece of crap, Georgia. It broke down once a week."

"But it was mine." The words come out sharp and loud. "Where is it?"

"The junkyard."

Rage blinds me. "What?"

"It's probably a tin can by now."

I'm speechless, I'm so furious. I feel shaky and weird. My pulse beats in my ears. Even when he threw my shoes in the garbage, I wasn't this mad. Back then, I expected nothing better.

Beneath the anger, though, I feel stupid. Disappointed. Whatever's been happening these past few weeks, how we've been talking without wanting to kill each other, I thought things were changing. He seemed different.

I stare at the stubborn set to his jaw. He's not different. He's exactly as controlling and high-handed as I'd thought he was.

My crush on my husband bursts like a balloon. I was right all along.

"Did you grab the bracelets from the rearview mirror?"

"What bracelets?" His expression turns confused, then irritated. "Do you realize what I did to get that car here, Georgia? It's back-ordered for six months."

I barely hear him. The girls at soccer made me those bracelets. They're silly and cheap but they say *PAGING DR. BADASS* on one and *FEMININE RAGE* on the other and I love them. When I see them, I smile.

And this asshole got rid of them without a second thought.

"That car was a death trap, Georgia. It was for your own good. I did this for you."

Something inside me snaps. I've heard those words before —*for your own good*. "Fuck you, Alexei."

Is that hurt behind the angry outrage in his eyes? I don't care.

"What the hell is wrong with you?" He gives me a *what the fuck* look. "I bought you a car. A *nice* one. The safest one on the market with every fucking bell and whistle available. I had to pull every string I had to get it here for this morning. Do you know how many women would kill to be in your position?"

"Oh, I'll kill," I laugh without humor, pulling out my phone. I need to get to work and I need to get away from him.

"Your car was a piece of shit, and *your* problem was becoming *my* problem, so I handled it. Why don't you show a bit of gratitude instead of acting like a spoiled brat?"

I choke on the air, blinking. Wow. Just wow. Five minutes ago, I kissed this guy on the cheek. What the hell was I thinking? This is what I get for letting my guard down.

"What are you doing?" he demands.

I won't look at him. "Booking a ride."

He curses under his breath, shaking his head. "Take the car, Georgia. It's why I bought it."

"I'm not driving that thing."

"Yes, you are. As my wife—"

I whirl on him, my blood boiling. "I am *not* your wife. You —you—" God, I can barely get the words out. I'm choking on them. "This is exactly why I never wanted to get married. This is exactly the kind of thing Liam would do. What I want doesn't even matter to you, does it? You steamrolled right over me like you do everyone else. You didn't ask, you just *took,* because what's mine is yours, right? Because what I want doesn't even register on your radar."

My chest aches. I feel like crying and burning the house down at the same time.

"I thought I was wrong about you. I was actually starting to like you."

Something shifts in his expression. My eyes sting and I turn, blinking furiously, clearing them. I hate that crying is my body's anger response, especially in front of him. It's the best way to weaken my argument and make me seem like a hysterical, hormonal, emotional woman.

I walk out the door and close it behind me without looking back.

I THOUGHT *I was wrong about you.*

A puck bounces off my chest, padded by my equipment. Walker stands twenty feet away with a curious grin, waiting.

You steamrolled right over me like you do everyone else.

"Sorry." I give myself a shake.

I was actually starting to like you.

We resume the defensive drills. The best way to get her out of my head is to focus on hockey.

"Do I steamroll people?" I blurt out a few minutes later.

Walker gives me a strange look. "Huh?"

"Steamrolling." I can feel the frown between my eyebrows, and when I swallow, there are rocks in my throat. I flex my hand, feeling my wedding ring beneath my glove. "Do I, uh, steamroll you?"

"If by *steamroll* you mean you think you know best and aren't really interested in hearing anything different, uh . . .yeah. Definitely."

Once again, the doctor was right.

I am not your wife.

Walker hesitates. "Do you want to talk about it?"

"No."

He leans on his stick. "Is this something to do with your pretty, new wife?"

"No."

His eyebrows go up. "It has nothing to do with the *smoking hot super babe* that you married?"

I stare at the ice. She kissed me on the cheek this morning. How'd I go from that to *Fuck you, Alexei*? She told me all that stuff about medical school. She was just starting to trust me.

I can't stop picturing the hurt look in her eyes.

I don't know why I keep thinking about her. I don't know why I can't get her out of my head.

Walker laughs. "Volkov, what's going on? Normally, you'd have my head on a stake by now, talking about her like this."

"I bought her a car."

Pleased surprise flickers in his eyes. "Nice."

"Her car was always breaking down. It wasn't safe." I was worried about her. With hockey, I can't always be there if she gets into a bad situation. "I got rid of her car without asking."

Walker huffs a laugh. "Yikes."

I pull my helmet off, raking a hand through my hair, pushing it back. It sounds bad, out loud.

Owens skates to a stop between us, spraying ice on the boards. "What's going on, Chatty Cathys? Are we scrimmaging or what?"

"Volkov bought Georgia a new car."

Owens gives me a big smile of approval, nodding. "Nice."

"And he got rid of her other car without asking," Walker adds.

Owens' smile drops. "You didn't."

"I didn't think it was a big fucking deal," I rush out. How does everyone know this stuff but me?

Because you're an asshole, a part of my brain whispers.

Owens glances up at the glass offices overlooking the ice. Her office is up there. I doubt she's watching, though. "How did she react?"

"She was mad." My gut twists, thinking of the way she looked at me this morning, so hurt and shocked. "Really mad."

I hurt her. Pain writhes in my chest and I blow out a heavy breath. Fuck.

Owens gives me a wary look. "How did *you* react?"

My eyes close. "I told her she should be grateful and that most women would kill to be in her position."

When I open my eyes, they're both staring at me with wide eyes.

Owens lets out a sharp laugh. "Well, it was really nice knowing you, Volkov."

I make a frustrated noise. "Probably not the best thing to say."

I was actually starting to like you. I don't know which stabs harder, that or her hurt expression which I keep replaying.

Even with Emma, I never felt like this. "I need to fix this."

Miller skates over with his arms out in a *what gives?* gesture. "What, is this the golf course or something? Let's play."

"Volkov needs help," Owens says.

"He got rid of Georgia's car without asking her," Walker explains, and I wish they'd stop repeating it, because it sounds worse every time I hear it.

How could I think that was okay? *This is* exactly *the kind of thing Liam would do.* Who the hell is Liam? Nausea and frustration rolls through me. I don't even know what he did, but I *hate* being in the same group as that guy.

Miller whistles. "Bad boy, Volkov. I'm shocked you're even standing right now. Hazel would have my balls for that."

"She already has your balls," Owens says.

He wiggles his eyebrows. "Yeah, she does." He sobers and points to me. "Fix this."

"I want to." I exhale a hard breath. "I don't know how," I admit. "I need to get that car back."

"At least." Miller turns to Streicher in net and waves him over. "Practice is over. Volkov needs our help."

WHEN MY RIDE drops me off in front of the house late that evening, my old junker car sits under the streetlight, clear as day.

Compared to the new car in the garage this morning, my old car looks laughably shitty. It could be part of the set in an apocalypse movie. It's sitting on a flatbed, like a truck hauled it here, and the wheels are gone already. One of the windows is smashed, and the passenger door looks dented, but maybe that was there before? It's concerning that I can't be sure. The driver-side door's unlocked, but the bracelets that used to hang on the rearview mirror are gone, and when I pop the hood—

Yep. The engine's gone. I stand there with my hand on my hip, thinking about the flowers he sent to my office today.

Hyacinth—I'm sorry, forgive me, your loveliness charms me.

I overreacted this morning. I've been replaying it all day. My emotions got the best of me.

He didn't ask me, though. I didn't matter, and I thought I did.

The lights are on inside the house, and he's sitting in the front room when I step inside. Upon seeing me, he stands.

"Georgia." He clears his throat and glances out the front windows. "You saw the car?"

"Yes."

"Here." He steps forward, holding his hand out. The friendship bracelets sit in his palm, and something in my chest squeezes.

I pluck them out of his hand, my fingertips accidentally brushing his warm skin.

"I overreacted this morning." I chew my lip. "I'm sorry."

"No, you didn't." He holds my gaze as he rubs the back of his neck. "I shouldn't have gotten rid of your car without asking you. That was a fucked-up thing to do."

That's . . . not what I expected him to say.

What do I do with this version of Alexei? I didn't know he was capable of this. Men like him never apologize, never take accountability, and nothing is ever their fault.

But maybe I was wrong about him the way he was wrong about me.

"I'll put it back to the way it was."

I let out a short laugh. "There's no engine."

"I'll get a new one installed."

"The window's smashed."

"I'll replace it."

"Tires."

He nods. "I'll get those, too."

I twist my mouth to the side, fiddling with the beads on the friendship bracelet.

"Why'd you do it?" Something about our relationship looking more realistic for the citizenship process, I'm sure.

His jaw tightens, and something flickers in his eyes. "I was worried about your car breaking down and your phone being dead and you being stranded."

Deep down, beneath all the anger and frustration and stubbornness, something melts. Liam unenrolled me for his own gain.

Alexei bought the car because he was worried about me. He didn't mean to hurt me.

"You hate me," I say quietly, even though I know it isn't true.

I don't know what else to say, though.

"I know," his mouth flattens, "but I was still worried about you."

He's not supposed to be like this. He's supposed to be brutal and condescending and controlling.

"I don't like how things have been between us the past two years. I don't like how I acted. It doesn't sit right with me."

Something unfurls in my chest, and I grapple to close it back up. Where's the asshole who called me incompetent? Where's the guy who sneered at me about hunting for a rich husband so I could be a lady of leisure?

"So you want to buy me a new car and pretend the past never happened."

"No. I want to buy you a new car and start over."

A strange emotion catches in my throat. If we had met differently—if I weren't his doctor and he weren't my patient, would everything have been different between us? Of course it would have.

I don't want to think about that, though.

He holds my eyes, expression unreadable. "Or we can go in a new direction."

A new direction. I think about us hate-fucking at the benefit. About sleeping in his bed, curled around him.

"I can't accept this kind of gift. It's too much."

"I'm rich, Georgia."

I let out a short laugh. "Humble, too."

He smirks. "If you really were my wife, I'd be happy to spend money on you." He looks away, then back to me. "And I'd feel better with you driving something safer. If you want to keep driving your car, I'll get it fixed up and I won't say another word about it." His throat works. "But I'm going to ask my dad to look at it regularly."

"It doesn't make sense to source all those car parts." I glance at the floor, the giant pink crystal he hates so much, the photo of us from the team dinner. Anywhere but at him. "Your dad's already so busy." Maria mentioned his garage is booked for weeks.

I can't believe I'm about to do this.

"I'll drive the car for as long as we're married, and then you can do whatever you want with it after that. Sell it, keep it, give it away, whatever."

Alexei doesn't say anything, and when my gaze lifts to his, I'm struggling to read his expression. His lips part and he takes a breath like he wants to argue, but he stops himself.

"Okay." A short nod. "Thank you."

"Okay."

Part of me worried he'd look smug, like he won something, but he doesn't. He just looks relieved. His eyes dart to the window, though, and a frown passes over his features.

"How did you get home?"

"I got a ride."

Our eyes meet. "Dr. Handjob?"

My stomach dips at the possessive flash in his eyes. "So what if he did?"

His jaw ticks. "I deserve that."

Another opportunity to act like a jealous asshole, and he passes it up? "Volkov, relax. I took a rideshare home."

He's visibly relieved, and I don't know how to feel. "Okay, well, goodnight."

"There's a dinner for the league in Toronto next week," he says, stopping me. "Come with me."

A few weeks ago, Ward asked me to accompany the team on the road trip. I wonder if he assumed I'd join for this dinner.

"You owe me a date," Alexei adds, but with a twitch to the corner of his mouth. "It would look weird if my wife didn't show up."

It *would* look weird.

"I'll buy you a new dress."

I raise my eyebrows. "And shoes?"

His eyes dip to my feet. Another jaw flex before his chin dips in a nod. "And shoes."

"Anything I want?" Now I'm just teasing him. If this is the new direction he's talking about, fine by me.

His mouth slants. "Anything you want."

I stare him dead-on, starting to smile. "I'm going to burn a hole in your pocket, baby."

Volkov. I meant to call him Volkov, not *baby*. From the way his eyes flare with interest, I guess he doesn't mind, though.

"Fine."

"Fine." My heart flutters. I thought I'd enjoy spending his money, but I'm more intrigued by him buying me things.

I've always been independent. I'm proud that I can unapologetically buy myself things. I don't need some guy to buy me shoes. I think about Alexei buying me a pair, though, and a fizzy little shiver of delight rolls through me.

A beat of silence passes where we just stare at each other.

"Who's Liam?" he asks, watching me closely, and my stomach drops.

I didn't mean to bring him up during the argument. The woman who let herself get swept away by Liam is long gone, so different from the person I am today. Even if things are changing between Alexei and me, I'd never tell him what happened. I'd never show him how truly stupid I can be when in love.

"No one." I look away. "I should go to bed."

He watches me for another beat, looking like he wants to press, but instead, he just nods. "Okay. Goodnight."

"Goodnight."

Later, I lie in bed, thinking about his expression of regret and shame as he apologized. I don't think Liam apologized once to me. Before I fall asleep, I'm left with one concerning realization.

My crush on my husband is back with a vengeance.

SATURDAY MORNING, a fist pounds on my door.

"Go away," I groan into my pillow. "It's my day off."

Another loud thumping noise. When I ignore it and pull the pillow over my head, the door opens. There's a clinking noise from my bedside table, and a second later, the pillow is whipped away.

A big hand comes to my back and he shakes me.

"Mmm," I moan into the bed, "harder, Dr. Handley. Harder."

Alexei growls, and I grin before rolling over. His hair is damp from his morning shower. A navy T-shirt. Brown eyes a little sleepy, with those under-eye circles. Something pulses between my legs.

I'm distracted, though, by the latte and breakfast sandwich on my bedside table.

I squint at him, frowning. "Did you make that?"

He shrugs. That means yes.

"I already forgave you. You don't have to keep doing this."

"All you eat are those fucking protein bars, and I don't want you getting hungry and cranky halfway through your dress fitting."

I sit up straighter, starting to smile. "Dress fitting?"

His eyes glint. "Mhm."

"Today?"

"If you ever get out of bed, yes. I have an appointment for a suit fitting. The designer is going to meet us there to get your measurements."

"Designer?" My vocabulary has been reduced to repeating things.

"Yes." He sighs like I'm getting on his nerves, but reaches for the coffee and puts it in my hand. "Eat. Drink." He looks at his watch. "We leave in twenty minutes."

Without another word, he leaves, closing the door behind him, and I look down at Damon, cuddled against my legs.

"Dress fitting," I whisper, wiggling with excitement.

———

At the tailor's shop, Alexei introduces me to the designer—who I recognize from a recent *Vogue* spread about up-and-coming designers—before he disappears with the tailor to do his final fitting.

"I'm thinking something like . . ." The designer's pencil flies over her sketchpad before she shows me what she's drawn.

"Yes." I blink at the simple line sketch of me in a floor-length gown with drapey sleeves. "Is that a cape? A thousand times yes."

She laughs. "I'm thinking less superhero and more high fashion, but yes. Toronto is cold as hell. The draping will need a lightweight fabric, probably silk. Something bold. Something fun." Her eyes move over the swatches.

My eyes go to one like a magnet. A soft gold that catches the light with a barely perceptible sparkle, so subtle it looks like a sheen.

"That one," we say at the same time, before we look at each other and laugh.

After she has my measurements, we say a quick goodbye, and I wander into the area where Alexei's being fitted for his suit.

He stands in front of the mirror while the tailor finishes tucking pins in a few places. They talk quietly, and I take a moment to admire my husband in the wool three-piece suit. Navy blue, like his T-shirt this morning, with a subtle check pattern. Fits him like a glove. Sharp and handsome.

There's something about brutal, cold, callous Alexei Volkov in a sharp suit that makes me frustratingly horny.

"Georgia."

"Hmm?" I snap to attention. The tailor's gone, and Alexei's eyes are on me. He's saying something.

His mouth twitches. "I said, what do you think?"

"Yes." I blink. "Looks great. What's this dinner for again?"

"A league thing," he says. Same answer as before.

No one on the team has mentioned it. "Are the guys going?"

"Just Ward and me."

I give him a strange look. What kind of dinner would single the two of them out?

"If you want to pick another fabric, I'll have the same one made for Miller's wedding."

My pulse stops. "You're going?"

"I'm going." He turns away without another word, heading back into the change room.

I stare after him, confused. It's the first word he's said about it since we learned that the team gifted us a week in the honeymoon suite at the Silver Falls resort. I assumed I'd go myself.

He doesn't go to weddings, so what's changed?

It's just for show, I tell myself. Maybe after our wedding, he doesn't care about going to them anymore. Maybe he feels bad about missing Jamie Streicher's wedding last year. Maybe he regretted it. Maybe he knows it would look strange if I went and he didn't.

Nothing to do with me.

THE NEXT WEEKEND, I hurry in the door of the hotel room Alexei and I are forced to share on another team trip. The week has been a whirlwind—work, soccer, traveling. It's one of those weeks where everything whizzes past, time races, and I feel unsettled and harried.

I have less than an hour to get ready for this mysterious dinner. Not ideal. The team went straight from the airport to the arena to practice for tomorrow night's game, so I haven't even unpacked my bag. My dress, delivered this morning in Vancouver before we left, hangs on the back of the door.

Two beds, I notice, with a weird dip in my stomach. Relief, most likely, that I won't be forced to inhale his addictive scent all night.

I'm about to open my bag and lay out all my hair and makeup products when there's a knock at the door. Alexei was still at the arena working with a physio when I left—maybe he got locked out.

At the door, though, a woman and man wait, each with their own rolling black case.

"Hair and makeup," the woman says.

"I didn't . . ." I shake my head, confused.

"Alexei arranged for it. He said you wouldn't have a lot of time to get ready."

Warmth spills through me and I grin. "Come on in."

———

An hour later, I head downstairs to the hotel lobby where Alexei texted me to meet him when I was done.

In the elevator, I study my reflection. No wonder the designer is an up-and-comer. I smooth a hand over the soft, lightweight fabric that drapes across my body and makes me feel like a Grecian goddess. *This* is what I love about fashion—a couple pieces of fabric arranged into art. In this dress, with my hair done in shiny waves and my makeup highlighting my favorite features—my eyes, my lips—I feel so beautiful. The shoes the designer included are bloodred and vicious, mostly hidden by the hem of the dress but peek out as I walk. Even the undergarments she sent along with the dress are pretty—a soft, feminine lace, undetectable beneath the thin fabric. I didn't even have to open my bag.

Getting ready with two professionals has been a nice distraction from the realization that tonight I'm just a woman on a powerful man's arm. Again. Liam would bring me to events, but instead of introducing me as his girlfriend who was about to enter medical school, I was his girlfriend, Hugo Greene's granddaughter.

I always felt erased at those events. I was there in physical form, but I didn't matter. Liam didn't even look at me. I was an accessory to make him seem more important.

My stomach wobbles. I hate that I'm repeating history like this. *Not real,* I remind myself. I'm just holding up my end of the bargain.

The elevator opens and as soon as I step out, I spot him sitting in a club chair, leaning back, legs spread, taking up a ridiculous amount of space. Handsome in that scary, bad boy way, wearing the hell out of that suit. In a busy lobby with a sea of people, his energy feels different. Magnetic. Heavier. Calm. Steady. Solid. That unsettled, harried feeling I've had all week quiets.

Our eyes meet and his gaze hardens, jaw flexing. I force myself to straighten and hold his gaze while I stride over.

"Well?" I put my palm up, gesturing at myself.

"Well, what?" He moves to standing.

I don't need him to tell me I look hot. I feel hot. That's all that matters.

I let out a dry laugh to myself, checking my clutch for everything I need. "All right, Volkov. Let's go." We start walking toward the ballroom. "What's this dinner for? You never told me."

"An award."

"Oldest player in the league?"

His unamused gaze slides to me. "Hilarious." His gaze drifts lower, down my dress, before he looks away.

"Wait, I know. Least teeth."

The corner of his mouth ticks. "Hellfire, keep running your mouth like that and you're going to regret it."

"What are you going to do, spank me?"

My stomach dips at the flare of heat in his eyes. "Maybe I will."

He looks away again, throat working.

"What's wrong?" I ask.

"Nothing."

He's tense. More than usual. "Is your shoulder hurting?"

"Shoulder's fine," he says tightly.

"It's the sparkles, isn't it?" I gesture at my dress with a mock crestfallen expression. "You hate them."

He gives me a flat look. "You look nice."

"Even though I'm wearing 'sparkly shit'?"

"Your sparkly shit is growing on me."

We're about to step through the door of the ballroom when his warm hand encircles my wrist, stopping me. I look up; he's so impossibly tall and broad. I'll never get used to it.

"You look beautiful," he says. "As always."

My pulse skips a beat. I didn't mean to fish for a compliment, and I don't need it from him, but I still float a couple inches off the ground. I don't care what he thinks. It's only because his compliments are scarce that I feel this way.

"As always?" I start to beam as we walk into the ballroom, and he rolls his eyes.

I'm about to start teasing him when we're surrounded by three enormous hockey players.

"Volkov." It's Rick Miller, Rory Miller's dad, a retired Canadian hockey legend. He shakes Alexei's hand with enthusiasm. "Good to see you again, and good to see you getting the recognition you deserve."

Recognition he deserves?

"Thank you." Alexei gives a tight nod before gesturing at me. "This is Dr. Georgia Greene, my wife."

Rick's gaze moves to me and we shake hands. "Ward has mentioned you. Nice to meet you. You work with the team?"

"I do."

"She works in injury recovery research at Lionsgate," Alexei adds.

Rick's eyes light up with interest. *"Really."*

I give Alexei a strange look. His hand is still on my waist, keeping me close. "Yes. I run a research program and work with athletes in their rehabilitation."

"Volkov." A man I recognize as a coach in the league interrupts, shaking Alexei's hand and slapping him on the back. "Congratulations. Well deserved."

"I'll find you later," Rick says to me while Alexei's pulled into the conversation. "I'm going to pick your brain."

He disappears, and I edge away, wanting to give Alexei space, but his grip on me tightens.

"Where do you think you're going?" he says in my ear.

"Just giving you space."

"Stay."

Again and again, people come up to him, congratulating him, and he introduces me. The athletes learn what I do and have a million questions, and I answer them with half my attention on my husband, and how he's treated like royalty among the players. People are eager to meet him and say hello. They hang on to the few words he says to them. Despite the attention and admiration from every level in the league, from current players to retired ones, from coaches to owners, he seems unfazed, deferring their praise and introducing me instead. *Dr. Georgia Greene, my wife,* he keeps saying. My profession first, my status as his wife second, I can't help but notice.

This is Hugo Greene's granddaughter, Georgia, Liam would say.

"Lucky guy, Volkov," the New York coach tells him after we talk about new methods of inflammation reduction. "Lucky guy."

"I'm aware." My husband's hand smoothes over my lower back, and a thrill runs through me.

"Dr. Greene." Ward appears at my side, giving me a friendly nod.

"Hi, Tate." I send a pointed glance to his suit. "Great suit." He always cleans up nice. It's probably why he's getting an increasing amount of attention in the media for his single status.

"How's Bea?" His daughter.

He smiles, his eyes crinkling. "She's great. Eight going on thirty-five."

"How's the harem?"

He lets out a short, tired laugh. "Relentless."

I try not to laugh *too* hard. "I heard about the field trip."

A couple weeks ago, Tate invited his daughter's class and the parents to a game, providing seats in the lower bowl so the kids could watch the game up close and arranging for a meet and greet with the players in the owner's box after.

A handful of parents monopolized Tate's attention. A lot of arm touching, hair flipping, big laughs at his jokes. Hints at getting the kids together for playdates.

"The, uh, single parents are kind of aggressive," he notes, the tops of his ears going pink.

"What do they call you online?" I act like I don't know. "Daddy Ward?"

"Please stop." His eyes close, and I laugh harder. "I don't think Ross likes how much media attention this is getting."

Ross Sheridan, the owner. Tate used to play for him when Ross coached the Storm, years ago. "Ross, or you?"

"Both."

"It'll blow over."

"I hope."

My attention is snagged by Alexei saying my name in conversation with someone, and our eyes meet.

Tate leans in and lowers his voice. "I'm glad you could make it." His gaze slides to my husband, deep in conversation with another hockey legend. "He needed you here tonight."

I almost laugh in Tate's face. No, he didn't. Needed me to distract from the hoards of people trying to shake his hand, maybe.

When I turn back to Tate, though, he's watching me with a

serious expression. "This kind of thing—" He glances around the room, at all the hockey greats eager to talk to my husband. "It can be hard. I don't think he'd have shown up without you, and he might have regretted it." He shrugs. "I regret not going to mine."

To your what? I'm about to ask, but he's beckoned over by a staff member.

"Talk to you later," he says, stepping away, "and if not, see you at warm-up tomorrow morning."

He disappears, and Alexei's big hand comes back to my waist, pulling me to his side. His warmth permeates the fabric of my dress.

"Let's find our seats," he says, leading me away.

"What's this award for?" I ask as he pulls my chair out at a table near the front of the room.

He clears his throat, looking away. "Lifetime achievement."

"Lifetime *achievement*?"

He makes a low, displeased noise of acknowledgment, and I let out a short laugh. They don't give this award to just anyone. Rick Miller has one. Tate has one. It's given to the best of the best—players who don't come around very often.

"Alexei, you're getting a lifetime achievement award and you look like you're bracing yourself for an ice bath. What's the deal? Is it the attention?" He should be used to it after so many years. These guys learn to ignore it. "You're getting one and you're still playing. Has that ever happened before?"

The strong line of his throat works and his expression darkens. "No."

What is his problem? "You haven't even retired yet and—"

"Exactly." Our eyes meet, his flashing with something. Oh. My stomach tightens. Whatever I see in his eyes, I don't like. "They give this award to guys who are *retired*."

Oh. I sink further.

The ceremony begins. A few guys are getting the award tonight, all retired except for Alexei. When it's his turn, a reel of his career highlights plays on the screen behind the stage.

It starts with him as a child, playing at the local rink. My heart does a funny flip as I recognize him from the photos. There's Nikita on the ice with him, smiling proudly. Video footage of a game at another local rink, where he must be a young teenager, already bigger than every other player on the ice. A clip of him in the minors, taking big hits without effort, like a brick wall. His first season in the NHL, stunning everyone with his power and strength as he kept up with the stars and proved his merit. Him receiving the Calder trophy awarded to the rookie of the year. More footage through the years of him on the ice—playing for Montreal, winning the Stanley Cup, winning the Norris trophy several times.

Clip after clip of Alexei Volkov being incredible at what he loves.

At my side, his arms are folded across his chest, shoulders tense and stiff while he watches the reel with an indiscernible expression.

That look in his eyes? Determination, longing, and a tiny shard of sadness? That's how I would look if someone was playing a highlight reel of my career moments in medicine, if I knew it was all about to end.

God. My chest aches and I run a hand over my sternum. Alexei's eyes cut to me, and my heart aches again. If someone said I couldn't do what I love, I'd die. I'd just die.

But first I'd fight like hell.

No wonder he wears that stupid watch with the stupid heart rate alarm. No wonder he goes to bed at nine on off nights, like an old man. No wonder he eats clean, does his daily sauna, and spends hours in the gym.

Hockey is everything to him the way medicine is everything to me, and it's about to go away. It's inevitable. It doesn't matter that he's one of the best. He can't play forever, and he knows this.

I find myself reaching over to Alexei and slipping my hand beneath his, folded under his bicep. He uncrosses his arms and looks at me in confusion, like he isn't sure what I'm doing, but he wraps his hand around mine and settles them in his lap.

What am I doing? The warm contact of his palm against mine is almost uncomfortably intimate. I sit frozen, holding his gaze, before the eye contact is too much and I turn my attention back to the screen.

The clip changes, and nausea spikes through me, tightening in my stomach, rising up my throat. His injury two years ago. A head shot that sent him to the hospital. The opening game of the season, after our first meeting. I watch the footage of him being carted off the ice, every cell in my body screaming at me. The room is silent, watching. There's me on the ice, crouching over him, checking him for spinal cord injuries before watching the trainers move him onto the stretcher. Beside me, Alexei's eyes are on me, a frown pulling between his eyebrows at whatever he sees on my face.

The reel changes to Alexei working with trainers and physio during his time away after the concussion. Joining practices again with a no-contact jersey. His first game back. His first assist after returning to the Storm. Playing with Hayden Owens, water to Alexei's oil, but a pair who turned out to be incredible together. More clips of Alexei's dominance on the ice.

The reel ends and applause thunders through the ballroom. Tate steps onstage, up to the podium.

"Alexei Volkov is one of the toughest bastards I've had the pleasure to work with." Ward wears a wry smile, and chuckles rise around the room. "Full of determination, grit, and passion for the game, he's an inspiration to everyone who has the privilege of working with him. I am proud to present him with the award for lifetime achievement in the National Hockey League."

Another roar of applause as Alexei gets up. Before walking up to accept his award, though, his gaze swings down to me, he takes my hand, and he pulls me up to standing before he lowers his mouth to mine. The kiss is brief, hard, and quick, but something warm and fizzing and desperate loops through me.

He needs you here, Ward had said, and my heart aches again.

As fast as it started, the kiss is over, and Alexei strides onto the stage, shakes Tate's hand, gives the room a terse nod, before he's seated back beside me, and the ceremony moves on.

I hate Alexei Volkov for what he said about me and my incompetence, but for the first time, I wish his impending retirement wasn't a given.

WHEN THE CEREMONY ENDS, I lean toward my wife, inhaling the scent I've been clinging to this entire evening. Whenever the panic about retiring started to gnaw at me, I'd pull her closer, take a deep breath, and shove the feelings away.

"Come with me to the bar," I murmur.

She arches an eyebrow.

"I'm going to get mauled. You're a good deterrent."

She rolls her eyes, smirking, but stands, and doesn't even say anything when my hand comes to her lower back. Gazes follow her, sweeping up and down her dress, until they spot my hand on her and look away with respect.

I'm not surprised guys are staring. She's a fucking knock-out. She's always beautiful, but tonight, in that dress, I just—the second I saw her in the lobby, walking toward me like some kind of siren, some dream, my heart stopped.

Doesn't mean I like them looking at her, though. Possessive feelings course through my veins. She's my wife.

She hasn't said a word about what I put in her suitcase, which makes me think she hasn't seen it. My pulse picks up with anticipation.

And then there's what I found in her bag. An old book from

my mom's flower shop, with the meanings of flowers. As a teenager helping her out after school, I read it a hundred times.

How did she get it? She must have found it in the library at home. An odd, playful feeling pulses in my chest, cutting through all the weird tension and worry about tonight. The flowers started as a private joke with myself, but now that she's in on it, I don't mind nearly as much as I thought I would.

At the bar, I order her another drink and a water for myself before I step in front of her, backing her against the bar. I'm not hiding her from the room, I tell myself, I'm closing myself off from everyone. I need a fucking break, is all. One hand leans on the bar counter, the other comes around her waist and I pull her close. Close enough so that her hair brushes my shoulder, and her ear is inches from my mouth. Close enough to feel her warmth against my side.

"Feeling possessive tonight, Volkov?"

Yes. More than ever. "If we look like we're busy, no one will interrupt us." No more fucking handshakes. No more fucking congratulations on the end of my fucking career.

Our drinks arrive, and we sip in silence, me inhaling her perfume and her staring off into space. I count seventeen freckles across her nose and cheekbones before I interrupt her daydream.

"What are you thinking about, Hellfire?"

"Why aren't your parents here?"

My gut tightens. "I told you. They give this to retired guys."

She studies me. I don't know how to feel, under her scrutiny like this.

"They worked to the bone so I could play hockey," I tell her, not looking into those fascinating eyes. "If they weren't working, they were driving me to hockey at the crack of dawn." Finally, I force myself to meet her gaze. "Playing in the NHL showed them it was worth it."

"Alexei." Her teeth sink into her bottom lip, a little frown pulling between her brows. "They're proud of you. That's not going to go away when you retire."

"I know. I just—" I shake my head. "They didn't flee Russia so I could retire and spend all day cooking and watering my plants."

"They're proud of you," she says with conviction, like back at the benefit when she told me about loving her work at the hospital. "No matter what."

A beat of silence passes. When she held my hand, my entire world anchored to her, all the panic and worry subsiding for a brief moment. I don't know what's going on anymore.

"I'm sorry I recommended you for retirement." Her eyes are wide with an unreadable emotion. Regret, maybe. "I shouldn't have done that."

Pain twists in my chest at the memory, but I keep my voice steady, my gaze across the room, and my expression neutral. "You called me a lost cause."

Silence. She's chewing that tempting bottom lip again. "I may not enjoy watching you get hurt, but you're definitely not a lost cause." She shakes her head, gesturing around the room. "All these people are here for you, Alexei. The applause for you was ten times the other guys'. Everyone thinks you're incredible, not just me."

Under my hand on her waist, she tenses, eyes flaring with surprise like she didn't mean to say that.

"You think I'm incredible?" I arch an eyebrow, holding tight to my cold, undeterred expression, even as warmth and pride spread through me.

She gives me a tiny nod. "Sure. Yes. You're clearly a great hockey player."

"Are you sorry you transferred me to another doctor?"

Wordless, she shakes her head. I want to pry that head

open and read every thought. I want to know her and understand her. If she didn't think I was on my career deathbed, why'd she shove me onto another doctor?

"So." Her eyebrows lift, eyes curious. "You're going to Rory and Hazel's wedding now."

I'm about to press on the previous subject, but I want her to trust me enough to tell me herself. "Yeah. I'm going."

My mind flips to that incredible fuck at her work benefit, and my groin tightens. I probably should ditch Miller's wedding, or I should find another place to stay for the week, but I'm not going to do either.

"I thought you didn't go to weddings," she says lightly.

"I don't." A pause. "I was engaged," I admit. Telling her this makes me feel like I'm balancing on a tightwire. I scan her face, gauging her reaction, but she just nods.

"Emma."

An ugly spike of alarm shoots through me, both at the name I haven't said out loud in years, and that Georgia knows.

"Your mom brought that photo album of you as an ugly baby." Her eyes tease me before she sobers. "Your wedding invitation was tucked in the back."

Right. She texted me a bunch of pictures. Jesus, that was a month ago. "I wasn't an ugly baby."

My mom sent me a flurry of rabbit photos that night, and it hits me: she didn't like Emma. She tried to, and she never said a word against her, but she didn't connect with her like she has with Georgia.

"What happened?"

I sigh, rolling my bad shoulder, but stop when Georgia's eyes flick to it. "I was young and stupid."

"I was engaged, too."

"You were?" Another spike of alarm. She didn't want to get married. What kind of guy would she actually say yes to? Is it that Liam guy she didn't want to talk about? Does she still think about him? I hate the idea of another guy's ring on her finger. "What happened?"

"I was young and stupid."

Curiosity has me by the throat. "They might ask this in the citizenship interview."

Her eyes turn wary. "You first."

I hesitate. I never talk about what happened. I want to know her side, though. I want her to trust me like she did the night she bandaged my broken finger. "She didn't show up to our wedding."

Her back muscles tense, and she turns to face me. I can feel her body heat in the inch between us.

"What?" she asks in a cold, deadly voice that I kind of like. "She left you at the altar?"

I snort, shaking my head. "No. The morning of."

Her nostrils flare. "Was she stupid?"

"Now who's feeling possessive, Hellfire?"

"I hate that stupid nickname." Her eyes flash.

"No, you don't." I stare down into her eyes, counting every color in her irises. "Her family didn't like me. They were wealthy. Old money." I give her a significant look. "Very close with the Greenes."

She makes a face. "Not this Greene."

"I know that. Now."

I watch realization dawn on her face before guilt stabs me in the gut. "You thought I was like her."

"Yeah." A tight nod. More regret pinching behind my sternum. "You reminded me of her." I gesture at her hair. "Well-dressed, beautiful, charming. Outgoing. Charismatic."

She blinks, stunned.

"They didn't think I was from a suitable family." I can't believe how many cards I'm showing her tonight.

Her jaw drops. "What?"

I grunt, nodding again.

"If I ever meet that bitch, I will kill her."

In an instant, all the weird feelings evaporate, replaced with the urge to laugh. My head drops to her neck, and I smile into it so she won't see. "Easy there, Hellfire." I take a deep breath, inhaling her.

"Do you miss her?" she asks quietly.

My relationship with Emma was nothing like what I see between my teammates and their partners. I never looked at her the way Streicher looks at Pippa, I didn't joke around with her the way Owens and Darcy do, and I didn't tease her like Miller does to Hazel.

"No." Easy answer.

I barely saw her during the season. Weeks would pass without seeing her. None of those guys could do that. All I cared about was hockey, though.

When we were apart, I never thought about her. I can barely go five minutes without thinking about the woman next to me.

I frown. That's not good.

Georgia pulls back to study me. "I'm still sorry."

"I'm not cut out for marriage. Maybe that's why this is working so well. We're a good pair." I give her a look, gripping the bar counter. "Your turn."

She looks away, shrugs like it doesn't matter. "He wanted a pretty little thing on his arm, taking care of his home, raising his kids. And being engaged to Hugo Greene's granddaughter opens a lot of doors for a new doctor."

"Was this Liam?"

She nods, and her mouth tips. "Thanks for not treating me like a piece of arm candy tonight, by the way."

"How'd it end?"

"He unenrolled me from medical school."

I stiffen. "What?" She's still not looking at me, and my hand comes beneath her chin, tipping her face up. "Georgia."

At the sharp edge to my voice, her eyes flare.

"Now who's jealous?" she whispers, but I ignore it. I'm not jealous, I'm furious. No wonder she lost it when I got rid of her car.

"Explain."

The delicate line of her throat works, and I feel the urge to kiss it. Kiss her better. Make her forget this asshole ever existed. I'm still holding her chin.

"We were here in Toronto, where his residency was, and I was about to start medical school back at UBC. He wanted me here, with him. He said he was doing me a favor. That it was for my own good, because medical school would be hard. I don't have the right personality, I think he said." She studies her nails. "He said we could get married, and I was so stupidly in love, which I now realize was infatuation, not love, that I almost let him convince me."

I want to find this guy and kill him. I want to ruin his life for hurting her. Off the ice, I never fight, but I would knock this guy's teeth out.

For your own good, I said when I bought her the car. Shit. "I'm sorry again about the car. I should have talked to you about it. We could have made the decision together."

Her mouth curves into a humorless smile, and she shakes her head. "Forget it, Alexei. I have. I let old wounds get the best of me. You're nothing like Liam."

Hearing her say that does something to me, hooks my attention on her even harder. My fascination with my wife triples.

This isn't supposed to happen. The more I learn about her, the less I'm supposed to think about her.

"That's why you don't want to get married."

She shrugs like she doesn't care. "I thought I wanted to marry him, but he just wanted to control me. Marriage doesn't always mean the same thing to people."

Emma viewed marriage as a way to move up in the world. *What I now realize was infatuation,* Georgia said about her ex. I never loved Emma, either. I was hurt and humiliated and protective of my family. I was angry I ddin't see it coming and ignored every red flag. Not heartbroken, though.

"Has there been anyone since?" I ask. "Since him? For the citizenship interview."

"No one serious." She looks away before her gaze darts to mine. "You?"

"Nope."

We stand there in silence, every nerve ending aware of her so close to me. Before our agreement, I'd never admit those things to her. And I don't know what I would have done with the information she told me about her past.

Used it against her, probably. Now I just want to know more. My attention catches on her mouth. That pretty, perfect mouth. Arousal trickles into my blood.

Standing next to her isn't enough. My mind slides to the library, being buried deep inside her while I lost my mind.

I want her. It's as simple as that. I can't stop thinking about her, and I want more.

"You want to get out of here?" I ask.

She glances around the event space. "Are we allowed to leave?"

"Sure. Dinner's over. We can do what we want."

"Okay." She holds my gaze, and I can't read her expression. "Let's get out of here."

WE MAKE our way back to the hotel room in tense silence.

She left him at the altar, a voice whispers, a protective surge rising in my blood.

And the way he looked tonight, watching his highlight reel. My chest aches. More than ever, I regret recommending him for retirement. I was acting on my tangled and blurry emotions.

In the elevator, our eyes meet, and my pulse skips a beat. The air is thick with tension. We're not supposed to mess around, but the knowing interest in his eyes says he doesn't care.

I don't think I care, either. I forget why we weren't supposed to.

Inside the room, he holds my gaze, removing his jacket and loosening his tie, undoing the buttons of his shirt while my heart pounds in my ears. His mouth tilts and he takes a seat in the chair across from the bed. He leans back, spreads out, and watches me, so wildly handsome and serious. The image is like an advertisement in one of my fashion magazines—stacked muscle, dark, possessive eyes, and a knowing smirk.

It's the *who can break first* game. My competitive instincts wake up.

A memory flashes into my head: his tight, jealous expression at my sleep shirt, the one from an old hookup. That shirt is how I'm going to win this game.

When I open my suitcase, though, it's not there. None of the undergarments I packed are.

I hook a finger beneath a plum lacy strap, lifting the garment. It's high-end, similar to what the designer sent along with my dress. My blood starts to hum. I'm smiling, though.

"Volkov." I turn, holding it so he can see. He lounges in the chair with an undeterred expression. "What the hell is this?"

"No idea."

"Where's my stuff?"

"What stuff?"

"My panties, Alexei. You messed with my bag."

He must have done it this morning. He said he'd bring my bag to the arena. Why am I smiling?

"Maybe I just like buying you things."

I let out a high laugh of disbelief. "After years of making fun of me for shopping? I doubt it."

It's some kind of sick power game he's playing. I should hate being controlled like this, and yet I get a flutter between my legs at the idea of wearing lingerie he bought for me.

He wants to play a game? I'm in.

"How thoughtful of you." It's the hotel room all over again. *I am here to play.* "Guess I should try it on."

"Guess you should."

I can't get a full breath as I turn my back to him, feeling the weight of his attention. It's different than the hotel room. I don't know how. Maybe it feels like we're playing for fun now, instead of a way to get back at each other.

Off comes my dress and heels, leaving me in the undergarments the designer sent.

Nerves trickle through me. He's not backing down. Neither am I.

My hands shake as I take the undergarments off, but not from fear. Hookups have always been so dull and predictable, so unsatisfying. I've never been with someone that'll play with me like this.

With my back to him, I stand naked, Alexei's eyes burning marks in my skin. I don't know what the hell I'm doing. I can't stop, though. I feel alive, like I'm sprinting down a hill. If he rejects me, I'll explode into a thousand pieces of humiliation.

The man bought me lingerie, though. He's not going to reject me. I hope.

Slowly, so painfully slowly, I put the bra and panties on. Perfect fit. My tits look amazing and I feel like a goddess. My respect for him grows.

Before I can turn, though, he's at my back, warm and bare-chested. He reaches past me to lean on the dresser, caging me in. His lips meet the sensitive spot between my neck and my shoulder, and my thoughts scatter.

"You look like a fucking dream, Georgia."

"You don't think I look like a . . ." I pause, heart hammering. "Rotten tuber?"

I feel the curve of his lips on my shoulder. Just once, I wish I could see him smile. I bet it would blow my mind.

"Yes, I know all about your little term of endearment," I laugh. "We could have been caught, you asshole."

Another curve against my shoulder. Another scraping kiss, stubble against skin. Goosebumps rise down my back. We're supposed to be competing, I tell myself. Not laughing.

"I couldn't help myself." His low voice rumbles through his chest, which is pressed against my back. He's warm, and I fight the urge to lean into him. "Turn for me, Hellfire."

"Don't tell me what to do." And yet, I'm turning, leaning

back against the dresser, heart in my throat as his gaze drags down my body.

Our eyes meet; his flash with heat.

"You look fucking incredible." He sounds like he's in pain as his hand comes to my thigh, brushing his fingertips up my leg. "But you knew that."

"So this is the new direction you had in mind, huh."

"Tell me to stop."

His hand drags closer to my center, and my heart pounds everywhere—my throat, my ears, my chest, between my legs. His head dips to my neck again, his lips skating over my skin, still trailing his fingers over me. Over the seam at my hip, over my waist, up to the lace at my ribcage. Under his touch, I don't breathe.

"Why did you buy this?" I whisper, my focus narrowing to his fingertips at the top of my thigh, four inches from where I need them. Where I'm getting damp for him.

"Buying you things makes me feel a certain way."

My gaze drops. He's hard, huge, and my mind races with the memory of how he felt inside me. The deep, pleasurable burn as my body worked to accommodate him. A delicious ache forms between my legs.

"Are we doing this again, Hellfire?"

God, yes, I want to say. *Fucking finally.* "I don't care," I say instead. This is a game, I remind myself, and caring means I lose.

Slowly, he shakes his head, just like that time on the ice when that drunk guy was talking to me. "Not good enough."

I reach for his erection, but he catches my wrists, pinning them together in one hand. "No." He nips my shoulder. "You ready to beg?"

Determination roars through me. "Never."

"We'll see."

He brings his hand between my legs, brushing his knuckles over my center, over the panties he bought. The barest contact against that bundle of nerves has my head falling back, has my hips arching into his fingers, but he keeps his touch light and teasing.

"Wet already." He sounds like he's won something, dragging slow, leisurely strokes over me.

A frustrated noise slips out of me.

"The magic word is *please*."

"Bite me."

He pinches my clit firm enough to send pleasure racing through me, but it's not enough. I curl forward, clamping my teeth together to hold in the moan.

"*Bite me* is not the magic word, Hellfire."

"You're doing this because you hate me."

His mouth tips up. So cruel. So callous. So fucking hot. "I'm still going to make you come."

While he continues that hypnotic work between my legs, I hardly notice us making our way to one of the beds. I fall back as he climbs up beside me, leaning on one propped elbow, bicep bulging, while his other hand brushes over my panties. For a guy who's made his name being brutal, aggressive, and powerful, he's shockingly gentle.

Too gentle. I need more.

"You need to go harder and faster if you want me to actually feel anything," I manage, baiting him.

There's that annoying smirk again. "I'm aware, sweetheart."

"Don't call me that."

"Don't call you sweetheart? What's the matter?"

I like it too much. Instead of forcing me to answer, though, he slips beneath the fabric covering me. Pleasure whirs through my body at the friction, so much more intense with skin against skin. His fingers move faster, circling and swiping, and pressure builds behind my clit. My eyes close. I can feel his gaze on my face, can feel him watching me intently, but I don't care.

"Oh my god," I whisper before pressing my lips together to hold in the moan.

He winds me higher, kissing my neck and shoulder and chest. My thoughts begin to blur.

"All right. You want more?" His touch stops, his hands come to my waist, and he flips me onto my stomach. "I'll give you more."

MY EYES GO WIDE, face pressed into the duvet. "I wasn't
—*oh*."

His fingers sink into me. Intense pleasure radiates from
where he rubs my G-spot.

I shudder, toes curling as desire courses through me. In the
back of my mind, I find it annoying, how quickly and easily he
found it. It's probably just the angle of him kneeling behind me
on the bed. Urgent heat gathers between my legs, and I clutch
the duvet. He delivers a sharp slap to my ass. Another wave of
heat rolls through me.

"You love this, don't you?" His voice is low in my ear as I
shudder and clench on him. "You love being filled and fucked
by my fingers."

I close my eyes, trying not to disintegrate yet. That would
be way, way too good for his ego.

"Answer me."

"Yes," I rush out, before I curse myself for letting him win
that round.

His hand smooths over my backside. "Good girl."

Another shiver of delight moves through me. "Shut up," I
huff.

"What else would you be, with those pretty bows on your ankles?"

My shoes earlier. He always notices.

"Are you going to come tonight, good girl?" he asks in a low, smug voice.

I clench around his fingers, the tight spasm as pleasure rolls through me. Something about Alexei calling me that makes my brain melt.

"I doubt it." My strained voice betrays me.

Another sharp slap on my ass, and the coil of need between my legs winds, tightening.

"You know what I think, Hellfire?"

My teeth sink into my bottom lip so I don't cry out as he strokes his fingers in and out of me a little faster, a little rougher. God, that's so good.

"I think you're so in your head all the time, so in control, that it's nice to let me take charge."

With his free hand, he gathers my wrists and holds them against my lower back. I choke back a whimper as lust tightens between my legs.

I guess I like this.

"You're doing so good for me, sweetheart," he murmurs, trailing his lips over the back of my shoulder, and deep inside me, something shifts.

Everything heightens. The coil of need winds another notch, and sparks start going off at the center of my spine.

Oh god. He's rubbing exactly the right spot. I can't think. I can barely breathe. My arms flex, tugging against his hold, but he holds tight.

Shit. *No.* I think I'm going to—I can't actually be—pleasure tightens through my body, spiraling, spinning, whirling, expanding. My mouth falls open.

I'm going to come.

Pleasure washes over me, and as I tip over the edge, I bury my face in the pillow. I'd rather suffocate than give him the satisfaction of knowing I'm coming, but it only makes it worse. I only come *harder* on his fingers. His scent, the urgent feel of his fingers inside me, the way I know he's looking at me, so focused and hungry and intense, like I'm the focus of his full attention, they all fold together and the sensations within me double, triple, quadruple. I'm shaking on his fingers, clamping my teeth together, making fists with my bound wrists, and staying silent with every shred of control I have left.

"Did you just come?"

"No," I croak. I'm panting. My pulse races. Floaty, languid feelings drift through my bloodstream. Delicious serotonin has melted my brain.

"Liar."

I can't look at him. I don't think my vision works anymore.

His hand returns between my legs and my eyes go wide.

"What are you doing?" I gasp, tensing up with sensitivity as his fingers slick over my clit. I'm soaked.

"You said you didn't come." His breathing sounds ragged but he gives my wrists a teasing squeeze. "So we're not going to stop until you do."

My lips part. This wasn't part of the plan. I don't know what to do now. He swirls the pads of his fingers across my oversensitive nerves and my eyes close. Every nerve ending in my body melts with his slow touch. I think I sigh with pleasure.

"Throwing in the towel so soon, Doctor?"

"Fuck you." My voice is a thin rasp as another wave of heat ripples through me. My god. His fingers speed up. My muscles tighten again, pleasure cresting higher, insides going molten.

No. Nonono. Again? How?

I let out a desperate groan into the pillow, shuddering as the pressure between my legs peaks, firing through me, heating my blood and making my mind go blank. It's the best form of torture, this. I don't know how long this one goes on for—it could be seconds or hours, I'm not sure, but when I descend back to earth, I'm breathing hard, heart racing and limbs so heavy I couldn't stand if I wanted to.

A pleased noise rumbles out of his chest. "Again, huh?'

"No," I protest. I hate losing like this. I hate that he can make me come so easily. "You didn't. I didn't."

"Mhm." I refuse to look at him, but I can hear it in his voice —he loves this. He loves winning. "You're beautiful. I've always thought that."

"Shut up," I gasp. He's lying. "You hate me."

"I always thought you were beautiful, though." His eyes tease me. "It made me mad."

He guides his fingers back inside me. Moments later, I shatter again into a thousand pieces.

With a word, I could end this. There isn't a single part of me that believes he'd push this further than I want. He'd stop the second I say stop.

I don't say stop, though. For some reason, I hang on.

And I'm not quite sure I hate him anymore, not after tonight. Not after he apologized the other week. Not after he coached soccer for me, and they liked him.

"Done yet?" he asks.

"Done what?" I manage, panting. "I'm bored."

Alexei makes me come so many times, I lose count. One turns into three, which turns into five. I think we're around seven or eight by now, but they're starting to string into one another, so does that count as separate or just one? Who cares. I'm a disintegrating mess, coming on my husband's hand while he looks, doling out pleasure.

"There," he says with satisfaction when a moan finally slips past my clenched teeth as I come again. "There we go."

"I hate you," I gasp.

"Uh-huh. I know. I hate you, too."

It doesn't sound like he does, though. It sounds like he's enjoying this more than I am. Deep down, his smug satisfaction thrills me. I'm disgusting. I hate myself for that. Where's my fantasy of the faceless hot guy who doesn't talk and follows orders?

That guy could never make me come like this.

I sob another involuntary moan into the pillow.

"You could end this, you know, if you just admit it."

Never. Not while I'm still conscious. I'd pass out before I admitted defeat. He'd be so smug. He'd lord it over me for the rest of our deal. Every time he looked at me, every time he spoke to me, we'd both be thinking about this.

I don't even want to think about what this means, that he can make me come so easily.

"Fine!" I shout. "Fuck. Fine. Okay. You made me come. Once."

"Once?" His hand presses at my entrance like a threat.

"I lost count." I don't care if he knows. I don't care about anything.

I steel my spine and haul in a deep breath. My pride is about to get the bruising of a lifetime.

A kiss on my lower back. Soft, sweet, barely more pressure than a butterfly. His breath fans over my skin. "Good girl."

I shiver.

"Such a good wife for me," he says in a low voice, and threads of warmth trickle through me at his praise. A kiss on my left wrist.

"Stop that." He's just messing with me. He just loves winning.

"You did so well," he adds, pressing his lips to my right wrist, and I like that, too.

"What the actual fuck is happening here?" I whisper at the wall as he trails a soft line of kisses across my back. His hand is on my ass, smoothing over my skin. He chuckles.

That fucker actually *chuckles*.

He delivers a sharp slap to my ass, and my pussy tightens around nothing, the traitor. He lifts off the bed, and I feel the cold loss of his hands on my body.

That's my cue. I rise to my elbows, dragging my lifeless corpse up. I weigh approximately twelve million pounds.

In an instant, he's back, hand pressing to my lower back, pushing me down. "Stay there."

Opening my mouth to argue is an instinct.

"Don't argue," he says, but softly. Almost sweetly.

I don't know who this is. He body-swapped with someone else while my face was buried in the pillow.

Still, I sink into the duvet, catching my breath while I listen to him in the en suite. The tap runs. A rustle of fabric. His heavy footsteps return, and my lips part in surprise as a warm, damp cloth presses between my legs.

"What are you—" I start.

"Shut. Up." Again, that soft, soothing voice.

"You're not actually taking care of me right now?" I ask in my own soft, dazed voice as he swipes gently against my center. I want to wrench around and look at his expression to get a goddamned handle on what we're doing here, but I don't want him to see my baffled look of concern and confusion. Keeping my eyes open is proving difficult, anyway.

"This is what people do after sex, Hellfire."

No, they don't. We didn't, not last time. This wasn't anything like last time, though.

The cloth disappears. I hear it land in the bathroom before the bed dips. I crack one eye open. He's sitting on the edge.

"Are you going to sleepwalk tonight?"

"No," I lie, replaying the sickening stomach lurch as I watched the footage of his head shot, of him being carried off the ice.

"You remember what I said?" His voice teases me, low but gentle, and the stubborn part of me digs her heels in. "About you sleepwalking?"

If I sleepwalk again, he's getting rid of my bed. He wouldn't.

I think about him buying me that car, and I'm not so sure.

"If I wake up with you in my bed," he warns, and I squint at him, half-awake.

"You won't," I promise, too sleepy and orgasmed-out to deal with tomorrow's consequences. Around Alexei, I can't seem to stop running my mouth. It's a problem. It gets me into trouble, again and again.

The fun kind of trouble, though. The kind that made me come over and over.

He sweeps my hair aside and his breath skitters over the back of my neck. "Close your eyes," he murmurs.

"Don't tell me what to do."

I close my eyes because I want to, not because he told me to, but within seconds, I'm fast asleep.

The next morning, I wake with my leg trapped under Alexei's, tucked into his chest.

His erection presses against my hip and my eyelids fly open. His skin is impossibly warm and his heart beats steadily under my palm. Slow, steady breathing lifts his expansive chest.

Fuck, I mouth, cursing myself and my stupid problem.

When the footage of his career started last night, I should

have made an excuse and hid in the bathroom, checking my makeup, so I didn't have to watch.

He needs you here, Ward had said, and an ache forms in my throat at the memory.

I sneak out of bed without waking him, tiptoe into the shower, and wash every trace of what we did last night off of myself.

I don't want to think about it. I don't want to feel like this, like I'm starting to care.

This crush I have on my husband isn't going away, but I'm going to ignore it until it does.

"VOLKOV," Ward calls as I pass his office at the arena in Vancouver. He and Darcy sit in the chairs in front of his desk, watching game tape on her laptop screen. "You got a second?"

Their gazes drop to the bouquet in my arms as I step into his office. I was planning on dropping these off before Georgia gets in.

"Nice flowers." Ward's eyes shine with interest, and Darcy grins at me. He glances at Darcy with a smile. "Seems like Volkov has caught on to this whole married thing."

Calla lilies—beauty. My mind slips to the hotel room after the awards dinner, and how addictive making Georgia come was. How she looked in that dress and lingerie. How it felt to see her wear what I bought her.

How I loved holding her wrists together and taking control. Making her lose it. Watching her shudder with pleasure.

It's all I've thought about since.

"Thanks." I clear my throat, trying not to smile. "What's up?"

"What do you think of this guy?" He restarts the game tape. "Number eight."

On the laptop, we watch a defenseman in a minors game.

Big guy. Young, from the quick flashes of his face that we can see. He knocks players out of the way with ease, disrupts the play so his teammates can snag the puck. When he can, he passes to his defensive partner or a forward.

"Good team player," I murmur. He looks like a younger version of me. "He's young and needs work but he's good."

In the right situation, he could be great. Like Walker. My gut wrenches with guilt and anguish.

I still haven't figured out how to help him. It's early December. Ward can make trades until early March. We only have a few months to get Walker playing at a higher level.

"Watch him," Ward tells Darcy about the guy in the minors. "If anyone makes any moves, I want to know."

Any offers, he means.

"You got it." She closes up her laptop and stands.

"Thanks, Darcy." Ward gives her a smile before he looks at me and gestures at her seat. "Stay for a second, would you, Volkov?"

"See you, Darce," I call as she waves and heads out of Ward's office. "Are you going to sign him?" I ask, settling into the seat across from him.

Ward sits back, hesitating like he's choosing his words with care. "Thinking about it."

The Storm roster is full. My gut tightens. So he's either thinking about trading Walker or ushering me into retirement.

"Relax, Volkov. It's normal for us to have guys on the back burner. You know how it is in this game. Things change fast." His mouth tips as he shifts in his seat, glancing at his knee. "I'm glad you decided to accept the award."

I think about how Georgia looked at me that night, like she finally understood why I'm doing everything I can to delay retirement. If anyone would get it, it would be her.

I have a feeling we're a lot more similar than I thought. The realization isn't as uncomfortable as it would have been months ago.

"Fine." I rub the back of my neck. "I'm happy it's over."

Ward's mouth quirks. "It must have been nice to have Georgia with you. I know it wasn't easy."

It wasn't just *nice*. I can't imagine enduring it without her. *You hate me,* she'd said later that night, but I don't. Not anymore.

Not even close. It's a problem that I'll solve another day, though.

"Thanks for what you said." I give him a brief nod. "I appreciate it."

He nods back, pride in his eyes. "All the truth."

I think about what he keeps saying—that hockey can't be everything. That he regrets not accepting his award.

"What happened after you retired?" I ask.

He laughs, short and dry. "I was a mess. It's probably a good thing I didn't accept my award. I probably would have made a scene and humiliated myself."

I stare at him, confused. Ward's the most composed, collected guy I know.

Off my expression, he gives me a wry smile. "After I retired, I spent a good two years hating myself, hating the world, hating the guy who I collided with on the ice. Wasn't his fault." He shrugs. "It wasn't my first knee injury, but I blamed him and blamed the doctors who couldn't fix me. At one point I actually blamed my brother—he's a biomechatronics engineer—because he wouldn't even consider building me a new knee. Said he wasn't in the business of bionic body parts. I didn't talk to him for a year after that." He sucks in a tight breath. "I blamed the world because I made hockey everything and when it was gone, I had nothing."

Fear trickles into my bloodstream. I don't want that. I don't know how to avoid it, though. Hockey is everything to me. When it's gone, what will I have left?

Nothing.

"And I drank way too much." He reaches into his pocket and pulls out his keys. On the keyring is what looks like a large coin with a tree on it. "Nine years sober."

Jesus. I didn't know any of this. "What changed?"

"Found out I was going to have a daughter. Well," he smiles, "I didn't know she was going to be a daughter at that time. But I found out I was going to have a kid. I didn't know what to do, so I went to Ross"—he nudges his chin toward the ceiling, where Ross's office is on the floor above us—"and he shoved me in rehab. Once I completed the program, he got me a job coaching women's hockey at UBC. And now we're here." A calm, steady smile. "Just keep looking forward, Volkov."

"How do you cope with not playing anymore?" Asking this is the closest I've ever come to accepting my fate.

He folds his arms, thinking. "I realized helping players perform at their best and achieve their dreams is just as rewarding."

Good for him, but it's unlikely I'll ever find something I love as much as playing hockey.

"Think we have a shot at the Cup this year?" I ask.

He takes a deep breath, thinking. "Yes. Maybe. I hope." His mouth slants. "God, I fucking hope. More than anything, I want that Cup again."

The year before he was forced to retire, in overtime of the last round of the Stanley Cup playoffs, he scored the game-winning goal. A golden goal, those are called. The Storm haven't made it to the final round of the playoffs since. I won it with Montreal sixteen years ago, and I still remember the roar of the fans in the arena and around the city.

Winning the Cup is like nothing else.

"You think it would feel the same, winning the Cup from your side of the bench?" I ask.

His eyes meet mine, sparking with determination. "It would be better."

"WHAT DO you like about Coach Georgia?" one of the girls asks Alexei at practice the next week, when he insisted on joining.

"She's mean to me."

They giggle and I hide a smile.

"And she doesn't let me push her around."

"Do you think she's pretty?"

"Girls." I give them a look.

"Yes," Alexei says at the same time, and we exchange a look. My stomach does that annoying rolling thing again, warm and languid and fluttery. Is he thinking about what we did after the awards dinner?

I haven't. Not even once. Not when I wake up, not when I'm trying to work, and not when I'm falling asleep at night.

The girls grin at one another. "Do you think she's *beautiful?*"

"Yes. But she's also smart, and hardworking."

An odd-looking potted plant arrived at my office at the arena this morning. *Lady's slipper—sudden and unpredictable attraction.*

I avoid looking at him, but I can feel my face heating. What kind of game is he playing now? "All right, ladies, no more stalling. Let's do some passing drills."

"What was that you called me a few months ago," Alexei murmurs in my ear while the girls run passing drills up and down the field. "Ugly?"

His eyes shift to mine, the tiniest spark of amusement flaring in them. I laugh and then cover it with a cough. We can't tease each other like this.

"And I stand by it," I lie, keeping my eyes on the girls.

His eyes cut to mine, glittering. "Really."

"Mhm. A face only a mother could love."

He shrugs, turning his gaze to the field. "Because you look at me like you think I'm hot."

My jaw drops. "I don't."

Of course I do, but I'm not going to admit that.

His mouth slants and even though he isn't looking at me, smugness radiates off him in waves.

"I *don't*."

"That must be the sound of someone else's panties dropping when I wear my glasses."

"Keep dreaming, Volkov. And stop flirting with me." I blow my whistle and call the girls in, giving them a few general pointers before I split the teams up for a scrimmage. After a few minutes, my gaze snags on someone on the field, and I frown.

"What?" Alexei asks.

"Teddy's holding back."

"Teddy . . ." He studies the field. "Black ponytail?"

I nod. "I see this with athletes sometimes after an injury. They're so afraid of reinjuring themselves or slowing their progress that they take it too easy. You don't have this issue." Just the opposite.

He watches, listening with a serious, thoughtful expression.

I turn my attention back to Teddy. She's shy, conflict-averse, very sweet, and helpful. Helpful. Hmm.

Oh. A lightbulb goes off in my head, and I blow the whistle. "Time out," I call to the field. "Take a break, grab some water."

When the girls reach the sidelines, I gesture at Teddy.

"When you're handling the ball," I tell her quietly while everyone talks and drinks water, "it's no fun for the other team if you hand it over without a fight. If you make it too easy, they'll get bored." I tip my chin at Tasha, one of our most competitive players. "Look at Tash. She loves to win, but only if it's earned. If you make it too easy for her, she doesn't feel like she deserves it."

Teddy gives me a flat look. "I see what you're doing."

"Good." I smile at her. "So when Tash is coming at you, tell yourself, *I'm going to make this really difficult on her because that'll be more fun for her.* Play harder, Teddy. It'll do you good."

Teddy takes a deep breath. "Okay."

I blow my whistle, the girls hit the field, and the game resumes.

Someone passes to Teddy. She brings the ball toward the net, Tasha running to intercept. I hold my breath as Teddy tenses, pauses, but then flips the ball up and away with her feet like we practiced the other week.

I whoop, but cover my mouth with my hand as Teddy takes off toward the net, Tash on her heels.

"Here we go," I whisper, heart lifting, eyes on Teddy as she kicks the ball at the net.

The goalie leaps for it, arms outstretched, but the ball sails right past.

I whoop and clap and cup my hands to my mouth. "Nice work, Teddy!"

The girls surround her, hugging her and congratulating her, and even from the sidelines, I can see her ear-to-ear grin.

"Come on," Tash yells at the sky, falling to her knees in defeat, but she's smiling, the competitive part of her activated.

See? I mouth at Teddy, pointing at Tash and then making a smile gesture. She nods and smiles back at me.

"How did you know to do that?" Alexei asks. He regards me with a curious, searching expression, like he's seeing something new in me.

I shrug. "I didn't. But Teddy has a heart of gold. Helping others and contributing to the team motivates her, so I used that to get what I want out of her. Every athlete is different. They're all motivated by different things."

His eyebrows lift. "Very impressive, Coach Georgia."

Warmth spills through me at his approval.

"Are we going again?" one of the girls asks, and I check the time on my phone.

"That's all for today." I point at Teddy. "Nice goal, Teddy." I list off some more pointers before turning to Alexei. "Anything to add?"

He shakes his head. "Great work, girls." He sends me a questioning look. "Want me to lead them through the stretch?"

"Uh. Sure. Thank you."

While I make notes about today's practice and start cleaning up the field, bringing in the pylons, I listen to the girls ask him questions about recovery, his diet, his training, and the answers in his low voice.

Later, Alexei and I are walking to the car, carrying the equipment, when Teddy catches up to us.

"Wait," she says, handing something to Alexei. It makes a clinking noise.

"We made you these." She drops them in his open palm and I start to smile, heart squeezing.

Friendship bracelets, just like mine, with the cheap plastic beads strung on elastics, with letters arranged into silly sayings.

My first thought is that he'll make fun of them, or say something dismissive.

"I love them." He nods at her. So handsome in his serious, stern way. "Thank you."

"No problem. Bye!" She grins again and sprints to the car waiting for her.

TOUGH GUY, one bracelet says, with skulls and crossbones.

"Very manly." I nod with a serious expression. NO MULLETS, the other one says. "What's with that one?"

He snorts. "They asked why I don't have hockey hair."

"A mullet?"

We get to my car and he opens the trunk, reaching for my bag and hoisting it in the back. "Apparently they're back in style."

"Oh no." I cringe. "You're never getting a mullet. Wife's rules."

Our eyes meet and there's a funny flop in my stomach. "I mean, no one would believe I'd marry a guy with a mullet."

His mouth twitches. "True."

"What does the other one say?"

He shows me. ASS-ISTANT COACH VOLKOV, with peach emoji beads between the words.

I press my lips together so I don't laugh. "Should I be concerned?"

He looks a shade embarrassed. "They asked me about exercises to get a bigger butt because they said whatever I was doing was working."

I dissolve into laughter. "I can't believe I missed that."

He shakes his head, but looks like he's fighting a smile. "You want me to drive home?"

"Sure." I smile at him. I don't love driving, and it's nice to have someone do it for me.

And I like the way he says *home,* like it's ours.

"Assistant coach." I wiggle my eyebrows at him when we're in the car, driving home. "That has a nice ring to it. You going to join me every time?"

"Maybe I will." The bracelets clink on his arm, adorable and ridiculous against his thick, muscled forearm. Only a guy like Alexei could make friendship bracelets look hot.

When we get home, he pulls into my side of the garage and hauls my gear out of the trunk.

"Want me to leave this here?" He gestures at an empty rack in the garage.

"Sure." I frown at it. "Wasn't there stuff there before?"

He lifts the heavy bag like it weighs nothing. "I cleared it off. You need space for your soccer bags."

I hold the door open for him, feeling funny about this. "That was nice of you."

"Don't mention it." He follows me into the house, and at the junction where the kitchen and foyer link up, we pause, him watching me closely.

"Thanks for helping out tonight." I feel weirdly self-conscious in front of him.

"Don't mention that, either." He folds his arms over his chest, watching me carefully. "We have a game tomorrow night. Maybe you can come. If you have time."

"Oh, um. Yeah." I blink. "I can make time."

A beat of silence. Is he thinking about the hotel room after the awards dinner? Starting over, he said, or a new direction. Maybe he changed his mind. Maybe he won the weird power game we played by making me come and now it's not fun anymore.

So typical. Men love the chase, but then they catch you and they're no longer interested.

What was with that flirting earlier tonight, then? Why did he tell the girls I was beautiful?

See, this is why I do the one-and-done thing with hookups. So I'm not worrying and thinking about things after. I don't have the mental energy to worry about men.

This is an agreement. We got turned on and messed around. That's it.

He pauses, eyes lingering on my mouth, and my fluttery pulse takes off at a gallop.

"Goodnight," I rush out before heading upstairs, feeling his gaze on me the entire way.

———

The next afternoon, a gift box sits on my bed with a big silky navy blue ribbon tied in a bow. My pulse jumps as I open it and lift up the Storm jersey in my size.

I check the back—*VOLKOV* is stitched on in block letters. Number 70.

Buying you things makes me feel a certain way, he'd said. Something pleasant twists low in my stomach.

As soon as his citizenship and my inheritance come through, I'll have to either donate this to a thrift store or bury it at the back of my closet, where I won't be reminded of it. That's a problem for future me, though.

I look to my closet, starting to smile. I know just the heels for tonight.

WE HIT the ice for the last warm-up before the game, and when I skate behind the net, my eyes meet Georgia's.

She's wearing the jersey I got her, and fucking hell, she looks good in it. I nod at her and while Darcy talks to her, she gives me a little nod back, eyes dragging over me in my Storm uniform.

Is she checking me out? Pride beats through me.

My gaze lifts to the owner's box reserved for friends and family, where our parents are watching the game and hanging out. It's still strange, seeing our parents get along after the image I had in my head. Strange, but not unpleasant.

At the bench after the anthem, I take a seat beside the rookie.

"Today—" I start, but he's already nodding.

"I know. Be more physical. Get them up against the boards. Disrupt the play."

"No."

The rookie pauses.

"Let's try something different."

All night, I thought about what Georgia did at soccer practice, tailoring the training to the player's personality. She found what motivated Teddy and used it to help her.

"I reviewed your old game tape with Darcy this afternoon," I tell him.

"From my college games? Why?"

"Darcy saw something in those tapes that made her recommend you to Ward, and Ward saw something that led him to signing you." It's so obvious when I lay it out like that. "I was encouraging you to play like me, because that's all I know. But now you're going to play like you."

You steamroll everyone, Georgia had said when I screwed up and got rid of her car. *You always think you know best.*

I don't want to be that guy. Not anymore.

On the game tape, Darcy pointed out his sharp, shifty turns and the ease at which he moved the puck around the ice. Forget getting physical, he barely touched other players, because they couldn't catch him. He doesn't have the hardest shot in the league but as soon as he has time and space, he's deadly. He picks corners of the net with proficiency I've only seen in the most highly skilled forwards. He'd give Miller a run for his money.

And most importantly, Walker could read what was happening on the ice before it took place. Before the other team had even passed the puck, he was intervening, and he's so fast and nimble, the other team doesn't have time to respond.

We watched this happen again and again and again. He was like nothing I've ever seen in defense—and I've been so hardheaded that I almost missed it.

I think about the rookie's playful, competitive spirit. All the kid wants is to have fun.

"Don't let them touch you and don't let them get the puck."

A light sparks in his eyes.

He could be great, with the right mentoring. He could be great, if I let him. This whole time, I've been in the way.

"I've been pushing you to play in a physical style that doesn't work for you." I swallow, guilt writhing inside me. "The fewer injuries you sustain, the better. You'll have a longer career."

The way I was forcing the kid to play, he'd be out of the league by his early thirties, battered and beat up, and it would be my fault for pushing him to be like me.

I clear my throat and look away, embarrassment tightening in my gut. "I'm sorry."

"Wow." Walker doubles over. "I need a moment."

I shake my head, trying not to smile. The little shit reminds me of Georgia sometimes. "Yeah, yeah. Very funny."

"Are you okay? Let me check your temperature." The rookie tries to put his glove on my helmet but I smack him away.

"Volkov, Walker," Ward calls to us as the forwards hit the ice for the first face-off. "You're up."

Walker and I climb over the boards and skate into position.

"Ready, Rookie?" I call.

He just grins, a new light shining in his eyes.

The whistle blows and the other team steals the puck. While their forwards pass back and forth, I glance at Walker. He watches the play with hawk-eye focus, a little smirk on his mouth.

I do what I do best—use my size and strength as a weapon, disrupt the play, and pass the puck to Walker.

He's off like a shot, dodging and swerving the other team as he handles the puck with a deftness I've only seen from Miller and his dad, a Canadian hockey legend. The fans are on their feet as the players trail Walker. He's on a breakaway. The noise crescendos, energy heightening as he approaches.

He snaps the puck up and it hits the back of the net. The arena explodes with noise.

Walker crows with victory, skating past the fans as they slam their fists on the glass, jumping up and down. Nothing gets these fans going like a goal less than sixty seconds into the game.

"There you fucking go," I yell as I wrap Walker in a tight hug, jostling him. "Now you're playing hockey, Rookie."

"There *we* go," he yells back, beaming, and pride expands through my chest, so strong and sharp it takes my breath away.

I hope his parents are watching. I hope they see Walker soar. My fucking god, that was fun to watch. The skill, the surprise, the way the game can change in an instant—it's what I love about hockey.

Does this ever get old? Walker asked me at the beginning of the season. To my shock, watching Walker score feels even better than a goal of my own.

Behind the net, Georgia's on her feet with Darcy, Hazel, and Pippa, smiling and cheering. Our eyes meet and my heart jumps into my throat, pounding.

Nice job, she mouths with a wink, that gorgeous mouth of hers grinning ear to ear, eyes sparkling. At the sight of her in her jersey, the one I bought for her with my name on it, I smile.

"WE SAW photos online of the award ceremony," Maria tells me and my mom in the box after the game. "You looked beautiful, *solnyshko*."

Warmth hooks behind my ribcage at her endearment for me—an actual endearment, unlike his rotten tuber one.

The NHL social media account posted a picture of Alexei and I, with his arm around my waist, his dark, serious expression and my smile. The Storm fan accounts went nuts. Even the account dedicated to my outfits reposted it. I've stared at that picture for probably twelve hours total. *Liked by @alexeivolkov.*

"He looked good, too," I tell her. "Your son knows how to wear a suit."

The two women look at me with something sparking in their eyes. I clear my throat.

"And the ceremony, it was, um...really incredible to see what he's accomplished over his career—"

Alexei steps into the box, and the air changes. Our gazes meet, my heart trips, my lungs feel tight, and I can't look away from him as he approaches.

He can't seem to look away from me, either. Has he gotten even taller? A shiver runs down my spine. I try to think of something cool and witty to say about his play with Walker at the beginning of the game, but my brain is blank, hooked on the way his muscles move under his T-shirt and the way he prowls toward me like I'm being hunted.

"Hi—" I start to say when he steps into my space, but he wraps a big hand around the back of my neck, hauls me toward him, and kisses me.

My body responds to being kissed by Alexei Volkov. His mouth presses to mine and I melt against him. Without hesitation, I open for him. His stubble scrapes me; I think I moan. His hands frame my face, then sink into my hair, and the way he kisses me like he wants me more than anything is so deliciously addictive.

I can't stop. It's too good. Too intense and electric and warm.

This kiss feels different. Everything goes quiet, stops, realigns, and points in a new direction, like my true north has shifted. *This,* my body seems to say, *is exactly what we needed.* Alexei can just keep kissing me like this, with these deep, searching kisses that are somehow still soft and careful, and everything will be okay in the world. My hands fist in his shirt, made of the softest cotton I'm already scheming to steal and wear to bed, and beneath the fabric, his heart slams against the front wall of his broad, firm chest. He smells fresh and clean, his damp hair brushes my cheekbone, and a low, rumbling noise of pleased surprise slips out of him, making goosebumps rise down my spine.

I like this too much, and it's on that jarring thought that he pulls away, looking down at me with darkened eyes. "Hi."

"Hi." I sound a little breathless. My heart's doing that frustrating fluttering thing again. Tomorrow, first thing at work, I'm going to hook myself up to the EKG.

"You okay?" he asks, raising an eyebrow.

"I'm great." I swallow, not even wanting to blink and miss a split second of what he looks like right now.

His tongue runs along the edge of his teeth, still smiling. He knows what he's doing to me, and I don't even care. I'm vaguely aware our moms are blatantly staring with big grins, and clutching each other's arms.

I rise up on my tiptoes. "We said no kissing," I whisper in his ear.

"I don't care," he murmurs in my ear. "Do you?" His mouth is slanted in a cocky, pleased, arrogant way, like he knows the answer.

When I don't answer, his gaze trails over me, eyes flaring with heat, and beneath my jersey, I'm suddenly too warm. "You look good with my name on your back, Hellfire."

I can't get a full breath. In another version of this reality, I'd make a sharp, biting remark that I'm not some piece of property, not his lunch that he's putting his name on.

I don't feel like his property, though. I'm proud of what he did tonight with the rookie, proud that the huge, brutal hockey player out there on the ice is my husband.

Concern prickles at the edges of my mind.

His eyes drop to my shoes, a navy blue velvet heel. With our rainy winters, velvet is deeply impractical, but the universe aligned and tonight is a cold, dry evening.

He raises an eyebrow at them, the corner of his mouth tugging up again. "New?"

I still feel dazed from that kiss, but I shake my head and find my voice. "I was saving them for a special occasion."

His gaze lingers on them for a long moment, and flashing

with that look he used to give my heels, disapproving and angry. Although he doesn't seem so disapproving anymore.

He's holding my eyes so intensely that another shiver runs down my spine.

"I like those, too."

JAMIE, Pippa, Hazel, Rory, and a few other teammates are already at the Filthy Flamingo when we arrive later that night. Jordan mixes drinks behind the bar. She looks up, sees us, and tips her chin in greeting before turning back to the drinks.

"Go sit." Alexei takes my coat and hangs it up. "I'll get our drinks."

At the table, Rory whistles. "That was some kiss back in the box after the game."

"Don't tease her," Hazel tells him. "You kiss me like that."

"I know." He grins at her. "Because I think you're hot, I love you, and I score every goal for you."

My face goes hot. It's not the same with Alexei and me. He's just getting good at this pretending thing.

Start over, he said. *A new direction.*

Even I'm having a hard time believing this is just pretend, but I don't want to acknowledge the other option. Not yet.

He reaches the booth and slides in beside me, pushing my drink toward me. He rests his arm on the top of the booth, just above my shoulders. The smell of his body wash makes me feel the weirdest mix of woozy and horny.

"Nice bracelets," Hayden says to Alexei.

He's wearing the friendship bracelets the girls made him. With his towering, broad frame and the hard, brutal lines of his face, they look laughably silly.

And yet extremely hot. Annoying.

"Thanks," he says, unfazed, unembarrassed, and that's hot, too.

"Heyo, party people." Luca slides into the booth, and everyone cheers.

Alexei shifts over, and his arm drops so it's resting around my shoulders now. I'm tucked against his side. I'm still buzzing from the kiss after the game, and now all this touching feels strangely intimate and comfortable.

"First goal, buddy." Rory claps Luca on the shoulder. "First of many."

Luca smiles ear to ear. "I hope."

"You will, man. It's your first year." Hayden nudges Alexei with his elbow. "And you got this guy on your side, helping you."

"You did good tonight," Alexei tells Luca.

"I *felt* good," he admits. "I felt like I was flying."

Something changes in Alexei's expression, but he just nods. "That's what it's supposed to feel like."

"We're proud of you," Rory tells him. "All of us." He looks to Alexei. "Including Volkov." He raises his eyebrows at Alexei, waiting.

Alexei clears his throat and nods at Luca. "Proud of you, Rookie."

Everyone goes *awww* and Luca grins, the tips of his ears going red.

Darcy joins the booth, but there's no room. Alexei stands, holding out his hand to me.

"Let's go sit over there," he says, tilting his chin to an empty table at the other end of the bar.

"Where are you going, Volkov?" Luca asks.

Alexei holds my eyes. "I want my wife to myself."

A shiver of delight runs through me and I take his hand. Darcy grabs Hayden's arm as they exchange a private look, but I ignore them. Alexei leads me to the quiet booth, and I feel the weight of our friends' gazes on us. Jordan and I meet eyes—her brows lift, eyes sparking.

When I sit down, he pulls me into his lap, warm and solid beneath me.

"Does your shoulder hurt?" I ask quietly. He collided with a guy tonight, hard.

He makes a low noise, hands still on my waist. "It's not so bad."

"Not so bad, or not as bad as usual?"

He gives me a wry look. I reach up and press into his shoulder gently, feeling for tension.

"Ow," he groans, pretending. "You're hurting me."

"I'm barely touching you, you big baby." I don't know why I'm even doing this. I can't help myself, I guess. It's the injury recovery specialist in me, knowing he's in pain and wanting to do what I can to help.

"It hurts."

"This is why you need regular massages." I push my thumb along the muscle. "It won't hurt so much next time."

"There won't be a next time."

I meet his eyes, raising my eyebrows. "Yes, there will be."

With his eyes on mine, he makes a low, humming noise, and electricity zings through me. I pull my gaze back to where my hand's working, working the tension out of his shoulder.

"Hellfire."

"Mmm?"

He stares at my shoulder. "Is that one of the things I bought you?"

I glance down, where the edge of my bra strap peeks out from the jersey's collar. My body flushes with heat.

"Tell the truth."

My mouth tips up but I keep my gaze on his shoulder. "Maybe."

He makes a low, pleased noise, chest rising and falling with a deep breath. Delight crackles through me. Wearing the things he bought me should feel like losing the game—but it doesn't.

It just feels fun. A wave of self-consciousness hits me.

"So, you figured it out with the rookie," I say, glancing at the bar, where Luca's now flirting with Jordan while she ignores him.

When I look back at Alexei, his eyes are on me. "I figured things out with the rookie thanks to you. Soccer practice. Watching you coach. It helped me. *You* helped me."

"I didn't do anything."

"Yes, you did, Georgia. You're a good coach." He tilts his gaze to where my hands work on his shoulder. "And a good doctor."

My thoughts drift to a question that's been rising in my mind more and more these days.

"What's that look?" he asks, studying me.

Nerves tumble in my stomach. "Why did you call me incompetent, two years ago?"

I've replayed that meeting a thousand times, read over my notes again and again. He said I reminded him of his ex, and I know he was upset that I recommended him for retirement, but I feel like there's more.

"Did I do or say something that made you think I wasn't good at my job?"

He takes a deep breath. "Are you sure you want to know?"

I brace myself for criticism. "I can handle it."

A tiny shard of vulnerability rises in his eyes. "You called me a lost cause."

I sink. I did call him that.

"Even if you hadn't, though, I would have asked for another doctor."

"Why?" I breathe, and he hesitates.

Here it comes. Whatever Alexei's about to say, it's going to hurt so much worse now that I know him. Now that I have this ridiculous crush on him.

"While you examined me," his eyes meet mine, dark and intense, "I was hard as a rock."

HER JAW DROPS, but her eyes flare with lust.

That first meeting was excruciating with her running her soft, delicate hands all over my body, feeling out my previous injuries and how they've healed. I remember biting back a groan as her nails grazed my knee. At one point, her hair brushed my bare shoulder and I almost came in my shorts.

"You're kidding." She blinks.

How could I work with a doctor I was attracted to? I could barely concentrate on what she was saying during the appointment.

"Not kidding. I never told Ward you were incompetent, but I did tell him I was attracted to you."

A slow blink, like she's processing all of this. "You never told Ward I was incompetent."

I shake my head as the sharp knife of regret and embarrassment twists in my gut. "I was pissed off about the *lost cause* comment and let my emotions get the best of me. It was childish and immature. I'm sorry again."

She's silent for ten agonizing seconds before she claps once and crows with victory, bouncing in my lap. "I knew it."

"No, you didn't." The tension in my chest melts away. Not mad, then. That's good.

"Sack of *potatoes*," she whispers, eyes glittering like diamonds. "Sack of potatoes, my ass. Or maybe you've got a thing for potatoes."

"What are you two hooting and hollering about?" Owens calls over.

"Volkov thinks I'm hot," Georgia says proudly, and I roll my eyes, but I think I'm smiling again.

"Everyone knows this already," Miller calls from the bar.

Her mouth turns up more and mischief sparks in her eyes. It's nice, her smiling at me like that. "So now we know the truth. You've got a thing for me."

"I don't," I lie quietly. "I definitely don't."

I do. I definitely do.

She laughs. "Sweetheart, I hate to break it to you, but that's what an inconvenient boner means." She lowers her voice again, studying me with that annoying, pretty smile. "You're attracted to me. I bet that pisses you off so much, that you've got the hots for me. Ooooh, I bet that makes you mad."

"'Got the hots'? What are you, sixteen?"

"Is that why you were in such a bad mood over that trip earlier in the season?" She says it in this teasing, overjoyed way, like she knows the answer. "Tell the truth. The citizenship people might ask about this."

"They're not going to ask if I'm attracted to my wife!"

Her head falls back and laughter spills out of her. Something warm and crackling expands in my chest.

Georgia Greene's laugh is something else. "I never would have told you if I knew you'd gloat like this."

"Mhmmm." She smiles at me, all smug and knowing, eyes sparkling. She fans herself, sliding me a coy look. "Is it hot in here or is it just me?" Her eyes drop to my mouth. "Volkov, your mouth is doing that weird turn-uppy thing again. Do you like my laugh or something?"

More than anything, but I can't tell her that. I need to distract her.

"I like you in my jersey," I admit. "The color's nice on you. Looks good with your eyes." My gaze moves to her auburn hair and I tug on a lock. "And your hair."

What am I talking about? What am I saying?

She narrows her eyes, still smiling. "What's wrong with you tonight?"

The bottom falls out of my stomach. I don't *know* what's wrong with me. I can't think around her. I can't concentrate. She's constantly on my mind.

Can she tell?

Her eyes skim over me, over my shoulders and torso, over the collar of my half-zip sweater. "You look nice, too."

"Yeah?"

She looks away, smiling. "Yeah."

After a beat, I give her waist a squeeze. "My turn."

"Go for it."

"Why didn't you want to help me? Why'd you call me a lost cause?"

She's not lazy, I know that now. She cares about her patients and she works hard. She loves what she does. She wants to help people.

So why didn't she want to help me?

The amused spark dies from her eyes. She won't meet my gaze. "I couldn't be impartial."

I'm confused. I can feel myself frowning.

"When you got your concussion, I just, um." She presses her lips together, looking like she's going to be sick. "I couldn't check out emotionally the way I can with other patients. It wasn't ethical to keep you as a patient."

"You didn't transfer me because I was too injured to play?"

She rolls her eyes like I'm exasperating. "Alexei, are you serious? No matter how many times you get injured, you're still one of the best players in the league. You're like Wolverine or something. You got a career achievement award while you're still playing."

There's that pulse of warmth again behind my sternum, like her opinion of me matters. "What do you mean, you couldn't be impartial?"

She looks at her hands. "I don't like watching the physical side of hockey."

"With me."

A nod.

"It's a contact sport." That's one of the things I love about it —the rush, the intensity, the chaos.

"I'm a doctor," she says lightly. "I don't like it when people get hurt."

"When *I* get hurt."

Again, silence. So that's a yes. And I get hurt all the time. "What about fighting?"

Her arms fold across her chest, tucking into her sides like she feels sick. "Not my favorite."

I feel weird. Unhappy and worried. "It's part of the game. That's my job as an enforcer, to make sure the other team knows they can't get away with things."

"I know."

"I need to protect my guys."

"I know." Her eyes meet mine, soft and sad, and the quiet way she says it does something unwelcome to my heart.

"You don't like it when I fight."

She lifts a shoulder.

"You don't like it when I get hurt."

She doesn't say anything, just keeps her gaze on the rest of the room, shoulders tense.

"Do you watch my games? The ones you're not at?"

"I try not to." Her eyes dart, wild and worried. Like I'm learning her secrets.

"I have to fight," I say, almost desperately.

"I know." She fiddles with her necklace, looking away. "I'm going to grab a drink. Do you want anything?"

I shake my head, watching her walk away with an uneasy feeling in my gut. The puzzle pieces slide into place.

I know why she sleepwalks.

I WAKE the next morning in Alexei's bed, with his big arm looped around my waist and his firm, warm chest flush against my back. I'm warm, cozy, and so incredibly comfortable.

Goddamnit. I sleepwalked to his bed again—I think? After we left the bar, we got into the back of the car Alexei booked on his app. I don't remember getting home, though. I just remember being warm and comfortable. Gentle hands around my ankles, taking my heels off. Being tucked into bed.

My bed or his, though?

I shift to crawl out of bed before he wakes, but his arm tightens around me, pulling me against his body. My breath catches; he's hard like steel. Heat slides south between my legs, gathering and tightening, and I picture a million things I would do to that cock. Touch it, trail my fingers over it, run my tongue up it. Take it all the way to the back of my mouth so I can hear him groan. Ride it. Watch him fall apart.

Memories from last night roll through my head. That life-changing kiss. Sitting on his lap at the bar. Our conversation.

He never thought I was incompetent. He thought I was *hot*. His feelings were bruised over what I had said. That changes things—I think it might change everything.

"Morning," he murmurs into my shoulder, like his rock-hard boner isn't pressing into me. His voice is a low, sleepy rasp.

"Morning." I try to sound normal, like I'm not so turned on I can barely think. I try to sit up, but he holds me against him. "Did I, um—"

"Sleepwalk? Yes." A pause. "You know what this means, Hellfire."

My stomach does a slow roll forward. "Very funny."

"I wasn't kidding. What if you sleepwalk and hurt yourself?"

"I'm not going to hurt myself."

I glance over my shoulder. His hair's a mess, eyes all sleepy, under-eye circles still there, and god, he looks handsome first thing in the morning.

Last night's kiss was different. Real, careful, and special. Something flutters in my stomach.

Far away in my head, an alarm goes off. What part of this is detached?

His eyes move over me, a tiny spark growing in them. "Lionhead."

"I'm sorry?"

The corner of his mouth tips up. "That's what you look like in the morning. A lionhead rabbit."

I start laughing, smoothing down my bedhead. "So, heartbreakingly adorable?"

His mouth tips higher. "Something like that."

My face is going hot. This is too intimate.

"You hate me," I point out, smiling a little.

"I do hate you." He smirks like he doesn't, though. "But you're cute when you wake up."

Something in the corner of the room catches my eye.

"Alexei." I sit up, frowning. "What's Damon doing in your room?"

He doesn't look surprised to see my giant bunny lounging on the chair by his bed. "I left the door open and he hopped in here."

My heart stops like I've found my size shoe at a set sale. He's being nice to my bunnies? That wasn't on my bingo card.

"You said they stink."

He shrugs, eyes on my hair again. "They do, but they're growing on me."

The way he's looking at me right now makes me want a repeat of last weekend, after the awards ceremony. The way he made me come so many times I couldn't see straight, couldn't think straight.

It's happening again, I realize. It's not just sex; I'm starting to like him.

Detached, my survival instincts screech.

"I should get ready for work." This time, when I slip out of bed, he doesn't stop me.

"Georgia? You sleepwalk when I get hurt, don't you?"

I freeze at the door, stomach sinking. I knew I shouldn't have told him the real reason I transferred him to another doctor. He told me the thing about getting hard during our exam—oof, I'm going to be thinking about that a lot—and I was so proud of him for how he worked with Luca, and I just—I don't know. When I told him about medical school and why I didn't want to get married, he listened, so I had the urge to tell him more. Let him in a tiny bit further.

I don't like this, though. I don't like him seeing right through me. Seeing all the things I don't want to acknowledge.

Staring at the floor, I nod, before I head to my room without another word.

———

A bouquet of coral roses arrives in my office that afternoon, and I don't even need to look them up in the book.

Coral roses—fascination.

"EXCUSE ME," I say to Alexei the next day when I step into the living room.

He's lying on the sofa, reading emails on his phone, the bunnies on either side of him. I don't think I've ever seen any of them so relaxed.

He's wearing a black T-shirt that looks unfairly good on him. Dark colors suit him. God, he's hot.

"What is this?" I gesture at him and the bunnies.

He shrugs. "They wanted out of your room."

"They were making noise?"

"I could just tell they wanted out." He absently strokes a hand down Stefan's back and the bunny's eyes close.

Interesting. I start to smile. "Find any tumors?"

He gives me an annoyed look and I'm fully grinning now. "No, but I better keep looking."

God, my heart. This is too freaking cute. "Are you guys all friends or something now?"

"Hellfire," he sighs, and I'm fully grinning, because that means yes. "Do you need something?"

"Nope. Just finding this extremely interesting." And adorable. I'm on the bottom of the stairs when he calls after me.

"I've got an idea for soccer practice tomorrow night."

With narrowed eyes, I turn.

"I'm going." He rests his arm over the back of the sofa, watching me.

Wait. "So are you coaching with me every week now?"

For the past month and a half, since he first helped me out, if he didn't have a game and wasn't traveling, he came with me to soccer. He never talks over me or tells me how to coach, he just watches, listens, and asks he can help.

And he always wears the friendship bracelets, which the girls love.

He studies me. "Ward says our lives are about more than hockey." His Adam's apple bobs. "I'm not ready to retire but," he takes a deep breath, letting it out on a heavy exhale, "I don't want to be left with nothing when I do."

My heart feels funny. Achey and tight. It's on the tip of my tongue to say, *I'd never let you be left with nothing*, but I can't say that. That's the kind of thing people say when they're in relationships.

And I don't know what this is.

He shrugs. "And someone has to stop you from teaching them that bend-and-snap thing from the movie the other night."

"So you *were* watching." I had *Legally Blonde* on downstairs the other night when he got home and he kept walking through the living room, lingering. "Okay, what's your idea?"

"Luca's such a heartthrob," Darcy whispers the next evening at the rink as we stand at the bench.

I grin. The girls in his group are hanging on to his every word. Half of them are blushing. "They do seem obsessed with him."

"Don't be afraid to fall," Alexei calls across the ice as they all start the skating drill. "Your equipment will protect you."

"This was a good idea." Hazel appears at my other side. "Cross-training is so important." She's led a few yoga classes for the soccer team.

"And the girls seem to be having a ton of fun," Darcy adds.

My gaze goes to my husband, yelling out encouragement as the girls skate. "It was all Alexei."

He did everything: got permission from the parents to change the practice location, booked ice time, arranged for skates and gear, and convinced the available Storm players to participate. Hayden, Rory, Luca, Jamie—they're all here. Even Ward showed up to watch and support.

In the seating behind the glass, parents watch, talking and enjoying hot beverages and snacks that Alexei had catered.

Some sad, limp, listless part of my mind croaks *detached*, while the devil inside me rolls her eyes. How can I stay detached when he does things like this?

Hazel spots a parent who goes to her fitness studio and heads off to say hi, and Darcy gives me a sidelong look full of meaning.

"Stop it."

Her smile pulls higher. "I didn't say anything."

"Good." I suppress a smile of my own. "Keep it that way."

"But if I *were* to say something, I'd say, *wow, he must really like you.*"

"He doesn't, but okay." I think about how working with the rookie seems to bring him happiness. "I think he's just considering what to do after hockey." A thought strikes me, something I've been meaning to ask Darcy. "Hey, you know when he brought you flowers last year, on the double date?"

She smiles. "The ones Hayden called *funeral flowers*?"

We laugh. "Yes. Those. Do you remember what they were?"

"Lotus." Her eyebrows knit together as she thinks. "Kind of an interesting choice." She catches sight of my expression and gives me an odd look. "What?"

My heart's doing that funny flip again. "Lotus flowers —*strength, resilience, and rebirth.*" The perfect flower for Darcy's transformative year. I look away to avoid her pleased, inquisitive gaze. "He has a book of flower meanings."

"That's surprisingly thoughtful of him."

We look over to the man in question, working with the girls. "*He* is surprisingly thoughtful."

Darcy turns that curious gaze back to me, about to say something, but Tate approaches with his daughter.

I beam at her. "Hi, Bea."

"Hi." She gives me and Darcy a shy smile. She has Tate's green eyes and his dark hair. Ugh. My heart. She's so freaking cute.

"Look at how much fun they're having," Tate says, gesturing at the ice. "You want to play hockey?"

She grins. "No," she says firmly, and we laugh.

Tate pretends to look heartbroken. "Aw, come on."

"No." She shakes her head.

He smiles at her like she's everything to him. "The queen has spoken." She tugs him toward the catered food. "All right, I promised her cookies."

We smile after them but my attention is snagged by my husband, skating to a stop in front of the bench to speak to Luca.

"Rookie." Alexei gestures to him. "You want to lead them through the stretch?"

"You bet, boss." Luca grins and the two of them gather the

girls into a circle on the ice, Luca sitting in the center, while the rest of the Storm players head over to us at the bench.

Hayden pulls his helmet off and drops a quick kiss on Darcy's mouth. "Hi, honey."

"Thanks for coming tonight," I tell him. "I really appreciate it."

"Don't worry about it. That was fun." He gives me a good-natured smile. "Besides, I didn't have a choice. Volkov said it was mandatory."

He wiggles his eyebrows at me before he and Darcy head over to where the other Storm players sign autographs and take pictures with the parents.

Alexei skates to a stop in front of me. "Why are you hiding behind the bench?"

"I was giving you room to coach."

"You're the coach. Not me."

I lift a shoulder, smiling. "I didn't mind letting you take the lead tonight."

"Oh yeah?" He arches an eyebrow, eyes sparking. "You don't mind me taking the lead?"

"Controlling," I say lightly, but I'm smiling, and from the way his mouth tips up, he knows I don't mean it.

"Come here," he says, watching me with a look that makes my stomach dip with excitement.

"Why?"

"I'm going to kiss you."

Another dip. "Because everyone's going to see."

"Sure. We'll go with that."

I lift my chin in defiance. "You come here, then."

He grips the front of my jacket, holding my eyes, slowly pulling me toward him, before he gives me a soft, sweet kiss.

I like this too much. It's a problem.

"Was that so bad?" His voice is a low murmur against my lips.

"I guess not."

He lets out a light puff of air. "Stubborn."

On the other side of the rink, the players glance over at us, smiling.

ON THE DRIVE HOME, Georgia's quiet, staring out the window with a pinch between her eyebrows.

Something's wrong. I thought tonight went well. Everyone had fun, and we spent an hour with the parents and kids after, signing stuff and taking photos.

Going to practice with her every week is something I look forward to. I'm already annoyed that I have a game next week and can't join. I love seeing this side of her, warm and funny and encouraging, with all her walls down. Like no one ever hurt her.

I don't know what went wrong. I pull into the garage and cut the engine. "Was tonight okay?"

"Uh-huh." She gets out of the car.

"And you didn't mind that I brought the guys?"

"Of course not."

Tension twists in my gut as we head inside. There's something she's not telling me. Something I can't see is brewing under the surface with the doctor.

"Tell me what's wrong."

In the foyer, she glances over, raising an eyebrow at me. Something sparks in her gaze. "Everything is fine, Alexei."

It's not, though. I rub the back of my neck. I can't force her to talk to me if she doesn't want—

The doctor strides over to me and, holding my gaze with a small smile, pushes me against the front door. I frown, but she rises onto her toes, mouth covering mine in a hungry, desperate kiss.

"What—"

"Be quiet," she murmurs in between kisses.

Her tongue slicks against mine, hot and greedy. Arousal races through me before I can string thoughts together.

"You're not mad?" I rasp before she tugs my bottom lip with her teeth.

She loops her arms around my neck, and her lips move to my throat. A shudder moves through me. "No, baby, I'm not mad."

Baby. Jesus. I'm half hard.

She gives me her mouth again, so soft and pliable and generous that I'm losing my mind in her. I thread my fingers into her hair, extra soft tonight, and when I grip it to tilt her head back more, she lets out this breathy, needy noise that sends blood rushing to my groin.

This is all I've thought about for the past couple days, this and the way she sounds when she comes, when she finally moans for me.

Fucking hell, I love when the doctor lets go for me. When she trusts me.

"Fuck, you're so hot," I groan against her soft lips as my hand settles on her lush ass. "Georgia, the things I want to do to you."

I feel her smile. "Wait your turn."

I groan again, but I'm smiling, too. Nothing winds me up like this back and forth between us.

While we kiss, her hands go to my belt, working it undone.

My jaw drops as she looks up, holds my eyes with her mouth tilted in a sexy, teasing smile, before she slips her hand into my boxers and grips my cock.

My lips part, eyes falling closed as need races through me. I came in the shower this morning, fantasizing about this, about that smug look in her eyes.

She pulls me from my boxers and my cock juts out, already beading with precum, and the slight expression of surprise in her eyes is like a steroid shot to my ego.

"What's the matter, Hellfire?" I'm barely breathing as she trails her fingers up and down my length. "Intimidated?"

Her mouth curves. "A little."

She gives me a firm stroke and pleasure tightens in my groin. She's looking at my cock like it's a pair of those fuck-me heels she loves so much. I open my mouth to tell her we don't have to do anything, but she strokes me again, and the words fall out of my head.

"What were you saying?" She watches with a smug little smile that makes me even harder.

"I don't remember."

She grins, running her other hand over my balls, teasing me with light, exploring touches. Her manicured nails look so fucking hot, holding me like this. She tugs them lightly and a high, desperate noise slips out of me. My head falls back against the door as her hand finds a steady rhythm, applying the perfect amount of pressure, twisting a little at the tip like I do to myself.

I'm already on the edge, with her eagerness to please and the way she's touching me.

She drops to her knees and my cock jumps.

"Right here?" My voice is hoarse. I'm breathing hard. The image of my wife on her knees for me, looking up at me with that pretty, trusting smile, my cock inches from her mouth—I'll jerk off to this image for the rest of my life.

"Uh-huh." She wets her lips. My balls ache. We still have our jackets on, for Christ's sake. Why is that so hot, that she couldn't even wait?

"We should—" She strokes me again. *Oh, fuck.* "—go upstairs."

"No." Another long stroke. Heat wraps around the base of my spine and through my nose, I suck in a deep breath. "I want to do this right here."

She opens her mouth, holding my gaze, and stops. My chest rises and falls fast as I stare down at her.

"Remind me how this part goes again," she whispers, her eyes sparkling.

"What?" My thoughts slip and slur. I can't think straight with her holding me, with her breath skating over my length.

"I forget the next part."

She holds my gaze, parts her lips, and waits. Blood pounds in my ears, and it hits me.

She wants me to take the lead. She likes it, and she knows I like it. She trusts me. She wants this.

Holding her pretty gaze, I thread my fingers into her hair, firm but gentle, and feed my cock between Georgia's perfect lips.

"HOLY FUCK." Alexei's head falls back, eyes closed. "I'm never going to stop thinking about this. Jesus Christ, Georgia."

God, same. Seeing him tortured, agonized, completely at my mercy is the best thing I've ever seen. I'm wet, aching between my legs, but taking his cock to the back of my throat is a different kind of pleasure. In my hand, he is hot, heavy, and thick.

He looks down, his eyes dark and glazed, and holds my gaze as his hips begin to move, thrusting his cock in and out of my mouth. Like I expected, he's almost too big.

It's heaven. I haven't gone down on a guy in years, but I could do this for hours with Alexei. I'm not thinking about being detached, I'm not wondering where this is going, I'm just . . . having fun.

His eyes taunt me. "Don't forget to suck."

That resistant, playful feeling rises in me, but his hand comes to the back of my head, he pushes himself into my mouth, and I don't think about it, I just apply suction to his cock and watch his expression melt into pleasure.

"Good fucking girl, Georgia," he whispers, eyes closed. "Just like that, sweetheart."

A shiver runs through me, landing between my legs, and my eyelids flutter. Around his thick cock, I moan. I hate being told what to do, and I hate how much I enjoy being rewarded by him. I hate that I love it when he calls me sweetheart.

"I knew you'd be incredible at this." He casts a possessive look down at me, eyes hot with need. "I knew you'd make me lose my mind with that smart mouth. Keep going, Hellfire. Make me come."

We find a rhythm that has his jaw tensing and his breath turning ragged. His fingers flex on my scalp. Watching him unravel is intoxicating. Between my legs, my center throbs, desperate for attention. My nipples beg to be touched. This is too good, though, seeing Alexei lose it because of me.

His grip on my hair tightens and I relax my mouth to take him deeper. He rewards me with a desperate look I never thought I'd see from him, but which I'm already addicted to. Deep down, I love him fucking my mouth like this. The version of me from three months ago would be shrieking in outrage that he has me under this thumb like this. It's different now, though.

"I'm going to come in your mouth," he groans through clenched teeth, burning me with his gaze. I make another humming noise of acknowledgment and just as he swells in my mouth, I slow down, sucking harder. He makes a hoarse, agonized noise of surprise before filling my mouth with his release.

I've never swallowed in my life—it's never appealed to me —but Alexei comes in my mouth and I want this to be the best he's ever had. Long after we divorce, I want him to think of this. I want him to compare every blow job for the rest of his life to this one.

He holds my gaze while I swallow. His chest rises and falls fast with his breathing, his eyes are clouded with lust, and he looks at me like he can't believe we're doing this.

My heart skips a beat, but before I can say anything, he hauls me over his shoulder, and carries me upstairs.

"MY ROOM," I murmur against his mouth as he sets me down on his bed.

If we mess around in his room, it's going to feel too—I don't know. Like we're married for real or something.

"No."

Kneeling on the floor while I sit on the edge of the bed, he deepens the kiss, hot and searching, his stubble brushing my skin while he takes my heels off. It's intensely familiar—did he do this the other night, after the bar? When my top comes off, his expression turns arrogant and pleased.

"Wearing the stuff I bought you, huh?"

"You know I like nice things. The designer did a good job."

"The designer didn't choose those, Hellfire." He unbuttons my jeans and I lift my hips so he can pull them off. "I did."

I blink. "You did?"

"Uh-huh." His eyes trail down me, dark with heat and lust. The front of his pants tents—he's hard again? "I told you. Buying you things makes me feel a certain way."

He stares at my chest before his gaze drops to between my thighs, jaw clenching like he resents the lace for blocking his view. "Seeing you wrapped up in something I bought you, seeing you feel like the fucking knockout you are," he rakes a hand through his hair, "I don't know, Georgia. I like it too much."

Oh god. It's hard to remember why all of this is a bad idea.

"Alexei?"

Our eyes meet.

"Enough talking."

"Agreed."

Our mouths crash together again in a hard, fast kiss. While he kneels and I sit, we're the same height, and my hands thread into his hair while he devours me. Every hot slide of his tongue pulls a noise from me, high and needy. Every tug of his hair has him making this low, addictive noise in his throat, like he can't get enough.

He takes my bra off, pulling away to stare at my tits before he lets out a heavy, frustrated breath. "Are you fucking kidding me?"

His lips meet my collarbones, palming my breasts, weighing them, finding the stiff peaks, playing with them, winding me up as if I'm a toy. All I can do is sit here, eyes open but staring at nothing as Alexei lavishes attention on my tits.

Every pull of his lips on the peaks tugs on an intimate muscle deep inside me. Have I always been this sensitive? I don't usually get wet from a guy touching my nipples, but no one has ever run their tongue over me with that expression— like I'm water in a desert. Like he's discovering something new and life-changing. Like this is all he needs. Arousal gathers between my legs, and while he explores me, I do the same, pulling his shirt off, running my hands over the hard muscle of his shoulders and arms.

I guess he likes that, because his eyes meet mine before he latches onto one aching peak, and he sucks hard. My lips part, my eyes close, and I sigh as heat spills through me.

God, this is fucking good. I should be furious that he knows exactly how to play me, that he's just as skilled with my body as he is on the ice, but I don't have the mental space to care.

He makes an impatient noise before I'm flat on my back, panties yanked down my legs and his thumb pressing against my clit. My hips lift—it's too intense, too good, holy shit—and his mouth catches the high, desperate sound I make before he's kneeling again between my legs, pressing my knees farther apart to make room for him as his lips brush up my inner thighs. He's doing these little biting scrapes in between soft, open-mouth kisses, drawing breathy noises from me. His hands slip beneath my backside, palming and squeezing me. My clit aches, desperate for attention again, but he denies me, taking his time.

This is different, a tiny voice whispers in my head. Alexei treats me like I'm something rare, something to be enjoyed and savored. Something to remember. A pinch of fear disperses through me, but I'm too turned on to care.

He's almost at the crest of my thighs when hesitation tenses through my body. I jolt, sitting up, reaching to push him away. His hands come to my wrists, though, banding them together.

"Alexei."

"Mmm." He sounds drugged, like he's not in his right mind. "Don't interrupt, Hellfire. Busy." He's a fraction of an inch from my center. The alarm blares louder, every muscle going taut.

"Alexei, stop."

At the panicked edge to my voice, he freezes, looking up at me. Eyes glazed but alert. "What?"

His hands loosen around my wrists as I pull them apart and press into his shoulder, pushing him away, but it's like trying to move a brick wall.

"It's okay."

He stares at me.

"We don't have to do that."

"I want to." His tone and expression are confused. Irritated, even. Like I'm taking away his toy.

"I don't."

Heat rises to the surface of my skin. It's an old bruise that never healed. *I really don't want to,* Liam had said with a repulsed wince.

I haven't done this since. Some guys have offered, and when I say no, they shrug and we move on to other things. Things where I'm not open and exposed.

Alexei's eyes narrow with competition and challenge, like he wants to fight me on this.

"Fine." His searching expression falls away, and I almost sink in relief.

Instead of climbing on top of me, he get ups and prowls out of the room. I stare at the empty doorway, thoughts suspended in the air—what's he doing? Heavy footsteps. A drawer opens. Is he in my room? A moment later, he strides back in, holding my vibrator with a slant to his mouth.

"I knew you'd have something like this in your bedside table."

"What else am I supposed to do when I wake up in the middle of the night, turned on from sex dreams about Dr. Handsome?"

His jaw flexes, and I press my lips together so I don't smile.

"I know you're messing with me," he walks over slowly, and my gaze drops to his erection distorting the front of his pants, "but you're still going to pay for that."

Thrills run through me, landing at my center. The worry of what we almost did evaporates as he settles on the bed bedside me, propped on his elbow.

"Here's the game, Georgia."

My stomach dips at the way he says my name. Possessive and dominant. For a moment, I forget to hate it.

"You say please, and I give you more."

Another shivering thrill. His dark eyes roam my body before our gazes meet.

"Why don't you just make me come, like a good boy?"

He laughs. I'm a tiny guppy picking a fight with a shark.

"That's not how this works," he tells me. "You do what I say, and I reward you."

Another burst of heat pulses through me. I wish I didn't like that so much.

"Why can't we just fuck like normal people?" I ask, almost desperately.

"I have a theory. You want to hear it?"

"No."

"Too bad. I think you need it rougher than you realize. You need to be told what to do, and rewarded for it. You need to hand control over to someone you trust."

Someone I trust. I swallow hard. "That isn't you."

"We'll get there." He winks before he lowers his mouth to my breast and drags his tongue over me.

Molten heat rolls through me—it's like there's a tether between my nipples and my ladyparts, tugging and tightening as he works his tongue and teeth over my nerve endings. With his free hand, he explores me, trailing over my waist, stomach, the inside of my knee, inches from my center. My breathing turns rapid, my eyes close, and need trickles into my blood.

After a few minutes of this, I squirm with desire and impatience. "Let's get this show on the road."

"Do you need a refresher on the rules?"

"The clit is the at the top."

A quick grin before he nips the underside of my breast. "The word is *please*, sweetheart."

He has me so worked up, so wet and frustrated, I can barely stand it.

"Fine," I spit out. "Fuck. Fine. Please." I stare at the ceiling, nostrils flaring. I hate losing.

The low buzzing begins, and he presses the toy to my clit. I arch, forgetting that I said *please*, forgetting that I lost, because pleasure races through me, sharp and sparkling, and it doesn't really feel like losing.

It feels incredible. My nails dig into his arms, my forehead pressing to his chest as I breathe hard. He's drawn this out so much that I'm already close.

"Was that so bad?" he murmurs in my ear.

"Shut up," I whisper. "Just shut up and make me come."

He pulls the toy away, and my hips lift, chasing it while his eyes spark.

"One more."

I'm going to explode. "Alexei!"

"Come on, sweetheart. Indulge me. I love it so much."

"I hate you."

"Mhm."

"Are you actually enjoying this more than me sucking your cock?"

He laughs into my neck. Not an answer. Annoying.

"Fine. *Please*." The toy returns to my clit and I moan, back arching as a tight, crackling feeling swells inside me.

"Good girl."

I'm starting to shake, tightening around nothing, getting slick all over my inner thighs. I wish we could go back to hating each other. Everything was simple and easy back then. He pushes me back down on the bed, and at the intensity in his gaze, I close my eyes, turning my head so I don't give in to the urge to kiss him.

"Look at me." His voice is a low growl, his breathing ragged.

"Shut up, Volkov. I'm pretending you're someone else." I tilt my hips for more friction against the toy but he pulls it away.

His hand threads through the hair at the back of my head and he grips, *hard,* before he turns my head to face him. I shiver in pleasure.

"Look at me," he grits out.

Our eyes meet, his dark, dominant, and clouded with lust. I hate being told what to do, but my toes curl. My hands fist the duvet. I can't get a full breath, and around the base of my spine, heat gathers.

He presses the toy against me again, and a jolt of lust spikes through my body. He's so different from every guy I've been with. Liam was lazy and selfish, and everyone since has been hesitant and deferential, letting me take the lead and control every aspect.

I hate that this works for me. I hate that nothing will compare to this.

The corner of his cruel mouth slides up. "Good girl. What a good wife you are."

The pleasure spills over. My lips part, my scalp prickles from his grip, and I come hard around nothing, clamping down as waves of heat pound through me. My thoughts blank out, my whole body tenses, and my nerves tear apart as I ride out the wave, holding his eyes the entire time. His gaze sharpens, watching me come for him, flashing with possession I shouldn't find so hot.

"A little longer," he says when I think I can't take it anymore, and I have the disgusting urge to do what he says. "Just for me."

I make a high, desperate noise as the toy buzzes against me, holding on to the last shreds of myself, before he tosses it aside and I collapse on the bed. I've barely taken one heaving breath before he kisses me, hard and consuming. The kiss slows, turning gentle and soft, and I don't have the brain cells to care that we shouldn't be kissing like this. That we probably shouldn't be doing any of this.

He breaks away, looking down at me with an expression I can't read.

"Just to be clear, you're not mad about practice tonight."

I burst out laughing, and I catch the corner of his grin as he buries his face into my neck. That orgasm obviously knocked something loose in my head. We don't joke like this. Maybe this is all a weird dream, with some version of Alexei conjured by my subconscious.

"Perfect, Hellfire," he says into my hair, and my chest swells. "That was . . . I think I died."

"I'm glad."

"That I died?"

I laugh. "No. I'm glad you enjoyed it. And thank you for organizing the practice tonight."

He pulls back to search my eyes, brows knitting together. "I didn't do it because I wanted this."

"I know," I add quickly. "I know you didn't."

That just made me want to do it more.

"I don't want this to be a transaction." He swallows, holding my gaze. "Don't do something unless you want it."

I press my palm over his mouth. Yes, I lost the game tonight, but defeat had its rewards, and I'm overcome with the urgent need to make sure Alexei knows this. "I wanted to. I promise."

He lets out a breath, studying my face, and my pulse does a weird gallop, off beat and uneven. *Too intimate,* the warning voice whispers.

I should go back to my bed. I start to get up, but his arm bands around me, pulling me to his chest.

"No."

"I won't sleepwalk tonight." A rush of vulnerability hits me, and I'm glad he can't see my face. He *knows* why I sleepwalk, and there was no game tonight. He didn't get hurt, so I'll sleep soundly.

"We shouldn't risk it." A scrape of teeth over my shoulder. "I'd feel better with you in here."

I ignore the way my heart skips a beat. "You just want to fool around in the morning."

He doesn't care about me. This isn't anything.

"I do want to fool around in the morning." His mouth curves against my skin. "But I'd also feel better with you here."

"You're actually asking? What happened to the big bad enforcer? You said you were going to get rid of my bed. I'm surprised it's still even there."

He hesitates. "I'm trying not to make decisions about my wife without her input."

A warm flush moves through me and I suck in a deep breath. He's just doing this because . . . I don't know. I'm having a hard time thinking of reasons, after that orgasm. "Fine."

"Thank you," he says, like I'm doing him a favor.

He pulls the duvet over us, tucks me against his warm torso, and in seconds, I'm out.

A SMALL POTTED plant sits on my desk when I get to work a few mornings later. The flowers are a pretty pale pink with dainty petals.

Hibiscus—delicate beauty. A frisson of electricity runs through me, making it hard to breathe as I smile at the plant.

I'm no gardener, and this plant will die in a week, but I don't care. I love it.

I'm not getting feelings; I just love presents and being spoiled. I haven't seen him since the night we messed around, after he brought soccer practice to the rink. When I woke up the next morning, he was gone.

I had to leave for training and didn't want to wake you, he texted. *It was too early to incur Satan's wrath.*

Good boy, I texted back, ignoring the disappointment.

That night, I got home late from soccer. His bedroom light was on, and against the headboard, he was fast asleep. I slept in my own bed like a scaredy little chicken.

Between my fingertips, I stroke the soft pink petals. "I'll water it," Alexei says from my doorway, leaning on the glass.

I school my dopey smile into something neutral. "It's lovely. Thank you."

My dumb little heart hopes he'll say something like *you're lovely* but he just continues to give me that affectionate look.

"And thank you again for soccer practice—"

He sighs.

"—which you absolutely didn't have to—"

He strides over and kisses me. His stubble brushes my face, his scent whooshes up my nose, and his warm hand wraps around the back of my neck. I forget what I was saying. My hands are on his chest, though. His T-shirt is the softest thing I've ever felt. It's the same one he wore months ago, at Darcy and Hayden's engagement party.

He pulls away to study my eyes. "Stop thanking me."

I don't even remember what I was thanking him for. He holds my eyes, and my stomach dips at the intensity in his gaze. He lowers to a crouch so we're at eye level with me sitting. His hands come to my upper arms, firm but gentle.

"If you get home and I'm asleep," he says in a low voice that makes the back of my neck prickle, "wake me up."

I swallow. "You need your rest. You're very old."

His gaze sharpens. He looks like he wants to say something but thinks better of it, exhaling. "Don't wake me up, then. But don't go to your bed. Not anymore."

My stomach does a funny flip.

"I'm getting rid of it today."

I should protest. I should tell him to get fucked. That's what I would have done before.

"Okay," I say instead, like some besotted dumbass. "Fine."

"Fine."

His mouth quirks and he drops another quick kiss on my mouth before straightening up, sitting on the edge of my desk, and folding his arms over his chest.

Again, my gaze drops to his T-shirt. If I stole it, would he notice? I bet it smells like him.

"What's that look?"

"Your shirt." I swallow. Get a hold of yourself, Georgia. "It's soft."

"You like my T-shirt?" He arches an eyebrow, amused at whatever he sees on my face.

I'm trying to think of something cool and witty to say when my eyes drop to the keys he set on my desk when he walked in. There's a tiny pink crystal on his keychain.

"What is that?"

He glances at it, unfazed. "That's a keychain, Hellfire."

A *crystal*? He said they were stupid. He made fun of me for mine. "What, do you think it gives you powers or something?"

The corner of his mouth tips up at me throwing his words back at him. "I saw it and thought of you."

Oh god. No. Nonono. He can't just say things like that.

"You saw this crystal and thought of me?"

He nods.

Damn it. I can't deal with sweet Alexei. I can't.

I suck in a tight breath. "I have something terrible to tell you. You're not going to like it."

His eyebrow arches.

"I bought that crystal just to annoy you."

He huffs. "It worked."

"I know. I'm very, very good at getting on your nerves."

His mouth tips again, eyes warm, and my stomach dips. I don't understand this game. I don't know the rules.

He looks away first, shifting on the desk. "Are you free Saturday?"

I squint, thinking. "Yes. Why?"

"We should have everyone over for dinner."

I stare at him. He stares back. "*You* want to have people over."

"Sure."

"I've lived with you for two and a half months, and you haven't had company over once. And your parents don't count."

He narrows his eyes at me, but the corner of his mouth ticks up. I love when he gives me this look, like he wants to be annoyed but he's entertained and amused.

"How many people are you thinking?"

He shrugs. "Ten? Twenty? I'm not sure."

"Ten or *twenty*?" My eyes bug out of my head. "Alexei, this is going to be a ton of work. You should have it catered. Or have everyone bring a dish, potluck style."

"I'll do everything," he adds, off whatever he sees in my expression. "I'll get all the food, I'll cook, I'll clean up. It would be nice if you were there and doing your..." He waves a hand noncommittally at me. "You know."

"My what?"

"Smiling. Laughing. Charming everyone."

"You think I'm charming?" I'm smiling now.

"More than me, that's for sure."

"Oh my god." I brighten. "Think of how many people I could get to lick the crystal."

He makes a horrified noise. "That's disgusting. You should have your medical license taken away."

My laugh comes out loud and bold, and something warm flashes in his eyes. "Just admit you licked the crystal, Alexei. You think I haven't noticed the string of good luck you've had since I moved in?"

He doesn't answer, just swallows and watches me, mouth starting to curve up like mine is, dark eyes moving over me with pleasure.

My heart flops over in my chest. He really is handsome.

I glance at my nails. "I'll be there, and I'll be my delightful, charming self. No promises about not forcing people to lick the rock, though."

———

That night, I get home from work well after dinner. There's a container of pasta in the fridge with a sticky note on top. *Eat it,* written in tight, scratchy writing. I sit at the bar counter, devouring the penne arrabbiata while answering emails on my phone, listening for any noise in the silent house. He's an incredible cook, I realize, as I polish the food off. After, I play with the bunnies for a few minutes in the front room, which they seem to have staked out as *their* room now, and when I can't stall anymore, I head upstairs.

My bed is gone from my room. No surprise there, but my heart still does whirly loops.

In his room, the light's on but he's asleep, chest rising and falling, a peaceful, relaxed expression on his face. E-reader flat against his bare chest. Wedding ring glinting on his finger in the low light.

I glance down at my own hand, at the ugly ring that's growing on me. How extremely *married* of me, gazing at my husband while he sleeps in the bed we now share.

I undress, pull on the lacy sleep romper I grabbed from my room, and slide into bed beside him. He bought it, I'm sure he'll enjoy waking up to it. Still asleep, his arms come around me like an instinct.

"Georgia?"

"I'm here," I say quietly, reaching for the light, and he relaxes, tucking me into him.

I lie there in the dark, his heart beating against my back, his warmth and his scent surrounding me.

I don't know what we're doing. I don't know what any of this means anymore. We're going to get divorced. Neither of us are cut out for marriage. This isn't detached, though. This *thing* we're doing is quickly becoming more than an arrangement.

And yet, I can't stop.

ON SATURDAY, I wake to Alexei setting a coffee on my bedside table. I squint at him in the morning light, wearing a dark green T-shirt and those athletic joggers he looks so good in.

"Drink your coffee, lionhead. We've got a busy day."

"You're wearing too many clothes."

His eyes darken, trailing over me in bed, before he lets out an impatient sigh.

"I can't. I have too much to do and if we start something, we'll still be up here when people start knocking on the front door. Besides, you've got a massage in an hour." He starts making the bed.

God, I love it when he's bossy like this. "Hi, can you not make the bed while I'm still in it?" I'm laughing. "Also, what are you talking about?"

"I booked it for you at the place Jordan said you liked. You've got a whole morning of things to go to." He squints, thinking. "Japanese head something?"

I gasp, sitting up higher. "A Japanese head spa?"

"Yeah. That."

"Oh my god." I've totally wanted to try that. Apparently it

makes your hair all soft and glossy. "Wait. I can't leave. I was going to help."

"I told you I'd take care of everything." He glares at the neckline of my camisole—one of the items he bought. "You're too distracting, Georgia. Especially wearing that thing."

––––––––

"*Lick the rock*," we all chant that evening while Alexei glowers, hands on his hips in defiance.

Everyone's here—Rory, Hazel, Darcy, Hayden, Jamie, Pippa, Luca, a few of the other players. Even Jordan, an introvert who prefers spending her nights off alone, showed up.

"I'm not licking the fucking—"

"*Lick the rock*," we keep chanting. "*Lick the rock*."

Our eyes meet and I give him a look like, *well?* and he rolls his eyes with exasperation, but he looks like he wants to smile.

"We've all licked it," I tell him while our friends grin. "It's your turn. It's bad luck. A witch will put a curse on you if you don't."

"Fine," he snaps before bending down and touching his tongue to the tip of the crystal.

Everyone hollers, clapping and laughing, filling the home with joyful noise. Luca snaps a picture.

"Happy?" Alexei demands, coming over to me and pulling me against him as we head to the dining room to eat.

I bury my face into his neck, smiling. "Extremely."

––––––––

"The food's incredible, Volkov." Hayden lifts his beer to my husband as we all sit in the dining room.

It's the first time I've seen it used since I moved in. Around the table, our guests chorus praise for the Italian dinner Alexei made us—caprese salad, steamed clams and mussels in tomato sauce, some kind of kale caesar salad that tastes like heaven, and a seafood pasta with squid ink.

My husband clears his throat, nods once. "It's good to finally have everyone over."

He reaches for one of the bottles of wine he brought out from the cellar and refills my glass. I don't know whether my face is warm because I can't remember how many times he's refilled the glass, or because it's actually nice, having our friends over and—

Our friends? This is suspiciously couple-y.

"Where did you learn to cook like this?" I ask quietly, because as his wife, I should probably already know this. "And don't say you helped out at home. Teenagers don't cook like this."

His mouth tilts. "Italy."

I stare at him.

"I have a place there," he explains.

I continue to stare at him. "But what about hockey?"

There's that mouth tilt again. "We have something called an offseason, Hellfire, and it has a gym. The caretaker used to own a restaurant in town. She likes to teach me recipes."

I'm struck with an intense need to know more. To see this for myself. "It's kind of annoying, how good you are at everything you put your mind to."

"I could say the same about you." His eyes meet mine. "I like having people over to our home."

Our home?

My heart flips. *Don't even start*, I scold myself. This isn't our home. It's his home, and when we divorce, I'll find an apartment near the arena, or maybe Jordan and I will move in together again.

Disappointment pangs in my chest at the idea of moving out, and not just because I love the morning light in the front room or the way the forest air smells so fresh or the quiet serenity of the mountains.

I'm going to miss Alexei.

My stomach twists into a tight knot. What was the one thing I wasn't supposed to do? Get attached. We even said it in our vows.

When this is all over, I won't miss you.

And now I've gone and gotten feelings over the whole thing.

Alexei's in the middle of a conversation with Luca and Rory, but like he can sense my worries, he reaches out and takes my hand, pulling it into his lap, lightly playing with my fingers while the guys talk about some trade Ward was trying to make. At his light, warm touch, my worries dampen, the jagged edges turning dull and harmless.

Maybe this could work.

As quickly as the thought appears, I strike it, blinking in shock. Maybe this could *work*? What *this*? We're getting along, but that doesn't mean this is an actual marriage.

Some guy cooks and cuddles with me and I lose my head over him. It's like I've learned nothing after Liam. I'm not cut out for this kind of thing. When I fall for someone, I lose my head over them. I make bad decisions. I dissolve into their life. Their career.

I give them everything, and I'm left with nothing.

"All right, ladies." Rory leans back and folds his arms behind his head. "When you're finished cleaning, we'll come inspect your work."

Hazel tries to punch him in the stomach but he catches her fist, laughing, pulling her into a hug.

He presses a kiss to the top of her head while she tries to

fight him off, both of them smiling. "We'll clean. You all hang out. You, too, Alexei. You can get the good gossip to pass on to us later."

"I'll go with you." He stands. "Otherwise you'll put everything back in the wrong place."

"*I* will stay," Luca says. "I need to keep Jordan company."

She smirks. "Get lost, dork."

Luca grins at her, handsome and cheeky. Alexei gives him a light push toward the kitchen, making him laugh. He's already a heartthrob at twenty-two. My soccer girls are obsessed with him. In about five years, he'll be deadly.

While the guys head to the kitchen, the women move to the front room, draping over couches and taking seats on the floor, complaining about how full we are.

"Alexei and Luca are so cute together," Pippa says.

We can hear the guys in the kitchen, cleaning up and talking and horsing around.

"Don't throw that," Alexei orders, and I smile.

"I know. They've got this *big brother, little brother* thing going." I think about the game the other week. "Alexei's proud of him, I think. Ward did a good thing, pairing them together."

At the mention of Ward's name, Jordan stiffens.

"Speaking of gossip," Hazel says to Darcy, "how about that press conference last night?"

"Oh my god." Darcy rolls her eyes.

I frown. "What happened?"

"They were hounding Ward about his dating life." Darcy shakes her head. "So unprofessional."

"You know those reporters." Hazel smirks. "They want a good story, and Ward's dating life is interesting. It helps that he's hot."

"He was so embarrassed," Darcy says in a low voice. "I think the media attention is really getting to him."

"Is he seeing anyone?" Pippa asks.

"Why?" Hazel asks with a teasing smile. "You interested?"

Pippa laughs, a little embarrassed. "No, but he *is* handsome."

Jordan gets up to leave the room.

I catch her hand. "You okay?"

"Yep. Just going to get the bunnies."

She heads upstairs. I had put them in my room during dinner so they weren't begging at the table like starved wildlings.

Something isn't right, but Jordan's so hard to read sometimes. I've learned not to try to pry her open until she's ready, though.

"I don't think he's dating anyone," Darcy says with a shrug. "I don't think he has time. If he's not coaching or on the road, he's with Bea."

Pippa plays with the stem of her wineglass. "What kind of woman do you think he'd go for?"

"Someone his total opposite, I'm sure," I say without thinking. "It always happens like that."

Their gazes swing to me.

"Right." Hazel's mouth curves into a knowing smile. "You and Alexei are looking very comfortable together tonight."

The way she says it, the sharp, inquisitive way she's looking at me, it's like she *knows*. My eyes narrow. Does she?

"Why wouldn't we? We're in love." My face heats.

"Cut it out. We know something's going on." She gestures between herself and Pippa.

"You know . . . what?" I prompt, holding my expression neutral despite a hammering heart.

"I don't know the details but we know it's fake. Or," she smirks, "it *was* fake."

And here I thought we'd done a good job at faking it. My

gaze swings to Darcy and she gives me a subtle shake of her head.

"Darcy didn't say anything," Pippa adds, "but now we *really* know." Her smile softens. "You can trust us. We won't tell anyone."

"It's how Rory and I got together," Hazel adds with a wry look.

I think back to the beginning of last season, when I didn't know Hazel as well. Realization dawns on me and I stare at her, starting to smile. "It *was* weird how you didn't like him, and then the next week, you were dating."

"I was trying to get back at Connor."

Her ex who had just been traded to the Storm. Right. He was my patient and I couldn't stand him. One of those condescending, know-it-all types who thinks every woman has a thing for him. Gross.

Darcy and I meet eyes. "You can trust them," she says.

"I know." I give them the rundown on the agreement. "We didn't say anything because we didn't want anyone getting in trouble. What tipped you off?"

"At first," Hazel surveys me, "I thought this is just how you are in relationships. Reserved, not good at PDA, private." She shakes her head, smiling. "You're acting different now, though. I think you might not be acting at all."

My heart lurches, exposed and uncertain.

Thankfully, Jordan returns to the living room with a bunny under each arm.

I gesture at the Hartley sisters. "They know about the agreement."

"Good." Her mouth tips, eyes sparkling. "Because I noticed something in your room." She buries her face into Stefan's fur. Those two have always loved each other. "A *lack* of something."

Oh god. I'm not ready to talk about this with her. I should have retrieved the bunnies myself.

"What?" Darcy asks, and my mouth starts to pull into a wince.

"There's no bed in there." Jordan studies me. She knows. She *so* knows. "Isn't that weird, Georgia, that there's no bed in your room? Are you sleeping on the floor?"

My face is going red. She knows I'm not sleeping on the floor.

"No, I'm not sleeping on the floor." I stare at her, giving her my *shut the fuck up* eyes.

"Are you sleeping on the chair?" she wonders aloud with an innocent expression.

"No." I'm going to kill her, and yet I'm smiling. "I'm not sleeping on the chair."

Darcy sucks in an excited breath, clutching her hands together, eyes lit up bright and sparkly.

"Are you sleeping on the—"

"I'm sleeping in Alexei's bed. Happy?"

"Yes," Darcy bursts out, bouncing up and down. "Very."

"I'm a sleepwalker." I can't make eye contact with anyone. "It's for my own safety."

Silence, before they all burst out laughing.

"Are you fucking kidding me?" Hazel asks.

"I'm serious," I sputter, face burning hotter than the sun. "And it was his idea. Pippa, you believe me, right?" I gesture at the younger Hartley sister. "You're the nice one."

"Hey," Hazel says, but she's smiling.

"I thought I was the nice one," Darcy says, pretending to pout.

"You and Pippa tie for being the nice ones, but I already know you don't believe me." I look to Pippa. "But you believe me, right, Pips?"

She presses her lips together, giving me a wincing, sympathetic look. "No."

Hazel and Jordan smile at each other. Hazel starts walking around the room with her arms out like a zombie.

"*Alexei,*" she moans in a low voice like she's possessed, and we're all shaking with laughter. "*Take your pants off so we can make a baby.*"

Pippa chokes on her wine. Darcy is horizontal on the floor, shaking with laughter, and Jordan just smiles.

I'm helpless with laughter. "I'm a sleepwalker, not Frankenstein's monster."

"And what are you doing in this bed you share?" Jordan is enjoying this too much. "Just sleeping?"

"Who are you, my mother?" I sound so defensive. Even she'd want to know.

She shrugs, smiling. "He's touching you a lot."

"At every opportunity," Pippa adds, also smiling.

"He really likes your hair," Darcy adds. "He always stares at it. And the shoes."

"Right." Hazel nods. "He's obsessed with her shoes."

Jordan arches a dark eyebrow. "He held your hand tonight. He licked the rock for you."

"Okay—"

"So are you hooking up yet, or what?" Hazel prompts. "Give us the details we actually want."

"This is private!"

Darcy gives me a surprised look. "Since when are you such a prude?"

My jaw drops, but I start laughing. "I've turned you into a monster. Okay, fine. We've messed around."

They exchange knowing looks.

"Stop that." I cover Darcy's eyes. "Stop exchanging looks."

She laughs, swatting me away.

"Is it good?" Hazel asks.

"Yes," I blurt out.

"How good?" Darcy prompts.

"Like, brain-melting." Shit. Why did I say that? Now, when this is all over and I'm bummed, they're going to know why.

"The best you've ever had?" Jordan wears a knowing smile.

"Yes." I guess I'm saying everything in my head now. "The best I've ever had."

A low throat-clearing sound makes us freeze.

ALEXEI STANDS at the side of the front room, watching with an unreadable expression, holding a bottle of wine. We all sober. How much did he hear?

"Hi." I clear my throat. My face is so hot my freckles are probably sizzling off. "Can we help you?"

Slowly, holding my eyes with a funny, knowing spark, he walks over, sets the wine on the coffee table, before he leans down and, in front of everyone, kisses me. I hear someone's sharp intake of breath but Alexei steals my focus with his gentle but firm mouth, clean scent, and hand on the back of my head.

"Having fun?" he murmurs against my lips, like all of my friends aren't watching and listening to every word.

I nod, holding his eyes, smiling.

"Good." He drops another quick kiss on my lips and my heart flips over.

The room is very silent, very tense, and very still until he leaves, when everyone's heads whip toward me.

"What?" My voice goes too high as I fiddle with Damon's ear, smoothing it down, not meeting their gazes.

"Someone say it." Jordan lifts her eyebrows.

Darcy raises her hand. "I volunteer as tribute. He loves you."

My heart drops through the floor. I keep my eyes on Damon. "No, he doesn't."

"Yes, he does." Hazel nods. "He so does."

"Let's take a vote," Jordan says.

"No." My eyes go wide. "No voting."

"All those who think—" Her gaze cuts to the direction Alexei came from. "—Volkov is in love with Georgia, raise your hand."

I'm staring at my bunny but in my periphery, four hands go up. My heart does a somersault of delight. Fuck.

Jordan reaches out and lifts Stefan's paw. Darcy giggles, lifting Damon's paw in my lap.

Jordan gently pokes the side of my head. "It's unanimous."

"Okay," Hayden bursts into the room like a golden retriever, carrying two plates of something chocolate, "enough lazing around, ladies. Eating, round two, is about to begin." He tries to sit in Darcy's lap while she dissolves into laughter, trying to push him off, and the other guys wander in.

"I'll help." I get up fast and hurry out of the room, eager to get the hell away from their knowing gazes.

In the kitchen, I find Alexei plating more of the dessert. I was hoping for a pile of dishes to distract myself, but the kitchen is spotless.

"What is this?" I ask, leaning on the counter, folding my arms over my stomach. I don't want to go back into the front room, with everyone and their knowing glances, so I linger.

"Raspberry chocolate torte."

He focuses on cutting perfect slices. Like everything else about him, his sharp focus is hot.

"You know what I just realized?" he asks after a moment, eyes on the raspberry stuff he's drizzling over each slice.

"What?" *Please don't say anything about whatever he might have overheard in the other room,* I pray.

His gaze swings to mine, hot with teasing. "I never got you back for the team dinner."

When I smeared cake in his face. Up his nose. My pulse picks up. "I have no idea what you're talking about."

He tilts his head, eyes on me like a predator, and a laugh bubbles up my throat.

"You don't remember smearing cake all over my face?"

"Alexei." I start to back away, and he follows, gaze locked on mine. "No."

"It's only fair." His eyes flare with amusement. It's a good look on him.

"Alexei," I put my hands up, "I'm serious. This dress is silk."

"I'm rich. I'll buy you a new one."

I swallow, trying not to smile so hard. "I'm smiling but it's because I'm nervous."

"Good." His expression turns wolfish. He's enjoying this, the sick fuck. "You should be."

I bump up against the counter. He braces a hand behind me, blocking me in.

"You ready to beg, Hellfire?"

I start giggling helplessly. "Never."

"Maybe you just need some encouragement." He dips his hand into the bowl and I laugh harder, pushing against his arm to scramble away, but it's like trying to move a steel bar.

His arm loops around my waist and I shriek with laughter as he smears raspberry sauce across my mouth, trying to fight him off but laughing too hard to succeed.

"Oh my god, get away from me," I laugh as he tries to kiss my mouth. "If you're going to cover me in dessert, at least fuck me after."

He lands a kiss and grins down at me. My heart jolts hard, racing, spinning, careening through me like I've never felt before. I'm smiling up at him, swooning and dizzy.

Deep in my mind, I'm aware that this is one of those moments I'll remember for the rest of my life. Every time I see a piece of chocolate cake, I'm going to think about standing in his kitchen, covered in raspberry sauce, breathless with laughter as I gaze up at my pretend husband.

I don't want to be married, but maybe I could be married to someone like Alexei.

Someone clears their throat and we freeze. Everyone is standing at the edge of the kitchen, watching us with a mix of amused and knowing expressions.

"We heard a scream," Rory says, grinning.

My face starts to go red. I feel like I've been caught with my skirt tucked into my underwear. I try to move away, wiping at my face, but Alexei keeps me close.

"We're fine." I can't meet anyone's eyes.

I excuse myself to go clean up, he lets me go, and when I return to the front room, Alexei pulls me onto his lap. Thankfully, Jordan, Darcy, Hazel, and Pippa take mercy on me and don't give the *told you so* eyes.

"I'M NOT GOING to run away," my wife says as she takes her makeup off in my en suite.

I'm leaning on the doorframe, arms folded across my bare chest, fascinated. I watched her get ready this morning and now I'm watching her get ready for bed.

I like it. I like it all. I like seeing her first thing in the morning with bedhead and a grumpy frown because I woke her up. I like having people over to our home for dinner, I like cooking for her, and I definitely like overhearing her friends tease her about our relationship.

Best sex of her life? Damn fucking right. Pride beats through me.

"What's that look?" She arches an eyebrow at me, gaze snagging on my black boxer briefs.

"Just interested in this process."

My thoughts slide to the other night, when I tried to go down on her and she wouldn't let me. I keep seeing the flash of worry and self-consciousness in her eyes, so rare for her.

It's something to do with that fucking ex of hers, the one who unenrolled her from medical school.

She leans up on her tiptoes to reach something in the cabinet, one of the bottles I moved over from her bathroom, and my gaze goes to the long line of her legs, her toned calves, the teasing curve of her ass beneath the hem of those silk shorts. Her wild hair is tied up into a knot on top of her head. The sight of her like this, something almost no one else gets to see, sends arousal through me.

In an instant, I want her so badly I can't stand it.

I come behind her, hands sliding up her sides, my lips pressing to where the tiny, delicate strap sits on her shoulder. With care, I pull the elastic from her hair, watching it cascade in soft waves around her shoulders.

"I'm not done," she says, but she sets the bottle on the counter, hands clutching the marble edge as my teeth scrape her soft skin.

"Yes, you are."

I open a drawer, pull out a condom, and her breath catches when she sees where this is going. Against her ass, I'm already hard. Another breath catch.

Our eyes meet in the mirror. "Impatient asshole."

"Mhm." My mouth slants. "I'll make it up to you."

Holding her against me, I reach into the front of her shorts, where my fingers find wet, slick heat.

"No panties."

Those defiant eyes flash. "I didn't do it for you."

I swirl my fingertips over her clit and her eyelids dip. Fuck, I love how ready she is for me. I love that this works for her as much as it works for me.

"Yes, you did."

Her lips part like she has a smart comment lined up, but I sink my fingers into her and her eyes close, words forgotten.

"What were you going to say, sweetheart?" My tone is smug and teasing as I work that sensitive, ridged spot inside her.

"Uh."

Her eyes stay closed as I fuck her with my hand, her pussy soaked and tight around my fingers. A flush of pink grows across her cheeks, down her neck, and across her chest. So fucking pretty and perfect. My other hand slips up her camisole, palming her breast. At the quick pinch of my fingers on her nipple, her teeth clamp together like she's trying not to moan.

A sense of challenge floods me and I shove my boxers down, reach for the condom, and roll it on. While she's still blinking from the loss of my fingers inside her, I yank her shorts down, push her forward, line myself up with her entrance, and sink inside.

"Holy fuck," she breathes as I push deeper.

She's so fucking tight and hot, I can barely think. My first thrusts are slow and steady to get her used to the snug fit, but she's wet and ready for me, hands flexing on the countertop, breathing hard. Watching her bent over while I fuck her is the hottest thing I've ever seen, though, and before long, my hips are flush against her ass as I sink deep.

She braces an elbow on the countertop, covering her mouth with her hand to muffle a low noise.

"Oh no, you fucking don't." I pull her wrist away, grab her other one, banding them behind her back. "Don't you dare hide from me, Georgia." I sink my hand into the back of her hair, gripping the soft strands to hold her head up so I can see her expression in the mirror. "Open your eyes and watch me fuck my wife."

Our gazes meet in the mirror—hers unfocused, needy, and cloudy with lust, mine sharp and hot—and I almost come right there. Her pussy clenches around my cock, her eyelids dip, and the pressure around the base of my spine coils tighter.

This is not the hate fuck from the benefit. This is so, so

much more. I'm addicted to this woman, to her pleasure and the way she trusts me with it.

"You love it like this, don't you, Hellfire? Rough and hard?"

Her teeth grit together. Stubborn little brat.

"Answer me."

"Yes," she rushes out, and another pulse of heat moves through me.

"You're made for this. Made for taking my cock."

She nods. Something about Georgia admitting how much she wants me, following my commands, letting me take control over her, makes me feel like a fucking king. My lips come to her ear, still gripping her hair, her wrists.

"If I let your wrists go," I murmur while I fuck her, "can I trust you to be a good wife and keep your hands behind your back?"

She looks like she wants to argue, so I drop a kiss to her neck.

"It'll be worth it," I add, and she huffs a laugh.

"Fine."

"Good girl."

Her throat works, and she tightens around me again. When my fingers slide through the wetness between her legs, she lets out a choked gasp. A few tight, firm circles on her clit and she's already coming, letting out high, breathy moans that I hoard like treasure. Her muscles begin to spasm, tightening and pulsing around me, and my hands come to her hips, gripping them for leverage as I fuck her hard.

Something about reducing this smart, mouthy woman to a desperate, shuddering mess sets me on fire. The urgent pressure in my groin overflows, heat roaring through me, shattering my senses. I can't think, I can't breathe, I just clutch her against me and spill into the condom, feeling like my DNA is being rearranged. Wishing I was coming inside her with nothing in between us.

Wishing I could call her my wife for real.

The last thought isn't even a concern anymore. That's how far gone I am. I don't care if she's not there yet. I'll be patient. I'll wait until my wife is ready.

We catch our breaths, gaze meeting in the mirror. Her face is still flushed, her chest rising and falling fast. Hair wild. I'm still inside her, not ready to pull out just yet.

"That's a good look on you."

She lets out a silent laugh. Once we've cleaned up and are lying in bed, I turn to her. Her hair spills over the pillows, golden strands glinting in the dim light from the bedside lamp. A pretty pink glow still on those cheeks. She stares at the ceiling, a pinch between her eyebrows.

"Did I go too hard?"

"A little." Her gaze slides to mine, embarrassment and something a little sly in her eyes. "But I didn't mind."

"Would you say I melted your brain?"

"That's it." She starts to get out of bed, face flaming with embarrassment. "I'm sleeping on the couch."

I catch her in my arms, pulling her against me, caging her in. "Like hell you are." My fingers lift her chin so our eyes meet. "Hey." I press a soft kiss to her lips. "Best fuck of my life, too."

She swallows as I search her gaze.

Pressure swells in my chest, so expanding and consuming I can barely breathe as I gaze into her eyes. It's Georgia, I've realized. Maybe it's been Georgia for a long time. The intense emotions I've always felt toward her—maybe they were never hate. Maybe they were the opposite.

"What are we doing, Georgia?"

"I don't know."

"I think you do." I want her to say it, though. I want her to trust me. And yet, I can't help pushing her limits. "I like you."

She frowns. Sits up and stiffens. "What?"

"I like you," I repeat slowly. I can feel the corner of my mouth sliding up.

She laughs, nervous and tight. "Well, not like *that*."

I nod. She's freaking out but it's fucking cute. "Like that. I like you like that."

"But we said—"

"I know what we said. I know what we agreed to. I still like you."

It's freeing, putting it all out on the line like this. Or most of it.

"Who just *says* that?" she demands. "What kind of game is this, Alexei?"

Don't laugh, I tell myself. It'll make her really mad. That could be fun, though.

"Don't look at me like that." Her tone comes out sharp, and I really do start laughing.

"Like what?"

"Like I'm cute or something."

"You are cute. I just pulled your hair, bent you over, and fucked you against the counter, but *this* is what makes you want to bolt?"

She sucks a deep breath in through her nose, folding her arms across her stomach. "You hate me."

Did I ever actually hate her? Or did I just hate that I wanted to fuck her so badly? Did I hate how much I thought about her?

I don't know anymore. I just like bickering with her in bed like this.

"I hate you," I lie, reaching for her, tucking her against my chest, turning off the light and pulling the duvet around us, "but I still think you're cute. And I still like you."

CHAPTER 74
GEORGIA

A WEEK LATER, Alexei appears in my row on the plane, lifting his bag into the overheard bin. My gaze catches on his toned arms, muscles flexing with the movement.

"Hello," I say, cool and disinterested, turning back to my work.

Coward, my brain whispers.

"Good morning, Hellfire." He sits beside me, his big frame taking up a ridiculous amount of space. His knee bumps mine.

I focus on my work. He's not looking at me, but I can feel his attention.

"You want to make out?" he asks, and against my will, I laugh.

"I'm working, you animal."

He's not supposed to be funny. He's not supposed to be a good cook and buy me pretty things and say *I like you* or *you're cute.*

"I think the term you used was *beast.*"

Telling Darcy he was a beast in bed at the team dinner feels like years ago. I press my lips together, trying not to smile at the irony of being right.

His knee bumps mine again. "Did you get the flowers?"

"Yes." *Yellow tulips—sunshine in your smile.* "Thank you."

I have that entire book memorized, I've flipped through it so many times.

My heart does that annoying pitter-patter thing. He likes me. There's no excuse anymore, no logical way I can tell myself he's just trying to make things look real. He's nothing like Liam, either. At the awards dinner, he talked me and my accomplishments up. He worries about my safety.

When I see him get hurt, I feel sick, and when I sleepwalk, it's to his bed. Forget about hiding from my feelings; they stare me down, challenging me.

I like him, too. I don't want this to end. My chest aches, vulnerable and exposed. I think it might be different this time, but that scares me even more.

I can't lose myself again. I can't be left humiliated and empty when it's over.

Just like at dinner with our friends, he takes my hand, pulling it into his lap, toying with my plain wedding ring, clinking his against mine, making me smile, turning down the volume on my worries.

Maybe I just shut up. Maybe I ignore the worries. Maybe I take a risk.

Maybe I just enjoy being married to Alexei.

BLOOD PUMPS in my ears that evening as Walker and I hit the ice for another shift.

Within seconds, Walker steals the puck, moving it to the other end of the ice, passing to the forwards. He's fast like lightning, sharp like a knife. My blood hums and I hold my breath. Here we go. Here we *fucking* go.

The puck comes to Walker. He skates back, giving himself space. A player barrels forward but in a split second, Walker goes right, and the player falls face-first onto the ice, sliding. The rookie's so agile, he makes everyone else look like elephants.

Walker snaps the puck at the lower corner of the net—it goes in. It's an away game so there's no roar from the crowd, but the few Vancouver fans cheer as we celebrate the goal.

"Feels good, doesn't it?" I say to Walker.

"Like flying." He grins before skating off to bump gloves with the players on the bench.

The next time we're on the ice, though, the rookie's about to intercept a play when the other team's defenseman cross-checks him.

Protective fury ignites in my chest as the ref blows the whistle. It's a two-minute penalty.

Moments later, it happens again. The rookie gets slammed into the boards. He bounces like a rag doll, and a wave of nausea hits me. Even the other team's fans behind the glass wince.

"You okay?" I ask him after, and he nods.

"I'm fine. Let's play."

We all look to the ref.

No penalty. Blood pounds in my ears.

"They're trying to take the rookie out," Owens mutters to us.

This happens sometimes, usually to Miller. They see what he can do, and they want him injured so he can't play.

"You good?" Miller asks me, a question in his eyes.

I know what I need to do. I hate this part, but I can't sit around and watch the rookie get the shit beat out of him.

Protective rage rattles through me. Not on my watch. Not one of my guys.

My gaze swings to the hallway behind the bench, where Georgia sits, watching the game and eating dinner. Hesitation twists in my gut, warring with my need to protect the rookie. She's not going to like this.

I nod at Miller. "I'm good. Let's do it."

While we line up for a face-off, I find the guy who hit Walker, and I smile at him. It's not my Georgia smile. It's my *I'm about to fuck you up* smile. Cold, calculating, and cruel. I think about the way Walker rag-dolled against the boards, and adrenaline hits my bloodstream.

Now I wait for my opportunity.

The puck drops, the game restarts, but before the next whistle blows, I'm hit from the side, slammed into the boards, and pain sears through my shoulder and face.

I WATCH Alexei take the hit. I watch his shoulder dislocate. Even through his pads, his shoulder's not supposed to move like that.

Nausea and pain roll through me, like it's *my* shoulder getting dislocated, and without realizing it, I'm pushing through the people to get to the medical room.

One of the trainers steps in my path. "Dr. Greene, maybe we should have the other team's doctor look at this one—"

"That's my husband," I bite out with an intensity I've never felt before, heart pounding, ready to claw this guy's face off if I have to. I think I'm yelling. "Back the fuck up and get out of my way."

He steps away with his palms in the air. "Jesus."

Another trainer helps Alexei into the medical room, and my heart beats so hard I think it might give out. His eyebrow is bleeding from where he hit the boards.

"On the table, Jason," I direct them.

"I'm okay," Alexei murmurs to me. "It's not too bad."

I don't answer. He's not okay. It *is* bad. He could have bent or broken the steel plate holding his collarbones together. He could have gotten another concussion. He's already going to have to play through the healing process. These guys can't afford to take the time off that they need, not until the offseason.

My hands shake as I go through my bag. He's going to need painkillers to get ahead of the swelling and pain.

"Dr. Greene." Tate appears in the doorway. The period must be over. "Everything okay?"

"Yes." I need to be in focus mode and put my emotions aside, like I don't care about this guy. I can't, though. I take a deep breath in through my nose and let it out slowly.

"Can you please have the other team's doctor supervise?" I ask Tate. "It's a conflict of interest for me. And I'm going to need help putting his shoulder back in."

He returns a moment later with Dr. Cheung, a woman about my age. Together, we get Alexei's jersey and pads off, ignoring him when he grumbles about having those pads for over a decade.

"The player's been ejected from the game," Tate says at the door.

"Good," I bite out, too aggressive to fool anyone. "Send him to me so I can make sure he's done for the season."

Beneath me, Alexei makes a noise that sounds like a stifled laugh.

Our eyes meet, and his pained amusement fades at whatever he sees on my face. I look away, fast.

Once we have Alexei's shoulder back in place and his arm is in a sling, I check him for a concussion. I check again, just to be safe, and then again, once more.

And then I have Dr. Cheung check him. I feel a little pulse of gratitude that she doesn't say anything about my overzealous care. When she's done, I thank her. She gives me a quick smile and heads out.

"Thanks, Doc," Tate says at the door as she leaves. "Dr. Greene, can I support in any way?"

I shake my head. "Just going to stitch his face up."

"I'll let you work." He leaves, closing the door behind him, and now we're alone.

The hand from his good arm comes to my hip. "*Now* do you want to make out?"

Against my will, I start to smile. I hate that he makes me laugh when I'm feeling like this. "I'm trying not to mess up your ugly face more than it already is. Stop talking."

He grins, but his lip is split, and he winces with pain. My eyes prick and I look away, blinking.

"You were like a snarling dog."

I cough out a laugh. "Don't call me a dog, Alexei."

"How about a demon, then?" His mouth tips up. "I liked it, you losing it over me."

"I didn't lose it."

I finish his brow, applying a bandage, before I move to his lip. I can't look him in the eyes. If I do, he'll see. He'll know.

"Hey." He runs his hand up to my neck to cup my jaw. "I'm okay."

"I know."

Worry threads through his gaze. "Because you're looking at me like you don't."

I nod, looking down at my hands. Not shaking anymore, so that's good. "I don't like watching you get hurt."

He studies me, starting to frown like he realizes it, too.

This is why we can't be married for real. Even if it's nice. Even if it's better than I thought it could be. I can't watch him get hurt, and I can't ask him to give up his career, not when it's everything to him.

———

"This is what you want to watch?" I ask him in the hotel room later as he hit 'play' on the TV's streaming service. "You know what this is, right?"

In the bed, with an ice pack tucked under his sling, he looks at me with glittering eyes. I can tell he's trying not to smile because his lip hurts. "Yes."

"This show is for teenagers."

God, every time I look at him, I replay the hit from tonight and feel sick all over again.

"I thought you said it was just about teenagers."

The Vampire Diaries opening credits play.

"Okay." He's going to be bored or asleep after five minutes. "If this is what you want."

"It is. You know what else I want?"

"What?" Where's the acetaminophen? I search through my bag.

"To play doctor."

With my back to him, I smile. "You need to rest."

"I'll make you a deal."

"The last time you wanted to make me a deal, I ended up married."

"Put on one of the things I bought you and I'll do whatever you say."

That, I can do. I search through my bag to find the lacy forest green romper, but pause when my fingers brush soft cotton. The softest, well-worn T-shirt.

I turn to him, holding it with a quizzical look.

"For me?" I ask, delight blooming throughout my body.

"If you want it."

"You won't miss it?" With my back to him, I undress and pull it over my head. His scent surrounds me, and I almost forget all the horrible stuff that happened tonight at the game.

When I turn, Alexei stares at me with a heated expression. "Alexei?"

"Hmm?"

I start to smile. "I asked if you'll miss it."

He exhales a heavy breath, dark eyes all over me, looking tortured. "Not when you look like that in it."

My stomach dips as I head over to the bed. The front of his boxers is already stretched out by his erection.

"I almost feel bad for you," I gesture at his erection, "but after today, you deserve it."

I slip into bed beside him, sitting against the pillows on his good side. Slowly, wincing, he leans down and presses a kiss to my temple.

"Thanks for taking care of me, sweetheart."

We watch each other for a long moment.

"You okay?" he asks quietly.

I nod.

"You sure?"

I nod again.

"Because you seem like you're not okay."

My throat aches at the memory of tonight. "I didn't like seeing you get hurt."

"I don't like seeing you upset over me getting hurt."

My heart wrenches, and I don't answer.

He searches my eyes. "I'm not ready to retire."

"I'm not asking you to."

The longest silence of my life. We both know it now. The reason this can't be real.

Disappointment pulses through me, cold and heavy.

He sighs with frustration. "Come here."

"You're supposed to be resting."

"I am resting. Come here," he says again, and I shift over.

Our lips meet and his kiss is soft, sweet, and searching.

Loving. Another crack forms in my heart. I reach up and run my hands through his hair, and his eyelids droop halfway.

We watch the rest of the episode, and when it ends, neither of us moves as the next episode cues up.

"We're away for most of December," he says in a low voice, not looking at me.

I know. I've been thinking about it more and more. The Storm have a few long away-game stretches throughout the season. He'll be gone for almost three weeks.

When we made the agreement, I remember looking at the calendar and thinking our time apart would be a reprieve. I couldn't *wait* for December so I could get rid of the horrible Alexei Volkov for a few weeks.

Now I'm dreading it.

"The bunnies are really going to miss you."

He's quiet for a beat. "I'm going to miss the bunnies, too. I'm going to think about them every day, Hellfire."

CHAPTER 77

ALEXEI

THREE WEEKS LATER, I wait with the rest of the team in the lounge for the private plane. Christmas is the day after tomorrow. Through the windows, snow dumps from the sky. Ward and the pilot talk in low voices while everyone darts glances at them. Two days, we've been delayed due to this blizzard.

"What the fuck is taking so long?" I mutter.

Miller leans forward, elbows on his knees, eyes on the falling snow. "We're not getting out of Denver."

Owens folds his arms over his stomach, an uncharacteristic frown on his face. Streicher sighs, staring at his phone background of Pippa and their dog. Walker dozes with the brim of his hat pulled low over his eyes.

On the ice, the past three weeks have been incredible. The rookie is soaring, racking up the goals and assists, catching the attention of fans, commentators, and the league. Solidifying his spot on the team, I hope.

The next Gretzky, people whisper. *The next Tate Ward.*

Off the ice, I miss my wife. Being away from her is torture. I hate sleeping alone. I hate having to see her life through the photos she texts me—her at soccer, her and the bunnies, at my mom's flower shop, helping her—instead of standing beside her, seeing it for myself. I like that picture she sent of her wearing my T-shirt, though.

Ward said it's dangerous to let hockey become everything, because when it's gone, you have nothing left. Seeing Georgia wear my clothes, though, makes me feel like...

Maybe I won't be left with nothing. Maybe I'll have her.

I think about how Georgia reacted when I got hurt at the beginning of the month. She sleepwalks because me getting hurt causes her stress and pain. I can't retire *now*, though, not when the rookie and I are making progress like this.

It's what I love. I can't give it up.

On my keychain, the little pink crystal catches the light. My wedding ring glints. The friendship bracelets from the girls at soccer sit on my wrist. One of the Christmas presents I got Georgia is tucked in my jacket pocket, a little black velvet box that I didn't dare leave at home in case she found it before she was ready to see it.

I love her, I said during the citizenship interview before I left. *I think I've loved her for a lot longer than I realized.*

It didn't feel like lying. I'm not sure what to do with that. I'm not sure what to do with any of this.

I'm in love with her. Maybe it's as simple as that. I love being married to her. I love waking up with her in my bed. I love hosting our friends for dinner, and I love sharing a home with her.

I want share a *life* with her.

My phone buzzes with a text. My background is the photo of us after we had everyone over, in the kitchen with her laughing, raspberry stuff on our faces. Miller snapped the pic and sent it to me.

I stare at that photo a lot.

The text is from Georgia. It's a photo of Stefan and Damon, wearing little Christmas hats. My chest aches. I miss them, too.

Another photo pops up—she's sitting on the chair beside the fireplace, drinking a glass of wine. An intense surge of motivation hits me. She's sitting at home, what the fuck am I doing here?

I'm on my feet, and the guys look at me.

"I need to get home to my wife."

Miller stares at me like I've lost it. "There's a blizzard, Volkov. We're stuck."

"Roads are open." We passed a rental car company on the way into the terminal. "I'm renting a truck and driving."

"Driving where?"

"I don't know. Salt Lake, maybe." I rake my hand through my hair. I can probably catch a flight home from there. "I need to get home. Tomorrow's Christmas Eve, and Georgia's at home, waiting for me. I need to get home," I say again, like some lovesick fool.

Maybe I am. Maybe I don't care.

"Volkov." Miller stands with a serious expression. "As your captain, I need you to know this is dangerous and stupid."

"I know."

He nods once. "Okay. Good." He reaches down to get his bag. "Let's go."

"What?"

His cocky grin appears. "I'm coming, too."

Owens stands. "Same."

I frown. "You don't have to."

He claps me on the shoulder. "You're not the only one with a girl at home, Volkov. Besides, we're not going to let you drive on your own. Where's the fun in that?" He smiles like he just thought of something. "We can listen to *The Northern Sword* on audio."

That's the fantasy series he and Darcy are always pushing on people. Miller groans.

"We're not listening to your fairy porn, Owens."

"There's a truck with four-wheel drive at the rental place here," Streicher says, frowning at his phone. "Want me to book it?"

"Book it," Walker says, bleary-eyed but awake and grinning. Off my curious look, he shrugs. "I never say no to adventure."

"Bad news, gentlemen." Ward sighs at our side. "The pilot doesn't think it's safe to fly. We're grounded until at least tomorrow."

"We're renting a car and driving to Salt Lake," I tell him.

His eyebrows lift. "You're going to be driving all night."

"I know."

For a moment, I worry he might stop us, but the corners of his eyes crinkle. "Tell Dr. Greene Merry Christmas from me."

"I will. Everyone ready?" I look to the guys, on their feet, holding their bags. "Let's go home."

"SNOW IS FALLING ON THE TREES," I tell Alexei on Christmas Eve morning, staring out the window at the forest behind the house as the soft flurries drift, coating the emerald trees in white.

Everything is pretty and quiet. It's my favorite time of year. At night, under the streetlights, the snow sparkles.

I wish you were here, I don't say. *I miss you. I wear your T-shirt every night to bed because it makes me feel close to you.*

Alexei has been away for weeks and I'm losing my mind. We leave for our fake honeymoon in Silver Falls the day after Christmas—if Alexei ever gets home. His flight has been delayed two days in a row.

Time apart was supposed to bring these feelings down, but I can't seem to get the guy out of my head, and he isn't helping. Every few days, flowers arrive at my office, at the hospital, at home.

Camellia (white)—you're adorable.

Red fuchsia—I like your taste. That one made me blush every time I looked at it.

Calla lily—beauty.

Honeysuckle—devoted affection.

Salvia (red)—forever mine.

I think about that last one a lot. I snipped off a bloom and pressed it between the pages of an old medical text like some wartime damsel pining for her beloved.

Who even am I anymore? If he ever found it, I'd die of humiliation.

"The money hit my bank account yesterday," I say offhand, like my balance increasing by ten million isn't a big deal. "Heather and I met with the bank yesterday to arrange the transfer."

On the other end, Alexei's quiet. "That's good, right?" he says, finally, a strange note to his voice.

"Yes," I lie. "It's great. It's a relief."

I'm thrilled to secure our research program for the next decade, but it's also one less reason to stay married to Alexei Volkov. Once his and his parents' citizenship comes through, there's nothing keeping me here. Nothing keeping me with him.

I hate the thought of this ending. Three weeks without him has been hard enough. It's not just that I miss the sex. A few nights ago in his hotel room after their game, Alexei demanded I use my toy while he watched on FaceTime, murmuring low encouragement in my ear as he stroked himself.

I miss having him around. Without him, the house feels empty and cold. Life feels a little more dull. Even the bunnies are bored and listless. Despite sleeping in his bed, with his scent surrounding me, my sleep is restless and uneasy.

"Hellfire, I have some bad news for you."

"Don't tell me your flight is delayed again." I keep my voice light and teasing. When he doesn't answer, my heart sinks, but I sigh with exaggeration. "How will I ever stay warm tonight? I'll have to borrow that man-chest doll Hayden got Darcy for Valentine's Day."

He gifted it to her as a joke after she broke up with her boyfriend. They bring it out at parties. Last time, they put a Storm jersey and sunglasses on it and brought it with us to the Filthy Flamingo.

There's a knock at the door.

My pulse leaps before I curse myself. It's probably just another delivery. I hurry to the door, though, almost tripping over my own feet to open it.

Alexei's standing on the doorstep, holding a bouquet, taller and broader than I remember. His gaze sears me, intense and determined.

"You're going to have to hold off on cuddling with that doll," he says, tucking his phone in his back pocket.

I light up, and when my gaze drops to the flowers in his hand, I feel that sharp, pleasant tug again.

Soft, pretty white petals, like a cross between a dogwood and a rose.

I clear my throat. "Gardenia?"

He nods.

That's what I was hoping for, but that's what I was also afraid of.

Gardenia—secret love.

"Welcome home," I whisper, heart beating wildly.

The corner of his mouth twitches up, eyes warm and soft. "Missed you, Hellfire. Missed you like crazy."

We stare at each other for a long moment before he wraps me in a tight, warm hug, his face in my neck, my head against his expansive chest. Even through his thick knit sweater, I can feel his heart beating fast.

My nervous system settles, and a deep sense of comfort falls over me.

"I missed you, too," I admit.

I pull back and glance at his healing shoulder. "How does it feel?"

"Good. Better every day."

"You're not just saying that so I don't worry?"

He shakes his head, pressing his mouth in a slanted line. "I have a different injury I need you to take a look at, though."

In an instant, I'm alert, stepping back to look at him. With a sharp intake of breath, he gives me a wide grin before his tongue flicks, popping his left central incisor out.

He's missing a tooth.

"No," I choke, clapping a hand over my mouth in horror. "Alexei." I stare at the gap before I burst out laughing. His grin is wide and boyish, pleased as punch. I laugh harder.

"The team dentist is giving me an implant on Boxing Day." The day after Christmas. "Before we leave for Silver Falls."

"I thought hockey players don't get implants until after they're done." Losing teeth is so common, most of them use temporary bridges like what he has now until they retire.

"I doubt my wife would allow that."

My mouth twists so I don't smile too hard. "You know what this means, right? Get ready for those soft foods, Grandpa. Lots of oatmeal and apple sauce."

His expression turns wolfish, eyes teasing but predatory. He steps toward me, and I take a step back, holding up a hand, still smiling.

"Do not."

His eyes dance. "I want to kiss my wife."

"No, thank you." That missing tooth looks ridiculous. I'm horrified, yet laughing. "Nope. Never."

"Come here, Hellfire."

"Get away from *meeee*—" I break off on a shriek, helpless with laughter as he hauls me over his shoulder. "I'll never kiss you now," I holler, upside down.

He delivers a sharp slap to my ass. "We'll see about that."

―――――――

That evening, we lie on the sofa in the front room, my head on his chest, the fireplace on, and the Christmas tree glowing with soft, pretty lights. Damon is curled up by our feet, Stefan is sleeping beneath the tree.

So this is what it's suppsed to be like. This is why people get married. This is why they choose one person for the rest of their lives.

"He likes it under there," Alexei murmurs.

I smile. I caught him snuggling them this afternoon, Alexei whispering something in their ears.

"I didn't know you were such a Christmas guy."

"I'm not."

"You had a ton of decorations." They were in the spare room, the one at the end of the hall, that we never go in. We spent all afternoon putting them up—when we weren't getting distracted by each other.

"I asked Svetta to hide them there as they arrived so you wouldn't see."

"Why?" I'm gawking at him, to his amusement.

"I wanted it to be a surprise."

Even as my heart pinwheels with delight, I give him a funny look. "We're leaving in two days."

"It's our first Christmas together. We can't do nothing."

First, like there will be more. Like we're a family. My dumb little hopeful heart lifts. It doesn't change anything, though. If we're together, I'm either watching him break bones and dislocate joints, or he's not doing the thing he loves. Either option breaks my heart.

Marriage didn't mean the same thing to Liam as it did to

me, but what about Alexei? Would it be more of this, more quiet, intimate conversations, more laughter, more coaching soccer together and having our friends over for dinner?

He pulls me against his chest, and I force the thoughts away.

"I asked you once if you wanted kids," he says carefully, and my body tenses. "And you didn't really answer."

I never thought it was an option, I'd said. My hopeful heart tries to rise again.

My throat works. He's given me so much. Can't I just be honest with him? "It's hard for women, because, um." I falter. "A lot of women still struggle to have families and careers. I know it's a decades-old problem, but it's still true. It's even harder when both parents put their career first."

I want one, though. It's a fact I've never admitted to myself because it was easier and less painful to pretend I didn't care, but it's the truth. I would love to have kids.

Especially with someone like Alexei. I picture him being a dad, playing hockey with them, cooking with them, carrying a tiny version of himself on his shoulders, and it's an image so sweet, my chest hurts.

"What if you had the right person?" He searches my eyes. "Someone to share the work and support you in the way you need. A partner. Fifty-fifty."

A partner, like what my parents have. God, I want it to be him. "With the right person, I would want kids."

He looks at me for a long time. I'd give anything to hear his thoughts. "Me too," he finally says. "With the right person, I want kids."

We gaze at each other, something yearning and expansive behind my ribcage.

"Remind me to thank Ward for getting you guys home this morning," I whisper, smiling.

"He didn't. The flight didn't leave Denver until an hour ago."

I frown. After he hauled me upstairs this morning, showing me how much he missed me must have scrambled my brains.

"I drove to Salt Lake last night and rented a private plane." The corner of his mouth twitches.

"You drove through a snowstorm by yourself?" I'm not even going to touch this private plane thing.

"Not by myself. The guys came with me."

I sit up. "That's dangerous. You could have been in an accident." Worry tightens around my heart. "What if you got hurt?"

He gives me an amused smile. "I played two seasons in Montreal, Georgia. I know how to drive in the snow. Besides," he eases me back down to lying against him, his hand in my hair, "I needed to get home to my wife."

Well, if I hadn't been in love with the man before, I am now.

"ARE YOU WARM ENOUGH?" I ask on Christmas morning as we walk through the snow-covered forest. She couldn't find her gloves so I have her hand tucked in my pocket.

She nods, giving me a small smile. "I'm fine."

"Your nose is red."

Her mouth curves, pretty and distracting. My phone rings, and I fish it out of my pocket. "It's the team's immigration lawyer."

Her eyes go wide. "Answer it."

I put the phone on speaker. "Hello?"

"Sorry to call on Christmas," the lawyer says, "but it's important."

I look to Georgia like a lifeline. "Is there another problem with the paperwork?"

Georgia presses her hands over her mouth, eyes wide and worried.

"No," the lawyer laughs. "It's approved."

Georgia and I stare at each other in silence. I'm trying not to jump to conclusions.

"Your citizenship has been approved," the lawyer repeats.

"And my parents'?" I'm holding my breath.

"And your parents'," she confirms.

Relief crashes through me. Georgia lets out a muffled yelp of excitement, jumping up and down in the snow, and I wrap an arm around her, tucking her against my chest. The lawyer talks me through the last of the process before we wish each other happy holidays and hang up. Georgia throws her arms around my neck.

"Call your parents," she urges. "Call them right now."

My chest squeezes with affection for her, and when we tell my parents the good news, her eyes well up.

"You okay?" I ask after we hang up, and she nods.

"Just happy for you all. And relieved you get to stay."

"Same." I sigh, taking her hand as we start to walk back to the house. "Finally, this nightmare is over."

At my side, her smile falters.

A frown snaps onto my face. "I didn't mean you."

I love her, but I can't tell her, because she'll panic, but fucking hell, I don't like keeping it from her.

She blinks, looking stricken like she just realized something. "Now that I have my inheritance and you have your citizenship, there's no reason to stay married."

Like touching a hot stove, my whole body reacts with repulsion to the idea of ending this. Is she ready to hear how I feel, though? One glance at her face tells me no. *I like her,* I'd said, and she was practically climbing the walls to avoid looking at me.

She's chewing her bottom lip. I wish I could wipe away the panic in her eyes.

"We should keep this going," she rushes out, darting a glance up at me. "It would look weird if we separated right away."

She feels the same way. I don't know if she loves me, but

she feels *something*, and she isn't ready for this to be over, either.

She's terrified, though.

"And the bunnies just got settled," I add, watching her pretty eyes.

"Yeah." She nods. "It would be irresponsible to uproot them again so quickly."

"How about another six months with me, Hellfire? Until the end of the season. Think you can manage that?"

She starts to smile, soft and lovely. "I can manage."

We walk back to the house, our boots crunching in the snow, and I'm flooded with resolve.

I'm going to do everything I can to make this woman fall in love with me like I have with her.

BACK AT THE HOUSE, I'm helping her out of her coat when she sucks in a sharp breath.

"I got you a present. For Christmas."

My eyebrows lift. "Yeah?"

"You don't have to get me anything," she adds, a nervous edge to her voice that makes me smile more.

"I did." The black velvet box in my bag upstairs tugs at my attention, but from the panic in her eyes earlier, she isn't ready for it.

"I didn't know if we were exchanging gifts."

"We are."

She bites her bottom lip, Christmas tree lights sparkling in her pretty eyes. "Okay."

"Well?"

"Well, what?" Her eyes dart around. She's nervous. Fucking adorable.

"I want my present."

Her eyes flicker with amusement. "So demanding."

I stare at her before she rolls her eyes and heads to the garage. When she doesn't return, I find her standing at the open trunk of her car, chewing her lip. She sees me and steps in the way, blocking my view.

"You know what?" She makes a face like she's laughing at herself. "I'm so sorry. I forgot your gift at the store."

Little liar. I try not to smile. "Georgia. You don't need to be nervous, sweetheart." And I need to see what's in those boxes.

"I'm *not* nervous—"

I gather the boxes and carry them inside. She follows at my heels.

"You're so hard to buy for, Alexei. Like, really, what do you get the guy who can buy anything for himself, you know?"

In the front room, I take a seat on the sofa and open the first box, hooking my finger into the strap of something emerald green, lacy, and hot as hell. I raise an eyebrow at her, already picturing her in it.

A pretty blush appears on her face. "That's for me." She presses her lips together, eyes sparkling. "But also for you."

We've been fooling around nonstop since I got home. Last night, the middle of the night, this morning. This morning again, in the shower.

And yet, I want her again. It still won't be enough, though. My appetite for Georgia Greene is insatiable.

"You bought this, thinking about me?"

The blush deepens.

"Hellfire," I warn, already getting hard. "Tell the truth."

"Yes," she says lightly.

I grip the back of her neck and give her a hard kiss, blood rushing to my groin. I groan against her lips. "Good girl. I love it. Thank you."

She smiles, and my heart expands. When I move to the next box, though, she folds her arms, then tucks them under her thighs, then folds them again.

This is the one she's nervous about. Curiosity courses through me as I open it.

My fingers find soft knit fabric, and I pull out an emerald green sweater.

"I know it's not the most original gift," she says quietly, "but my mom gets one for my dad every year. It's tradition."

My heart aches with affection. I want this to be the first of many Christmas sweaters from Georgia. I want a whole closet full of them.

I nudge my chin at the lingerie. "Are we going to match?"

She laughs. "I love the way men look in those sweaters." Her eyes dart to mine. "I saw it and I thought of you."

"I'm glad you did." I pull her into my lap. "I love it. Thank you."

Our kiss is sweet and soft, and deep in my chest, everything settles.

She's terrified, but she's trying. She's inching forward to meet me.

"All right." I give her thigh a squeeze before setting her aside. "Your turn. Stay here."

I return a moment later with a box.

"This is *one* of your gifts. The other wasn't ready in time," I lie about the velvet box.

The second she shakes the box I hand her, she smiles.

"Really," she says, like she can't believe it.

"Just open it."

Her eyes glow with excitement as she tears off the wrapping, and when she flips the box open, she lets out an excited yelp of surprise. "Shoes!"

"Like them?" I laugh.

A puzzled expression forms on her pretty face, and she narrows her eyes up at me. "I don't know these."

I stifle a grin. Her eyes narrow more.

"I know every shoe by this designer from the last five years. This is not one of them."

"I know." Most of the shoes in her closet are by this designer.

"Alexei."

"Keep looking."

Her expression is wary, like she's afraid to peek in the box, before she pulls out a card. She reads it and her eyes go wide.

I already know what it says. *The Georgia—for a woman who knows she's hot.*

"Shut up," she whispers. She sees me grinning. "Alexei, shut the fuck up."

She loves it. I knew she'd fucking love it. This husband thing? I was born to do it.

"You got her to design a shoe for me?" she screams, jumping up and throwing her arms around my neck, covering me in kisses.

"Mhm." I smile against her hair, my heart pounding and flipping over in my chest. "So you like them?"

"I love them," she howls into my neck.

"Put them on."

"No," she gasps, breaking away to gather the shoes against her chest. "I can't wear these. I'm going to keep them under glass." She gazes at the shoes like they're her bunnies. *I love you guys,* she mouths.

"Sweetheart, I bought ten pairs. And they'll be out next winter in stores. Put them on."

I ease back on the couch, one arm over the top of it, and when she reaches for the shoes, I send a pointed glance to the lingerie.

"Put all of it on."

She bites her bottom lip, her mouth curving up, and my

blood starts to race when she lifts her top off. I watch from the couch as she undresses.

"Close your eyes," she says when she reaches behind her to take her bra off, and I let my eyes close for a brief moment before they're open again. Her back is to me as she slips on the items I bought her, and my gaze trails down her soft curves, over her toned legs, to those sexy little fuck-me heels.

I sigh, raking a hand through my hair. "God, you're beautiful."

She smiles, turning around. "You were supposed to close your eyes."

We gaze at each other for a beat, my heart racing, arousal pooling in my groin and a heavy warmth growing in my chest.

"I can't close my eyes around you, Georgia."

Her mouth curves, eyes sparkling. "Because you can't trust me?"

"Because I don't want to miss a second of this."

The delicate line of her throat works. Does she believe me?

"Come here," I say quietly, and she does.

So obedient and trusting. God, I fucking love her.

She climbs onto my lap and her lips meet mine, kissing me, running her hands over my chest, tugging on my hair, making me groan as I wrap my arms around her. She opens up for me and our kiss is a perfect give and take as we lose ourselves in each other.

My hand drifts between her legs, where her panties are damp.

"Wet, already."

"It's the shoes," she whispers into my ear with that teasing smile. "They turn me on."

I glance down to them. Delicate yet deadly. "Me too."

She laughs, and I lift her off me before standing.

"Stay there." She gives me an odd look before I take a seat on the floor, my back against the couch, and maneuver her so my head is between her legs, her kneeling and facing the back of the couch with arms braced.

Her eyes flare with alarm.

"I wouldn't do this unless I wanted to," I say quietly, rubbing her thigh. "It's all I thought about while I was away."

Her throat works.

"Please," I add, with a crooked smile. "Let me get a taste of my wife. Let me change your mind about this."

She presses her lips together before she gives me a tiny nod. A deep sense of determination floods me.

"Like this?" She looks uncertain at the position.

I guarantee she's never ridden a guy's face before, and I *love* being the first.

"Uh-huh." My hands come to her ass, slipping my fingers beneath the lace to palm her soft skin.

"Right here?"

I grin, thinking about her sucking my cock so well in the foyer a few weeks ago. "Yes, sweetheart, right here."

Hooking my fingers beneath the fabric, I pull it aside and drag my tongue up her center.

"Oh god," she breathes.

I let her take what she needs, let her ride my face like I've thought about for years. Images of exactly what we're doing now have snuck into my head at the worst times—in the dressing room, during a face-off, during postgame press—and now that we're actually doing it, I'm so hard it hurts.

She finds a good rhythm, her breath coming out in shallow pants, and I pull my cock out, stroking myself as I work her clit with my tongue and lips.

"Who's the world's hottest wife?" I ask.

She laughs, head falling forward onto the sofa.

"Say it, Georgia."

"Fine." I can hear the smile in her voice. "I am."

"That's right. That's my girl."

I press my fingers at her entrance, pushing inside her to find the ridged spot that makes her fall apart. She moans, tightening around my fingers.

Against her pussy, I smile. That's the sound I wanted to hear. I massage that spot, lavishing attention on the bundle of nerves at the top of her entrance, and before long, her thighs tighten.

"Say my name when you come, sweetheart."

She sucks in a sharp breath, and around my fingers, her muscles clamp down, tensing and spasming.

"Alexei." She works her pussy against my mouth, riding my tongue and fingers, and my balls ache with need as I stroke myself faster. "Please don't stop."

Those words are heaven to my ears. Her hand threads into my hair, tugging, sending electric currents down my spine, and I suck her clit hard, driving her to the next level of orgasm. A rush of moisture coats my fingers, and the moan she makes is desperate, frantic, disbelieving.

When the last shudder rolls through her and she sighs into the couch, I flip her over, pull my clothes off, and retrieve a condom from my wallet before rolling it on.

Still catching her breath, she reaches to take her heels off, but I pull her wrists away, stopping her.

"Leave them on."

She grins, eyes still glazed. "I knew it."

"I think everyone knew it," I admit, laughing a little, before I sink into her and my laugh falls away.

It's like coming home. Like being exactly where I belong.

Together, we fit. Together, nothing else matters. Her tight warmth is so welcoming, I can't think. Need pounds through me as I lower my mouth to hers, kissing her, pushing in to the hilt. I pull her knee up over my shoulder to sink deeper and a broken moan slips out of her.

"The sweetest noise I've ever heard," I growl into her neck, my hips pulling back to thrust in again. "You're such a good wife, sweetheart," I gather a fistful of hair for leverage. Georgia's pretty lips part, her eyelids falling halfway as she accommodates my size. "Such a pretty wife. Such a trusting wife."

I pull her other leg over my shoulder, and as I bury myself in her again and again, her body tightens. Her heels dig into my back, sharp pricks of pain winding my desire higher. Around my cock, her pussy flexes. She's close again. Fire races through my blood and I have to fight not to let my head fall back with pleasure. I'm driving into her now, finding a fast rhythm. Punishing her for being so perfect, for changing my life, for making me want everything with her.

"That's so fucking good, Georgia." My voice is a low, gritty rasp. "I'm so close. You're a goddamned dream. Does my pretty little wife like me fucking her hard like this?"

I feel the shiver that runs through her. Her eyes meet mine, hazy and pupils wide with lust. She nods; heat pounds harder through my body.

The first flutters inside her, the way her eyes close in pleasure, the blush on her cheekbones, the sound of her moaning beneath me—the sensations blur together, pressure tightens at the base of my spine, and excruciating, incredible desire slices me into a thousand pieces.

"Fuck, I'm going to come," I manage, breathing hard, heart pounding. "I'm going to come inside you."

With her hair in my fist and her eyes on me, I fuck my gorgeous wife until the pleasure boils over, my balls tighten, and I release into her. Deep in my brain, everything locks into place.

I am *never* letting her go. I'll give her all the time and space she needs, but I will never give up on the woman I love.

Georgia is mine.

"A BACHELORETTE without a blow-up penis in sight?" Across the table, I raise my eyebrows at Hazel. We're finishing up our drinks after dinner. "This is your send-off. We need to make sure you have a good time."

The guys are out having their bachelor party, but they didn't say what they were doing.

Hazel grins. "No blow-up penises. Not my style." Her eyes move around the table, from her sister to Darcy to Jordan to me. "This is perfect. Besides, I don't feel like I'm marching to my grave or anything." She shrugs, a soft smile pulling up on her mouth. "I'm excited to get married."

Jordan raises her eyebrows, skeptical.

"Before Rory, I didn't think I'd want to." Hazel looks down at her drink, a funny smile on her mouth. "But it's so easy with him. The easiest thing in the world. He's my best friend."

My heart pangs with yearning, and even though we've spent every second of the past week together, even though I saw him two hours ago, I miss him.

Somehow, this man I used to hate has become one of the most important people in my life.

Six more months, my brain whispers. I don't know why I said that. I don't know why I'm prolonging something that'll hurt me either way.

Maybe it's because I'm in love with him. I think about things ending with Alexei and something crumples in my chest.

If he was traded, or retired and got a job in another city, maybe as an analyst or in player development on another team, I'd want to go with him. I couldn't, though, because I have the hospital program, but I'd want to.

That alone is cause for concern. Am I repeating the past? Am I handing over everything for a man again?

I was never in love with Liam, though. I thought I was, but we never laughed together the way Alexei and I do. I never felt the deep sense of comfort and peace that I feel with my husband. And with Alexei, I never feel the need to make myself small and invisible. To lessen my accomplishments.

He could crush me, if he doesn't feel the same way. He could hurt me so much worse than Liam did.

Pippa gives me a soft smile. "Are you two having a nice honeymoon?"

My face warms. "Yes. We love it here."

The mountain town is small, charming, and quaint, with crisp, fresh air, sparkling lights in the trees, and vintage-looking streetlamps, like something out of a Christmas movie. Pippa mentioned they film a lot of Hallmark movies here. Our suite overlooks the Silver Falls lake, frozen solid, surrounded by snow-covered mountains.

"What have you two been doing?" Hazel asks.

We haven't left the suite once.

All we do is have sex, sleep, order room service while watching *The Vampire Diaries,* to which Alexei is addicted but won't admit it, before we're making out and undressing each other again. We can't keep our hands off each other. Clothes are unnecessary when you have a big warm enforcer to cuddle with.

I feign nonchalance. "You know. Touristy things around town."

"You must have seen the steam clock, then, in the main square."

Hazel and Pippa know Silver Falls because their parents moved here for retirement a few years ago. They visit several times a year.

Darcy frowns. "Steam clock?"

"Yes," I lie. "We saw it." I have no idea what she's talking about.

"Cool, right?" Hazel's eyes sparkle.

"Supercool." I give her a bright, confident smile. "I think I remember it from a movie."

Pippa puts her hand over her mouth, and Hazel gives me a knowing look. "There's no steam clock. I'm fucking with you."

Pippa bursts out laughing.

"Busted," Jordan drawls, smiling.

"He's sent me flowers every day," I blurt out. I've already told them about the shoes. I'm wearing them now. "They have meanings. His mom gave me a book."

"Every day?" Darcy asks, leaning in.

"Every day."

The book is tucked into my workbag, although I hardly need to check it anymore, I have so many of them memorized.

Hazel makes an impatient *go on* gesture.

"The first day was sunflowers." They all wait. "*Adoration.* Daisies. *I love you truly,*" I add. "White lilies. *My love is pure.*" Darcy's jaw drops. Pippa and Hazel exchange a glance, and my pulse trips. "Red chrysanthemum. *I love you.*" Jordan's eyebrows go up. "And today, red tulips. *Declaration of love.*"

A long pause of silence.

Jordan's eyebrows lift. "The guy's got it bad for you."

No one says anything, and when I look up, they're all smiling at me, even Jordan.

I look down at my hands, trying not to think about the end. "I've got it bad for him, too."

"ONE LAST STOP," Miller says on our way to meet up with the girls.

He gestures at a tattoo shop on the main street of Silver Falls. The place is actually nice. Maybe Georgia and I will come back next year.

If we're still together, I remind myself with unease. If I can make this thing real.

She hasn't sleepwalked once this week, because I haven't been playing hockey. I rub my sternum, swallowing hard. I don't know what to do about that. Watching me get hurt causes her stress, but I can't give it up.

I can't give her up, either.

Miller smiles at a tattoo shop, and I remember last year on Boxing Day, when he and Hazel were still in the pretending phase of their relationship but Miller was head over fucking heels for her. He got very, very drunk, and then got a tattoo for her.

"I'm going to get another one," Miller announces.

Owens rubs his jaw. "Yeah, what the hell. I'll get one, too."

"I'm in," Streicher adds.

"Shit, really, Streicher?" Miller grins at him.

Streicher nods again. "I was already thinking about it."

The guys look to me.

"You okay to wait, buddy?" Miller asks.

"No." I straighten up, squaring my shoulders. "Because I'm getting one, too."

Owens crows, trying to put me in a headlock, and I shove him off, but I'm smiling.

Hours later, we leave the tattoo parlor.

Streicher got a minimalist outline of a guitar, identical to the one he bought Pippa the first year they were together. Her dream guitar, that she wrote and recorded her debut album with.

Miller got another dragon. That's what he calls Hazel, his tiny fire-breathing dragon.

Owens got a sword up the back of his calf, from *The Northern Sword* book series he and Darcy love.

I shift my shoulder back and forth, sore from keeping still for so long. My tattoo took a lot longer than the others, but they were happy to wait, talking and laughing and keeping me company while I lay on the table.

"What do you think, Volkov?" Owens asks. "You feel like you made the right choice?"

It didn't hurt as much as I thought it would, maybe because I thought about my wife the entire time.

"Without a doubt."

CHAPTER 83
GEORGIA

THE NEXT AFTERNOON, Alexei's on the phone in the other room, talking to his lawyer about some last immigration details, when I walk out in the dress he bought me. He's shirtless with his back to me, and I take a moment to admire the strong planes of his back.

My husband is so freaking hot.

He notices me standing there and stops talking, eyes flaring. He hangs up without saying goodbye, never taking his gaze off me.

"Hi." I smile.

"Hi, Hellfire." He hasn't seen this dress yet. "Jesus, fuck, my wife is hot."

I roll my eyes, smiling, and my gaze catches on the bandage across his chest. My stomach drops through the floor. He's hurt?

"Oh my god. Alexei, what happened?" When did this happen? I was half-asleep when he got home last night, and when I woke this morning, he was already awake, dressed, and giving me a quick kiss before he stepped out to get us breakfast.

I reach for the bandage but his hands wrap around my wrists.

"Let me take the bandage off," I insist, but he's way too strong.

"No." His gaze is steady on me, voice firm. "I didn't get hurt, but you can't see it."

I drop my wrists, confused.

"It's a tattoo."

"What?" I blanche. "You got a tattoo. *You* got a tattoo."

"Yes." The corner of his mouth ticks up. "I got a tattoo."

"Of what?" I'm desperate to see it.

"I'll show you when you're ready."

My heart thunks. "Ready for what?"

He smiles that quiet, secretive smile, and now I want to see it more than anything.

"It's of my face, isn't it?" I joke.

"No." He laughs, low and pleased, before he looks at his watch. "We need to go soon."

Rory and Hazel's wedding starts in half an hour. He puts his shirt, tie, and jacket on while I retrieve my necklace from the bedroom, return, and hold it up for him. "Help me with this?"

He takes it from me and I hold my hair off my neck as he does the clasp up, his fingers sending goosebumps over my back as his fingers brush my skin.

"You look great, by the way," I say over my shoulder. "You know how to wear a suit."

"Thanks to you." He presses a warm kiss to the back of my neck. "And you haven't even seen the lining."

I turn, and he opens his suit jacket. The lining is the same color as my dress. My smile is instant, delight bubbling through me.

"You wanted to match me?" This is the dumbest, sweetest, cheesiest thing I've ever heard.

"Mhm." His mouth tilts. "Got a little something for you to

complete your outfit, too." He strides across the room and opens his bag before placing a shoebox in front of me.

I bite back a smile, flipping the lid open. It's *The Georgia* heels in ice blue to match my dress. "Another pair?"

"You needed them for the dress."

I make a wistful noise and stroke his cheek. "You're learning."

He grins and kisses my palm before kneeling in front of me. He slips them on my feet, doing up the dainty straps. The sight of them between his strong fingers sends a weird twist of longing through me.

"You're spoiling me."

He smirks, working on the other shoe. "You deserve to be spoiled."

"Can you imagine saying that a few months ago?"

He looks up, hand encircling my ankle. "I didn't know what I was missing, Hellfire."

"So this is the last present, huh?"

He shakes his head. "Nope."

Excitement flutters in my stomach. "Are you going to give it to me?"

He stands, gazing down at me, so steady and warm. "When you're ready."

This again? I groan in frustration. "You're driving me nuts."

"Good. Now you know how it feels."

———

Hazel and Rory's wedding is beautiful, romantic, and fun.

"Hazel Hartley-Miller, I love you more than anything," Rory says during their vows, blinking away vulnerability and emotion from his eyes. He looks so dashing and handsome with his blond hair, sparkling eyes, and black tux.

Hazel is a vision, her chestnut hair up in an elegant pony-tail, her long white dress cascading down her form in soft waves.

"You are my world," he says, "and when we're a hundred years old, I'll still be flirting with you to get your attention."

He whispers something in her ear, something just for her. Hazel closes her eyes, like she can't believe how much he loves her. Like she can't believe this is real.

I look up to Alexei, holding my hand and watching the couple, and my heart twists at the sight of my handsome husband, with the strong lines of his face, thick hair, and dark eyes.

How could I ever think his eyes were cold? They're warm like the spring sun, one of those brilliantly sunny days after a winter of dreary rain. Everything's a bit brighter, lighter, and happier, like it's all going to work out just fine.

Alexei's eyes are like that.

He meets my gaze and his throat works.

"Are you thinking about your wedding?" I whisper. "It's okay. Weddings stir up weird emotions."

He lets out a soft, silent laugh, shaking his head. "Not even a little bit, Hellfire." He gives my hand a warm squeeze. "Just thinking about how hot you look in that dress." He sends a pointed glance down to my feet. "And those shoes."

"*Foot fetish,*" I sing lightly under my breath, and he shakes his head, but his mouth is twitching.

At the front of the grand room, the officiant smiles between the couple.

"I pronounce you husband and wife. You may now kiss the bride."

They kiss, everyone cheers and applauds.

"Remember when you didn't want to kiss me?" I ask Alexei.

He presses his lips to my temple. "We don't have that problem anymore."

Later, after dinner, a band plays and people fill the dance floor. Alexei's getting us drinks while I chat with Darcy and Hayden, only half listening as they playfully argue over plans for their upcoming wedding.

"We should have a *Northern Sword*–themed wedding," he says.

She smiles. "I love you, but no."

The entire team and most of the staff are here. Ward smiles down at his daughter, who's holding his hand and wearing a pink party dress, before he sneaks a glance at Jordan. She looks anywhere but at him. Rory's parents laugh with Hazel's parents, a new ring sparkling on Rory's mom's ring finger. His parents divorced when Rory was young but remarried this past summer, Hazel said.

While the band takes a break, Pippa gets onstage with her guitar amid cheers and applause.

"This is a song about true love," she says, smiling at Jamie, before she starts to play.

The newly wed couple dances, swaying on the dance floor, Rory looking down at his new wife with adoration. Their lips move as they talk quietly. My heart aches.

I wish I could lay it all out on the line. If I tell Alexei, though, I suspect he'll retire, and I can let him give up something he loves because of me.

My husband appears at my side with our drinks. He sets them down and holds out a hand to me.

"Let's dance, Hellfire." He takes my hand. "I want to dance with my wife."

On the dance floor, his arms surround me, and I loop mine around his neck. We sway to Pippa's soft, lilting voice, the strum of her guitar. Alexei's breath tickles my cheek, and I inhale his fresh male scent.

This song is familiar, and it hits me. I lean back to look up at him. "This is the song we danced to at the team dinner."

He nods, studying me. I think back to how I felt, dancing with him that night, hating him. Questioning Pippa's sanity for falling for someone so hard. Feeling like a phony in front of everyone.

I get it now. I'm the one who fell hard. I'm the one who let this get real.

I wish we could stay here forever, on the dance floor in a ski town in the middle of the mountains, where everything is an easy, effortless dream.

"Have I ever told you how beautiful your eyes are?" he asks, and I smile, turning away and pressing my face into his shoulder.

Of course I'm in love with him. I was always going to fall in love with this guy, the only man who ever made me feel something.

"Tell me it's real, sweetheart."

Does he mean this marriage, or what we're doing right now? I don't care. The answer's the same for both. For me, at least. "It's real."

He stops, breathing hard, gazing down at me. My heart pounds in my ears, my skin is hot, and my head spins. I can't believe I admitted that.

"I know about the flowers," I say against him.

He pulls back to meet my eyes, unsurprised and unfazed, his mouth slanting into that affectionate half smile.

"I know what they mean. I know that—" I break off.

"What, Georgia?" His deep voice is low and gentle. More gentle than I ever thought he was capable of. "What do they mean?"

My throat works but I hold his gaze, heart pounding. "That you love me."

His chin dips. "Mhm. And I think you love me, too."

My heart stops. He sees right through me. I'm stripped bare, naked and exposed, with no defenses left. Even if I don't say it, he can see it in my eyes. What's the point of hiding? This is going to decimate me regardless of whether I say it or not.

"I do love you." The words fall from my lips. After all this time, fighting it so hard, telling Alexei I love him is like breathing. It feels right.

He kisses me once, twice, three times. "I was trying to give you time and space. I didn't want to rush you."

"Rush me." My heart beats harder than ever, and my hands thread into his hair, tugging him down to me for another kiss.

"Okay." His breath tickles my lips. "I love you, then. I want you. This is real for me, Georgia."

Relief slams into me, so hard it makes me give a short laugh. "It's real for me, too." Him getting hurt, though. "But—"

"I know." He clutches me harder to him, his big hand moving over my back in calming strokes. "But maybe we save that for later. We can find a solution together." His mouth comes to my ear. "Let go for me. I'll be there to catch you."

I'm tired of fighting this. I'm tired of trying to not be in love with him, so I nod. Letting go of control had never felt so easy, so I lean against my husband, sway to the last verses of the love song, and give him my heart.

The hesitant, worried part of me demands attention, but I shove her down, so far down I can't hear her anymore. I want to be in love. I want it to be easy.

I want Alexei.

The song ends and he leans down to kiss me, a soft, slow kiss that warms me to my toes, blanks out every thought from my head.

"You want to get out of here, Hellfire?"

I smile against his neck and nod before he takes my hand and pulls me off the dance floor.

WAITING for the elevator to our suite, Alexei leans down and kisses my neck. The lobby is quiet, just a few employees, a couple of wedding guests passing through, but with one touch, we're the only people on the planet. Goosebumps scatter across my skin, and he presses another kiss to the sensitive spot beneath my ear.

Inside the elevator, he backs me up to the wall and presses more soft, sweet, slow kisses along my skin. My stomach flutters every time we touch. It's torture. The corner of his mouth twitches up like he knows what he's doing to me.

The elevator doors open but we don't break apart, don't stop kissing for one second, as we move to the door of our suite.

I stumble—he catches me with an arm around my waist. I laugh—he gives me the handsome half smile that's just for me. I nip his earlobe while he tries to use his keycard to open the door—he drops it, pushes me against the wall, and kisses me senseless.

We're perfect for each other, and I don't know how I never saw it before. We wasted years fighting when we could have been doing this.

Inside the suite, he undresses me, his lips moving over my

skin. My dress flutters to the floor and I stand there in my bra, panties, and heels. His eyes darken before he exhales a heavy breath.

"Are you okay?" I laugh.

"Yes." He rakes a hand over his hair, gaze snagging on my chest, my waist, the tiny lace thong. "No. I don't know. I see you and I can't think. It's always been like this. It's . . ." He takes a deep breath. "Overwhelming."

In the bedroom, he wears that handsome, just-for-me half smile as he peels the pretty lace off and I fumble with his clothes. My heart tugs at my husband carefully undoing the straps of my heels with a gentle hand around my ankle, treating me with reverence like I'm made of glass. So careful with me, and with the things I love.

He sets the heels aside before his lips find a pinched peak, sucking and teasing. Pleasure races straight to between my legs. He's already fully erect, heavy and hot in my hand.

"Hands and knees," he tells me in a low voice. At the flare of uncertainty in my eyes, his eyes soften. "Do you trust me, Georgia?"

"Yes." My heart dips. I do.

"Good girl." He nips my bottom lip. "Now, do what you're told so I can reward you."

Nerves trickle through me as I turn over and brace myself on my palms and knees. Being exposed and powerless like this is a new experience.

It's Alexei, though, and I trust him.

His tongue meets my clit, and I gasp at the hot, wet sensation.

"Good?" he murmurs against my pussy, and I make a stifled noise of affirmation. "Words," he demands.

"Yes," I rush out, heat expanding through my body already. "It's good."

He works my clit with his tongue, winding me higher. God, this angle. It's perfection. Pleasure swirls between my legs, my blood thickens, and I'm lulled into a hazy dream.

His tongue slicks over my back entrance. I let out a high moan, clenching with surprise and need.

"What about this?" He draws a light circle over it and heat gathers low in my abdomen. My toes curl. "How does this feel, Georgia?"

Lost in the sensation, so unfamiliar but shockingly good, I ignore his smug tone. Sparks gather around the base of my spine.

"I don't know. I've never done this before."

"Do you want to stop?"

Another swirl of his tongue sends arousal rushing between my legs. I forget to answer, and he pulls away.

"No." My eyes fly wide. "Don't stop."

"How does it feel, Georgia?" he asks again, patient but firm.

I hate that I find this bossy side of him so hot. I hate how he makes me bend like this, and I hate how much I love it. "Incredible."

"Keep going?"

"Yes," I beg.

He resumes those intoxicating, wet swirls. Even if I won't come from this, my brain is searing with pleasure. It's never been like this, so hot yet intimate. His hands grip my thighs before he delivers a sharp slap to my ass. Another jolt of heat races through me.

My head drops, hair falling forward. "Oh my god."

"Hands behind your back."

I don't even argue, I just lower my head to the bed and bring my hands to my lower back, heart beating harder at how exposed and vulnerable I am right now. His warm hand bands around my wrists, giving me a gentle squeeze.

"So trusting and obedient. Such a good wife for me."

I shiver. I don't have the brain space to fight him. I'm floating, waiting, desperate for more.

"Are you close?"

"Yes," I manage through clenched teeth, arching my back.

"Do you want to come?"

"*Yes.*"

"You going to let me buy you another ring?"

My clit aches with need. "Fine. Yes."

"You know what I think whenever I see you wearing my ring, Georgia?" His breath tickles my pussy, and I shiver. I'm hot and cold all over, right on the edge. "I think, *mine*. I think, *that's my wife.*"

His fingers press inside me, finding that ridged spot. My lips part as he works it with his thick fingers, stretching me. My climax is on the horizon, gaining energy, but then Alexei pushes his tongue inside me and my thoughts detonate.

Holy hell, Alexei Volkov has his tongue in my ass.

Sharp pleasure erupts and my orgasm slams into me. I shudder through it, listening to the low, pleased noises he makes, his free hand grasping my hip, pulling me back against his face. My hands fist the duvet, my toes curl, and my heart pounds harder than ever as I spin and hurtle and shatter.

As I come down, his hands smooth over me in calming strokes. He applies soft, loving kisses to my thighs, my backside, my lower back, before he's turning me over.

"Georgia?" Hovering over me, his eyes are dark, his expansive chest rising and falling fast. "I want to come inside you."

My pulse stumbles.

"I'm clean," he adds, voice rough, eyes never leaving mine. "I've never gone without one."

"Me neither. I never trusted anyone enough. I want you,

though." I run my hands over his chest. "All of you. Nothing between us."

He closes his eyes. "Hearing that . . ." He shakes his head. "Fuck, Georgia. I love you."

"I love you, too." I can't help but smile. "And I have an IUD."

"Right." He blinks like he didn't even think of that.

"I'm not sure if you know this, Volkov," I'm still breathless but I give him a teasing smile, "but sex can lead to pregnancy."

"I'm aware." He makes a frustrated noise. "I'm finding it really hard to care about that right now."

He can't mean—? He does. His expression is intense and determined. Heat washes through me at the idea of him getting me pregnant.

At my baffled expression, he smiles. "I want kids with you."

"*Now?*" I blanche, and he laughs into my neck. My career. His career. It'll be hard. It'll hurt. It'll change our lives forever.

Despite all of that, I want it, too. Just not yet.

"No, sweetheart." A kiss against my skin. "Not now. But eventually. When we're ready."

I relax. I'm going to be thinking about this for a long time. The besotted, head-over-heels-in-love part of me reminds me how loving and protective Alexei is, and that having a baby with him might be one of the best things I ever do.

"We'll talk about this later," he murmurs, bracing himself above me. "Right now, I need my wife."

My legs fall open, he positions himself at my entrance. I can barely speak, I'm so overcome with this fluttering, heart-pounding, all-consuming want for him.

He nudges inside me, and my eyes roll back at the intense, perfect burn between my legs. I'm never going to get used to his size. At the first deep thrust, we both groan in disbelief.

Already, another release stirs inside me, warming and aching as he fills me.

"Okay?" he manages, like he can barely stand how good it is.

"So good." My nails dig into his shoulders. "Don't stop."

"What's the magic word," he murmurs against my ear, and I smile.

"Please."

"That's my girl. That's my pretty little wife."

Under his praises, I melt, dissolving, re-forming, rearranging.

"Jesus, Georgia. You're so fucking tight. So fucking good for me. So pretty and perfect."

Sparks blur my vision as he moves inside me. It's not just sex. It's so much more. It's everything. It's all-consuming.

It's love.

He pulls my leg over his shoulder, hitting so much deeper. My thoughts dissolve as he nudges that spot only he can reach. It's not just his size. He knows my body. He knows what I need.

"Right there." His eyes are dark like sin, intense and greedy. "Right fucking there, isn't it, Georgia?"

I'm nodding, eyes starting to close, breathing hard and about to lose it, tightening around his thick length. My muscles begin to flutter.

We'll call that *the husband spot* from now on.

"Say your husband's name when you come." His voice is like gravel. "Please."

"Now who's begging?" I gasp, and he laughs, short and sharp against my neck.

"I'll beg for you, Hellfire, I don't care anymore. You own me."

I come undone. The pleasure spills over, washing through

me, and I clutch him as I spiral, muscles clamping down on him while he fucks me hard. "Alexei," I whisper, the crash of need and pleasure so strong that tears prick my eyes.

At his name, he loses it, strokes turning jerky and urgent, hips pounding against me while he wears that strained, agonized expression until his eyes close, his head tips back, and he lets out a low, tortured groan that sets off another wave of pleasure within me.

"Georgia, fuck." His release slips between us, wet and slick. "Nothing compares to being with you." Our eyes meet, his hands framing my face as he shudders through the last of it. "You're everything."

Later, as we lie in bed, he laces his fingers through mine, our wedding rings glinting in the moonlight.

"Happy new year, Hellfire," my huge, handsome husband says.

"Happy new year, Alexei." Our eyes hold. "I love you," I whisper, strangely shy.

Happy, though.

"I love you, too."

Reality slithers back in, cold and unwelcome. What does this mean for us? What about him getting hurt? Are we . . . married for real?

"Hey." He threads his hand into my hair, presses his lips to my temple, and my distress lessens in an instant. "I know you're not fully in yet, but I'm going to convince you."

His mouth hooks, his eyes warming with an affection that smoothes my worries away.

"Just you wait."

"DID you two end up leaving the hotel?" Darcy asks as we sit behind the net a few nights later with Pippa and Hazel.

I let out a soft laugh. "We explored the town on the last day. Silver Falls is nice." Walking hand in hand down the main street with my husband was nice, too.

Darcy grins. "Maybe you can go back for your anniversary."

Our anniversary. A pleased *huh* slips out of me. "I like that idea."

Alexei skates past, his eyes meeting mine through the glass, and when his gaze drops to my jersey, a possessive, proud look fills his eyes. My stomach dips with pleasant warmth.

He loves me. I don't know what the future holds, but he loves me, and I love him. I'm going to be happy, I've decided. I'm going to enjoy being in love.

On the ice, Alexei steals the puck from the other team before passing to Luca, who moves it up the ice with the forwards. Hayden scores after Luca assists, and the arena erupts with noise, the goal horn blaring, lights flashing. I'm on my feet along with every other fan, cheering and smiling ear to ear.

It's Alexei I'm cheering for, though. He gives Luca a firm nod of approval before slapping him on the back. As Luca and Hayden skate past the bench, bumping gloves with the rest of the team, Alexei watches with a proud expression. It's a good look on him.

We take our seats again, and I look over to Hazel. "Are you two going on a honeymoon?"

She nods. "Hawaii during All-Star week," most players have that week off in February, "and we'll do a longer trip in the summer."

Hazel Hartley-Miller, Rory had said during their vows. "You decided to change your name."

"Yes." She sighs, smiling. "I did."

"So much paperwork," Pippa groans. Professionally, her last name is still *Hartley*, but legally, she changed it to *Hartley-Streicher*.

"What are you going to do, Darce?" I ask.

She taps her lip, frowning. "I think I want to change my last name to *Owens*."

"Darcy Owens." My eyebrows lift. "It sounds good."

She glances between all of us. "Is that . . . un-feminist of me?"

"Not at all." I nudge her. "The beauty of feminism is that you can do whatever you want."

"Yeah." She watches Hayden through the glass as he skates past, giving Darcy a big, dopey grin.

"Besides," Hazel smiles at her own hockey player. "It makes them very happy."

"Yeah." Pippa gazes at hers. "Very, very happy."

I think about my own name. I never felt attached to it. The opposite, actually. It's a reminder of a horrible man who made my parents' lives very difficult.

Georgia Volkov. A pulse of warmth hits me in the chest as I find him on the ice, towering above the rest. The whistle blows for an icing call, the game stops, and he turns, giving me his handsome half smile.

Changing my name isn't as repulsive as it once would have been. I actually kind of like that idea.

"I'm still not used to seeing him smile," Darcy says.

"You two seemed to be getting along at the wedding." Hazel smirks at me. "Very *marital*." She makes a face. "Sorry. Rory keeps trying to make that word sound dirty but it doesn't work. You two just seemed happy together."

The guys line up for a face-off, and my throat squeezes with emotion as I remember the way he looked at me in bed, like I was everything to him. "We are."

"No more sleepwalking?"

A player from the other team cross-checks Alexei, and my stomach lurches. "Still sleepwalking." Probably tonight, although it doesn't look like he's gotten injured. "Alexei helps with that." Usually with a big arm around my waist, holding me to his chest, keeping me safe.

Another pleasant pulse hits me.

The others exchange smiles.

"Don't be smug," I tell them, and they laugh. "It's unbecoming."

Rory sends the puck to Luca, and while Alexei buys him time, the rookie shoots the puck at the net. He misses, but Hayden passes it back to him. He tries again, aiming for the top corner of the net—and it goes in.

The arena explodes with a volume particular to two goals in quick succession, a delighted roar of surprise and gratitude. On the bench, the guys all jump up, and on the ice, the players surround Luca again, slapping him on the back, jostling him with big grins.

Alexei just wears that proud look again.

"The rookie's pretty good, huh?" Pippa asks, and I smile.

"He's incredible, with the right coaching."

———

In the third period, the Storm are up three–nothing, with goals from Luca, Rory, and Hayden.

The thing about hockey, though, is that everything can change in a split second.

Alexei has the puck when a defenseman collides with him at speed, hitting Alexei's head with his shoulder. Alexei's head snaps back at an angle that makes fan gasp, before he drops.

Over the blood beating in my ears, the whistle blows. I'm on my feet, watching in horror as Rory and Hayden fly to Alexei's side. He's lying on the ice, not moving.

Fuck. Oh god. He's not moving.

He's not moving.

Rory shifts to let a doctor through. Blood runs down Alexei's face onto the ice. His eyes are still closed. The arena is a deadly, horrifying quiet.

He's still not moving.

I'm sprinting, pushing past people, until I'm in the arena concourse, rushing to the ice. No one stops me. I don't even show my ID.

At the bench, someone blocks my path.

"Georgia." Tate's voice is quiet, eyes worried and serious. "No."

"I need to get to him." I'm shaking. I can't breathe. My eyes stay glued to the group on the ice, waiting for a glimpse of him. Waiting for him to get up.

Get up, I pray. *Open your eyes. Glare at me. Call me your wife. Call me Hellfire. Tell me I'm your everything.*

"Let them do their jobs," Tate says, eyes full of patient

sympathy. "You can follow them to the hospital, but let them take care of this."

Every cell in my body revolts, but he's right. We keep family members out of the way during times like these because of how I'm feeling right now. Reckless, terrified, and desperate.

The arena is silent as Alexei is moved onto a stretcher and carried off the ice, and my stomach hardens into a tight, cold block. It's so much worse than two years ago.

I love him now. I can't be without him. Seeing him like this makes that clear as day. I'll stand by his side, watch him get hurt and take care of him after, even if it kills me.

MY BODY HURTS.

My head throbs, my back aches like something else, and stinging pain lances across my face. Did I get stitches? Feels like it.

The pain is nothing compared to how I feel when I open my eyes and see Georgia sitting in the chair beside my hospital bed, silently sobbing into her hands. Her shoulders shake, and my world collapses.

"Sweetheart."

My voice is a dry rasp, and her head jolts up. Red and puffy eyes. Tearstained face. My chest aches. I can handle the other pain, but this? No. I can't take this.

I'm done playing hockey. I know that now.

"You're awake." She sniffs and wipes her face, blinking away the tears.

In an instant, she's at my side, pressing a soft kiss to the corner of my mouth that doesn't hurt so much. Her scent is in my nose, her hair tickles my neck as it falls around me in a curtain of softness, and her hands barely touch my face, they're so gentle.

"Alexei," she breathes, and a fresh wave of tears shine in

her eyes. She sucks in a tight breath, blinking, slipping on her professional exterior. "Do you remember what happened?"

"No." I know it was bad, for my head to feel like this.

"Okay." She nods to herself. "You were playing a game and experienced a head shot."

"Feels like it."

She pulls out a penlight as her eyes well with moisture. "I bet. Can you tell me your last name?"

I've done this before. She's checking me for the concussion severity. "Volkov."

"Good. Do you know the date?"

"January third." I fucking hope.

She nods again. Good. "Who am I?"

My heart trips. "My wife."

Her eyes close for a brief moment and she nods. "Yes, baby. What's my name?"

"Hellfire."

"Alexei, I swear to god."

Teasing her dulls the pain. "Georgia Greene. *Dr.* Georgia Greene."

"Good. I'm going to shine a light in your eyes."

I study her face while she checks my pupils.

"What are you feeling? Headache? Nausea? Ringing in your ears?"

"Headache. Ringing in my ears. Back hurts."

She nods to herself.

"Am I still pretty?" I ask with a crooked grin.

She doesn't smile the way I want her to. "You've been unconscious for an hour."

"Shit."

"Yeah. Shit." Her throat works. "The doctor will do an assessment, but I think you have a Grade 4 concussion.

This woman loves me. Watching me get hurt hurts her. *I'm*

hurting her. It's so simple when I put it that way. I reach for her hand.

"I'm done with hockey." I knew it the second I opened my eyes and saw her curled up and crying. "I'm ready to retire."

"No, Alexei—" She starts shaking her head. "Don't retire because of me. It's everything to you."

She's so wrong. "It's *not* everything to me. Not anymore. You are." I swallow hard, studying every shade of whiskey, caramel, and amber in her eyes. "I won't cause you pain."

I never want to see her like this again. I never want her to cry because of me.

"I'm not going anywhere." Her hand comes to my hair, pushing it off my forehead, careful not to touch what I'm sure is a massive goose egg. "I meant what I said. I love you."

This woman. I can't believe I ever thought she was selfish. She's offering to go through hell and back so I can keep playing hockey.

"I meant what I said, too. I love you. Besides, I think I found something else I love more than playing hockey." My mind goes to the rookie. I remember his goal tonight, and his assist, and the searing sense of pride and purpose in my chest, watching him celebrate.

"Walker is a cocky little fucker," I admit with a laugh, and she smiles, too. It's like a shot of morphine to my blood, relaxing me. "But seeing him grow and develop has been . . ." I trail off, unable to find the words. Challenging, but rewarding. "What if I can do that with other players?"

"You can." Her smile is soft and encouraging. "I know you can."

We smile at each other. She's so fucking beautiful, it makes my heart ache in the sweetest way. I don't deserve her.

I want forever with this woman, and I'm about to tell her that, when she sends a pointed glance to my chest.

"Nice tattoo."

I look down, wincing as pain races down my neck. I'm in a loose hospital gown, but beneath it, the bandage has been removed. Across my chest, the tattoo is still healing, but the flowers and vines are vibrant, bold, and beautiful.

"They took the bandage off when you were admitted."

My gut tightens with nerves. She saw it. It's now or never. "Do you know what those flowers are?"

She shifts the neckline down, studying them. "Yellow roses."

"No, sweetheart. They're golden roses."

Her eyebrows slide together, eyes narrowing. "That one isn't in my book."

"I know. It goes by another name, though." My pulse trips. "The Teasing Georgia rose."

THE TATTOO IS BEAUTIFUL.

The flowers span Alexei's broad chest, the soft, lovely roses such a shocking contrast to the hard and brutal lines of his face and body.

His eyes never leave my face. God, my heart breaks all over again at the bruise around his eye. He looks like hell. My nerves are still fried from the breakneck speed at which the ambulance drove here from the arena.

The Teasing Georgia. My heart skips every other beat. If I were wearing that watch of Alexei's, the battery would be on fire right now, it would be going off so hard.

"Tell me you didn't get a tattoo for me, Volkov."

"I got a tattoo for you." The corner of his mouth slants. "Before I tell you what the flowers mean, though, I want to give you something."

His gaze cuts to his bag on the other side of the hospital room. One of the trainers had brought it after the game.

"I think now is a good time to give you the rest of your Christmas present."

My breath catches at the look in his eyes, part nerves and part warm, glowing affection. He directs me to his bag, to the side pocket. My hands close around a small velvet box, and I freeze.

I turn, holding it. "This?"

"Mhm. Come here."

My heart begins to hammer for the second time tonight as I take a seat beside him on the hospital bed.

"You had this with you?"

"I've been carrying it with me everywhere since early December, waiting for the right moment." He gives me a rueful smile. "And I didn't want you to find it before the time was right, or you'd freak out. Open it, Georgia."

With butterflies in my stomach, I open the box.

A pear-shaped diamond the color of caramel and whiskey sits on a thin gold band. White diamonds stud the band, subtle but sparkling.

It's breathtaking. I've never seen something so beautiful.

"It's a cognac diamond," he explains in a low voice, gaze never leaving my face. "I found it in a vintage ring and had it reset in a more modern setting."

It's so pretty, so perfect and unique and special.

A long beat of silence. He stares at me and I stare at the ring. "Do you like it?"

I laugh in disbelief. "Alexei, I love it. It's easily the most beautiful thing I'll ever wear. *Thank you* doesn't seem like enough."

His mouth quirks, eyes warm and affectionate. "Say yes, then. Marry me for real. Be my wife forever. I love you. I love you so fucking much. I don't want this to end. There's no way I'm letting you go. Being married to you is everything I never realized I wanted."

He takes a deep breath, broad chest and tattoo rising and falling, and his throat works.

"I love being your husband. I said I'd never fall in love with you and that this marriage wasn't real and that I wouldn't miss you when it's over but . . ." He shakes his head. "I was so wrong, sweetheart. So fucking wrong about all of it."

He takes a deep breath, his gaze full of resolve and determination. There's my competitive hockey player, so determined and hardheaded.

"I'll never ask you to give anything up for me. I'll never get in the way of your career. If we want to have kids, I'll do whatever it takes so your career isn't affected. I'm in, Georgia. I'm all in. And I'll never stop taking care of you."

For a long moment, I'm speechless, staring at him, unsure if I heard right or if this is all the best dream I'm about to wake up from.

"Ask me what the flowers mean, Hellfire," he says softly, running his thumb over the back of my hand.

My heart's pounding now. "What do they mean?"

His eyes glint. "Come here."

I bring my mouth to his, and his hand lifts to thread into my hair with gentle pressure.

"Does that hurt?" I whisper.

"Yes." An inch from my mouth, his pulls into a smile. "But I want to kiss you. The *Teasing Georgia,* also known as the golden rose, means friendship." He presses a soft kiss to my lips, and my eyes flutter closed. "Joy." Another kiss. "Loyalty." His lips linger there for a moment, his breath tickling my skin. "Eternity."

"Eternity," I whisper back, eyes still closed but stinging with more tears as I'm seized with euphoria.

"Mhm." A beat of silence. "Georgia," he murmurs.

A tear rolls down my face, and he swipes it away, watching me with so much concern and affection, my heart breaks.

"What's wrong, sweetheart?"

My throat works. "Nothing's wrong. Everything's amazing," I laugh, another tear rolling down my face. "Eternity, though?"

"Eternity."

"That's a long time."

His mouth twitches. "I know."

"You want me forever, don't you, you sick fuck?"

He lets out a sharp laugh before he winces.

"Don't do that." I hold his eyes. "I love you, too."

His fingers come to beneath my chin and, so gently, he tilts my face up and kisses me. I feel it all the way to my toes. Our kiss is soft, sweet, and easy. Effortless.

"Be a good wife and say you'll marry me."

I laugh, lean down, and kiss him. "Okay."

"Yes?" He pulls back to look into my eyes. "You're saying yes?"

"Yes," I whisper, smiling, searching his gaze. "Are we ridiculous?" We've only technically been together three months.

"I don't care."

"Me neither."

He reaches for my hand and begins to pull the band off, the ugly, plain one he gave me months ago, but I snatch my hand back.

"Don't." I send him an accusing look. "I like it."

"You called it a *cheap little piece of shit*."

"It is. But I like it. It's mine." I give him my hand again, and he rolls his eyes, but he's smiling, too, as he slips the new ring on in front of the old one.

Alexei makes a face. "They don't match."

My grin broadens as I study my hand. The new ring is shockingly beautiful. I'm going to be gazing at this thing nonstop.

"At least let me get the old ring coated to match the new one," Alexei says.

"Okay." I smile at him. "I'll give you that. But only because I love you."

LATER, after multiple concussion assessments by the medical staff and visits from my parents and Georgia's, I lie in the hospital bed with my wife curled up at my side, her new ring sparkling in the dim lighting. She won't leave me.

"Georgia, go home to sleep." I tug on a lock of her hair.

"Alexei." She brushes a hand lightly over my chest, over the tattoo I got thinking about her, and gives me a smile. The warmest, sweetest smile. My Georgia. "Bite me."

I stifle a laugh. Her eyes warm.

"I'm not leaving you," she adds. "I'll probably sleepwalk back to the hospital." She gives me an arch look. "Through traffic."

I suck in a tight breath. "Okay. You can stay."

Ward appears at the doorway, dark circles under his eyes.

"You're awake," he says quietly, a small smile forming on his mouth at the sight of the two of us lying here together. "I won't interrupt, I just wanted to check in."

Georgia slides off the bed, and my instinct is to reach for her to keep her beside me.

"I'll give you two a minute." She presses a gentle kiss to my forehead. "I'm going to talk to the nurses and get him some food."

He nods at her as she leaves before he takes a seat in the chair beside my hospital bed. "How are you feeling?"

"Like shit."

"I bet." His mouth flattens and he glances away. I wonder if he's thinking about his career-ending injury. I wonder if he's thinking this is the end for me, too.

Here we go. "I want to talk to you about retirement."

He shakes his head. "We don't need to talk about this now, Volkov. I just wanted to check on you, and let you know we're all thinking about you."

I think about the guys and how tonight was probably the last time I hit the ice with them, and my heart aches.

It's right, though. I'm ready for the next phase, both in my career and with Georgia.

"I do want to talk about this now. I've made a decision."

He takes a seat, expression turning amused and wry. "You've made a major decision on your career hours after a head injury?"

I laugh, then wince. "Yes. But this has been a long time coming."

"You're going to be out for a while," he says. "You've got time to think and see how you recover."

"My decision is final. I'm ready. It's time."

He makes a thoughtful noise. "What changed your mind?"

"Seeing the rookie grow and succeed has been the most rewarding part of this season for me."

He waits. I glance at the empty doorway that my wife walked through moments ago. I can hear her talking to the nurses in the hall, the musical sound of her voice filtering in and making my heart rate monitor blip. Ward's gaze cuts to the screen and he smiles.

"But mostly, Georgia," I say, simply. "She's everything to me."

He sighs "Yeah. I know how that is."

"Your daughter?"

He nods, smiling. "Watching you and Walker work together has been something else."

"I see why you had your eye on him this season."

Ward gives me a curious look.

"You always pick a guy," I explain. "Streicher, Miller, then Owens. This season, it was the rookie."

Amusement glints in his eyes. "You think Walker was my guy?"

Something about his expression tells me I'm off. "Wasn't he?"

Ward's mouth twists into a smirk. "No, Volkov. Walker wasn't my guy. You were."

I stare at him, not following. Must be the head injury making things cloudy.

"What's the plan from here, then?" he asks.

"Nothing."

My future is a blank slate, and three months ago, that would have fucking killed me, but with Georgia, the possibilities are endless. Maybe I'll convince her to take a vacation. Maybe we'll have a real wedding. Maybe I'll volunteer more with the hospital program. Maybe I'll just help clean up pylons at her soccer practice.

Ward leans forward. "I've got an assistant coach position with your name on it, if you're interested."

Or that. Deep in my chest, I get the same *locking-into-place* feeling I get when I look at Georgia. Blindsided, but not in a bad way.

The second he says it, I can picture coaching. Of course coaching is my future. Images roll through my head: agonizing over Walker, watching Georgia at soccer, learning from her, feeling on top of the world when the rookie and I figured things out and he rose to his potential.

How the fuck didn't I see this all along?

Off whatever he sees in my expression, Ward grins again. "Don't look so surprised, Volkov."

"You knew."

"I had my suspicions. No matter where you end up, whether it's with the Storm or another team, I think you might love it. Maybe even more than playing. I know I do." His eyebrows go up. "What do you say?"

"Yes." Easy answer.

"That's what I hoped you would say." He nods. "I like it when things go my way. And I won't hold you to this. I'll give you a few weeks to heal up before I come at you with a contract."

"I'll sign it tomorrow."

"Sign what?" Georgia asks from the doorway.

"Volkov's going to think about coming on board as the assistant coach to the Storm," Ward tells her, and she lights up, turning to me with a proud, pleased, surprised smile.

"What do you think?" I ask her.

"You'd make an incredible coach." She sits beside me, handing me a water before she turns to Ward, all business. "Tate, he needs to rest. Get out."

"You got it." Ward stands, giving me a firm nod, but suppressing a smile. "Rest up, take all the time you need, and we'll talk when you're ready." He glances between the two of us, me with my arm around her waist, her applying ice to my bad shoulder. "Glad everything worked out with you two."

He leaves, and Georgia stares after him with a small frown. "Does he know?"

"About us?"

She nods. I think back to her walking past his office, and Ward saying *too bad you aren't married to a Canadian.*

"The whole thing was his idea."

EPILOGUE
ALEXEI

ON A SUNNY DAY IN SEPTEMBER, under the big oak tree outside Vancouver City Hall, Georgia and I get married.

Again.

My wife is breathtaking, with her hair down and wavy, freckles on her nose and cheekbones from the summer sun. She wears the same dress as when we got married last year, when we hated each other.

A vow renewal, we told everyone.

"Being married to you is a dream I never want to wake up from," I tell my wife in front of all our friends and family.

Nearby, someone sniffles. Probably one of our moms. Our parents have become tight-knit friends. They even took a group holiday to Italy this summer, staying at my and Georgia's vacation home.

Holding my hands, my new ring sparkling on her finger above the ugly one she refuses to take off, Georgia smiles. "When you're not around, I miss you."

Affection expands through my chest, warm and consuming. "I love you, and I always will."

She beams at me, recognizing the reversed vows from our first wedding. "Glad we're on the same page."

Between us, Ward, acting as our officiant, says a few words about love and soulmates. I'm not really listening, I'm just staring at Georgia. Under the big tree, light scatters across her hair, the golden strands sparkling, her whiskey eyes making my heart ache.

With a warm look, Ward nods at us. "You may now—"

I wrap a hand around the back of her neck and haul her mouth to mine. Her hands sink into my hair.

"—kiss your wife."

Our guests laugh, but my wife consumes my senses—her soft mouth, her dizzying violet scent, her hands on my chest, her body against mine. Her sigh.

We break apart, and she rises up on her tiptoes, bringing her mouth to my ear.

"Great job," she whispers. "Nothing like kissing the dead body at a funeral."

———

That evening, at the restaurant from the double date with Owens and Darcy, I hold my wife close with a firm hand on her waist.

Flowers from my mom's shop fill the room, bouquets made with every flower I gave Georgia during those life-altering few months. I even convinced my mom to hide blue tansy in a bouquet while Georgia laughed. Around the restaurant, soft lighting splashes a warm glow on everyone, and the sound of our friends and family's conversation and laughter puts me at ease.

"Christ, you're beautiful," I tell Georgia. "That dress is something else."

Her mouth curves, teasing and lovely. "I thought you didn't like it."

"Because I wanted to buy you a new one?"

She nods.

I turn her so she's facing me. Our own world, away from everyone. "It's not that I don't like it. I've been half hard since I saw you this morning, Hellfire. I didn't know if you wanted to wear it again, that's all. It could have been your something new."

"This is a great dress," she insists, palms smoothing over my chest, over the lapels of the suit she picked out for me. "It deserves it's moment. It deserves a wedding between two people who love each other." Her eyes meet mine, sparkling. "It's my something old."

"I thought I was your something old."

She laughs, and my watch goes off. I've been using the heart-rate monitoring program as part of my concussion recovery—but to Georgia's delight, it still goes off like clockwork around her.

"Besides," her delicate hand comes to the necklace I gifted her this morning. "I already have my something new."

The Teasing Georgia rose in golden yellow diamonds in marquise, round, and baguette cuts. I'm getting well-versed in diamonds, being with Georgia, because buying her things makes me feel like a king.

Friendship, joy, loyalty, eternity, I whispered in her ear as I put it on her.

"Have I told you how much I love it?" she asks, giving me a kiss on my cheek.

"Yes, Hellfire, but I don't mind you showing your appreciation."

She arches an eyebrow, smirking. "Later."

My watch goes off again.

As I silence it, she lifts the hem of her dress a couple inches, showing off the pale blue heels the designer made for her to match her dress at Miller and Hazel's wedding. "Something blue."

I nod, mouth crooking. "Something borrowed?"

She raises her wrist. A thin gold chain with violet-blue stones sparkles in the low light. "From Jordan. It was her mother's."

The bartender appears in front of us, looking slightly uncomfortable in a social setting on this side of the bar.

"Volkov." Her mouth tips in a quiet smile. "Congrats."

"Thanks."

She leans in for a hug. "Happy for you two," she tells me, giving me a squeeze, and I'm hit with a wave of gratitude. "If you screw it up, I will poison you."

I cough out a laugh. "Okay. Fair."

"I told you not to threaten him," Georgia says as they embrace. "That's my job."

At the bar, Ward's eyes flick to Jordan before he turns his attention back to his daughter, who's laughing as Owens gives her a piggyback ride.

"I'm going to talk to Ward for a moment," I tell them, sensing they need a moment. Georgia gives me another soft kiss on the cheek before I head over to him and nod hello.

"Ward."

"Coach Volkov."

Once I was cleared for activity, Ward and I made my assistant coach role official, and I moved into my new office beside Georgia's at the arena. Having my wife so close at work is both heaven and hell. She's too distracting to get much done when we're both there, but having her within reach is a luxury I'm grateful for.

I also resumed work with the rookie—along with the rest of the new recruits.

"I've had a few complaints about the rookie training camp,"

Ward says, eyes sparking. "They didn't expect it to be so grueling."

"It's nothing they can't handle. If they want to be ready for the NHL, they need to push themselves."

The corners of his eyes crinkle. "Do you really need to start at six in the morning?"

"If they want to succeed, they can't be out drinking and chasing girls and boys the night before. They need to be in bed by nine. It's good practice for the season." I give him a sidelong look. "They only hate me because they can hardly keep up with me."

Ward laughs. "No one can. You're still a machine, Volkov, retired or not. They respect you and they want to make you proud."

If I can be a tenth of the coach Ward is, that'll be enough for me. A warm pulse hits me in the chest. "I love working with those guys," I admit. "I'm already seeing incredible progress in them."

"Ready for the season?"

Opening night is next week. I think about last year, when everything was so uncertain. When the thought of retirement sent cold dread through my veins.

Another thing I was hardheaded and wrong about. My life in retirement is ten times as fulfilling as before. I'm already anticipating what the new players will do on the ice this season. I get to work with my wife, both with the Storm and the Vancouver Devils, whose practices I attend whenever I can. After the hockey season ended, I convinced her to spend a month in Italy, just the two of us. Four weeks of great food, wine, and skinny-dipping with Georgia.

I was clueless and ignorant to dread this life, like I was clueless and ignorant to dread marriage. My eyes go to Georgia, and a sense of calm settles through me. She hasn't sleepwalked once since I retired.

"I think this is our year," Ward says quietly.

My chest expands with anticipation. "I think so, too."

Last year, the Storm advanced to the final round of playoffs before losing in game seven to a better team. Fortunately, our guys walked away from playoffs without a slew of injuries.

Fucking hell, I hope it's our year. My gaze goes to Streicher, with his arm locked around Pippa's shoulders, murmuring something in her ear. Miller, teasing his new wife with a cocky grin while she pretends to look unamused. Owens, smiling and laughing with Darcy, his best friend. Walker, talking to Georgia and Jordan, his big fun-loving grin stretched ear to ear.

I've already won the Stanley Cup in my career, but these guys haven't. For them, I want it more than anything.

My gaze goes back to Georgia. Well, almost anything.

The team owner, Ross Sheridan, appears and shakes my hand. "Alexei."

"Ross."

"The rookies are looking sharp this year." On occasion, the ex–hockey player joins my early morning practices, watching with quiet interest. "Where's Dr. Greene? I'd like to say hello before I have to leave."

I tilt my chin to where Georgia and Jordan stand, talking. Walker's disappeared—to flirt with someone, I'm sure. Sheridan sees Jordan standing beside my wife, though, and seems to brace himself.

"I'll join," Ward says quickly, wearing an odd, serious expression.

When we approach the women, Sheridan hesitates. Georgia's eyes go wide like she's surprised; Jordan freezes and falls silent, expression shuttering.

What's going on?

"Dr. Greene." Sheridan shakes her hand before turning to Jordan, taking a deep breath like he's nervous or something. "Jordan."

This guy owns half of Vancouver. Jordan can be intimidating with her take-no-shit bartender stare, but still.

"You look lovely."

Her eyes flicker with anger but she doesn't say anything.

His throat works. "Can we talk?"

There's that stare of hers. "You're a decade late."

Abruptly, she walks away. Ross Sheridan watches her for a long moment, features full of regret.

Ward's eyes follow Jordan, jaw tight. I've never seen the guy look anything less than patient. "Excuse me," he says before he strides after her.

Sheridan turns to us with a polite but forced smile. "Thank you for inviting me. It was a lovely ceremony." His eyes go to the direction Jordan went before he shakes his head. "I should be going. See you in the office. Have a great night."

"Did you invite him?" Georgia asks as we watch him leave.

"Yeah. Is that okay?"

"Uh." She looks to Jordan. She and Ward are talking in the corner, glaring at each other. Why does Ward look so annoyed? I didn't even realize he knew Jordan. He almost never comes to the bar. "Ross is Jordan's father."

A frown snaps onto my face. This is news to me. "Her last name is *Hathaway*."

"She changed it after her mom passed." Her mouth tightens. "It's complicated. She doesn't want people to know they're related. They aren't close."

"Do you need to go after her?"

"She'll talk about it when she's ready." Her gaze trails over the suit we picked out together, and her mouth curves with appreciation.

"See something you like?"

She lets out a soft laugh, eyes dancing. "You're so hot, Alexei. I always thought that."

"Always?"

That pretty mouth curves. "Always. Even when I hated you."

Christ, I can barely stand how much I love her. How my heart beats solely for her. How she changed my life, helped me find a new purpose, made me whole.

"You want to get out of here?" I ask, and she bites her lip, glancing around at our guests.

"Can we?"

"It's our wedding." My lips are on her neck, inhaling her, skimming my mouth over her soft skin. "We can do whatever we want," I murmur in her ear, and she smiles.

My wife. My love. My everything.

"Come on, Hellfire. Let's go have that wedding night we never got."

ACKNOWLEDGMENTS

Thank you for reading *Gloves Off*! I've been excited to write these two since I started *Behind the Net*, and I hope you enjoyed. As you might have guessed, Ward's book is next! I dropped a couple hints about the tropes, did you catch them?

It seems a bit unfair that my name is on the cover when this book was a team effort. Many, many people propped me up and supported me during this process, and I have a few *thank you*s to hand out.

Thank you to my spectacular editor, Shauna Summers and her amazing team at Dell for taking a chance on me and making my dreams come true. Thank you to eagle-eyed copy-editor Pamela Feinstein for her endless patience with me. Thank you to the lovely Rhea Kurien and her team at Orion for their incredible work distributing my books around the globe.

Thank you to my fearless agents, Flavia Viotti and Meire Dias, for championing me and helping my books find homes with such wonderful publishers. I'm so grateful to have you in my corner.

My PA, Lauren Cox: thank you for keeping my head on straight during this chaotic year. Thanks for listening to my rambling voice notes, for being my right-hand woman, for reminding me thirty-five times to do the same thing, and for putting up with me when I fill out your forms as my alter egos.

Huge thank you to all my friends for their love and support.

The list gets longer with every book, and I am a very lucky lady to know all of you. Thank you to Grace Reilly for talking sports with me. Massive *thank you*s to Sophia Travers and Maggie North for reading a half-written messy pile of crap and giving insightful, smart feedback.

Thank you to Matt Leonhardt for enthusiastically talking hockey to me. Your passion for sports is contagious and your knowledge is staggering. Any errors about how the hockey world works are mine, not Matt's.

Thank you to my betas: Esther, Marcie, Ycelsa, Mahbuba, Tabitha, Brett, Cal, and Wren. Thank you all for reading an early draft, giving sharp and funny input, and following me on this journey. Thank you to Lizzie Hunsaker for her proof-reading eagle-eyes. I'm grateful for all of you.

Thank you to illustrator Chloe Quinn and designer Echo Grayce for giving me yet another beautiful cover. Every time we do this, I go "no, THIS one is my favorite!" I'm in awe of both of your talent!

Demon Baby, you showed up in the middle of writing this book and changed my whole life. You're even better than I thought you'd be. I count my lucky stars for you every day.

This book probably exists mostly because of Tim, the guy who used to sleepwalk when he was stressed, who has broken so many bones that we practically have a parking spot at the hospital. The guy who puts food in front of me and gave up his career to support mine. The best husband, the best dad. I love you.

And lastly, thank you to my readers! Every time you read my books, every time you tell a friend or post about them, you're making my dreams come true. Thanks for letting me live out my dream of writing romance.

Until next time,

xo Stephanie

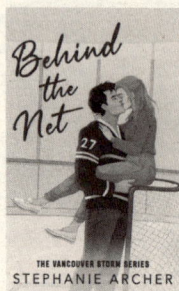

He's the hot, grumpy goalie I had a crush on in high school . . . and now I'm his live-in assistant.

After my ex crushed my dreams in the music industry, I'm done with getting my heart broken. Working as an assistant for an NHL player was supposed to be a breeze, but nothing about Jamie Streicher is easy. He's intimidatingly hot, grumpy, and can't stand me. Keeping things professional will be no problem, even when he demands I move in with him.

Beneath his surliness, though, Jamie's surprisingly sweet and protective.

When he finds out my ex was terrible in bed, his competitive nature flares, and he encourages and spoils me in every way. The creative spark I used to feel about music? It's back, and I'm writing songs again. Between wearing his jersey at games, fun, rowdy parties with the team, and being brave on stage again, I'm falling for him.

He could break my heart, but maybe I'm willing to take that chance.

Behind the Net is a grumpy-sunshine, pro-hockey romance with lots of spice and an HEA. It's the first book in the Vancouver Storm series and can be read as a standalone.

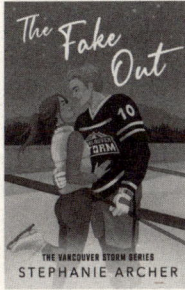

**The best way to get back at my horrible ex?
Fake date Rory Miller--my ex's rival, the top scorer in
pro hockey, and the arrogant, flirtatious hockey player I
tutored in high school.**

Faking it is fun and addictive, though, and beneath the bad
boy swagger, Rory's sweet, funny, and protective.

He teaches me to skate and spends way too much money
on me.

He sleeps in my bed and convinces me to break my just-
one-time hookup rule.

He kisses me like it's real.

And now I wonder if Rory was ever faking it to begin with.

*The Fake Out is a pro hockey fake dating romance. It's the
second book in the Vancouver Storm series but can be read
as a standalone.*

The best way to gain confidence after years with the wrong guy? Get lessons in love from my best friend.

Hayden Owens is the hottest defenseman in pro hockey, my confident best friend, and my new dating coach.

He'll teach me to be a player, but convinces me to practice with him . . . and our flirting lessons and practice kisses push the bounds of friendship.

All that relationship stuff he's always avoided? He doesn't seem to mind it anymore.

Rule number one of being a player is no attachments, but when Hayden sees me picking up other guys, he's jealous enough that I wonder...

Maybe my wingman's been waiting for me all along.

The Wingman is a pro hockey relationship coach romance. It's the third book in the Vancouver Storm series but can be read as a standalone.

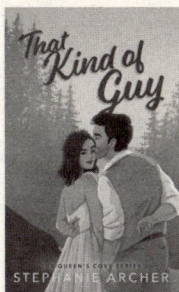

My arrogant fake fiancé? I can't stand him.

Cocky and charismatic Emmett Rhodes isn't a relationship kind of guy, but now that he's running for mayor of our small town, his bachelor past is hurting the campaign.

Thankfully, I'm the last woman who would ever fall for him.

We're total opposites—he's a golden retriever and I'm sharp and snarky, but he'll co-sign on my restaurant loan if I play his devoted fiancée. Between romantic dates, a prom night re-do, and visits to a secret beach, things heat up, and the line between real and ruse is lit on fire. I'm starting to see another side of Mr Popular, and now I wonder if I was all wrong.

We can't keep our hands off each other, but it's all for show . . . right?

A sizzling, hilarious, enemies-to-lovers, fake-dating rom-com with an HEA. This is the first book in the Queen's Cove series and can be read as a standalone.

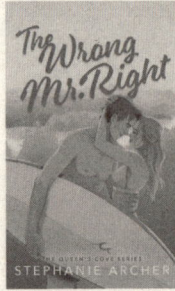

The hot, commitment-phobe surfer is the only one I can turn to . . .

In my small-town bookstore, I'm surrounded by book boyfriends, but I've never had one in real life. At almost 30, I've never been in love, and my bookstore isn't breaking even. Something needs to change, and I know exactly who's going to help me: Wyatt Rhodes, the guy everyone wants.

He agrees to be my relationship coach, but his lessons aren't what I expected.

Between surfing, mortifying dates and revamping my store, his lessons are more about drawing me out of my shell than changing me into someone new. But when we add praise-filled 'spice lessons' to the curriculum, it's clear he wants me. He's leaving town and I'm staying to run my store, so it can't work, but that doesn't seem to matter to him.

He's supposed to find me someone to fall for but instead, we're falling for each other.

A sizzling, hilarious, small- town, friends-to-lovers romantic comedy with a guaranteed HEA. This is the second book in the Queen's Cove series but can be read as a standalone.

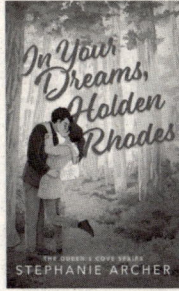

The deal is simple: the grumpy guy will pay off my debt if I find him a wife.

Holden Rhodes is grouchy, unfairly hot, and has hated me for years. He's the last person I'd choose to inherit an inn with. As we renovate the inn and practice his dating skills, I see a different side of him.

What if I was all wrong about Holden?

When we add 'friends with benefits' to the deal, our chemistry is so hot the sparks could burn down the inn. Holden's a secret romantic, and I'm secretly falling for him.

I'm terrible at bartending, a video of a bear stealing my toy went viral, and everyone in this small town knows my business, but Holden Rhodes is so much more than I expected.

I don't want him to find love with anyone but me.

A spicy, grumpy-sunshine, friends-with-benefits, small-town romantic comedy with an HEA. This is the third book in the Queen's Cove series but can be read as a standalone.

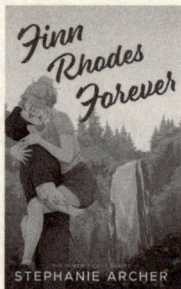

The guy who broke my heart is now an arrogant, too-hot firefighter . . . who's hell-bent on getting me back.

This summer, I have one goal: field work. I need it to finish my PhD. I never expected Finn Rhodes to offer help. He broke my heart twelve years ago, and now that he's back in town, I want nothing to do with him.

Finn wants one thing: me.

We were inseparable as kids until everything changed. Now, he's all grown up—tattooed, muscled, and unfairly hot . . . and insists we're meant to be together. I know he'll grow bored of me and this small town like before, but he'll never give up unless it's his idea.

I'll pretend to date him, but actually? I'm trying to get him to dump me.

Between hiking the back country and cringe-worthy dates designed to turn him off, I begin to remember why we were best friends. Despite how hard I try, Finn isn't interested in dumping me . . . and now I'm not sure I want him to.

Finn's always been trouble, but now he's a different kind entirely. The kind that might break my heart. Again.

Finn Rhodes Forever is a spicy, second-chance, reverse-grumpy-sunshine rom-com. This is the fourth book in the Queen's Cove series but can be read as a standalone.